Soylent Caravan

Screenplay

Paul D. Escudero

WorkBook
PRESS

WORKBOOK PRESS LLC
187 E Warm Springs Rd,
Suite B285 Las Vegas NV 89119 USA

Website: https://workbookpress.com/
Hotline: 1-888-818-4856
Email: admin@workbookpress.com

Ordering Information:

Quantity sales. Special discounts are available on quantity purchases by corporations, associations, and others. For details, contact the publisher at the address above.

ISBN-13: 978-1-965732-47-2 Paperback Version

REV. DATE: 05/13/2025

ARRIVAL

FADE IN.

EXT. CGI. SPACE. CARSOPIAN ARMADA FLYING PAST A FOCAL POINT (CAMERA). JUST LIKE IN MANY TRAIN VIDEOS AS THE HEAD OF THE FLEET PASSES OFFSET FROM THE CAMERA, THE CAMERA SLOWLY SPINS TO THE RIGHT SHOWING THE REARS OF THE SPACECRAFT AND PLANET EARTH COMING INTO FOCUS.

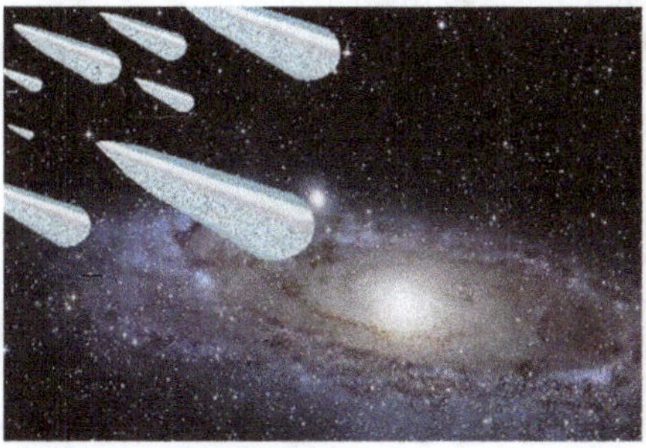

THE JOURNEY BEGINS.

VOICEOVER
(With Music background) https://www.youtube.com/watch?v=9jK-NcRmVcw

Carsopian Extraterrestrials who originated in the Regulus Solar System part of the Leo Constellation, were converging on Earth.

Leo exists as viewed from Earth between constellations Cancer (the crab) to the west and Virgo (the maiden) to the east.

Leo's name is Latin for lion, and to the ancient Greeks represented the Nemean Lion killed by the mythical Greek hero Heracles meaning 'Glory of Hera' (known to the ancient Romans as Hercules) as one of his twelve labors.

Because of the lack of effective space surveillance, the Carsopian's sailed through the ether unmolested and undetected towards Earth.

Earth wasn't specifically chosen by the Carsopian's, as there were several solar systems in this direction, it was simply one of the dozens that as they got closer appeared to have a more suitable atmosphere and surface water to support life in a temperate zone.

INT.SPACE.CARSOPIAN COMMAND SHIP CONTROL ROOM.

VOICEOVER
(With Music background)

The sophisticated Carsopian's monitored all electromagnetic emanations out of the dozen or so suitable planets as they approached, and the final deciding factor was Earth appeared to be the most primitive. Hence, planet Earth was viewed by Carsopian planners as the weakest and easiest to penetrate possible security systems and arrive unmolested.

CARSOPIAN PLANNER #1

On their technology scaling, Earth was given a score card of 1.5.

CARSOPIAN PLANNER #2

Most of the other planets to possibly visit were rated at 4.5, 5.8, 6.3, 6.9, 7.1 and even higher.

CARSOPIAN PLANNER #1

Since we are now committed to Earth, we now need to focus our study and analysis of the planet in all respects, and as we approach closer to the planet, I expect we will began intercepting vast amounts of communications.

The Carsopian's had very advanced Artificial Intelligence. Thanks to the video transmissions now being received from Earth, the Carsopian Artificial Intelligence was able to slowly put together a lexicon and designed electronic translators operated by Artificial Intelligence. These elaborate translators greatly speeded up Carsopian's analysis and knowledge base of Earth that helped chart their destiny.

INT. SPACE. CARSOPIAN COMMAND SHIP PLANNING ROOM NEXT TO THE MAIN CONTROL ROOM.

CARSOPIAN PLANNER #1

General Fukua de Hundan, we have determined there were only a few suitable locations for their arrival, that had acceptable climate and sparse density of population.

GENERAL FUKUA DE HUNDAN

What's the alternative? What do you recommend as the landing zone?

CARSOPIAN PLANNER #1

There is a sparsely populated area of China chose first, but a military base is too close.

GENERAL FUKUA DE HUNDAN

What's the alternative? What do you recommend as the landing zone?

CARSOPIAN PLANNER #1

A thinly populated area of the country of Mexico which speaks the language Spanish.

GENERAL FUKUA DE HUNDAN

Does our translation capabilities enable us to understand the Spanish language?

CARSOPIAN PLANNER #1

The Earth language translators were then tweaked to be extremely accurate in the languages corresponding to the prospective landing zones.

We have concentrated also on the English language since countries that speak English are our biggest threats.

Our Spanish translator is functioning very well as we have been obtaining vast amounts of information and conversations from the country of Mexico.

GENERAL FUKUA DE HUNDAN

Very well, we shall land in Mexico.

The Carsopian's Mexico arrival location existed near the path of one of the largest attempted migrations in world history. As America loomed on the verge of social upheaval, the political dynamics out of Washington D.C. that caused the Border Patrol to stand down fostered a frenzy of migratory activity.

***

VOICEOVER

(With music as the Carsopian Fleet lands in Mexico) https://www.youtube.com/watch?v=cQTO9n3FhhY

The best way to describe the average Carsopian would include an imagery of a very tall Asian with large almond shaped eyes. Since their eyes were approximately sixty five percent larger than human eyes, they would never pass as an Earth Human.

There would never be any possibility of desire of penetrating human society nor planetary conquest.

The Carsopian's were not here to stay. This was just a stopover from the long trip from their planet to another Empire Provincial stronghold Cui.

The normal space lanes from their home planet Shenqi Zhilong to Cui were secured due to the ongoing dispute with their traditional enemies, the Heisibing.

This powerful Heisibing enemy placed forces and obstructed the Cui Transit Lane, an ultra-fast space conduit created by a cosmic convergence channel that altered space and time just

like the event horizon of a black whole.

The Carsopian's going through this region of space past Earth and a dozen other solar systems to travel to Cui indirectly, added a significant period of travel being trapped aboard those spaceships breathing reprocessed air, living in half artificial gravity, and meager diets.

The Carsopian's were not well liked in the galaxy because they were known Cannibals.

Killing and consuming intelligent sentient beings did not set well with a large percentage of the galaxy.

Some of the Carsopian's delicacies were obtained from eating beings considered 40 to 50 times more intelligent than humans on Earth.

There was no plan to harvest Earth beings, and the standard Carsopian space food was to provide Carsopian all their requirements until arrival at Cui.

The Carsopian's stopped only to rejuvenate in fresh air, dump all the reprocessed water and take on all fresh filtered water, and allow the bodies to enjoy full gravity, that measured like the Carsopian home planet Shenqi Zhilong.

It all started innocently enough when commanders, feeling sorry for their troops allowed them to get a few Stragglers marching along with the Caravan just over a few hills away.

The security rover craft sent out to guard the perimeter and warn them of approaching entities easily manifested this Cannibalistic activity.

EXT.NIGHT.MEXICO HIWAY 23 NORTH OF GUADALAHARA ALONG THE CARAVAN ROUTE.

The stragglers, usually penniless with very little to barter were on foot and at the mercy of the Mexican people for food and water.

The Caravan traveled at no more than a three miles per hour and most of the time were doing less than two miles an hour or even less stopping as fuel and roads were problematic and they had to wait for many people on foot.

If you went down the same road a day later, you would know the Caravan just passed through with the local villages terrified and, in some cases, plundered if there wasn't good law enforcement nearby.

But worse than the locals, the stragglers at the end of the Caravan didn't know falling back cost them their lives.

Carsopian Security Rover-craft using infrared and ultraviolet technologies could fly in total darkness and track all their intended victims.

EXT.CGI.NIGHT CARSOPIAN SECURITY ROVER LANDING TO SNATCH MORE CARAVANERS DURING FOLLOWING VOICE OVER.

Once there was sufficient distance between the last stragglers and the main body, the Carsopian Security Rover-craft craft landed on the road just a few feet behind the last stragglers, and security men got out with their sophisticated hand carried beam weapons that instantly killed one or more stragglers.

It was all silent and people ahead simply thought the stragglers stopped, turned around and went home. No inquiry was made because most of the Caravan were out of sight from the stragglers, plus the nights were dark along the empty road with very few amounts of vehicle traffic.

The Carsopian's loaded the migrant caravanner bodies up in their craft and returned to base, where the growing number of Carsopian's were wanting to partake in consuming their fair share of barbecued humans.

The number of participants desiring such consumption grew spontaneously.

Just as the first morsels of cannibalized flesh invigorated the souls of the long-travelled spacers, the sudden new demand for more and more barbecued humans led to aggressive tracking, hunting and bagging of stragglers along the Caravan.

***

EXT. DAY. SAN DIEGO, CA. U.S. MEXICO BORDER. CROWDS FORMED TO RUSH THE BORDER.

With the progressives and socialists suddenly controlling the White House and American Congress, the word was out to all possible migrants around the world, unrestricted access to *The American Dream* beckoned call to them.

The only avenue of approach was via the southern border because the Northern Border, ports, airports, and other means of entry were well secured fearing terrorists crossing.

Corrupt politicians funded by special interest groups gutted any semblance of border control in the southwest region. From 2021 through 2023 it became a total disaster at the border. In 2024 the situation improved but with a pending turnover in the White House, the Migrants were coming in large numbers trying to get in before the new administration made it tougher, and the billionaire who hated America because of how WW2 ended was funding this migration that multiplied the numbers.

***

INT. DAY. HONDURAS. COFFEE SHOP. MUSIC DURING THE NEXT TWO VOICEOVERS AND FOLLOWING PARAGRAPHS. (https://www.youtube.com/watch?v=GB3zR_X25UU)

VOICEOVER

Delmy Áquilar, Yanuel Romero, Rony Nieto, and Eduardo Ordoñez grew up together and completed high school but since their families lived in borderline poverty, had little prospect of getting into a university since they could not afford tuition.

These young adults were the ultimate dreamers. Good grades, good families, staunch Catholics, and hard workers. Trapped in the cycle of poverty didn't appeal to them.

These teenagers socialized together. Delmy and Yanuel were attractive females and could easily find mates if they wanted,

But the two young women didn't want to be trapped in poverty like their parents and were the real instigators of the trek north to join the Caravan the ultra-rich Billionaire arranged, bent on destroying the United States capitalist system.

Honduran society is predominately Mestizo; however, American Indian, Black and White individuals also live in Honduras adding to the diversity.

Honduras has the world's highest murder rate and high levels of sexual violence. Delmy Áquilar and Yanuel Romero had both been sexually assaulted in the past and were eager to get out of that hell hole.

Rony Nieto, and Eduardo Ordoñez decided leaving Honduras partially because the threat of them being caught up in the Battalion 316 business made them fear for their lives.

But Rony Nieto and Eduardo Ordoñez real motivations came from their interests in Delmy Áquilar and Yanuel Romero.

The World Bank categorizes Honduras as a low middle-income nation. The nation's per capita income before 2020, was around $700 US dollars, making it one of the lowest in North America.

Rony Nieto, and Eduardo Ordoñez, thus had the added incentive they too would be trapped in insular poverty if they didn't escape Honduras.

Oddly enough, they were some of the many who proudly enjoyed observing the leaders of the convoy carrying Honduras national flags on their vehicles in the convoy.

Honduras economic growth in the last few years has averaged 7% a year, one of the highest rates in Latin America (2010). Despite this, Honduras has seen the least development amongst all Central American countries.

Owing to insufficient law enforcement resources, crime in Honduras is rampant and criminals operate with a high degree of impunity.

Consequently, Honduras has one of the highest murder rates in the world. Official statistics from the Honduran Observatory on National Violence show Honduras' homicide rate was 60 per 100,000 in 2015 with most homicide cases unprosecuted.

Highway assaults, especially carjacking at roadblocks or checkpoints set up by criminals with police uniforms and equipment frequently occur.

Although reports of kidnappings of foreigners are not common, families of kidnapping victims often pay ransoms without reporting the crime to police out of fear of retribution, so kidnapping figures are underreported.

Owing to measures taken by government and business in 2014 to improve tourist safety, Roatan and the Bay Islands now has lower crime rates than the Honduran mainland.

In the less populated region of Gracias a Dios, narcotics-trafficking is rampant, and police presence is scarce. Threats against U.S. citizens by drug traffickers and other criminal organizations have resulted in the U.S. Embassy placing restrictions on the travel of U.S. officials through Gracias a Dios.

***

VOICEOVER

Rony Nieto, Eduardo Ordoñez, just like Delmy Áquilar and Yanuel Romero knew they had few options.

Either they worked in a San Pedro Sula Honduras tobacco or coffee businesses as cheap laborers, or get trapped in the narco-trafficking and possible death from assassinations perpetrated by the Battalion 316.

On their own Rony Nieto and Eduardo Ordoñez probably would have glumly stayed and done one of those activities for the rest of their lives had they not had the acquaintances with Delmy Áquilar and Yanuel Romero who demonstrated they were real risk takers.

None of the teenagers had a lot of money, as they were expected to help their families unless they wanted to be kicked out of the home.

Rony Nieto, and Eduardo Ordoñez knew they were living on borrowed time as harsh conditions dictated, they either fork over most of their earnings to their fathers who would squander over half getting drunk or face going out into the cruel world on their own becoming instantly homeless and poverty stricken.

Sex was absolutely forbidden for Delmy Áquilar and Yanuel Romero, as they knew their parents would severely beat them if they were ever caught having sex and possibly even if they were mere rumors.

No matter how much Rony Nieto, and Eduardo Ordoñez wanted a physical embrace, unless they could demonstrate a reliable income capable of supporting a family and go through the full Catholic indoctrination of starting a family and marriage.

That was never going to happen despite the affection the two girls had for the two boys that already had the appearance of young men.

INT. DAY. SAN PEDRO SULA HONDURAS. COFFEE SHOP

Socializing occurred at festivals or at a coffee shop, where prices were reasonable, partly thanks to the abundant coffee product nearby. That's when it all started. The ladies were well read, as life sucked so bad in Honduras, simply reading the newspaper was a major daily activity and the coffeeshop usually had one laying around for the paying customers.

YANUEL ROMERO

What do you think of this Caravan business that's getting a lot of attention lately?

DELMY ÁQUILAR

I wish I had a way to join it and get the hell out of here. I think I could make it in America.

YANUEL ROMERO

Delmy, I bet American men would go after you. You are so beautiful.

DELMY ÁQUILAR

The American tourists I've met here were only looking for sex. None of them wanted a legitimate relationship.

YANUEL ROMERO

Well, you just saw crazy Americans who are here on vacation getting drunk or high. I bet if you went to America and met them in their natural environment, they would act differently.

DELMY ÁQUILAR

It seems it's impossible for me to ever get there. Plus, my English isn't too good, how would I survive?

YANUEL ROMERO

The first few years would be hard until you met someone.

DELMY ÁQUILAR

It's too bad we couldn't be on that Caravan.

YANUEL ROMERO

It would be too dangerous for us. A lot of bad men are in that Caravan. We would probably be raped and abused.

DELMY ÁQUILAR

Yea if we just had someone go with us and protect us.

It was quite a coincidence as Rony Nieto and Eduardo Ordoñez walked into the coffee shop, knowing the two beautiful ladies would most likely be there with several other young adults who made this more or less their rendezvous location.

As soon as Delmy spotted the two young men she smiled.

DELMY ÁQUILAR

Look who just walked in.

Yanuel suddenly had that inquisitive look on her face that seemed to always get Delmy in trouble. It was as if she could read her mind.

YANUEL ROMERO

Are you thinking what I'm thinking?

DELMY ÁQUILAR

I knew you would say that!

The two ladies started laughing knowing the solution had just walked into the coffee shop.

Now would be the hard part. To convince them to treat them with respect and not push themselves onto them throughout what could be a very tough journey and not expected to be entitled to their bodies just because they agreed to go with them and provide some level of security.

The next huge question would be how far they could trust them. Another inconvenience would be to attempt accumulating some travel money without their families knowing about it and confiscating it.

The logistics involved seemed enormous. Just getting ready to go would be a daunting challenge.

RONY NIETO

Hello.

Rony Nieto approached the table that had a bench on one side and two chairs on the other. One of the women was sitting on the bench and the other in a chair. That made it very convenient for the two young men who could quickly sit next to the lady they had personal inspiration towards.

Rony had incredible lust for Delmy whose mixed DNA included Honduran, British, Spanish, and other's that created a blend that formed a spectacular dark brown hair with natural auburn tendrils.

Delmy's freckles also conveyed that European DNA modulated the essence of her exquisite beauty. Delmy's ample breasts were of almost a mature woman, with perfect curves and dimensions.

Rony's behavior was often irritating to Delmy who often caught him spending too much time staring at her breasts.

Delmy had at times abruptly turned and caught Rony focused on her buttocks, so she wasn't entirely convinced his motives were not somehow influenced by desires to seek personal gratification at her expense.

Delmy quite simply didn't know how far she could trust Rony, especially if they were alone together in some obscure location.

Yanuel wasn't quite as beautiful as Delmy and often felt bad, she was considered second prize.

But Yanuel knew her friend Delmy was genuine and a true friend after all they had gone through together since they were toddlers. Delmy was her best friend, intelligent, sincere, protective, and a person that transcended the essence of friendship as if she were almost her own sister.

Yanuel had features one would expect from indigenous Mestizo people of that area. Her facial features and height fell right in line with the normal Honduran female teenager.

Though Yanuel too had a great shape and curves which provided a great distraction to her face. With proper makeup and proper dress, Yanuel seemed highly desirable.

Of the two young women, Yanuel would seem like the more domesticated type. Hence, men would more than likely seek her out ahead of Delmy who gave the appearance of a socialite verses a domesticated woman ready to be the consummate mother and provider for a noble man's children.

DELMY

Rony, how is everything going for you?

RONY NIETO

I'm a little tired from hauling sacks of coffee all day long."

DELMY

Well at least you make a man's salary.

RONY NIETO

Yes, but I don't think my body is ready to do this kind of work for the rest of my life.

Rony looked down at the table and saw the newspaper and the headlines of the Caravan.

RONY NIETO

Those people are stupid. Most of them will get turned away from the American border.

DELMY ÁQUILAR

Some of them will make it through.

RONY NIETO

America's new president is not too friendly towards migrants. They missed their chance with the former American President.

DELMY ÁQUILAR

The newspaper says that a new congress in Washington D.C. is disabling the president from conducting the stringent border security.

RONY NIETO

I bet many of them will be turned away and must come back.

DELMY ÁQUILAR

That's too bad since many of them gave up their jobs to go on those convoys.

RONY NIETO

The tobacco and coffee farmers always need strong backs. There will be jobs waiting for them when they get back.

DELMY ÁQUILAR

Would you ever consider going?

RONY NIETO

Not really, I would end up being a slave up there like I am here.

DELMY ÁQUILAR

What if I asked you to take me there would you go?

RONY NIETO

Does that mean we would be a couple?

DELMY ÁQUILAR

No, it just means you would be a good friend to help get me there safely. After we get established in America and start living normal lives again, then you and I could consider a possible future relationship.

RONY NIETO

You would be brave enough to join one of those convoys?

DELMY ÁQUILAR

Yanuel and I were just talking about it.

Rony didn't believe Delmy would consider such a trek.

After all Delmy was so beautiful, she could just about catch any upward mobile male in San Pedro Sula. Rony didn't realize Delmy didn't have the self-confidence to believe she was capable of transcending into a relationship with a person several stratums above her level that was borderline poverty in Honduras, but would be considered poverty in places like Tijuana, Mexico.

Delmy Áquilar's ideals were that she felt she had to make it on her own and the sooner she was away from her family and the confiscation of all her income the better off she would be.

But that's how it was in impoverished areas of San Pedro Sula, teenage children living at home with an income were considered essential towards helping the family's plight. And if she didn't hand over most of her income to her mother, she would be shown to the door and kicked out just like Rony would be.

The gloom and doom that settled down upon the four teenagers, feeling their families had an anchor around their necks, frequently manifested the melancholy. But at the same time, looking at the paper and discussing the Caravan added new measure to their lives along with the influences afforded by the notion of going to America.

Delmy understood that without Rony's protection, such a trip North would be a non-starter. The timing of their departure was also critical. They would have to leave at the same time as the next Caravan departed around payday before her mother could confiscate her meager funds as she would just about need every single Lempira, she earned that month to pay her expenses going North.

The current conversion rate between Lempira and Peso's and Dollars was not good right now so it was even more important Delmy departed the exact same day she received her paycheck from her job at one of the *maquiladoras* that cultivated shrimp where she started working in all her spare time even while in high school. Her friend Yanuel also worked at the same maquiladora *Sea Delight* often criticized for exploiting cheap Central American labor. On their days off from Sea Delight, they worked in a textile mill and had no time off working seven days a week.

DELMY

Rony, if I joined the Caravan, would you go with me to protect me?

RONY

I would probably consider it. However, if I left with you, I'm sure my dad would permanently kick me out. I could never go back.

DELMY

If I did ask you to go with me, you would have to promise to protect me and not attempt to do something before I was ready.

RONY

You know I would be the perfect gentleman with you.

DELMY

I would expect that out of you. Otherwise, I might as well start sleeping with the drug cartel people and you would never see me again.

RONY

What if we get separated in the United States or Mexico?

DELMY

There is always that possibility. My family does have a working telephone, you could call them on your cell phone.

RONY

If I leave with you, I will not be able to pay my cell phone bill, and they will shut it off.

DELMY

Talk to the phone company and see if you can pay a few months in advance.

RONY

I wish I could, but my dad takes most of my money.

DELMY

You will have to do what I'm doing, leave on Payday!

Yanuel Romero and Eduardo Ordoñez were observing the couple in almost complete disbelief. Neither one of them believed the two would do it nor were they expecting the next exchange.

Delmy stated, looking at the other two sitting directly across from her inside the coffee house.

DELMY

I would also think that Yanuel and Eduardo would come with us. If all four of us went together we would be safer and know we could depend on each other.

VOICEOVER

It started out as a dream and quickly turned into reality. Over the next few weeks as they gathered at the same coffee house scheming their departure and substance set in. All four were lucky they only got paid once a month and they were now a week away from payday and the point of decision.

If the two boys did not go with them, they would lose these girls forever and it was unlikely they would ever get a chance to have

relations with quality women as nice as these two.
The four teenagers had known each other a long time and were almost family. Failure to go with the girls would appear as an act of betrayal.

Motivation to go thus elevated on many levels and the pressure rose exponentially because the Caravan was leaving within a day of Payday for all four teenagers. Timing was everything.

It was not unusual for Yanuel to spend weekends with Delmy. Hence, if she went home, packed a backpack with changes of clothes, swimsuit, etc. it would not be unexpected.

Likewise, Eduardo and Rony would stay at each other's places and go on weekend fishing trips and hunting in some of the undeveloped countryside where certain wildlife could be found and was highly appreciated at the dinner table on Sunday.

Hence to take the family pistol along would not be unexpected and was done so they had some form of protection. However, against the heavy fire power of the drug cartel guys, those peashooters were useless, though it did give them a sense of security, especially if they had to keep some rapists at bay and away from the girls.

Friday came and the plan unfolded. Drunken fathers and lazy mothers expecting a paycheck who could now stay home and sit on their rear ends since they now had a daughter and personal slave earning for them.

Their parents, would be unhappy as evening came and went and the routine money, they had been spoiled over the past couple of years suddenly didn't arrive.

The four teenagers' absence created worry and consternation, but also concern that in such a violent part of the world where bad things happen, it might have touched them in some terrible way.

The four received their paychecks, cashed them at banks and converted Honduran Lempira currencies to dollars and peso's where they would be much easier to trade for goods and services. They then took a bus about 50 miles up the road where the Caravan had formed up and already 2,500 migrants were already attached.

Car seats in the Caravan could be purchased. It cost slightly more than bus fares, but for the group to be able to stay together it was more than essential.

The four teenagers were lucky they obtained a ride in a vehicle that was reliable until they reached the middle of Mexico where they were forced to continue walking when the driver one morning took off without them after hearing rumors the stragglers up ahead were paying almost three times the fares to beat the caravan to the border. In due time the dust and lack of sanitation started to take its toll on the four. The boys were getting tired of only being able to sleep half the night to keep the women alive.

More and more they were at each other's throats and strong bonds between them slowly turned into flimsy attachments to the point the young men almost considered selling the two girls to cartel people and a ride in an air-conditioned car up to Tijuana as a benefit in doing so.

Probably the best purchase they made early on purchasing a large box of old type matches easily to start campfires with thinking they would have to have to cook food and live roughly.
As they traversed up the road in the swelling numbers now up to almost 4,000 by the time, they reached central Mexico, they picked up pieces of wood and scrap lumber along the roadside that would be good for a fire which added measurably to their security.

In due time the four teenagers found themselves integrated with families with the same concerns about security, so they helped look out for each other. But the problem now existed that since their ride had abandoned them for higher profits ahead, they were walkers and stragglers, along with well over one thousand others.

This Caravan now stretched for over 10 miles along the two lane Hiway 23 the Mexican police forced them to take to prevent them from impacting travel along any of the four lane road networks.

The first night when the Carsopian Aliens harvested the first group of stragglers, the rag tag group including the four Hondurans teenagers and the family's they traveled with rounded out to 20 people.

This group had lost a lot of ground from the main body because of the children in the group could only move so quickly, probably one and a half miles per hour typically.

To keep up with the Caravan, they had to continue walking almost two hours past sundown when the camps were set up and fires started long before they got there. Thus, unsuspecting Caravanners almost three miles ahead of them were the first picked off by the Carsopian Aliens now enjoying their *Rest and Relaxation Period* with real air and gravity, before they had to get back aboard their ships and complete the second half of their journey towards Empire stronghold ***Cui*** their ultimate destination where the star system was being fortified for what was considered the final battle for hegemony over the galaxy.

Lucky for the Caravanners, the wealthy billionaire organizer had pickup trucks sometimes with bottled water and meals, especially set aside for families with children. The family they traveled with knew the four teenagers were helpless and would not receive any accommodations, so they lied to the organizers and claimed them as their own kids.

Otherwise, the two girls might have been pushed into prostitution just to survive the trip. Traveling with the family was a godsend even though it slowed them down.

On a few occasions traveling with families with children also influenced the decisions of the Carsopian Aliens to harvest other groups of adults only because butchering and eating children didn't go over too well with their mindset. Plus, some of the adults in other groups were obese and the resulting barbecue was far tastier than attempting to eat a skinny kid.

The billionaire and his organizers eventually got around to identifying who's who in the zoo. They sent "technicians" in to persuade caravanners to reveal their identity and promised to contact authorities in their countries to inform relatives they were still alive and approaching the U.S. boarder.
By the night of the seventh day of travel, the organizers felt they had identified all members of the caravan and high-speed communications via the internet was already forwarding to operatives in each country their status. They were also manipulating the media who always wanted *hot stories*. The major media outlets soon imbedded reporters trying to dig up tear- jerker stories of abuse from their former countries.

Some of the imbedded people obtaining identities as well as intercepted communications allowed the U.S. Government to identify over five hundred people associated with the Caravan that were hardened Criminals.

Some of the Caravanners were let out of jail by their countries if they promised to leave and never come back. Many had been involved in narcotrafficking, human trafficking, children soldiering, rape, kidnapping of teenage girls and forcing them into prostitution slavery, murder for hire, racketeering, assassination, and insurrection. Fundamentally, they were Bad Hombres.

EXT.NIGHT.MEXICAN HIWAY 23 NORTH OF GUADALAJARA.

ACTION DEPICTED IN THE VOICEOVER TO BE FILMED AND SHOWN DURING THE VOICE OVER.

VOICEOVER

There had been more than one occasion for those Bad Hombres to plan on taking Delmy Áquilar and Yanuel Romero and pass them around campfires as sexual toys for a fee.
On the eighth night of travel deep in the heart of Central Mexico, a group of Bad Hombres eventually made their bold move. Little did they know the Carsopian Aliens were tracking them as a potential source of a delicacy for dinner that night.

As usual, the group of twenty was far behind the rest of the Convoy because of the delays the children caused. In some cases, the teenagers carried the children on their backs to help speed up the travel.

The Carsopian Aliens were surprised the dozen men suddenly were walking south, which was alright with them because it means much easier means of obtaining them away from any possible detection of the Caravan.

Watching through their infrared and ultraviolet optics a half mile away right after sunset, the Carsopian's observed the violence that abruptly erupted.

The twelve Bad Hombres were well armed and took very little time to pistol whip and beat Eduardo and Rony who were suddenly laying in pools of blood as they were beaten within an inch of their lives.

Two husbands who did not join in thinking they and their families would be left alone were in for a terrible rude awakening.

Their wives were also selected for sexual slavery, and they too were pistol whipped and knocked unconscious, leaving their kids and their wives screaming.

The Aliens then watched the hombres snatch the two teenage girls and two of the mothers of the small children who were young.

As the Bad Hombres marched the women at gunpoint off the side of the road where they would soon be the sex toys of these horrible excuses for human beings, the Aliens pounced upon them.

With their helmets on, the women could not see their almond shaped eyes nor know they were aliens. The twelve Bad Hombres were quickly killed, loaded up into the Carsopian Security Rover-craft and suddenly the Carsopian's departed.

The beaten men and two teenage boys with the crying children were suddenly amazed in the darkness when they heard the women cry out. There was barely enough twilight left after sundown to see them coming out of the nearby field.

One of the husbands who was now missing half his teeth cried out to his sobbing wife.

CARAVANER HUSBAND

What happened?

CARAVANER WIFE

Some men in uniforms came and killed those twelve bad guys and took them away!

Eduardo and Rony could hardly move, they were in bad shape. The family and the teenagers decided they would just stay on the road and wait for morning and hopefully someone would come along, and they could get help and notify the authorities.

All through the night the children whimpered from the horror they witnessed. Little did they know what their mothers, Delmy, and Yanuel had witnessed. Even though they knew the twelve Bad Hombres were horrible beings they were mowed down in cold blood with no offer to surrender. It was like an assassination!

VOICEOVER

The organizers of the Caravan knew that if really bad things happened to the group, the billionaire would be called out for being responsible and possibly sued or sanctioned by governments representing the Caravan people.
The Caravan organizers were getting more and more conscious of the plight of the Caravanners especially with the imbedded media types.
The Caravan supervisors were keeping a loose watch over members of the Caravan, especially families with kids, and were now being heavily criticized by humanitarian groups for forcing families to walk.

When the family with the small kids and teenagers didn't make it to camp and were long overdue and rumors had gone around that twelve Bad Hombres were heading toward the family, organizers with firearms got into a couple crew cab pickup trucks used to haul water and meals and headed south down the two-lane Mexican Hiway 23 to look for them. It didn't take them long to find the group just five miles south of the camp.

The families and teenagers just sat in the middle of the road totally ignoring the oncoming trucks which immediately caused some major concern with the drivers who knew something bad must have happened.

The men left their lights on, and motors running in the pickup trucks and got out and approached the family with flashlights and could see a lot of blood on their clothes and on the pavement. It was a terrible mess, and God help them if the media suddenly showed up!

To their chagrin the media wasn't too far behind and within minutes quickly had their cameras on the bloody mess. Including the two young ladies holding their severely wounded male friends in their laps, with blood all over their clothes.

The organizers tried to keep the media away from the Caravanners, but the media always smells a story, especially if there is this much blood all over the place!

There was a shoving match, but the media people suddenly outnumbered the organizers and were talking to the victims.

MAINSTREAM MEDIA (MSM) REP
What happened?

DELMY
We were assaulted by members of the Caravan.

That's all it took; the news feed was going viral because some of the cameras and media people had satellite feed.

MSM REP
Which direction did the men go who attacked you?

DELMY
They're all dead.

MSM REP
Who killed them?

DELMY
Men wearing nice uniforms.

MSM REP
Where's the bodies?

DELMY
The men who killed them took them with them.

MSM REP
Can you describe what the men looked like and what was their uniforms like?

DELMY
They were strange looking uniforms. I've never seen anything like that before in my lifetime. They didn't seem like military uniforms; they were a moth pastel like color.

MSM REP
Which direction did men in uniforms take the bodies?

DELMY
They put them in some kind of aircraft and flew maybe south. I couldn't really see which direction they were going.

The MSM Reporters started asking more questions when Delmy suddenly injected:

DELMY

These two young men are hurt very badly and need a doctor, and those men over there are beat up bad too. Can you get us medical help instead of asking any more questions?

The organizers understood they had to get this bloody mess away from the press as quick as possible and were already checking the internet for the nearest hospital. One of them said:

CARAVAN ORGANIZER REP

Let's put all the wounded in our trucks and we'll drive back to the camp and send some more vehicles down to pick up the rest as we try to get these men to a hospital.

DELMY

I must go with him, I'm traveling with him, and he's in bad shape from trying to save my life.

YANUEL

I must go with Eduardo. He's like part of my family.

MEDIA REP

We can put some of them in our vans and take them.

CHIEF CARAVAN ORGANIZER (Bill)

Okay, let's load everyone up since we probably have enough room if we put a few of them in the news vans. We'll locate and drive to the nearest hospital.

The assistant caravan organizer responded with a grim look on his face.

CARAVAN ORGANIZER ASSISTANT (JACK)

Okay, boss.

CHIEF CARAVAN ORGANIZER (Bill)

Jack, I want you to notify law enforcement and let them know we are all on the way to the nearest hospital.

CARAVAN ORGANIZER ASSISTANT (JACK)

We probably need some police protection tonight for the Caravan considering what we just witnessed.

By the time the group were heading North on the road which happened to be in the direction of a small town 30 miles ahead that had a doctor and a clinic as well as police, the Carsopian Aliens were 50 miles away at their current Rest & Relaxation site preparing the 12 bodies for cooking on a spit like device and explaining to their superiors what all happened.

***

NORMAN

EXT.NIGHT.SAN PEDRO SULA, HONDURAS. BARNEY AND BETTY LOGAN'S HOME. VOICEOVER DURING ACTION DESCRIBED IN THE VOICE OVER.

VOICEOVER

Barney and Betty Logan moved to Honduras with their dog Norman. The dog Norman was quarantined at huge cost for 90 days then released to Barney and Betty Logan after going through extensive checks by veterinarians.

Betty didn't like the idea of moving to Honduras, but Barney a penny pincher had determined they could live well on his government pension in such a place. After selling their home in San Diego for $800,000 they were able to buy an equivalent home in a nice area of San Pedro Sula for $175,000.

The home was totally fixed up, painted, ready to move in. The owner had to sell at a much lower price because he just received an H1B visa to work for a company in Silicon Valley. He'd make up for the loss of equity in the home after working just six months.

The neighbors quickly took a liking to Barney and Betty and their lovely, sweet dog Norman who had been around a lot of people and was as loveable as could be.

The Logan's didn't realize the chip in Norman wasn't going to work out too well in San Pedro Sula if the dog got lost. His dog collar had the name Norman on it, but no other identifying information.

Norman was an inquisitive dog. It wouldn't be the first time he got out and went exploring. Just after a mere two months out of quarantine, and adjusting to the new home, Norman seemed impatient. Everything including scents seemed strange to him.

That night Barney made a blunder and forgot to lock the back gate which led to the recycling containers in the back when he took the trash out.

Norman spent as much time outside as he did inside and with the mild temperature this time of year, outdoors suited him

just fine as he lay there in slumber and Barney went in the house with the door cracked open knowing Norman knew how to get in the house without any assistance.
Barney was reading and Betty was already in bed. Barney fell asleep in the recliner chair and didn't wake up again until 2:00 a.m.

Norman was still outside, and if anyone approached, the dog would of course bark loud and wake up the entire neighborhood, so there was no fear in leaving the back door unlocked and open a few inches so Norman could come in when he would eventually feel like it.

Barney went to bed unsuspecting of anything and soon fell into a deep sleep. What he didn't know, Norman had already left and had been gone almost five hours.

Norman the inquisitive dog, heard strange sounds outside the back of the fence and approached it. All he had to do was put his paw on the gate and it moved open. Norman then walked out and saw something off to the distance which got his attention which he went to check out.

As Norman wound up down at the very end of the alley, across the street was a stray dog. That dog barked at Norman which was the wrong thing to do.

Norman was gentle around humans whom he loved, but another dog in his territory would simply upset him and he gave chase.

The two dogs were already two blocks down the street before the scared mongrel Norman was chasing suddenly darted into a yard, where he probably belonged, and Norman quickly lost interest.

Norman's problem now was, chasing the other dog, he forgot which direction was home and there wasn't enough scent to follow it back.

Norman helplessly started cruising the nearby area looking for his new home, hoping Barney would call for him so he would know which way to go.

<u>EXT.NIGHT.SAN PEDRO SULA, HONDURAS. RANDOM STREET</u>

Alexandro Solórzano and Reynaldo Mejía were walking in the morning along the road where Norman was cruising when they spotted the huge Pitt Bull. The dog looked menacing and at first the two boys were scared. The dog didn't bark and looked at the two boys in some way hoping they would figure out how to take him back to his home. Norman slowly approached the boys and gave no bark or any sudden moves.

ALEXANDRO SOLÓRZANO
Hola perrito.

Alexandro reached out to pet Norman.

Norman was glad to have found a human that could get him home and acted friendly and sniffed the boy who petted him some more.

ALEXANDRO SOLÓRZANO
Me pregunto de quién es este perro? [I wonder whose dog this is?]

REYNALDO MEJÍA
Look at its dog collar.

ALEXANDRO SOLÓRZANO
It just says Norman on the dog collar.

REYNALDO MEJÍA
Maybe there will be a reward for it, the dog looks good, probably worth some money.

ALEXANDRO SOLÓRZANO
Let's take him home and post some flyers around here about the lost dog.

Good idea. If we can get a good reward, we can buy a seat on one of the Caravan buses and get to the USA.

The boys lead Norman home which was more than a mile away from Barney and Betty Logan's home.

Within a few days, Barney and Betty Logan realized their prized pet Norman was gone for good. He simply disappeared and any attempt to locate him, including posting rewards, turned up negative.

Norman soon started enjoying his new situation. Lots of people were fussing over him and playing with him. Barney and Betty Logan simply bored Norman and didn't provide enough activity for him. Also, Norman preferred the table scraps instead of the dog food he was used to eating. It didn't take Norman long to forget about Barney and Betty Logan.

***

EXT.NIGHT.SAN PEDRO SULA, HONDURAS. OSCAR GODOY'S PARENTS HOME.

VOICEOVER

A few other teenagers looking at joining the Caravan were Oscar Godoy, Gabriela Zelaya, and Javier Pineda.

Oscar owned a used Honda, that was good in every way except the transmission was shot from previous owners abusing the car.

The car's front end was now jacked up on blocks in front of the home as the two boys tinkered with it and slowly figured out how to get the transmission out of the car using tools Javier's dad owned.

Once they got the transmission open and looked inside, it quickly became evident, several of the parts were damaged beyond repair.

OSCAR GODOY

What are we going to do now?

JAVIER PINEDA

Unless we can figure out how to get this transmission fixed, there is no way we'll be able to get with that Caravan in time to travel up to the United States.

OSCAR GODOY

I think I have an idea.

JAVIER PINEDA

What's that?

OSCAR GODOY

When you drive around San Pedro Sula you see a lot of parked Honda's, some are broke, like this one, but with other types of problems keeping them from driving. Maybe they have the transmission we need.

JAVIER PINEDA

Yea, there's a Honda just like this one about four blocks, has been sitting there with a flat tire for over a month. Maybe the owner is out of town?

OSCAR GODOY

Let's go there this evening and see if there are any lights.

JAVIER PINEDA

It took us over six hours to get this transmission out.

OSCAR GODOY

That's because we didn't know what we were doing. Now we know how to get it out. I bet we can have it out in an hour.

JAVIER PINEDA

If we get caught, we'll end up in prison.

OSCAR GODOY

Let's not get caught and by the time they discover the transmission stolen, we'll already be up in Mexico.

JAVIER PINEDA

You sure you want to do this?

OSCAR GODOY

There is no future in bananas. We might as well risk going to jail than having to spend our life helping some rich guys grow bananas for people up north.

JAVIER PINEDA

Okay, let's take our tools with us and use Gabriela as the lookout. The car is in the yard so unless someone comes close, they will not know what we are doing if the owner isn't home.

OSCAR GODOY

You sure she will agree?

JAVIER PINEDA

I'm sure she will. I think I already got her pregnant.

OSCAR GODOY

Okay, I'll be back around sundown. We'll go then.

JAVIER PINEDA

See you then.

The day passed by quickly and around sundown the three were once together again, though *Gabriela* didn't look so happy. *Javier* didn't know if it was *Gabriela* simply was scared or because she was upset, she missed her period, and they had been screwing without protection.

The three trudged on four blocks fully loaded down with tools and a jack they needed to raise the car up so they could get under it to work.

The neighborhood appeared to be almost abandoned. There were only lights on one home almost an entire block up the street. Everyone else was either gone or already sleeping.

JAVIER PINEDA

We can go look in some windows and see if there is anyone inside.

They looked around, the coast was clear. Nobody was inside, though it appeared people lived there.

OSCAR GODOY

What can we put under the car when we raise it up?

JAVIER PINEDA

See those concrete blocks over there on the flower bed?

OSCAR GODOY

Yea?

JAVIER PINEDA

Let's grab a couple of them and after we raise the chassis, we'll put a couple of them under the chassis to hold it, just like we did at home.

OSCAR GODOY

Alright.

Soon, operating with flashlights the car was up on cement blocks and the boys had the hood up thanks to the car being left unlocked. Having gone through the drill with their own car, getting this transmission out was far simpler and in one hour it was out of the car sitting to the side.

OSCAR GODOY

What do we do about the car?

JAVIER PINEDA

We should put it back down on the ground and put those cement blocks back at the flower bed, so nothing looks suspicious.

Within 10 more minutes, the car was back down on the ground on its tires and the cement blocks back in place in the flower bed as if nothing happened.

It took both Oscar and Javier to carry the transmission the four blocks and it was a good thing that *Gabriela* was strong enough to carry some of the tools.

Back home they immediately went to work and installed the new transmission, though it was three hours later before they were all done because they were careful in putting everything back correctly so the car would work.

JAVIER PINEDA

Shall we drive it around the block to make sure it works?

OSCAR GODOY

Sounds like a good idea.

The boys hopped in front and *Gabriela* got in the back and they started the car up. The motor had no issues, and just like the transmission, it wasn't the motor the car had been delivered with!

They drove the car around the block, it sounded good, the transmission was satisfactory.

OSCAR GODOY

Let's all get some sleep then we'll take off around noon tomorrow and go find the Caravan.

JAVIER PINEDA

Ok, see you tomorrow.

The three then split up, and sleep would be hard to get as it was now only a few more hours before sunrise and their adrenalin was pumping.

ALEXANDRO SOLÓRZANO

<u>EXT.DAY.SAN PEDRO SULA, HONDURAS CENTRAL BUSINESS AREA.</u>

VOICEOVER

Alexandro Solórzano and Reynaldo Mejía met at the bank the day they were leaving to join the Caravan.

They had been unlucky in obtaining a reward for Norman, but they had one advantage other *dreamers* didn't have, their parents didn't confiscate their earnings.

Their parents were more pragmatic and realized the sooner the boys saved up some cash, the sooner they would be able to leave home and live on their own.

With dollars and pesos and instructions from the bank on how to wire home money after they got a job in America, they had their next big problem: *what to do about Norman.*

ALEXANDRO SOLÓRZANO

What can we do with Norman? If we just desert him, he might get killed.

REYNALDO MEJÍA

Yea nobody around here wants the dog, they fear it will cost too much to feed him.

ALEXANDRO SOLÓRZANO

We have one option.

REYNALDO MEJÍA

And what is that?

ALEXANDRO SOLÓRZANO

Take Norman with us.

REYNALDO MEJÍA

They will never let us on a bus with the dog.

ALEXANDRO SOLÓRZANO

Let's try hitch hiking. Maybe Norman will help us get a ride.

REYNALDO MEJÍA

Okay, but if that doesn't work, let's take the dog back to where we found it and turn it loose.

ALEXANDRO SOLÓRZANO

Sure.

Nobody was home at the boy's residence because everyone was working as they were expected to be working as well.

They packed lightly, fed the dog a good meal and gave it several bowls of water, then headed towards the main Hiway.

There were hitch hikers now and then, but due to the high crime rate, few people these days stopped picking up hitch hikers for fear of being robbed. Two boys with a dog would present a different picture and disarm the thoughts of many good people who otherwise would stop to give a stranger a ride. The boys were clean, and the dog looked immaculate and expensive.

Larissa Cortés and Daphne Vasquez were in one of Larissa's family's cars. This was not their primary car, so Larissa was allowed to drive it as much as she wanted if she filled it up with gas. It was a good second car, but her parents seldom drove it any longer as they had a new car. It was her father's intention to give her the car to help her out.

Larissa Cortés parents both worked. One in real estate and the other at a tourist hotel as a clerk/receptionist. Compared to most people living in San Pedro Sula, Honduras, the Cortés family lived well, had a nice house and had no problems affording the new car sitting in their driveway.

Larissa Cortés probably could have gone to the Universidad de San Pedro Sula but Daphne Vasquez who came from a family of not so well off, living down the street a block, just didn't have the grades to enable her enrollment.

Daphne Vasquez was not the good friend that Larissa Cortés needed that would inspire her to apply herself and attend the Universidad de San Pedro Sula. Instead, she was content to bring Larissa down to her level of an unachievable lackluster future.

It was later learned that Daphne Vasquez had the audacity to conspire and convince Larissa Cortés to go with her and join the Caravan and make that memorable trip north. They both had jobs and neither of their parents confiscated their money, so as far as they were both concerned it would be a simple matter of driving North and somehow make it through American customs officials and start their lives out in the United States where they knew because of their exquisite beauty, they would quickly latch on to Daddy Warbucks and live the good life.

Of all the people set off, these two girls were probably the best prepared in the sense they had substantial cash with them, and the car was well maintained, full of gas, recent oil change, and they both had Tourist passports because they had traveled outside the country on girls' soccer trips sponsored by their school and generous contributions by local businessmen.

As Daphne and Larissa were driving up CA13 Hiway heading Northeast for Choloma a short distance away they would pass through and follow the road up to the coastline where it abruptly turned west and headed for Guatemala and Belize and then turn off on CA14 that would be where they expected to meet the Convoy that would soon head through Mexico up to the United States; Daphne spotted the two boys and the dog hitch hiking.

DAPHNE

Should we stop and give those two boys a ride with their dog,
maybe they are going to the Caravan?

LARISSA

They might rob us and rape us.

DAPHNE

They look too clean cut to be that type, and the dog looks so well kept.

LARISSA

Somehow, I feel we will regret doing this.

DAPHNE

I'm sure it will be fine. They probably just want a ride to Choloma.

Larissa, with huge regret, slowed down and pulled over to the side of the road. The two boys and the dog came up running from behind.

DAPHNE

Where are you guys heading?

ALEXANDRO SOLÓRZANO

We are going up the road a way, we want to catch up with the Caravan heading North that you might have heard about.

DAPHNE

You mean the one to the United States.

ALEXANDRO SOLÓRZANO

Yes, that one.

Larissa looked at Daphne.

LARISSA

Don't get any ideas. We'll give them a ride then drop them off.

About that time Larissa was hoping Daphne didn't divulge to the two boys that's where they were heading as well, as it could easily create a scenario that Larissa wasn't ready for, plus she didn't know much about the boys or what kind of young men they were.

As Larissa pulled out back onto the Hiway Daphne asked them:

DAPHNE

What's your names?

ALEXANDRO

I'm Alexandro Solórzano and this is Reynaldo Mejía.

DAPHNE
Do your families live in San Pedro Sula?

ALEXANDRO
Yes, they do.

DAPHNE
Do they know you are leaving?

ALEXANDRO
They will figure it out a little later tonight or tomorrow, I'm sure. How about you?

DAPHNE
Yes, we live in San Pedro Sula.

ALEXANDRO
I appreciate you giving us a ride. I was worried when people saw our dog they wouldn't want to stop.

DAPHNE
The only reason why we stopped is because of your dog. It's well-kept and groomed, so it tells us something about you.

ALEXANDRO
Well thanks.

DAPHNE
What's the dog's name?

ALEXANDRO
Norman.

DAPHNE
Is he friendly?

ALEXANDRO
Very friendly, Norman loves all people and is very gentle.

DAPHNE
Be sure and let me know when he needs to use the restroom.

ALEXANDRO
Norman will let you know, he's a smart dog.

The ride was very pleasant. Popular music on the radio and nice perfume of the ladies made the young men's day. It was also cool they gave them a ride all the way to the Caravan.

LARISSA

Here you are, the Caravan. Good luck in the United States.

ALEXANDRO

Thank you for the ride.

The boys and the dog got out of the car and smartly walked up to the organizers who had bus seating or private car seats for all those going north.

ALEXANDRO

We would like tickets for the bus.

BUS EMPLOYEE

I'm sorry but dogs are not allowed on the bus.

VOICE OVER

The boys were sad when they learned *they were not allowed on the bus because of the dog.* They decided they would not abandon Norman.

As expected, the girls had disappeared but were now in line about 50 cars back. The boys didn't know these girls were joining the Caravan. This was the day it started moving North with some walking and some riding. Sadly, even families were walking, in some cases having been swindled out of their cars by people faking they were Caravan organizers, and the people had to get on a bus. But they didn't know they had insufficient funds for the bus and by then, their cars were long gone.

The vehicle traffic went almost double that of those walking after an hour the girls spotted the boys walking with their dog and pulled over.

DAPHNE

How come you are walking?

ALEXANDRO

They would not let us on the bus with our dog Norman.

LARISSA CORTÉS

I'll probably regret this but hop in the car. And don't get any ideas,
I'm just being nice.

Daphne Vasquez looked at Larissa Cortés in total disbelief. Her parents would be stunned if she left in this manner, but even more so picking up those two boys and their dog!

The Caravan made slow progress. The organizers purposely kept the speed of advance down to make sure the maximum number of people could make it.

LARISSA

Well, at this speed we'll get good gas mileage.

ALEXANDRO

We have money, we can pay for your gas.

LARISSA

Thank you.

Before long Norman was conked out laying on the lap of the two boys napping. Norman didn't know this yet, but he would soon become the most famous dog in the world as he was the only dog in the Caravan.

EXT. DAY. MEXICO COMEMOS CARAVANOS HIWAY 23

The Mexican two lane Hiway-23 had seen better years, but it was still good for almost 70 miles per hour even though the speed limit was 50 for safety reasons and lack of patrolling and close by hospitals for traffic accidents.

The media feed was soon showing and spinning the missing twelve Bad Hombres. They gave inferences that our American President had ordered their assassination and a lot of other baloney perpetrated by fake news to bolster ratings.

The police stopped the Caravan for over a day, getting statements and finding out who exactly was missing. The troubling part is there were suddenly people missing over the past few days that were unaccounted for and in some cases, they were normal decent people and not the Bad Hombres that were also missing.

With the help of the Mexican Policía Federal Ministerial (PFM) the missing twelve Bad Hombres were identified. Each one of them was a hardened criminal and roadblocks were set up south and north of the Caravan to find them because PFM agents didn't initially believe the story of the Caravanners.

The incident caused one additional outcome. The four young individuals were identified and their parents down in Honduras was notified about their disposition and location.

Circumstantial evidence and anecdotal information provided by other criminal elements and eyewitnesses also conveyed the notion the 12 Bad Hombres had nothing to do with the mystery of the other missing individuals. Checks made up to 100 miles south of this position on the roads they took derived no information on the whereabouts of the missing people.

Suddenly the Caravan had more protection and visibility than the 500 criminals traveling in the caravan cared for. Any exploitation or abuse by the criminals quickly evaporated as they were stuck with nowhere to go and nothing, they could do but follow along without attempting any nefarious activities.

Even though beat severely and in a lot of pain and suffering the two young men refused to be put on a bus to be sent home to their parents. Since they were able to prove they were 18 years old, there was nothing the authorities could do to compel them to return.

Because of the public pressure the billionaire was now starting to feel, he dispatched additional pickup trucks and drivers to carry resources for all 20 of the members struck by the Bad Hombres now admitted at a nearby hospital.

By the time the group had reached the hospital, they did not feel physically fit to continue the journey, however, just like they predicted, they didn't really have a case for asylum they soon learned by the authorities. And as they learned their fate, they would eventually have to go to plan B, give their remaining money to coyotes to get them past Campo and into San Diego proper where they could easily be recognized because of the film clips the media broadcasted. Plan B didn't seem viable either.

Out from the horror of the unimaginable brutality inflicted by the twelve Bad Hombres who were now missing persons of interests with man hunts on them, came a more light- hearted news feed. Norman was now in the camera's lenses. People around the globe who are dog lovers instantly focused on poor Norman.

One day unexpectedly a convoy of vehicles came south to meet the Caravan, and one vehicle sent had copious amounts of dog food for poor Norman.

The news media and representatives from the dog food company were there with cameras and ready to exploit the dog for advertisements on Television. They approached Alexandro Solórzano and Reynaldo Mejía to offer food for the dog.

Unfortunately for the dog food company, kids in the Caravan kept feeding Norman. He had no appetite and the last thing in the world Norman wanted was dog food!

Once the cameras were turned off the dog food company official asked the two young men:

DOG FOOD COMPANY OFFICIAL

What kinds of food did the dog like?

ALEXANDRO

His favorite is hot dogs.

DOG FOOD COMPANY OFFICIAL

He prefers hot dogs?

ALEXANDRO

Yes, he loves hot dogs, sometimes we wrap it in bread, but he often removes the bread and gets it out of the way and just eats the hot dogs.

20 minutes later the dog food truck was up the road getting away from all the Television cameras!

Alexandro Solórzano and Reynaldo Mejía behavior had impressed Larissa Cortés and Daphne Vasquez up to this moment. They turned out to be unusually kind and accommodative.

They were true gentlemen and had never been treated with such exaltation by attractive young ladies in their lifetimes. When they were alone from time to time as Larissa and Daphne visited porta-potties and these young gentlemen stood guard outside portable showers brought in so they could remove the grime of several days on the road.

The strangers slowly became friends that would last a lifetime. It didn't take long for Alexandro Solórzano and Reynaldo Mejía to figure out Norman preferred the two girls.

In one of their near misses, the only thing that saved Alexandro Solórzano, Reynaldo Mejía, Larissa Cortés, and Daphne Vasquez from becoming one of the entrées for the Carsopian Aliens dinner, was Norman.

The aliens could not bear to destroy such a magnificent looking animal and were curious as to why he had such tremendous affection towards the Humans, especially the females.

***

EXT. DAY. MEXICO COMEMOS CARAVANOS HIWAY 23

MUSIC DURING THE FOLLOWING VOICEOVER: **Liszt: Dante-Sinfonie**

[https://www.youtube.com/watch?v=A7x-la2AbjE]

VOICEOVER

Mexican Policía Federal Ministerial (PFM) Agent Carlos Guerrero's called in to investigate the matter.

PFM Agent Carlos Guerrero's was intently studying the missing twelve criminals while he read the police report about the four women almost raped as well as the two boyfriends and two husbands who were severely beaten and found almost crippled in the middle of the road, unable to move.

PFM Agent Carlos Guerrero read the reports made by the police investigating the matter but knew eventually he would have to interview these people because their story didn't seem possible.

All 20 people even the children interviewed by the police had said the same stories, except only the four women, witnessed the assassinations *as they termed it.*

The women said it was unprovoked murder even though they knew they were just about to be raped and mistreated.

It all happened very quickly according to the police report.

All four women stated the twelve Bad Hombres, fully armed with some powerful weapons soon lay dead on the ground with no gun shots heard.

But there was a strange sound when the twelve Bad Hombres bodies were blown apart and as the forensic teams searched the area, they found large amounts of DNA and entrails of all twelve men suggesting they received some terrible blunt trauma.

No spent gun casings from spent rounds or anything found to suggest what types of weapons were used. The lack of gunshot sounds reported seemed rather perplexing. Nobody in the Caravan heard gunshots, sounds of aircraft or anything else related to the case.

There was an extraordinary development in the case. The aliens left behind footprints. None of them matched any type of footwear ever worn or known of on planet Earth. The feet were unusually large and wide. Chills went down the Chief investigator's spine, as it all started to seem terribly surreal.

The Carsopian Aliens had several landing zones selected. They purposely did not want to stay in one spot too long.

EXT. CGI. DAY. CARSOPIAN FLEET LAUNCHES AND RELOCATES. 20 SECONDS.

VOICEOVER

On the following day they repositioned next to Grande de Santiago River located not far from Mexico's Pacific Coast.

EXT. CGI. DAY. CARSOPIAN FLEET LANDS AT NEW TEMPORARY LOCATION. 20 SECONDS.

VOICEOVER

This landing zone accommodated a lot of ships and was far away from the public or towns and cities. After a couple days here resting pumping and filtering water for their continued trek they planned to depart in a couple days.

Some of the crews were getting restless and at the same time, the earlier ease to which they obtained the human carcasses, led them to want to obtain a few more humans to satisfy the troops who knew soon they would be back on a space food diet and artificial gravity and reprocessed water.

Permission was granted and Carsopian Security Rover-craft

were sent West towards the coastal cities to acquire a few more carcasses to accentuate their next evening meals.

La Cantera which is a suburb of Tepic, Mexico was chosen, and the time of night coincided with a lot of drunks leaving bars and lovers parked out in lover's lane in romantic discourse.

Systematically a dozen people were snatched and grabbed. Some of them would not be missed until morning based on their routine behaviors.

The police found a couple of empty cars out in lover's lane parked in seclusion where lovers embrace occurred since they had no other place to go this late at night.

When the cars found had no signs of foul play, just missing bodies, it was apparent the cartels were not involved. The mystery deepened.

One of Mexican Policía Federal Ministerial, PFM Agent's Carlos Guerrero's who assisted in investigating the twelve missing Bad Hombres but also the growing list of unaccounted for Caravanners was sent to Tepic, Mexico with a forensic team.

PFM Agent Carlos Guerrero and the forensic team would try to provide some insights into how suddenly a dozen people came up missing. There was little or no evidence left behind except one lucky footprint found.

The hairs on the back of PFM Agent Carlos Guerrero's neck stood up when the cast of the footprint showed a shoe size of approximately 16G was left behind.

Comparison to the Caravan Incident footprint came back almost identical with a shoe print extraordinarily unusual.

The large footprint and patterns the Carsopian's left behind was due to the size and the technology used allowing them to march over far more rugged terrain than what armies on planet earth experienced.

The nature and the confidentiality of the investigation due to the sensitivity of the issues, none of this information could be brought to the public's attention. PFM Agent Guerrero previously had numerous interactions with the United States FBI who often cooperated in solving cases that affected both countries. Such would be the case with terrorism, human and narcotrafficking, and money laundering.

Several FBI agents were invited to Mexico and look over the evidence at the Mexican Policía Federal Ministerial, Headquarters. *PFM Agent Carlos Guerrero* was curious *if the FBI had ever come across similar footprints.*

<u>EXT. DAY. LA CANTERA SUBURB OF TEPIC, MEXICO</u>

FBI agents Bentley Boyd and Charles Gable had investigated some of the most bizarre crimes ever committed.

FBI AGENT BENTLEY BOYD

Quite frankly I've never seen a size 16G shoe at a crime scene before.

FBI AGENT CHARLES GABLE

I remember a crime solved in Hamamatsu Japan where the police went to every shoe store in town asking owners if they had ever sold a shoe that would leave the type of footprint discovered. It was the key to solving a very difficult case.

PFM AGENT CARLOS GUERRERO

Did they find any store that sold any such shoes?

FBI AGENT CHARLES GABLE

No, but they reached out to us and one of our agents in Hong Kong working with Hong Kong police went to several shoe stores and discovered a match.

PFM AGENT CARLOS GUERRERO

Did that help solve the crime?

FBI AGENT CHARLES GABLE

It did since one of the potential suspects had traveled to Hong Kong six months prior. Japanese police officers visited Hong Kong with pictures of the suspect and the shop owner recognized him. They eventually got a search warrant and found the shoes with DNA evidence in the perpetrators home.

The next question they were trying to reconcile in Mexico:

FBI AGENT BENTLEY BOYD

How could such disappearances of individuals more than 500 miles apart happen almost simultaneously, especially if the footprints were connected to the case?

***

EXT. DAY. CARSOPIAN NEW TEMPORARY LANDING ZONE AT GRANDE DE SANTIAGO RIVER LOCATED NEAR MEXICO'S PACIFIC COAST.

The humidity and moisture from the Pacific Ocean did not feel pleasing to most of the Carsopian's so after the water loading and filtering was completed, it was decided to move further inland into more arid land that would have a sparse population, and the cool evenings would be refreshing and more like their home world.

Long before anyone came looking in their direction near the lake where criminals could conceivably hide out, the Carsopian's were long gone. There were many footprints left behind to be found.

But since no individuals were reported seen when the locals were questioned by Agent Guerrero's men, there wasn't any point in expending vast man hours out looking for additional clues because like in previous incidents, human DNA and footprints was all they ever discovered.

The assumption was the perpetrators had driven to La Cantera via the Mexican Hiway network and were long gone. The motive could be human trafficking or simply robbery and eventually the bodies would show up. The cartels were possibly involved, and INTEL would attempt to discover if they were, and why?

Ironically when the Carsopian's relocated, they were once again near the path of the Caravan.

Word had reached out to migrants that *a "soft" caravan was heading north, and a billionaire was supplying the travelers with food, water, and security*. Several other impromptu caravans rendezvoused with this one which then soared over night to 7,000 plus including several of them on foot without transportation.

Also imbedded in these branches of Caravan's was more Bad Hombres. The Billionaire was pleased to learn the level of mass chaos he was creating. Civil Rights and Immigration Attorneys descended upon the Caravan the closer they got to the U.S. boarder. Instead of being strung out 10 miles, the security apparatus worried they no longer had the capacity to deal with the growing crowd and sent out requests for more backup.

The Mexican Policía Federal Ministerial, PFM on the other hand believed in safety in numbers. The crowd was so large, and the number of stragglers had doubled.

At the same time, the Carsopian troops demanded more barbecued humans because more than half did not receive any portions with their meals. Carsopian Security Rover Craft were sent out in larger numbers to assess their security and any possible threats. During the security sweeps the Carsopian's discovered the long convoy almost double what they had observed.

After reporting this migrant convoy, the Carsopian's decided to send out additional Carsopian Security Rover-Craft to obtain more humans for their cannibalistic ritual that often was done before major battles to build up zeal of the shock troops.

The troops were elated because this would be a huge boost for their psychology because the continued consumption of space food put a damper on their enjoyment of the Rest and Relaxation period.

Since no further incidents occurred along the caravan route for a while and the organizers had a good handle on the original four thousand Caravanners, the presence of imbedded security caused a level of vigilance decrement.

Out in this sparsely populated area north of Guadalajara, they could see car lights approach from a long distance and a rear-guard escort would then escort passing cars up the side of the Caravan who were instructed to stay in the right lane while cars passed the caravan with an escort.

On the next moonless night, a Mexican rancher came up the road from behind the Convoy in his pickup truck. He was carrying hardware and materials to his ranch another 30 miles up the road. While the escort was driving and escorting the Mexican rancher around the Caravan, the rear of the scattered Caravan was unprotected and exposed.

The last group of 50 Caravanners were almost a full half mile behind the Caravan, and the security escort had been rotating rides with them to help speed up the group to catch up with the main body. He dropped off a half dozen people to the head of the convoy as he completed his escort mission and turned around to get back to the rear, which he had to go slow to avoid hitting someone walking out on the wrong side of the road.

While the escort was gone, a group of Carsopian Security Rover-Craft landed on the road behind the last group of stragglers. Since their propulsion made no noise and they had no lights, they were not spotted in the moonless night.

The Carsopians got out of their security rover craft, lined up and targeted the fifty stragglers. It only took a minute, and the beam weapons tore through the bodies and killed every single straggler. Sadly, there were a few children in the mix.

Because the Carsopian security forces were a good fifty percent taller and larger than American and Mexican soldiers, it took little time for them to load up the fifty carcasses into the security rovers then fly back to their camp.

By the time the Carsopian's could see the lights of the caravan security pickup truck heading their way now about two miles away, they lifted off and were on their way to their bivouac area fifty miles to the West and far away from any roads. The two pieces of evidence left behind was a lot of blood on the Hiway and one large footprint created by stepping in a pool of blood and entrails.

The security pickup truck had a rough idea of the clusters of stragglers and since the driver had been alternating giving that last group rides to help speed them up, he knew who to look for and about how far back of the Caravan they were and what kinds of clothing they were wearing.

The security person Mark expected to find the last group of migrants probably a half mile behind the last cluster of the main body of stragglers. The security man was surprised they disappeared and were nowhere to be found. He then thought possibly they might have given up and turned around to go home. They needed to know that too. Therefore, he drove further south searching for them and didn't see a soul.

The security man went so far as to drive his pickup truck in a weave pattern so the lights would show out in fields in case that's where they stopped for the night. Because of the current season, there weren't many crops standing, and he could see far out into fields and there was no sign of any of the fifty or so stragglers. He then made that fateful call up ahead to the coordinators reporting in.

CARAVAN SECURITY MARK

Jack, this is Mark. My last group of 50 stragglers has just come up missing.

CARAVAN SECURITY MARK

The Caravan has stopped for the evening making campfires,
I'll be down there in a few minutes to help investigate this.

Several pickup trucks followed Jack to the rear of the Caravan where they saw Mark's pickup truck stopped but its headlights turned on and motor running.

CARAVAN SECURITY MARK

No sign of any of the stragglers?

CARAVAN SECURITY MARK

None. They simply vanished.

CARAVAN SECURITY MARK

Ok, I'm going to drive down the road a few miles and look for
them. You wait here and stay with the end of these stragglers.

CARAVAN SECURITY MARK

Okay.

Jack drove on down the Hiway and about a half mile south of where Mark was currently parked, he noticed a slight shimmering on the Hiway. It suddenly hit him; this was just like the gruesome find they saw with the 20 stragglers that included the four teenagers and the two families laying in pools of blood on the Hiway just a few days ago when the 12 bad hombres disappeared!

Jack stopped the pickup truck, got out with his flashlight and instantly revulsion hit him as he realized the carnage he was looking at. There was blood and entails all over the Hiway, just as if it were the floor of a slaughterhouse processing meat.

Jack then called the authorities and waited for their arrival.

Getting Mexican Policía Federal Ministerial, PFM agents into Guadalajara was simple as it was a short plane ride from Mexico City.

PFM Agent Guerrero currently assigned to the abduction cases and briefed about this new incident, he was just caucusing with his two FBI crime experts and invited them to go with him.

A short while later they were on a Mexican Policía Federal Ministerial, PFM jet flying to Guadalajara where they would be driven from to the crime scene about 80 miles to the North.

It was morning by the time the PFM and FBI agents arrived on the crime scene on the Hiway. Caravanners were slowly getting ready to start moving North which is what Agent Guerrero wanted as he wanted the crowd to get as far away from the crime scene as possible. The Hiway was shut down about a mile further south and to the North and as soon as the forensic examination of the crime scene would soon took place. Forensic technicians were on the way out of Guadalajara to take pictures and collect evidence.

Thanks to the canvassing of the stragglers by the Caravan organizers, they already had a list of names determined to be the missing people. Staunch measures had been taken right after the last murders to clearly identify everyone on the Caravan in the event they would become suspects.

But now this huge slaughter brought a new dimension to the case. It would be impossible for members of the Caravan to carry out this level of violence without leaving behind some clues, especially in such a short period of time, how did they disposed of the bodies and what would be their motive? Robbery? No, most of these people had the shirt on their back. They were desperately poor. There was nothing to rob. More than half were men and in this latest case there were a few children involved.

FBI AGENT CHARLES GABLE

Whoever did it was sophisticated, had elaborate transportation especially if what the four women stated from the original case was true, *they flew away.*

PFM AGENT GUERRERO

Based on where the blood evidence exists, we can almost determine who died and where.

FBI AGENT CHARLES GABLE

Some of them must have been running since the blood was smeared over a distance.

PFM AGENT GUERRERO

No shell casings or anything to describe the caliber of weapons used.

PFM AGENT GUERRERO

One thing is certain, based on the time Mark stated he went to escort the rancher to the time he got back, all the deaths and body removal had to have been accomplished maybe in 15 minutes.

FBI AGENT BENTLEY BOYD

And not one eyewitness?

FBI AGENT CHARLES GABLE

I've never seen anything like this in my 20 years with the FBI.

PFM AGENT GUERRERO

Nor have I even dealing with the Cartel's, we've never seen anything like this before.

FBI AGENT BENTLEY BOYD

Quite remarkable.

PFM AGENT GUERRERO

The women in the first case said it was some kind of aircraft, yet nobody heard any propulsion sounds from it.

FBI AGENT CHARLES GABLE

How's that possible?

FBI AGENT BENTLEY BOYD

The FBI would probably fire me for saying this, but what if it was not manmade?

PFM AGENT GUERRERO

I understand the gravity of your statement. The forensic team should be arriving shortly.

FBI AGENT BENTLEY BOYD

I hope you asked them to bring us a lot of coffee.

PFM AGENT GUERRERO

Yes, I probably need a gallon of coffee.

The PFM and FBI men silently waited, standing in almost disbelief. Had this been a one- time event it would not have been such an extraordinary affair. But now they have within a short period of time a second event, like the first, but a lot more people involved, but unlike the first scenario, but this one had zero eyewitnesses.

With the explosion of violence in Mexico caused by the Cartels, the Mexican forensics technicians were getting good at their work since they had significant proficiency. Now and then, Cartels have gang land type shootouts and as many as 50 or 60 bodies are involved. Because of their continuous activity the Mexican forensic technicians had more proficiency than the FBI who were considered the best in the business.

Numerous blood samples were taken, photographs of blood pools, and the holy grail of the event manifested when one of the Technion's said, "I got a footprint of possible perpetrator. Agent Guerrero led the two FBI men over to where the technician had photographed the blood-stained footprint.

MEXICAN PFM FORENSIC TECHNICIAN

Because the footprint is on the asphalt, all we can do is photograph it.

PFM AGENT GUERRERO

Any estimate on the size of the shoe?

MEXICAN PFM FORENSIC TECHNICIAN
It's huge. I'd say probably size 16G.

PFM AGENT GUERRERO
The killer is some sort of giant.

MEXICAN PFM FORENSIC TECHNICIAN
Shoe size is sometimes deceptive, but generally speaking it does give credence to a high probability the person who left this footprint is a tall, large person.

PFM AGENT GUERRERO
Whoever struck twice, will most likely be back a third time. We need to set a trap for them.

***

EXT. DAY. CARSOPIAN ALIN BIVUOAC AREA NEAR MEXICO COMEMOS CARAVANOS HIWAY 23

VOICEOVER

Fifty miles away, the Carsopian's were preparing for a grand meal. With 50 carcasses, this would be a feast. Very little space food with the consistency of soy would be ingested today. There were always crafty chefs aboard some of the transports who brought along special supplies that included special sauces to please their high-ranking leaders.

With such an auspicious moment, the capture and butcher of many humans now slowly rotating on spit like shafts like the way Greeks cook lamb, these enterprising chefs brought out the secret sauce. It was going to be delicious Caravanners tonight!

Most of the troops would forgo eating the little ones, but there were Carsopian assault troops who engaged in child cannibalism in a baptism of fire ceremony. The idea was to put unbridled fear in your opponents if they didn't surrender.

Barbecuing their children and allowing a few of them to escape on purpose quickly sent the message through many villages on planets they conquered with very few casualties as survival as a Carsopian slave was still a lot better than watching your children's skin boil away under the intense heat of the fires.

Tonight, those shock troops would rejoice in this ceremonial feasting and their leaders knew this would help prop them up psychologically for their continuation of their trip to the Carsopian Empire provincial stronghold Cui.

The Carsopian opponents, the Heisibing, they would soon fight, would feel more reviled had they known what the Carsopian's were doing to these poor helpless human creatures.

The Carsopian's were now just starting to feel normal again. The relatively short period of getting over space lag and cosmic sickness slowly ended for most of the troops as ninety percent of them were now physically and psychologically ready to commence crack assaults and deliver devastating blows to their enemies.

Even though several weapons now possessed by both the Carsopian's and the Heisibing could easily lay a planet to waste, the idea wasn't to kill the planet. It was more towards forcing submission by brute military coercion.

Some of the planets in the contested area had already changed hands a dozen times and the residents simply surrendered quickly to avoid the tremendous damage inflicted before by resisting.

Usually by the time a large Heisibing or Carsopian fleet arrived, the Garrison troops left behind to guard the spoils of war, would have deserted their posts and bugged out and off the planet as soon as they knew a large force was coming which they could not hope to defend against suddenly arrived in nearby space.

As the Heisibings slowly and systematically encroached closer and closer to the Carsopian Empire stronghold of Cui, the Carsopian's could no longer abandon planets. They had to stand and fight and risk irreparable damage to their planets to repel the Heisibings or eventually all would be lost.

Harvesting 50 humans for this ritual was considered trivial considering the possibility 50 billion Carsopian's could be dead in the matter of less than a year.

Earth was lucky it existed far away from most of the galaxy populated areas and clear out of the war zone. With a technology rating of 1.5, the evaluation indicated Earth was a pushover.

Humans would receive no respect from the Heisibings, Carsopians, or even the nearest dozen solar systems that had planets that had intelligent life like the planet Earth.

Just like an assembly line, the carcasses cooked to a medium rare and were deposited on a large table where the chefs cut out chunks of flesh for the big footed Carsopian's who slowly filed through getting their servings and feeling invigorated with the consumption.

A separate table was setup to carve up the smaller bodies and much fewer Carsopian's lined up here. All that did line up carried the special patch of a shock trooper. They were the tip of the sword, those who most likely would be killed in combat as they led the attack into withering hell.

The ceremony and psychology seemed no different than Japanese Generals in World War Two, on the communications outpost on the Island of Chichi Jima. As narrated in the non-fiction book "FLYBOYS," several Generals in charge of that Island, ate the livers of downed American Pilots to lift their spirits. No different than the Carsopians.

[https://en.wikipedia.org/wiki/Flyboys:_A_True_Story_of_Courage]

Former President George H. W. Bush was shot down near the island of Chichi Jima where eight POW pilots lost their livers to the top military commanders there for ceremonial dinners. Bush was rescued by the U.S.S. Finback virtually a few minutes before the Japanese from Chichi Jima would have capture him and cut out his liver.

It might seem terrible, but so was Dresden, Tokyo, Hiroshima, and Nagasaki which Sun Tzu would never condone. Imagine what Confucius would say if he observed it?

Another important aspect of this *Carsopian cannibalistic feast* was that it also occurred with their schedule to leave the planet. In a few more days. Every trace of them would be gone, except the footprints they left behind and Human remains.

General Fukua de Hundan toasted to the Carsopian troops sipping a special *Nuo Li Yaojì Elixir* he ordered made available for this auspicious occasion. They would not know when he would be ordering them to mount up and leave the planet, but the celebration seemed to suggest sooner rather than later.

The *Nuo Li Yaojì elixir* fortified the soul and gave the Carsopian Troops the invincibility syndrome. It was often dispersed to the shock troops in small dosages just as they deployed to the combat areas in the initial assault.

GENERAL FUKUA DE HUNDAN

The men are starting to look healthy again.

CARSOPIAN EXECUTIVE OFFICER

Real sunlight, real gravity, fresh water and fresh meat has had quite an impact on their physiology.

GENERAL FUKUA DE HUNDAN

Do you think they have rested enough to continue our transit to Cui?

CARSOPIAN EXECUTIVE OFFICER

Yes, I think we can depart at any time now.

GENERAL FUKUA DE HUNDAN

Alright, I recommend we give them another day here, then we'll load up and ship out.

CARSOPIAN EXECUTIVE OFFICER

As you wish General.

The two Generals surrounded by staff officers sitting in shaded bivouac chairs and sitting at portable tables covered with a nice tablecloth and equipped with shined silver place settings, were thoroughly relaxed and reflective knowing that they would soon be completing the second half of their voyage where they would have to send these brave Carsopian assault troops into the jaws of hail.

***

EXT. DAY. MEXICAN HIWAY 23 CRIME SCENE

Meanwhile back at the Mexican Hiway 23 crime scene the forensics were completed.

MEXICAN PFM FORENSIC SUPEREVISOR

The entire area of the slaughter was photographed, and blood samples were taken from each pool of blood.

PFM AGENT GUERRERO

It's unlikely we'll need to do DNA analysis because these people probably have nobody that is concerned about their wellbeing.

MEXICAN PFM FORENSIC SUPEREVISOR

The DNA samples would not do us any good unless someone comes forward trying to locate a missing relative.

PFM AGENT GUERRERO

The Caravan organizers provided a list of names we think are those deceased.

MEXICAN PFM FORENSIC SUPEREVISOR

If someone makes an inquiry and it matches the list, if they can provide some DNA from another source, we could validate it.

PFM AGENT GUERRERO

All right, we must soon open the road, because even though there are only 20 cars lined up to pass through this area, we need to get the road open for public conveyance as there were a number of ranchers in the area that required access to this road for their daily operations.

MEXICAN PFM FORENSIC SUPEREVISOR

What about all this blood on the road?

PFM AGENT GUERRERO

Contact the Hiway Patrol and have them send out some guys in a water truck with push brooms and clean off as much as possible. Keep the public away and the media until we get it cleaned up.

MEXICAN PFM FORENSIC SUPEREVISOR

Those camera men are upset you are not allowing them to film it.

PFM AGENT GUERRERO

It's a crime scene, they have no business filming it. Any requests for pictures will have to go through Mexican Policía Federal Ministerial Public Relations.

SPECIAL AGENT CHARLES GABLE

They're not going to appreciate that.

PFM AGENT GUERRERO

This is Mexico, not the United States where the public prefers freedom *from* the press.

MEXICAN PFM FORENSIC SUPEREVISOR

What about these 20 cars waiting to pass?

PFM AGENT GUERRERO

Have an officer direct traffic and get them moving through the area. After the cars pass by close it down until the hiway gang cleans off most of the blood.

In a short while the 20 cars waiting to pass down the Hiway were gone wondering what that was all about.

First car passing the crime scene:

RANCHER

There was a lot of blood on the road, maybe a car crashed into the Caravan.

RANCHER'S WIFE

We have a few drunks that drive up this road, one of them could have hit the crowd.

PFM Agent Guerrero and FBI agents Bentley Boyd and Charles Gable were soon on their way back to Guadalajara where they got back on the Mexican Policía Federal Ministerial, (PFM) jet and flew to Mexico City for meetings with Mexican Authorities. FBI agents Bentley Boyd and Charles would soon be in the U.S.

Embassy in Mexico City discussing the matter with the ambassador who was urgently requested to inform the State Department all the details.

The press feed was now viral and even though Mexican Hiway Patrol Officers kept the press at a distance, their telephoto lenses zoomed in and could record Mexican Hiway Workers cleaning the blood off the gray pavement, and when they were all loaded up and gone, a lot of comments about the ditches being full of human blood now permeated the airwaves. Unfortunately, there wasn't much more they could do about the clean-up due to the nature of the blood spillage in such a concentrated area.

Because of the gruesome television coverage and conversations recorded from Caravanners, the Caravan murders turned into sensational news.

There were now film crews arriving from around the world. Japanese, French, Israeli, British, Chinese, German, and Spanish Speaking Television Vans with Satellite feed were imbedded in the caravan which slowly grew as more tendrils of migrants now scared, they would be picked off sought the refuge of the growing crawling human wave. By the following day, there were now an estimated 8,500 Caravanners and an additional 1000 news crew people following along.

By orders of the President of Mexico, the Mexican Army now had a Calvary Squadron in Mexican Marked Military vehicles following and shadowing the Caravan. Several times a day helicopters were observed doing flyovers. Fixed wing aircraft appeared now and then but didn't know who they were. They could have been government officials or media types surveying the group and filming it from above.

One of the jets that flew over carried PFM Agent Guerrero and FBI agents Bentley Boyd and Charles Gable surveying the Caravan and flying over the crime scenes looking for any possible clue of how the perpetrators might have attacked. There simply wasn't any evidence left behind other than the very large footprints.

***

INT. DAY. INSIDE PFM GS650 JET FLYING OVER THE LATEST CARAVAN.

Another new revelation became apparent during one of those flights as they were gazing over briefing packages from the forensic lab. From the two crime sites they had almost a dozen good footprints. All of which were large shoes, but the most sensational detail now revealed created a surreal conversation.

PFM AGENT GUERRERO

We got really good foot imprints in the dirt at the first crime scene and the surface of the blood-stained footprints from this latest incident have the texture and identifying marks on each footwear that identifies multiple perpetrators involved with large feet.

PFM AGENT GUERRERO

This seems rather incredible, but the foot sizes are between size sixteen and seventeen.

FBI AGENT CHARLES GABLE

How many of them could you distinguish?

PFM AGENT GUERRERO

The forensics technicians categorically stated beyond a shadow of a doubt, that twelve different sets of footprints did not match any of the others.

FBI AGENT BENTLEY BOYD

Are they claiming that over twelve sets of footprints are unique and can be identified and they are all size sixteen or larger?

PFM AGENT GUERRERO

Correct. Our Forensic Lab footprint analysis equipment and software use the latest technology.

FBI AGENT BENTLEY BOYD

How well does it work?

PFM AGENT GUERRERO

I'm told the process is similar to what your FBI Forensic Lab uses.

FBI AGENT BENTLEY BOYD

Then I'm sure it works well.

PFM AGENT GUERRERO

Indeed, it does. The PFM Forensic Lab supervisor informed me that identifying twelve individual footprints was straightforward and if you look on page 15 of the report you will see some of the artifacts identified that helped determine individual shoe footprints.

FBI AGENT BENTLEY BOYD

Those highlighted artifacts definitely show exclusivity as good as fingerprinting.

PFM AGENT GUERRERO

On page 17 you will see a map showing the area at the crime scene where each footprint was found with a letter designation A through L.

https://www.cbc.ca/radio/sks/if-the-shoe-fits-what- forensic-detectives-can-learn-from-footprints- 1.4928159

FBI AGENT BENTLEY BOYD

That's remarkable that many individuals were involved in the slaughter. Almost unbelievable there were no eyewitnesses in this latest slaughter.

FBI AGENT CHARLES GABLE

Maybe the criminals wore some type of shoe bottom to hide their prints?

PFM AGENT GUERRERO

Whatever may be the case, we need to keep a tight lid on this information. If the conspiracy theorists get their hands on this information, stories will erupt that will defy human logic and cause unimaginable chaos.

FBI AGENT CHARLES GABLE

Right. The UFO freaks will get huge mileage out of this if they discover any of it.

PFM AGENT GUERRERO

Ok Bentley, let me ask you this question: If the perpetrators were not wearing fake souls on their shoes to cover up their shoe footprints to throw us off and that's their real shoe size, then why not some kind of extraterrestrial related entity?

FBI AGENT BENTLEY BOYD

Agent Guerrero the FBI would officially tell you UFO's and Aliens do not exist, it's all fabrication and embellishments by the UFO community.

PFM AGENT GUERRERO

This is why I think it could be extraterrestrial:

A dozen or more perpetrators with size 16 or larger shoes with a pattern we've never seen before.

FBI AGENT BENTLEY BOYD

That alone creates quite a lot of notions of intrigue.

PFM AGENT GUERRERO

Whoever it was, killed twelve bad Hombres who were well armed.

FBI AGENT BENTLEY BOYD

Not to mention killed before they could give off return weapons firing.

PFM AGENT GUERRERO

Now we have a new case where another 50 caravanners were

killed and disappeared in a very short time. That tells me our conventional wisdom may not apply here.

FBI AGENT BENTLEY BOYD

Most crimes usually are simplified once we know the facts.

As Agent Guerrero continued reading his copies of the briefing papers, his eyes just about jumped out of his head, and he announced to FBI agents Bentley Boyd and Charles Gable:

PFM AGENT GUERRERO

The report says they have a match on a footprint taken at La Cantera with the latest Hiway massacre.

Bentley Boyd looked at Charles Gable.

BENTLEY BOYD

This case is getting stranger by the minute.

CHARLES GABLE

I think we should go visit those people that are in the hospital that were pistol-whipped by the Bad Hombres and ask them a few questions.

PFM AGENT GUERRERO

I'll ask the pilot to land at Guadalajara and we'll take a PFM car from there to the hospital which is about 80 miles away. Hopefully they are still there.

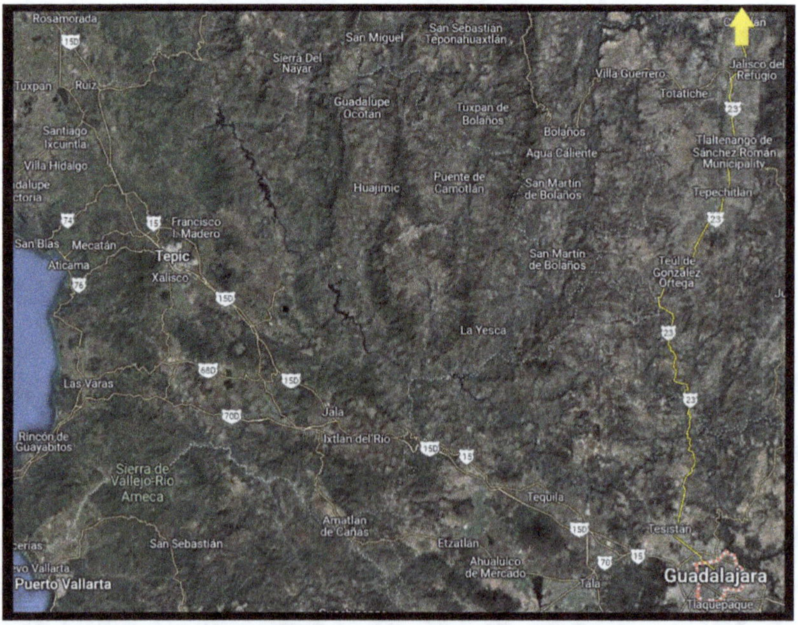

FBI AGENT BENTLEY BOYD

If they were released from the hospital, they would probably go back to the Caravan, I'd think.

EXT. DAY. COMEMOS CARAVANOS HIWAY 23. HOSPITAL

A few hours later they were driving up into the hospital parking lot. They were not alone; a Mexican Army car and another PFM car accompanied them.

The hospital was modest, but clean and well organized. Ran by Catholic Nuns, it had a couple doctors who would come out from Guadalajara as needed and they had a full surgical room if an emergency surgery was required, but in most cases, patients were ambulatory to hospitals in Guadalajara where critical surgery was performed.

The receptionist was well mannered and polite and expected a lot of law enforcement visits. She did have her patience tested a few times by the pesky news media types who demanded access to the patients.

Thanks to Agent Guerrero who recommended they station police officers at the hospital because of the sensationalism of the case to provide security, the news media people were easily constrained and eventually figured out they would not get access to the patients until they were discharged. They would then descend upon them like vultures.

The hospital had seen better days, and the local population shift towards Guadalajara where jobs were plentiful and pay much higher, slowly thinned out this once proud area which meant the hospital had plenty of empty beds and all 20 people were allowed to stay there.

The Nuns took good care of them and through their Catholic network provided the families with some essential items and the rest in the hospital did them all a lot of good. The psychological torture the kids went through watching their fathers beaten by the Bad Hombres and their poor mothers taken away to be molested left an indelible mark on all of them.

VOICEOVER

Delmy Áquilar, Yanuel Romero, Rony Nieto, and Eduardo Ordoñez were now very close friends. The valiant attempt to protect their lady friends that resulted in their brutal treatment by the Bad Hombres was sickening to watch.

Rony Nieto, and Eduardo Ordoñez lost teeth and had cracked ribs. Rony came close to losing a testicle. The boys were in such terrible pain they had to receive prescription pain relievers the Nuns had to administer at least every eight hours. By the time Agent Guerrero arrived at bedside, Rony Nieto, and Eduardo Ordoñez were slowly getting to the point they no longer needed extensive pain killers, but it was quite evident they would not be in any shape to be walking in a Caravan any time soon.

Delmy Áquilar and Yanuel Romero were slowly coming to the realization the consequence of their decision to join the Caravan had negative results.

However, this one event shaped their lives. They were already close to Rony Nieto, and Eduardo Ordoñez but when those two boys fought to save them from the 12 Bad Hombres and incurred such terrible bodily harm, it created a bond few others could ever know.

These two young women Delmy Áquilar and Yanuel Romero knew in their hearts they would do anything to help these two young men who proved their true love by their actions.

Very few women ever get the chance to see their grooms tested in a baptism of fire to demonstrate their profound love.

The boys never gave up, they fought courageously until they were knocked unconscious, and the twelve Bad Hombres only stopped beating them when the girls begged them to stop, including promising everything to stop it.

The adrenalin rush of beating boys was quickly overcome by the sensation of sex with these two young girls.
A couple wives in the group were not bad looking either even though they had children, they were taken and their husbands who could have lent a hand helping the boys and possibly reduced the impact suddenly discovered they also received similar treatment so delaying helping the teenage boys turned out not to be so wise after all. Had they given the boys a chance, they might have subdued enough of the Bad Hombres to force them away.

These horrors and memories were still in the minds of the young adults and now the officials questioning them forced the details and memories out again. To say it was a very unpleasant experience was an understatement.

PFM AGENT GUERRERO

I'm Agent Guerrero of the Mexican Policía Federal Ministerial and these are American FBI agents Bentley Boyd and Charles Gable.

The young females seemed almost in a panic looking at the officials wondering if it meant they would be hauled back to Honduras.

PFM AGENT GUERRERO

The reason why we are here, is we are investigating the men who attacked you as well as what happened to them.

The two females sitting in chairs next to the two beds Rony Nieto and Eduardo

Ordoñez were laying in remained quiet and stared with intensity towards Agent Guerrero.

PFM AGENT GUERRERO

I know talking to you about your ordeal is upsetting but there remain a lot of unanswered questions. If you can assist us in making sense of all of it, then it will help us to close the case.

The young girls remained quiet and were fearful to talk because they didn't know what would result from their statements. Their lives were already complicated enough as it was, they didn't want to go back to Honduras and their situation was now bleak with their boyfriends terribly beat up and not able to even walk.

PFM AGENT GUERRERO

If you will help us, we promise we'll do as much as we can for you. As an example, we know you are no longer able to walk in the Caravan, we can arrange for you to ride in an automobile for the rest of the journey.

Agent Guerrero's statement seemed to rectify Delmy Aquilar's concerns who now viewed this situation as possibly something that might help their plight.

Delmy Aquilar responded looking very intensely towards Agent Guerrero.

DELMY ÁQUILAR

Alright sir, I'll help as much as I can.

PFM AGENT GUERRERO

When the Bad Hombres took you away from the family and out into the field where they planned to do bad things to you, they were suddenly killed.

DELMY ÁQUILAR

That's right.

PFM AGENT GUERRERO

Have you ever seen someone killed before.

DELMY ÁQUILAR

No.

PFM AGENT GUERRERO

Have you ever heard or seen someone firing a gun before?

DELMY ÁQUILAR

Sure, I saw it on TV all the time.

PFM AGENT GUERRERO
How about in real life?

DELMY ÁQUILAR
No sir.

PFM AGENT GUERRERO
When you watched TV and saw people killed by guns, you are familiar with the sound?

DELMY ÁQUILAR
Yes sir, especially in the movies. I think the sound must be genuine.

PFM AGENT GUERRERO
Indeed, the sound is real and sometimes too genuine. When you saw those twelve Bad Hombres killed did you hear anyone shooting a gun.

DELMY ÁQUILAR
No sir.

PFM AGENT GUERRERO
No sound at all?

DELMY ÁQUILAR
There was a strange sound, it was dark, and the men started screaming in pain. A couple of the bastards had flashlights, and I could see the men screaming had body parts suddenly flying off and the men falling to the ground. One man's head exploded, who was carrying a flashlight. It was a horrible sight.

PFM AGENT GUERRERO
You mentioned there was a strange sound?

DELMY ÁQUILAR
Yes, I've never heard anything like it before.

PFM AGENT GUERRERO
Could you describe what that sound seemed like.

DELMY ÁQUILAR
It was kind of a whoosh-whoosh sound. It wasn't very loud. The men's body's exploding was much louder.

PFM AGENT GUERRERO
How long did it take for the men to be killed?

DELMY ÁQUILAR
They were all dead in less than a couple minutes it seemed.

PFM AGENT GUERRERO
What happened then?

DELMY ÁQUILAR
Men with uniforms suddenly appeared and they turned on lights and looked us over.

PFM AGENT GUERRERO
What did their uniforms look like?

DELMY ÁQUILAR
Very strange, almost too pretty to be uniforms.

PFM AGENT GUERRERO
What color were the uniforms?

DELMY ÁQUILAR
They were a purplish moth color.

PFM AGENT GUERRERO
Could you tell how tall or how big they were?

DELMY ÁQUILAR
They were very big. I've never seen men this big before. I thought they must have been some Mexican Special Forces out protecting us.

PFM AGENT GUERRERO
Would you say they were at least six feet tall?

DELMY ÁQUILAR
Much taller. You might think this is crazy, but I think a few of them were 8 or 9 feet tall.

PFM AGENT GUERRERO
Have you ever seen someone that tall before?

DELMY ÁQUILAR
No, and I've watched basketball players. These guys were taller than basketball players and physically looked a lot stronger.

PFM AGENT GUERRERO
Are you sure about all this.

DELMY ÁQUILAR
Ask everyone else what they saw.

PFM AGENT GUERRERO
We will, I promise. What did their faces look like.

DELMY ÁQUILAR
I could not see any of their faces. They were all wearing some kind of helmet with a face shield. Their faces were covered up by that.

PFM AGENT GUERRERO
Did those men talk?

DELMY ÁQUILAR
Yes.

PFM AGENT GUERRERO
Did you understand what they were saying?

DELMY ÁQUILAR
No, they were not speaking Spanish or English.

PFM AGENT GUERRERO
Russian perhaps?

DELMY ÁQUILAR
I'm not sure what Russian sounds like.

PFM AGENT GUERRERO
Let me play some Russian voices I have on my cell phone. Tell me if it sounds anything like this.

After playing a few sound clips of Russian mobsters talking, Agent Guerrero asked:

PFM AGENT GUERRERO
Did they sound anything like that?

DELMY ÁQUILAR
No, nothing like that and they seemed to talk a lot faster.

PFM AGENT GUERRERO

What happened next?

DELMY ÁQUILAR

Suddenly a strange-looking aircraft came near us and landed. Those soldiers put the dead men in, then they all left.

PFM AGENT GUERRERO

Did they say anything to you that you understood?

DELMY ÁQUILAR

No, they did not seem to want to communicate with us, they just took off.

PFM AGENT GUERRERO

Did they have a helicopter sound? Did you ever hear a helicopter flying?

DELMY ÁQUILAR

Sir, I know you might think I'm crazy, but their aircraft made no sounds.

PFM AGENT GUERRERO

No propulsion sounds at all?

DELMY ÁQUILAR

Those aircraft made no sounds. I could hear the men moaning from the road, but I could not hear any sound from those aircraft when they took off.

Agent Guerrero looked at the facial expressions of FBI agents Bentley Boyd and Charles Gable. This case was just now getting a lot more interesting!

Agent Guerrero looked at the young woman.

PFM AGENT GUERRERO

What is your name?

DELMY ÁQUILAR

I'm Delmy Áquilar.

PFM AGENT GUERRERO

Do your parents know you are here?

DELMY ÁQUILAR

No.

PFM AGENT GUERRERO

Would you like us to contact them and let them know you are, okay?

DELMY ÁQUILAR

I'd prefer you didn't. They would try to get me to come back. I don't want to be their personal slave any longer.

About that time Bentley Boyd interrupted.

BENTLY BOYD

Agent Guerrero could Charles and I talk to you outside for a few minutes.

PFM AGENT GUERRERO

Sure.

The three men adjourned outside the hospital to discuss and talk over strategy of the interview.

BENTLEY BOYD

What that woman had to say is rather incredible. Either she's a good liar, or she has just divulged something our governments are not going to like to hear.

PFM AGENT GUERRERO

Yea, aircraft with no sound will go over like a lead balloon.

BENTLEY BOYD

I'm pretty sure my government is not going to want her story in the News Papers.

PFM AGENT GUERRERO

What about the other three women, they might have the same story?

BENTLEY BOYD

We'll find that out soon enough, but I have an idea.

PFM AGENT GUERRERO

What's that?

BENTLEY BOYD

We have a couple hospitals in the USA where we could take these boys that cooperate with the FBI for the purposes of the witness protection program. We could place all 20 of them in the witness protection program to keep them away from the media and systematically vet their story.

PFM AGENT GUERRERO

I would have to get permission from my government to allow you to remove witnesses from a major crime scene before our government completes its investigation.

BENTLEY BOYD

We would of course invite you to accompany us to the United States and be part of a combined task force into the disappearance of the twelve individuals as well as the other two unsolved cases.

PFM AGENT GUERRERO

All right, as soon as I finish questioning these individuals, we'll fly to Mexico City and request a meeting with the head of Mexican Policía Federal Ministerial, to get permission to proceed.

BENTLEY BOYD

We appreciate your cooperation. This will be a sensational story that will cause every UFO freak in the world to descend upon this area.

Agent Guerrero stated with a grim look on his face.

PFM AGENT GUERRERO

All right, us go back in. I know it's going to make them uncomfortable, but we need to interview them.

The men walked back into the hospital and the look on Sister Margarette was not pleasant. She didn't want law enforcement badgering these people, but she also understood she couldn't stand in the way of the PFM because people that did had bad things happen to them as their reputation throughout Mexico was *Pure Effing Magic.*

Delmy Áquilar appeared irritable when they arrived back. She wasn't ready for a bunch of questions. But she soon discovered she was no longer the focus of their attention. The police men were no looking directly at Yanuel Romero.

PFM AGENT GUERRERO

What is your name young lady?

YANUEL ROMERO

I'm Yanuel Romero.

PFM AGENT GUERRERO

I take it you are friends with Delmy Áquilar?

YANUEL ROMERO

Yes, we've known each other since early elementary school.

PFM AGENT GUERRERO

Were your experiences during the incident like Delmy?

YANUEL ROMERO

Yes, I was standing right next to her.

PFM AGENT GUERRERO

What about when the Bad Hombres marched you out into the field?

YANUEL ROMERO

We stayed together the best we could.

PFM AGENT GUERRERO

Did the Bad Hombres molest you?

YANUEL ROMERO

No, they were just about to start I think, when their bodies started blowing up.

PFM AGENT GUERRERO

Their bodies were blowing up?

YANUEL ROMERO

Yes, it was so strange, we could not have known it except two guys had flashlights shining on everyone when it started.

PFM AGENT GUERRERO

Can you describe what you saw happen to the Bad Hombres?

YANUEL ROMERO

It was the most horrible sight I've ever seen. Their stomachs were split wide open, one guy's head exploded. One right after the other were hit and dead within seconds.

PFM AGENT GUERRERO

Were most of them hit in the mid-section of their body?

YANUEL ROMERO

Yes, however I saw one guy lose his arm and cry out.

PFM AGENT GUERRERO
Did this all take about a minute?

YANUEL ROMERO
It happened very quickly; it could have been a minute or two.

PFM AGENT GUERRERO
You saw the craft that came down near these dead men?

YANUEL ROMERO
Yes, I did.

PFM AGENT GUERRERO
Did it look like a helicopter or an Airplane?

YANUEL ROMERO
I thought it was some kind of Airplane with very short wings.

PFM AGENT GUERRERO
How large would you say the aircraft were?

YANUEL ROMERO
They were good size, maybe larger than a city bus.

PFM AGENT GUERRERO
Could you see what color they were painted?

YANUEL ROMERO
It seemed like a real dark gray, almost black.

PFM AGENT GUERRERO
What kind of sound did it make?

YANUEL ROMERO
I heard no sound from it.

PFM AGENT GUERRERO
While the aircraft were coming and going could you also hear moaning from men out on the Hiway?

YANUEL ROMERO
Yes, one of the men lost a lot of teeth when the bad hombre hit him in the face with a rifle butt. He was calling out to

God to save his wife.

PFM AGENT GUERRERO
And when the ships left, they made no sound?

YANUEL ROMERO
No sound. I was amazed.

PFM AGENT GUERRERO
The men who left in the ships, were they tall?

YANUEL ROMERO
Yes, they were very tall. I've never seen men this tall before.

PFM AGENT GUERRERO
As tall as a basketball player?

YANUEL ROMERO
Taller. My father watches American Basketball on Television. These men were taller than those basketball players.

PFM AGENT GUERRERO
How much taller than you were those men?

YANUEL ROMERO
This might seem rather strange, but they seemed twice as tall as me.

PFM AGENT GUERRERO
You saw them gather up all the Bad Hombres and put them in the aircraft?

YANUEL ROMERO
Yes, they took the dead men away

PFM AGENT GUERRERO
Did you see what direction they were going?

YANUEL ROMERO
I couldn't see too well, but it seemed like they were heading down the Hiway, like they were going to Guadalajara.

PFM AGENT GUERRERO
Are you physically ok now?

YANUEL ROMERO

Yes, I wasn't hurt in any way.

PFM AGENT GUERRERO

These are your male friends?

YANUEL ROMERO

Yes.

PFM AGENT GUERRERO

How are they doing?

YANUEL ROMERO

They're in a lot of pain; they were beaten very severely.

PFM AGENT GUERRERO

You don't have a problem with what happened to the Bad Hombres?

YANUEL ROMERO

I don't like to see people killed, but I felt rescued.

The two young men were sedated and obviously sleeping so the investigators decided to leave them alone for the time being and approached the women and children associated with the other men who were also beaten and in a lot of pain and suffering. These women who were in a separate room with their husbands, gave an exact accounting of details associated with the incident.

Several hours later, the investigating team was back in Guadalajara getting back on the Mexican Policía Federal Ministerial Jet heading to Mexico City for the big meeting.

<u>INT. DAY. U.S. EMBASSY MEXICO CITY AMERICAN AMBASSADOR'S OFFICE.</u>

The meeting with Mexican Policía Federal Ministerial was delayed until the next day which allowed the FBI men to brief the American Ambassador.

BENTLEY BOYD

Sir, our recommendation is to take twenty eye witnesses and place them in the witness protection program to keep them away from the press and shut them up permanently.

AMERICAN AMBASSADOR

Mr. Gamble, what's your thoughts on this?

CHARLES GABLE

Mr. Ambassador, two weeks ago if someone came up to me and said we would soon be dealing with Aliens, I would have thought they were nuts. But with the Forensic evidence PFM Agent Carlos Guerrero showed us and these eyewitness accounts, I'm convinced they encountered Aliens and saw them kill the twelve bad Hombres.

AMERICAN AMBASSADOR

Mr. Gamble, how do you feel about putting these 20 people in the witness protection program?

CHARLES GABLE

I think I share Bentley Boyd's rationale for moving the 20 to the USA and put them in the witness protection program. I do not thing that should be a huge problem since we allow a million immigrants in each year.

AMERICAN AMBASSADOR

I hope your meeting with Mexican Policía Federal Ministerial turns out positive but there is something else you need to know.

BENTLEY BOYD

Mr. Ambassador, is there something we should be aware of?

FBI Agents Bentley Boyd and Charles Gable could not stop other agencies from wanting to get involved and take over the case.

Within hours of hearing the possibility aliens were involved in killing the 12 hombres and snatching 50 others, and possibly killing a few more a long distance away in La Cantera, Mexico, Majestic 12 and the CIA were suddenly making their move.

Little did FBI AGEENTS Bentley Boyd and Charles Gable know, the American Ambassador articulated for them.

AMERICAN AMBASSADOR

U2 and SR-72 flights have started flying over the area of the abductions and killing areas looking for clues and Aliens.

BENTLEY BOYD

It's too bad the CIA didn't give us a chance to talk to Mexican Policía Federal Ministerial before these flights started. We may be walking into a hostile reception tomorrow and that is probably why the Mexicans delayed this meeting.

AMERICAN AMBASSADOR

I agree with you, but now it's too late for me to intervene. Prepare for the worst.

***

The SR-72 carried a pod that recorded emanations that might be construed as Alien propulsion signatures. CIA had one thing FBI didn't, instant access to the planes and KH- 14 satellites built specifically for the detection of aliens.

Preceding President Trumps June 25th, 2018, speech about the United States Space Force, the Airforce and the CIA were already moving in the direction of detecting and figuring out what alien intentions were. KH-14 satellites were soon a priority.

As soon as the females from Honduras stories reached Majestic 12 and the CIA, they already had a theory as to what transpired.

VOICEOVER

Unlike the FBI and PFM agents on the case who could not quite cross the line of beliefs that Aliens somehow were involved, the CIA and Majestic 12 had already determined that's exactly what happened. Now the search was on to discover just who and where they were.

Since Tall White Aliens had visited Area 51, it was not a surprise to CIA and Majestic 12 agents that other tall races existed and may have visited Earth.

Some of the 38 feet tall remains found in South America and the tall red head Giants that lived near the area around Detroit, and elsewhere clearly demonstrated giants had been here before.

Biblical story such as the battle between David and Goliath also conveyed the fact that giants had been involved on this planet. Therefore, Christians and Jews had some beliefs in involvement with giants.

The reports the CIA obtained from the FBI trip report written by FBI agents Bentley Boyd and Charles Gable clearly indicated the young Honduran woman claimed the Aliens were twice as tall as herself. That indicated they might have been as tall as 10 feet and the shoe sizes of 16G and 17 supported the allegations Giants killed the 12 Bad Hombres, and probably took the 50 other people missing from the Caravan.

Mexican officials were tight lipped about La Cantera. But the CIA and Majestic 12 agents who got copies from the CIA spy imbedded within the FBI, did a computer match of a La Cantera shoe footprint with the abduction of the 50-missing people from the Caravan, they knew it was most likely the same aliens that took them.

***

INT. DAY. CIA HEADQURTERS, LANGLEY VIRGINIA.

Two CIA analysts poured over the data to come to grips with why they killed the people and took the bodies.

CIA AGENT ROGER

There can be only one explanation. They were taken on purpose.

CIA AGENT KEVIN

What purpose?

Roger knew Kevin was a good Catholic and had a brother as a priest. His family friend, Father Marian, a Jesuit Priest who managed the Jesuit's finances, had clearly had a religious impression on Kevin who believed in JESUS, the all mighty and the Catholic Conventions. Even though Kevin didn't necessarily believe in the Pope's politics, he understood Catholics stood for humanity and decency which current trends in America severely tested.

ROGER

Either they took them away for scientific experiments, or they're cannibals.

KEVIN

Why would an advanced alien race capable of traveling between solar systems do such a terrible thing as cannibalism?

ROGER

Why do we eat cattle? Its rather offensive to Hindu's.

KEVIN

But to kill and eat an intelligent sentient being, that is barbarism, and I just can't believe, and advanced intelligent Alien civilization would condone such practices.

ROGER

Once we find the remains, we just might find out.

KEVIN

If they are capable of snatching people as easily as they appear to have demonstrated, don't you think they can easily dispose of the remains and never allow them to be discovered?

ROGER

At this point in time I would not bet on anything.

KEVIN

You realize if we put this crap in a report management will think we are a couple of goofballs and probably give us the boot.

ROGER

Well Kevin, what other explanation do you have. Using your own words, advanced Alien species, why would they brutally kill anyone in the first place?

KEVIN

I could understand if they observed those 12 criminals beating those families which resulted in their hospitalization, they might have considered those horrendous acts offensive and may have had no choice but to go about it the way they did.

ROGER

I'll give you that, but what about those fifty missing people whose blood was spilled all over that Hiway, clearly were massacred.

KEVIN

Not a good way to conduct a science experiment is what you are going to say next?

ROGER

Why else would they systematically lay in wait and snatch 50 bodies right after they killed them?

KEVIN

That's the million-dollar question.

ROGER

The only answer I can come up with is they're cannibals.

KEVIN

We can't put that in the report as much as we want. Our jobs are on-the-line if we do so.

ROGER

Alright then how can we handle this?

KEVIN

I think it would be better to just lay out the facts, the fifty migrants were murdered then hauled away for reasons unknown and allow management to conduct the dots on their own.

ROGER

You know that some of the dumb son of a bitches that will read this report are political appointees that don't know Shit from Shinola and if we don't spoon feed them basic information it will go over their heads.

KEVIN

Yea and they are dumb enough to fire us if we report something, they're not ready to hear that sounds rather preposterous.

ROGER

Kevin, you need to grow a set of balls if you want to stay in this business.

KEVIN

I plan on retiring. I want the paycheck. I'm more than happy to let some other dumb asses be the messenger, because management always loves shooting the messenger.

ROGER

Okay Kevin, I'll go along with what you want to say in the report. But I'm warning you now. If I'm put on the spot to clarify, I will freely articulate the aliens are probably cannibals and these people were their next meal.

KEVIN

Roger, say what you want during your own time, but I'm not putting my name on a report that says to the world the Aliens are cannibals.

ROGER

Fine. Leave it at that. I'll make corrections to the report and send it back to you via email to endorse and send it up to the Queen Bee.

KEVIN

She'll really love you if she finds out you have been calling her the Queen Bee.

ROGER

Everyone in this division calls her that so what's new.

KEVIN

Careful, she's a political appointee. The QB has big connections.

ROGER

Sure, when she spreads her legs for the promotion.

KEVIN

You don't believe that nonsense, do you?

ROGER

You would be shocked at who told me what.

KEVIN

If I were you, I would avoid talking about it. She's a ruthless bitch and if she finds out you have been bad mouthing her, she'll have your ass fired.

ROGER

Alright then. I'm going to go work on the changes.

KEVIN

Good, I'll see you later.

***

It was not unexpected the first few U2 and SR-72 flights came back with no indications of alien craft or power plants anywhere near the path of the Caravan or around La Cantera, Mexico. A swath north of Guadalajara was checked and then Mexican Radars spotted the U2 flyovers and started complaining most vociferously.

<u>INT. DAY. MEXICO CITY. MEXICAN POLICÍA FEDERAL MINISTERIAL HEADQUARTERS.</u>

About the same time the Mexican Government started squawking about U.S. violating Mexican Air Space, FBI agents Bentley Boyd and Charles Gable were led into the head office of the Mexican Policía Federal Ministerial, by PFM Agent Carlos Guerrero.

The receptionist led the men to a conference room which had a long table and chairs and bottled water and placemats with writing materials and paper.

The administrator of Mexican Policía Federal Ministerial, Jose Mercado stepped into the conference room in prompt fashion quite animated as he had just been involved in discussions concerning the U.S. infringement on Mexican Air Space without permission from Directorate General of Civil Aeronautics (DGAC, Mexico).

FBI agents Bentley Boyd and Charles Gable had just been briefed about the flareup in relations and to expect an explosive environment when they met Jose Mercado.

The men stood up and Agent Guerrero introduced them.

PFM AGENT GUERRERO

Sir, I would like to present to you FBI agents Bentley Boyd and Charles Gable who are here to discuss with you the situation with the Hondurans currently in the hospital north of Guadalajara that were involved in the incident at the Caravan.

JOSE MERCADO

Gentlemen, please have a seat.

Jose Mercado didn't offer his hand to shake and immediately sat down in his chair at the end of the table instantly appearing as if there would probably not be much cooperation in this meeting.

The other men followed his lead and sat down focusing on administrator, Jose Mercado who didn't parse words and got right to the point.

JOSE MERCADO

I've been notified you men want permission to take the primary witnesses in the murder investigation to America, place them in the witness protection program and interrogate them over the incident.

BENTLEY BOYD

That's correct sir, the Bureau feels if we can get them to a hospital where we have controlled access, provide the wounded men needed urgent medical treatments and help reduce their stress, they will be more reliable witnesses and provide good quality evidence on the perpetrators of the crimes.

Name placemats in front of each man made it easy for Jose Mercado to use their names as he talked to them.

JOSE MERCADO

Mr. Boyd, in a way what you are proposing is insulting to my government.

BENTLEY BOYD

Mr. Mercado, I have no other way of expressing it to you without upsetting my own government, but since we are all cleared here for classified information, I think I need to be blunt as to why my government has instructed me to take this course and present you with our plan and explain why.

JOSE MERCADO

Mr. Boyd, with all due respect, I believe we have already examined the witnesses' statements in our internal reports and know everything they have to offer in statements regarding what happened.

You FBI Agents taking the witnesses to America will not derive any new information that we do not already know.

BENTLEY BOYD

Mr. Mercado, you are correct, there is probably not more we can get out of the witnesses. I personally interviewed them and share with you in equal agreement, there is not much more we can get out of them to help solve the case."

JOSE MERCADO

Okay Mr. Boyd, then why do you want to take them away and put them in the witness protection program?

BENTLEY BOYD

I believe my government wants to keep them away from the news media and their stories away from reporters.

JOSE MERCADO

Is there something your government wishes to hide?

BENTLEY BOYD

I think my government wants to hide the same information your government will wish they hid, if this story truly breaks.

JOSE MERCADO

And what is precisely that?

BENTLEY BOYD

The perpetrators are Aliens.

JOSE MERCADO

You got to be shitting me.

BENTLEY BOYD

With all due respect sir, no I'm just like you. I would prefer to see the case closed, and all the information suggests criminals brought to justice. But who do we go after? Who will we indict and arrest?

JOSE MERCADO

You believe in this Alien nonsense?

BENTLEY BOYD

As you stated sir, you read the reports and know what the witnesses reported. You are also I'm sure have looked over the forensic data which provides an element of anecdotal information, the veracity of the witness statements.

JOSE MERCADO

Why should Mexico be concerned like you Americans that UFO's and Aliens were involved?

BENTLEY BOYD

Mr. Mercado, the very instant the press starts reporting that's exactly what happened, you will have all the whackos of the world descending upon Guadalajara to go look for aliens. Your worst nightmare is just about to occur.

You think that Caravan was a pain in the ass. Wait until you see 10 times that many people come here looking for the aliens.

JOSE MERCADO

Well maybe our tourist industry might just like all their business.

BENTLEY BOYD

What if the Aliens are not done?

JOSE MERCADO

What do you mean by that?

BENTLEY BOYD

There is nothing to suggest they are finished killing or abducting people.

JOSE MERCADO

Mr. Boyd, you are crazy if you think for one minute, I'll go along with your stupid belief Aliens killed those people.

BENTLEY BOYD

Minister Mercado, whether you believe the Aliens committed the crimes or not, if you do not allow us to take those 20 people and put them in our witness protection program where we know we can keep them away from the press, then you will be responsible for the mess the people up in Guadalajara will experience when every whacko from China, Japan, Russia, England, Germany, America, Canada, South America, and elsewhere shows up in a frenzy looking for aliens.

JOSE MERCADO

How's extra tourists going to affect us negatively?

BENTLEY BOYD

Minister Mercado, your crime rate will explode and if you think you got problems with the Cartel's now, wait until all these people show up and your police and PFM is taxed doing investigations you could have avoided.

As a conscientious person I plead with you to give it some

thought and simply not dismiss our plan just because you feel Aliens are not involved.

Our plan is to mitigate the perception Aliens took those people and the consequences that will be bestowed upon the people of Mexico who will have to deal with it.

JOSE MERCADO

You Americans push you way around Mexico too often. Even now we are dealing with your government violating our air space with spy planes flying over it.

Bentley Boyd knew *the resentment welling up inside Jose Mercado and these overflights probably pissed him off even more. The timing was terrible. Had the CIA cowboys had not jumped the gun like they always do and instigated those over flights, Jose Mercado might have been willing to go along with the witness protection plan.*

BENTLEY BOYD

Mr. Mercado, I'm not in agreement with the U.S. Government agency who conducted those flights without Mexico's permission.

JOSE MERCADO

Mr. Boyd, us not beat around the bush, in fact your Cash in Advance boys pull crap like this all the time and a lot of the mess down in Honduras and Nicaragua is of their making.

Some of our INTEL indicates they were involved in the overthrow of the Guatemalan government in the 1950's.

BENTLEY BOYD

Minister Mercado, I'm involved in crime investigations. I don't know anything about my government's operations in Central America. I'm not involved and quite frankly I just want to solve crimes and put felons in prison.

JOSE MERCADO

Okay, Agent Guerrero, what's your opinion in all of this?

PFM AGENT GUERRERO

Sir, I felt Aliens were involved before Mr. Boyd and Mr. Gable concluded as such. I'm sorry to report I swayed their thinking in this direction.

JOSE MERCADO

So, you were the first to come up with the speculation, Aliens did all this?

PFM AGENT GUERRERO

That's correct sir, I had to persuade Special Agents Boyd and Gable that Aliens were involved based on my interviews with the eyewitnesses.

JOSE MERCADO

That sheds a whole new light on this matter.

PFM AGENT GUERRERO

Indeed.

JOSE MERCADO

Okay Agent Guerrero, what made you think Aliens did all this?

PFM AGENT GUERRERO

Sir the two Honduran mothers that are eyewitnesses are not sophisticated women.

They come from an area of poverty, seldom ever watched TV and quite frankly were very seldom exposed to modern technology and entertainment that would feed fantasies about Aliens.

They don't even know what an Alien is or what has been said or written about them. They are the perfect eyewitness.

Their concise reports on what they saw was identical to the other two young females that were on the verge of being gang raped by a dozen low life's when the Aliens struck.

JOSE MERCADO

Maybe they talked to each other and formed a group opinion?

PFM AGENT GUERRERO

All four women stated independently in three different interview rooms identical stories that none of them heard gunshots and bodies simply exploded.

JOSE MERCADO

Which means what?

PFM AGENT GUERRERO

The Aliens have some type of weapon that can administer this type of lethality we are unaccustomed to or have ever experienced.

JOSE MERCADO

I'm not sure we need to take excessive actions.

PFM AGENT GUERRERO

Sir, the other compelling information is the people who killed the Bad Hombres were almost twice as tall as them and the footprint evidence supports the size.

Furthermore, sir, scientists working on the footprints say based on how far down they compressed the soil, they had to weigh perhaps as much as 500 pounds each, which would explain some type of combat person that's 10 feet tall.

JOSE MERCADO

Agent Guerrero, do you agree we should allow the Americans to take the eyewitnesses away?

PFM AGENT GUERRERO

Sir, I agree with Special Agent Boyd, we need to isolate these people from the public as they are the only eyewitnesses in the three incidents that occurred.

JOSE MERCADO

Why so?

PFM AGENT GUERRERO

We know from our own experiences dealing with the U.S. witness protection program they do a very good job of hiding individuals so that criminals can't get to them before a trial is conducted.

JOSE MERCADO

What good will that do us?

PFM AGENT GUERRERO

It will also buy us time to further investigate these incidents and make a better report to the President of Mexico allowing him time to develop a policy on how to handle it.

Jose Mercado was slowly starting to exhibit a different persona. Perhaps it was his realization that what Bentley Boyd stated started to resonate his own thoughts of the chaos that might erupt if the media started graphically showing the multitudes snippets of these eyewitnesses talking to the press and worse yet coerced into embellishing a grimmer tale.

Jose Mercado realized some of the yellow journalists would soon be offering the 20 people especially the four women a lot of money for their stories. He was damned if he did and damned if he didn't.

JOSE MERCADO

I need to think about this a while, I can't make an abrupt decision.

I'll let you know in a couple days. In the meantime, we will staff more police at the hospital and forbid all visitors who are not police or PFM agents.

BENTLEY BOYD

Thank you, sir, for your consideration.

JOSE MERCADO

One other item Mr. Boyd, I want you to relay to your government we do not want any more flyovers without Mexican Government permission.

BENTLEY BOYD

Mr. Mercado, I will certainly inform them they need to halt all flights until they receive permission from Directorate General of Civil Aeronautics (DGAC, Mexico). Otherwise, they will cause a lot of issues in international relations.

JOSE MERCADO

That will be all gentlemen.

Jose Mercado then stood up and promptly and pompously walked out of the room.

THE CARSOPIANS

Caravan security would have been optimized had the additional groups not attached themselves as the Hondurans continued Northward. Branching out of Guadalajara, Guatemalan's, El Salvadorians, and Nicaraguans were soon in line and growing the ranks.

It was a foregone conclusion; the organizers of the Caravan no longer knew *who was who in the zoo.*

The plan developed in the morning, organizers would take pickups south and use tape recorders to get all the names of everyone and those recordings would be attached to emails and sent to be transcribed and lists printed out and emailed back from a remote location.

At the rate the Caravan was growing, the Caravan would no doubt have upwards 10,000 migrants by the time they reached the American Border.

The Carsopian's were not yet quite ready to leave the planet and General Fukua de Hundan granted permission to send Carsopian Security Rover-craft out to snatch more bodies and INTEL had reported the Caravan had just grown as other new arrivals added to their numbers.

Mexican Police were attached to the tail end of the Caravan. What they didn't know is more migrants were following behind them now several miles urgently trying to catch up with the main body and insert themselves into the organized Caravan

VOICEOVR

Caravan late comers had been told by Mexican families who wanted Caravanner's to move along and get out of their towns, embellishments of all the social services and facilities provided by the Caravan organizers.

Plenty of food and water.

Women with children are put on buses and they attempt to make sure families are not separated.

They have a barbecue every evening, the food is great.

Reporters are paying large amounts of money for good stories about your plight.

Safety and security because Mexican police are with the Caravan protecting it.

Your ride to the land of milk and honey and money, is just two miles up the road. Better get there before the buses leave!

There were many stories told to these caravan new comers who then had added incentive to leave town even though they were tired and filthy and needed a break.

By the time they were two or miles up the road and figured out they had been duped, they had no incentive to turn around. Some of the more gullible people in the group said: We just need to keep going, we'll probably see them soon.

The two miles thus turned into five miles and on a hilltop, they could see what appeared to be lights on the horizon and then shouted with joy:

CARAVANERS

That must be the caravan!

One group believed such to the point they kept walking all night long. The lights were real, unfortunately they were just a rancher's house who had a dozen well-armed men with high powered rifles and suggested they keep moving and trespassers would be shot.

When the Carsopian Security Rover-craft headed out to collect what now appeared to be one of their final terrestrial meals before they boarded their craft and departed

Earth, one of the groups of migrants now five miles behind the Caravan was slowly running out of steam. Not realizing how close to salvation they were, slowly disintegrated as some simply decided to rest there for the night while the more anxious in the group continued without them.

In a matter of minutes, the group was divided in half with those staying put for the night, and those inspired souls who just knew they would probably spot the Caravan over the next hill.

The Carsopian Security Rover-Craft flew to the south of the Caravan and were working their way north observing the formation to determine the most practical area to obtain what was going to be their largest haul since they knew it would be their last meal before they were stuck back on space food.

Flying parallel to Hiway 23 they spotted the stretched-out formation of stragglers and continued flying towards the main body. In due time they spotted the security patrol in vehicles traveling along with the last group of stragglers in the main body.

The Carsopian's knew instinctively they would have to avoid the security patrol who might get lucky and wound some of their forces if they got into a fire fight. Even though Earth weaponry was a pushover, at close range it was lethal. The leader directed them south again and their focus would be the group that now seemed to be stalled on the Hiway.

There were almost 75 Guatemalan Migrants in that group. Many of them knew each other and this was not their first trip north. Most of them had been caught and deported from the U.S. before, and due to the ravages of a Hurricane and criminal elements who car jacked them, they were now on foot and very unhappy because they had assumed, they would drive up to the border in these second-hand cars they purchased they realized they might have to abandon at the border.

Sadly, this group had the largest concentration of kids. Those who continued the trek leaving them behind were mostly teenagers and single. All that remained huddled on the Hiway where they felt safe from snakes and wild animals were mom and pops and their children.

Several hours past sundown, the Carsopian Security Rover-craft landed quietly on the Hiway 50 meters south of the huddled migrants. The huge Carsopian's quickly converged on the migrants and because they were huddled in a mass, it was like shooting ducks in a barrel.

Bodies were exploding, people were screaming and some started running like scared dear, but none of them made it to safety. The 500-pound shock troops took no time in loading the Carcasses up in their security rover craft. And just as quickly and quietly as they had arrived, they left the bloody mess on the Hiway behind and flew 50 miles to the West well behind a large hill that had a dry creek bed next to the bivouac area.

The final feast was merely a couple hours later as the chefs did their magic on the carcass employing some of their secret sauces that made the troops quite pleased with the unexpected delight.

The survivors who had the motivation to continue walking in the dark finally came across the Caravan that had completely stopped and people were lined up at the soup kitchens getting a belly full of delightful stew before they would attempt getting sleep on the hard pavement. None of them wanted to sleep in the fields where snakes, coyotes, and other vicious animals roamed the nights.

The teenage boys startled the security men as they suddenly appeared out of nowhere.

GUATEMALAN MIGRANT

Is this where we can get water and food?

CARAVAN STAFFER

Who are you and where the hell did you come from?

GUATEMALAN MIGRANT

We are with a group of Guatemalan's spending the night on the road about five miles south of here.

CARAVAN STAFFER

How many of you are there?

GUATEMALAN MIGRANT

I'd say we had about seventy-five people. Probably 50 people stayed behind with their children because they were too tired to continue walking.

The security men radioed the organizers and asked for instructions.

ORGANIZERS

Take the newcomers to a soup tent and take some trucks south and pick up the stragglers.

CARAVAN STAFFER

All right.

After directing the young men to the nearby soup kitchen tent, several security men headed south to pick up the stragglers. About five miles down the road all they could see is what appeared to be a wet spot on the Hiway.

CARAVAN STAFF DRIVER

Nobody is around here, but what the hell is that wet spot on the Hiway?

The men got out of their trucks with flashlights and went up to the wet spot that wasn't expected out in the middle of a dry desert like area especially after sundown on a hot day.

The men were aghast when they saw the color of red.

CARAVAN STAFF DRIVER
It's blood.

CARAVAN REP
It's a lot of blood too, it's draining into the ditches.

CARAVAN STAFF DRIVER
Whoever did this was probably just here.

They immediately called the organizers who then sent the Mexican police down there right away.

ANOTHER MASSACRE

FBI agents Bentley Boyd and Charles Gable had just left the Embassy when Bentley received a call on his cell phone a number, he recognized immediately from the offices of the Mexican Policía Federal Ministerial, PFM. Agent Guerrero was on the line.

PFM AGENT GUERRERO
Bentley?

BENTLEY BOYD
Yes, Agent Guerrero. What's up?

PFM AGENT GUERRERO
We just had another incident.

BENTLEY BOYD
What happened?

PFM AGENT GUERRERO
At least 50 people are missing, blood all over the Hiway, just like before. Probably another massacre.

BENTLEY BOYD
Law enforcement at the site?

PFM AGENT GUERRERO
Yes, forensic technicians out of Guadalajara are on the way, and should arrive in a short while. The area is secured and the Hiway is shutdown.

BENTLEY BOYD

I see.

PFM AGENT GUERRERO

Say, I would like to pick you and Agent Gable up and take you up to the crime scene.

BENTLEY BOYD

Sure, we can go, we are currently at the Embassy if you could pick us up here?

PFM AGENT GUERRERO

I'll be right over, should be there in 15 minutes.

BENTLEY BOYD

See you then.

Charles Gable heard all he needed to hear. In crime cases bolden perpetrators often come back. If this was a terrorist act whoever was doing it was hoping for huge effect.

BENTLEY BOYD

Here we go again. I wonder if this latest crime will have some influence on Jose Mercado to release the 20 eyewitnesses to us."

CHARLES GABLE

No doubt Jose Mercado will start feeling the pressure now.

The teenage boys who had arrived out of nowhere in the night were rounded up and questioned by authorities. At first the boys thought they were some kind of criminals being accused of killing someone. They were almost in a panic.

The young male Guatemalans were asked if they could identify who they had left behind. Due to the close nit society, they knew most of the families they had left five miles down the road.

In some cases, they were relatives.

The boys had no weapons on them and certainly they were not covered in blood. They had no idea what had happened, and the police were not giving them any details.

But to their surprise they were only questions, none of them were arrested or handcuffed, in fact they were being treated as indigent people that were soon going to be told of a gruesome murder they were nowhere psychologically prepared to hear.

They would all bear responsibility and feel bad for the rest of their lives for abandoning the group just before they were all murdered. Most of them felt they could never go home again. They lost face in a major way.

The flight to Guadalajara aboard the Mexican Policía Federal Ministerial Gulfstream 650 was short and PFM had a couple cars waiting for them to take them up to the crime scene.

By the time they arrived the forensic experts had photographed the entire area and collected blood samples from the various pools of blood. They also bagged a few body parts that were strung around from exploding bodies.

EXT. DAY. MEXICO COMEMOS CARAVANOS HIWAY 23

Agent Guerrero asked the chief forensic supervisor.

PFM AGENT GUERRERO
Any interesting information?

CHIEF FORENSIC SUPERVISOR
Almost identical to the last Hiway incident. The perpetrators left without a clue almost, except for some shoe prints on the pavement.

PFM AGENT GUERRERO
Any estimate on shoe size and patterns?

CHIEF FORENSIC SUPERVISOR
The pattern matches the same from the last massacre, and two foot prints we estimate are size 17G and two size 16G.

PFM AGENT GUERRERO
How soon will you be able to match any of these patterns with previous attacks?

CHIEF FORENSIC SUPERVISOR
I'd say several hours after we get back to Guadalajara lab, we should know with 95% certainty whether any of the same shoe print patterns are a match to previous incidents.

PFM AGENT GUERRERO
Ok, inform me as soon as you can state any of these footprint patterns match any of the other incidents.

CHIEF FORENSIC SUPERVISOR
Will do. Want me to call you on your cell phone?

PFM AGENT GUERRERO
Yes, please do that.

PFM Agent Guerrero led FBI agents Bentley Boyd and Charles Gable back to the cars where they could speak out of range from others hearing their conversation.

PFM AGENT GUERRERO
So, what do you think now Bentley?

BENTLEY BOYD
Well Agent Guerrero, the key piece of evidence is someone with huge feet are killing these people and taking the bodies with them. Based on the interviews with the eyewitnesses, I believe we are dealing with Aliens.

PFM AGENT GUERRERO
No chance of extremist terrorism?

BENTLEY BOYD
None whatsoever. I seriously doubt terrorists have the means to pull something like this off, and the eyewitness account on the aircraft used to haul the bodies away is the only realistic explanation of how they can strike with impunity and get the bodies away before any security forces could intervene.

PFM AGENT GUERRERO
You know some crooked politicians will try to make it look like political conspiracy.

BENTLEY BOYD
Based on my experience dealing with extremists, they would have taken credit for it by now and used it as propaganda directed at the Caravan and its sponsors.

PFM AGENT GUERRERO
How about Terrorists along the lines of 9/11?

BENTLEY BOYD
They too would have made claims by now. Terrorism doesn't do much good for you unless you include the propaganda aspect with it.

PFM AGENT GUERRERO

You are convinced Aliens did this.

BENTLEY BOYD

Yes. Completely.

PFM AGENT GUERRERO

Do you think they will strike again?

BENTLEY BOYD

Most likely they will continue picking off stragglers. The Mexican Government must prohibit migrants from traveling unescorted North until we solve this case.

PFM AGENT GUERRERO

The migrants usually don't listen to us.

BENTLEY BOYD

Perhaps if you send patrols out and explain it to groups you catch and show them a few of these pictures, they might take to heart your warnings.

PFM AGENT GUERRERO

If it's aliens, we probably have no means of dealing with them.

BENTLEY BOYD

This case is a good reason why Mexico and the United States must cooperate in dealing with it, which will help us solve it sooner.

PFM AGENT GUERRERO

I suppose you are referring to the 20 eyewitnesses you want to move into the American Witness Protection Program.

BENTLEY BOYD

That certainly is one aspect of it, but if it truly is aliens involved, we need to keep performing those U2 and SR-72 flights.

PFM AGENT GUERRERO

Why is it your American Government claims the SR- 72 doesn't exist if you turn around and want to fly it over Mexico?

BENTLEY BOYD

I can't speak for the CIA and the Air Force, as to why they

deny the plane exists, but unofficially, I think it's prudent for your government to allow the flyovers so we can find where the aliens are hiding out and deal with them.

PFM AGENT GUERRERO

The aliens probably have nasty weapons, are you Americans willing to risk what they might be able to do to you?

BENTLEY BOYD

As my daddy once told me, you don't know how high the bullfrog will jump unless you punch him.

PFM AGENT GUERRERO

Okay, I'll contact Jose Mercado and press him to give you custody of the 20 eyewitnesses.

BENTLEY BOYD

We appreciate that, just like you we want to solve these murders and if we prove its Aliens doing it, then it might be a bigger problem than just for Mexico and the United States faces.

***

EXT.DAY.MARCH AIRFORCE BASE

The White House was ignoring Mexico and the State Department. There wasn't much either could do to the CIA crews flying the U2's and SR-72's now launching at March Air Force Base.

The 655th is the Air Force Reserve Command's first ISR wing at March Air Force Base was quite surprised when their commanding officer was informed, he had requirements to provide logistical support to specially modified U2's and a new type of aircraft never seen before, the SR-72.

EXT.DAY.MARCH AIRFORCE BASE, HANGER BUILDING 111.

One thing that upset General Collins he said to his Chief of Staff Colonel Peterson:

GENERAL COLLINS

The fact they also walked in and took over one of our hangers used to service the Cargo Planes that flew out of March like they owned the place, upsets me.

CHIEF OF STAFF COLONEL PETERSON

They brought out their own teams to empty the hanger of spare parts, tools, and just about anything that they could move.

GENERAL COLLINS

It appears they operate just like the way the Navy does.

CHIEF OF STAFF COLONEL PETERSON

How's that General?

GENERAL COLLINS

If it doesn't move, paint it.

CHIEF OF STAFF COLONEL PETERSON

What's the problem General? It's now the best- looking hanger we have.

GENERAL COLLINS

I do not mind that so much except it made the rest of the hangers look like crap.

CHIEF OF STAFF COLONEL PETERSON

Not much we can do about it now General; they start flight ops today.

GENERAL COLLINS

People driving up Interstate 215 would not have seen a hanger stand out like that but the contrast with the new paint job is an eye opener.

CHIEF OF STAFF COLONEL PETERSON

Not much we can do about it General.

GENERAL COLLINS

Colonel Peterson, I don't care who you must go beg, borrow or steal from, I want the surrounding hangers repainted on the exterior pronto.

CHIEF OF STAFF COLONEL PETERSON

General Collins, the OSHA Reps are not going to be happy about us repainting all those hangers.

GENERAL COLLINS

OSHA's complaint letters will remain in my in-basket until long after I'm retired, and my relief sends them to the circular file.

CHIEF OF STAFF COLONEL PETERSON

General Collins, I'll work on it and try to make sure we get the exteriors repainted before you retire.

GENERAL COLLINS

Colonel Peterson, thank you. I like the way you operate.

EXT.CGI.GROUND TO SPACE. DURING THE FOLLOWING VOICEOVER, SR-72 TAKES OFF AND FLIES MISSION TOWARDS THE ALIENS DURING VOICEOVER BELOW.

VOICEOVER

The U2 wasn't such a big deal because their local museum had a U2 parked in it and NASA's U2's did come into the base now and then. This ISR special equipped U2 really didn't look much different from a distance than the others.

What this new U2 did have was the same types of sensors and electronics built into the KH-14 Satellites designed to detect and track Aliens.

Alien space craft were extremely difficult to detect and track, but the more we attempted the more that was revealed.

Aliens that visited Earth used U115 reactors to power their propulsion and anti-gravity machines. CIA and Majestic 12 researchers had made a major inroad towards sniffing U115 reactors.

The U2 and SR-72 were loaded with prototype U115 sniffers as it appeared more and more aliens who visited earth employed U115 direct power reactors.

These U115 reactors did not give off dangerous levels of radiation like American nuclear power plants fission and fusion reactors used on space craft.

But the cosmic oscillations they created had resonances that a highly tuned chirp filter could process from an elaborate sensor assembly housed in the nose cone that could be lifted into scan position for a few minutes but would have to be retracted because otherwise it would eventually burn up.

Besides the upgraded U2, an SR-72 would also be flown from the same base and operated out of hanger, building 111.

The Lockheed Martin SR-72, colloquially referred to as **SON OF BLACKBIRD** *had a fuselage about the same size and weight of an SR-71 and shows the silhouette like a modern jet fighter aircraft, except the tail surfaces were shorter.*

SR-72 had angled edges and were canted at an angle to minimize radar returns and to minimize the radar cross section. SR-72 also had three engines vice two.

During the climb to high altitude the SR-72 jet engines operated like the SR-71 Pratt & Whitney J-58F turbo- ramjets. The centerline engine was an SJ-400 scramjet. Once obtaining cruising altitude of 80,000 feet and 2200 miles per hour, the SJ-400 cut in and powered up burning hydrogen injection and LOX provided thrust in the vacuum of space at the edge of the atmosphere.

SR-72 was more difficult to prepare for a mission because it required jet fuel for the outboard engines and hydrogen, and LOX for the centerline scramjet.

Most pilots feared that wicked combination would more easily produce a fireball followed with an unscheduled rapid disassembly.

Unless the enemy radar was above the SR-72 which was unlikely since it flew at heights greater than 100,000 feet, it's unlikely it would give a radar return an enemy could track.

People at March Air Force Base had no idea how fast people could work. When work commenced on the hanger, building 111, routine maintenance workers figured it would take a month to clean out and re-equip the building. The schedule that unfolded almost made onlookers dizzy with speculation.

Day-1 Hanger completely emptied out.

Day- 2 Internal and external surfaces of building 111 were painted.

Day -3 the floor of building 111, large enough to hold a couple U-2 spy planes with an SR-72 parked inside with the hanger doors closed, was painted a high gloss light gray to enable spotting lose hardware that might fall off the planes.

Day-4 the planes and squadron personnel arrived. Shipments of tools, supplies, and spare parts also arrived in cargo planes and were efficiently unloaded into the retrofitted building 111 special operations hanger via professional stevedores.

Day-5 test flights began.

Day-6 First Mission flown.

After a few days of missions, the flights were suddenly halted over complaints from Mexico. Then after the 4th alien abduction/murder incident, the flights resumed.

The search for the aliens was narrowed to swaths parallel to Mexico Hiway 23 the Caravan traveled over. If there was any hope of discovering the aliens it was assumed they had to be nearby where they did the body snatching.

The day before the aliens left, a detection of the sort was found. Had the aliens not been barbecuing Caravanners, they would never have been seen.

Infrared off the barbecue pits is what initially alerted the pilots of the U2 and subsequently an unmanned SR-72 flown in drone mode flew over the same area sniffing with its elaborate sensors and video recording equipment.

As soon as the planes landed and were parked inside building 111 at March Air Force Base, technicians immediately unloaded the mission packages and put them on carts. The carts were wheeled into a makeshift lab where the black boxes were plugged into a power source and fiber optic cables hooked up to download all the mission files.

Servers within the lab operating RED HAT LINUX slowly gzipped the files and transmitted them via high- speed private DARPANET built by the inventor of the internet Bolt Beranek and Newman (BBN) to Wright Patterson Airforce Base in Ohio where scientists and technicians analyzed the results.

[https://en.wikipedia.org/wiki/Raytheon_BBN]

Infrared and electromagnetic scans were plotted on a map where the coordinates were tagged with GPS fixes. The resulting eye candy was piped to the Pentagon where experts poured over the data and made assessments and advised the joint chiefs what they thought they had detected.

INT.DAY.PENTAGON. INNER D RING CONFERENCE ROOM.

PENTAGON BRIEFER

The maps showed there were no towns or settlements nearby. If there had been a camper or traveler it would stand to reason maybe one fire was going, but not several close together like this.

HEAD OF THE JOINT CHIEFS

Are the aliens doing a cookout/barbecue?

PENTAGON BRIEFER

That's what it looks like.

HEAD OF THE JOING CHIEFS

Is it possible this is where all the missing bodies from the Caravan went?

PENTAGON BRIEFER

This is the only area near the abductions which we conclude is quite possibly the case.

HEAD OF THE JOINT CHIEFS

If that's what they are doing, these Aliens are cannibals.

ADMIRAL LONG

Why would an advance race of Aliens be cannibals?

HEAD OF THE JOINT CHIEFS

Why do Americans go deer hunting?

ADMIRAL LONG

Deer are animals, not humans.

PENTAGON BRIEFER

Maybe the aliens view us so backwards to them as we are merely animals like deer?

HEAD OF THE JOINT CHIEFS

Any other information obtained by the flyover?

PENTAGON BRIEFER

Our new terrain profiler was used several days ago before we secured Mexico overflights until they resumed today. We have compared the areas during different days. This latest scan shows objects that were previously not seen before.

HEAD OF THE JOINT CHIEFS

What can you make of the contrasting backgrounds?

PENTAGON BRIEFER

Our conclusion is we scanned multiple Alien spacecraft.

HEAD OF THE JOINT CHIEFS

Any idea of their size?

PENTAGON BRIEFER

Flown from 100,000 feet the resolution is poor. But we have made some estimates, nevertheless. Those space craft are huge. Also, the infrared scanners indicate the possibility of a rather substantial sized Army down there.

ARMY GENERAL LUKE

Were you able to count the number of possible Alien combat troops?

PENTAGON BRIEFER

The resolution is too poor, we are scheduling another flyover and will do the next one at 50,000 feet.

AIR FORCE GENERAL KENNY

That would be kind of dangerous, the Mexican Air Force is liable to shoot down the craft.

PENTAGON BRIEFER

We are in direct talks with the Mexican Directorate General of Civil Aeronautics DGAC, of Mexico. We believe after this last Caravan Massacre; the Mexican Government will be more cooperative. They want to get to the bottom of this incident as much as we do.

HEAD OF THE JOINT CHIEFS
When will we expect to get the data from the next over flights?

PENTAGON BRIEFER
In approximately 12 hours.

EXT.DAY.CARSOPIAN ALIEN COMMAND SHIP.

The Carsopian aliens had detected the overflights and were alerted the flights were using some sophisticated scanning equipment.

GENERAL FUKUA DE HUNDAN
Do you think the Earth people are looking for us?

GENERAL FUKUA DE HUNDAN ADVISOR
That's a real possibility. They are probably trying to determine what happened to all those Earth people we abducted.

GENERAL FUKUA DE HUNDAN
Tomorrow morning, I want to load up the troops and depart after a brief memorial service for the few we buried and are leaving behind.

GENERAL FUKUA DE HUNDAN ADVISOR
The troops are rejuvenated. We have no reason to remain.

General Fukua De Hundan's Advisor knew tomorrow would be a painful day for General Fukua De Hundan, whose own son who died from space sickness was one of those buried.

***

INT. DAY. MEXICO CITY. MEXICAN POLICÍA FEDERAL MINISTERIAL HEADQUARTERS.

Mexican Policía Federal Ministerial, PFM Director Jose Mercado had been soul searching wanting to do the right thing. His superiors were too nervous to give him direction or authority over the 20 eyewitnesses.

But the longer the eyewitnesses stayed the greater the chance some police man would take a bribe and allow the cameras into the hospital. That's all he needed now was to wake up in the morning to watch live interviews on Television. Tension was mounting and he no longer could take the stress. He phoned Agent Guerrero.

AGENT GUERRERO
Hello

PFM DIRECTOR JOSE MERCADO
Agent Guerrero?

AGENT GUERRERO
Yes?

PFM DIRECTOR JOSE MERCADO
Agent Guerrero, this is Jose Mercado. I've come to a decision. I will allow you to hand the 20 witnesses over to the Americans.

AGENT GUERRERO
They will be happy to hear that.

PFM DIRECTOR JOSE MERCADO
Tell them if they want to take them into their witness protection program, they have this morning to do the move. After that I have no idea what restrictions the President may impose upon me.

AGENT GUERRERO
I will let them know immediately sir.

PFM DIRECTOR JOSE MERCADO
Make all appropriate arrangements, but I would prefer the Americans fly down and get them.

AGENT GUERRERO
Understand all, sir.

PFM DIRECTOR JOSE MERCADO
Good. Call me when the witnesses are gone.

AGENT GUERRERO
Yes sir.

In some respects, Agent Guerrero wasn't happy because it felt insulting to him, they had to rely on the Americans to hide the twenty witnesses.

But in another respect, Agent Guerrero knew those two boys and the husbands were in bad shape, and they would receive far better medical treatment in the USA than they would in that Catholic Hospital that wasn't really set up to treat men who had been brutally beaten to an inch of their lives.

The wheels of motion started very abruptly. FBI agents Bentley Boyd and Charles Gable personally oversaw the movement of the twenty eyewitnesses. They acquired several ambulances from Mexican Hospitals in Guadalajara so that the patients could be transported without a lot of pain. The good sisters of the hospital knew instinctively to shoot the men up with narcotics so they would not feel a lot of pain during transportation.

An Army evacuation plane equipped with doctors and medics was flown down to Guadalajara where the FBI caravan pulled up directly to the plane to load the patients up on the aircraft.

Rony Nieto and Eduardo Ordoñez and the two husbands were out of it drugged up to not feel pain during the flight. The doctors on the planes were notified what type of medications were given to the men.

In America their treatments would be altered, they would no longer enjoy the type and potency of the strong narcotics the Nuns had given them. But they would heal quicker.

Delmy Áquilar and Yanuel Romero were glued to the young men and inseparable. However, the medics and doctors assured them they would be looking after them and would call them if there was any need. The young men were already in hospital gowns which allowed the doctors to survey some of their wounds.
Likewise, the men of the families going with them were similarly treated and there were Spanish Speaking medics among the crew which went a long way to helping the women who were making all the decisions for their families since the men were incapacitated.

The twenty eyewitnesses were flown to Houston Texas where one of the best medical facilities in the world exists.

Built and funded by the late Howard Hughes, the medical facility had some of the best medical researchers and practitioners in the world. The Saudi Royal family used this facility exclusively.

Security was very tight and the personnel there were accustomed to working with the FBI as this wasn't the first time nor would it be the last time people beat up bad came through these doors on their way to the witness protection program. Some of the snitches of the MS13 gang had arrived in similar fashion.

The doctors knew what to do and what Jose Mercado would find out later, the one young man's testicle was saved only because he was brought here. Mercado's humane decision transcended the simple benevolent purpose he acted on and had a major impact on the young man's life.

Unfortunately for Delmy Áquilar, Yanuel Romero, Rony Nieto, and Eduardo Ordoñez, Majestic 12 and the CIA didn't want them ever to get near the media under any circumstances. As soon as the young men were stabilized and living in their drug induced painless world, their handlers explained to them how and why they got put into the Witness Protection Program.

These witnesses would never have to fear deportation since they were given a new identity. But they had to agree to the terms of the program. They could never reveal to their families their new identity, nor visit them any time soon.

In their new lives they would take on, they were made acutely aware that if they ever approached the media they would be stripped of their protections and immediately deported back to Honduras under their old identity with little hopes of ever legally obtaining access to the United States.

Another twist to this arrangement is councilors brought in quickly determined they were couples, and this extraordinary event had drawn the young women a lot closer to the men and had settled on the notion they would be with them the rest of their lives.

Seldom in life do men get the opportunity to demonstrate to what extent they would go to put their own lives at risk to defend their women. Rony Nieto and Eduardo Ordoñez had passed the test in flying colors.

Between providing housing, online college courses, and an income, the four lives had simply jumped several stratums. Their American Dream was starting. To the chagrin of the news media, these young adults and the other families now involved in the eyewitness program, had disappeared and were starting new lives in America under much better circumstances.

<u>EXT.CGI. DAY.HILLTOP OVERLOOKKING THE CARSOPIAN FLEET</u>

The Carsopian's completed their loadout for departure. General Fukua de Hundan's son had died in route to Earth from what is referred to as Cosmic Space Sickness. His son and several others were buried up on a hill next to the parked spacecraft.

General Fukua de Hundan gave his final respects, with a tear in his eye General Fukua de Hundan walked back to his command ship.

The Carsopians were probably ten minutes away from leaving when the next American spy plane flyover occurred at 50,000 feet. As soon as the surveillance craft had departed the area, General Fukua de Hundan gave the orders:

GENERAL FUKUA DE HUNDAN
Launch the fleet.

<u>EXT.CGI.MEXICO DESERT. CARSOPIAN FLEET LAUNCHES INTO SPACE.</u>

One by one the Carsopian spacecraft left and traveled along the electronic pathway their navigation coordinates and voyage construct guided them.

EXT. CGI. DAY. MARCH AIR FORCE BASE. SPECIAL U2 SPYPLANE TOWED INTO HANGER BUILDING 111.

Just like before, the reconnaissance flight landed at March Air Force Base where the mission modules were removed and taken to the lab to upload the data to Wright Patterson Air Force Base who would package it for Pentagon analysts and brief appropriate parties.

INT. DAY. PENTAGON.JOINT CHIEFS BRIEFING ROOM.

During the first briefing the comment that capsulized the framework of pentagon thinkers looking at the high-resolution images, included:

CHAIRMAN OF THE JOINT CHIEFS

That is a fleet of huge size space craft there in Mexico, no doubt about it. I think we should call the President immediately!

This was an extraordinary event, and the current administration had already started firing leakers from his administration. The joint chiefs feared they had no means of keeping this information compartmentalized. The joint chiefs feared one of the President's enemies would release it to cause him irreparable grief.

INT.DAY.OVAL OFFICE WASHINGTON

As soon as the President was informed, he did something nobody expected as he stated:

PRESIDENT OF THE UNITED STATES

Send a flight of fighter jets down there and see what the alien's intentions are. We might as well find out now.

SECRTARY OF DEFENSE

Sir, under the circumstances, it would be advisable to get permission from the Government of Mexico.

PRESIDENT OF THE UNITED STATES

Mexico has no real military power. We don't have time to kiss their ass and ask for permission. If it pisses them off that's too bad.

Those alien ships may pose a huge threat to the United States, so we don't have time for Mexico to dither and come to their senses. Get the aircraft airborne immediately!

The joint chiefs understood one thing vividly. The COMMANDER IN CHIEF was their boss, and like the previous President who fired a lot of Generals and Admirals, this guy no doubt would do so unremorsefully.

AIRFORCE SECRETARY

A couple dozen F22A's are already staged at Fort Worth Texas for another reason, War Games.

COMMANDER IN CHIEF

How soon can they fly?

AIRFORCE SECRETARY

The pilots were ready to take off. The aircraft are fueled and ready for immediate departure.

COMMANDER IN CHIEF

Will they be able to defend themselves if they encounter the Aliens?

AIRFORCE SECRETARY

They had live ordinance onboard because they were going to make bombing runs on targets and shoot aerial targets as part of the war games.

COMMANDER IN CHIEF

That's a good distance from Fort Worth to Guadalajara area, approximately 1000 miles. Do they have enough fuel to get there.

AIRFORCE SECRETARY

Refueling tankers were also on hand because they were going to fly out to California and Nevada as part of the exercise.

CHAIRMAN OF THE JOINT CHIEFS

Under normal circumstances, a strike could not be put together this quickly. The size and scope of this mission would most likely take 72 hours to prepare unless we were actually at war.

COMMANDER IN CHIEF

Why is that General?

CHAIRMAN OF THE JOINT CHIEFS

During wartime rules for engagement, the rule books are tossed, and the U.S. Air Force flies by the seat of their pants like they did in Vietnam.

EXT. CGI. DAY. F22AS LAUNCHING FROM FORT WORTH AIR BASE.

VOICEOVER

(During the F22A squadron takeoff)

By the time the F22As were lifting off the runway at Carswell Air Force Base north of Fort Worth, Texas, the aliens were already leaving the atmosphere happy for their time on Earth that allowed them to rejuvenate and overcome a high degree of Cosmic Space Sickness.

This pleasant stopover meant the Carsopian Space Armada would arrive at the provincial capital of ***Cui*** *in viable condition to immediately swing into action if required.*

American National Reconnaissance Office (NRO) was given orders to reposition one of its KH-14 satellites over the contested area. The orders came too late for the KH-14 to be of any value for the first F22A sortie.

Halfway to the target, the Mexicans had detected some of the formation, primarily because the air refueling tankers had no stealth. That immediately had some serious repercussions as the Mexicans were suddenly thinking they might be under attack from the United States who had been gradually becoming more and more aggressive due to the perceived lack of Mexican efforts to deal with the drug cartels.

Some administrators believed the Mexican Government was in bed with the Cartel's and took bribes from them, as one of the Cartel Leaders recently undergoing trial stated.

There was a lot of back and forth between the Americans and the Mexicans who had little ability to deal with a couple dozen F22As their airborne radars would have a slim chance of detecting. The Mexicans were warned to stand down and any Mexican plane that approached the formation would be shot down.

The Mexican Air Force sat on its hands as the leadership asked the question:

MEXICO AIR FORCE COMMANDER

Whiskey Tango Foxtrot?

At *super glide* it didn't take the F22's long to reach the target area. They only needed the tankers to get home.

From 20,000 feet the squadron leaders saw no targets but assumed the aliens might have good camouflage and radioed to his flock:

FLIGHT LEADER ZORRO

This is Flight Leader Zorro, I want Ka flight to follow me down, us see if we can locate the targets and light them up. The rest of you keep an eye out and stand by for further instructions.

Zorro (Ted's call sign) rolled his F22A and came down quickly looking over the area. His wingman Ka reported:

KA

Zorro, I'm not getting any signals from anything. There are no radars or lasers operating.

ZORRO

Roger that Ka.

Zorro flew all the way down on the deck looking around and only saw desert.

ZORRO

KA, I didn't see any possible targets, do you see anything?

KA

There was no sign of Alien ships or anything of concern.

ZORRO

I sure do not see anything. Did the Intel boys get some bum dope with Cash in Advance?

KA

The only thing I witnessed with interest, which I photographed with my gun camera video, was what appeared to be scorched spots where something was recently burned.

He then contacted the AWAC's plane that was probably 100 miles behind them:

ZORRO [F22]

Mother Goose, this is Zorro, there is nothing here but desert, recommend we return to base.

MOTHER GOOSE [AWACS]

Zorro, this is Mother Goose, understand no targets, standby for further instructions."

Within moments, the AWAC's plane came back with instructions.

MOTHER GOOSE [AWACS]

Zorro, this is Mother Goose, return to base.

ZORRO [F22]

Mother Goose, this is Zorro, understand return to base. Could you please vector those milk cows towards us. I would like to get another drink before I return to base.

MOTHER GOOSE [AWACS]

Zorro, this is Mother Goose, understand will vector the Milk Cows to your flock.

ZORRO [F22]

Mother Goose this is flight leader Zorro, understand line up for the Milk Cow, and standing by for instructions.

The flight of F22As then continued their way back to Fort Worth. This little trip down to Mexico was quickly *termed* another *Goat Fawk* that really screwed up their training plan for the Area-52 exercise.

The SR-72 recordings at 50,000 feet clearly showed the alien ships on the ground. The reconnaissance flights were sent out again immediately from March Air Force Base. The same flight crew who took 50,000-foot recordings was over the area again and in due time returned to March Air Force Base with new mission recordings.

To the consternation of the photo reconnaissance officers at Wright Patterson Air Force Base reported to the JOINT CHIEFS.

PHOTO RECONNAISSANCE OFFICER

The Alien ships are gone.

KH-14 flights scoured the area. There was no sign of any type of craft. No reports came from anywhere else in the world. Another clue supporting the Aliens left Earth was that abductions ended.

Soon after the State Department cooled off Mexican emotions a joint task group was formed.

On a very rare instance U.S. Army Calvary and Airborne troops were sent to a rendezvous point in Mexico where they met up with the Mexican Army.

American and Mexican Helicopter crews flew the airborne troops 50 miles West of Hiway 23 near one of the Massacres to the location the alien craft had been photographed and probably bivouacked.

EXT. DAY. ALIEN BIVOUAC AREA NORTH OF GUADALAJARA.

The former Alien camp site is where the gruesome Human remains findings were discovered that proved indeed these aliens are cannibals.

US ARMY COLONEL

Those sick bastards ate those people.

MEXICAN CALVARY RECONNOSSANCE OFFICER

Almost makes you want to puke.

Army intelligence people were then flown in to secure the site and prevent loss of intelligence by the army men walking around the site. Mexican and Americans were busy for a month photographing the alien bivouac site. A couple of the intelligence officers discussed the area.

INTELLIGENCE OFFICER

The Aliens didn't do a good job of cleaning up after themselves.

2ND INTELLIGENCE OFFICER

It's clear they didn't plan on staying long, so I can see where they had no interest in doing a camp cleanup.

INTELLIGENCE OFFICER

What kind of savages could do what they did?

2ND INTELLIGENCE OFFICER

I'm sure we are looked at for similar reasons for what we have done as well.

INTELLIGENCE OFFICER

With all the debris scattered around the bivouac area it was easy to piece together, the humans had been eaten by the alien cannibals.

2ND INTELLIGENCE OFFICER

I just don't understand how an advanced alien race that can travel to the stars could possibly kill and eat intelligent sentient beings.

INTELLIGENCE OFFICER

We have no idea what's normal for the rest of the galaxy or the Universe.

2ND INTELLIGENCE OFFICER

It could have been worse, what if they consider Humans as cosmic cockroaches and decided to use cosmic pest control on us.

INTELLIGENCE OFFICER

Do we have good photos of the imprints the alien ships left on the ground?

2ND INTELLIGENCE OFFICER

Yes, we have been feeding those photos with GPS tags on them to a lab in Rockville Maryland who's generating a computer graphic for us. We will be able to overlay the flyover images and more accurately assess the actual size of the Alien spacecraft.

INTELLIGENCE OFFICER
Any estimate on their weight?

2ND INTELLIGENCE OFFICER
Based on the depth of the indent into the soil and the surface area of devices, it's clear they all weighed millions of pounds.

INTELLIGENCE OFFICER
Must have been huge.

2ND INTELLIGENCE OFFICER
Some of the ground indentions we've measured are over 2,000 feet long.

INTELLIGENCE OFFICER
About twice as long as one of our Aircraft Carriers?

2ND INTELLIGENCE OFFICER
And more than twice as wide.

INTELLIGENCE OFFICER
Any chemical residue left behind from propulsion?

2ND INTELLIGENCE OFFICER
No traces of propulsion related chemicals. They are apparently powered by something other than rockets.

INTELLIGENCE OFFICER
Must be rather advanced to come here from far away.

2ND INTELLIGENCE OFFICER
Right, which makes it even harder to understand why they turned out to be cannibals.

Mexican Policía Federal Ministerial, PFM Agent Guerrero and FBI agents Bentley Boyd and Charles Gable flew in by helicopter from Guadalajara and were met by the Army Intel people. They had already read some of the reports the FBI obtained from the Pentagon.

It was a somber experience for the three agents as they were led over to the alien barbecue pits. Remnants of barbecued carcasses littered the area.

PFM Agent Guerrero
Looks like they had a little feast here.

FBI AGENT Bentley
Boyd Yea, sick bastards.

FBI AGENT CHARLES GABLE
Too bad they were wearing helmets; we'll never know what they look like.

As the day unfolded a group of soldiers approached the Intel Officers and the three agents.

SOLDIER
Sir, we think we have found shallow graves up on that hill.

INTELLIGENCE OFFICER
Let's go take a look, soldier.

2ND INTELLIGENCE OFFICER
Sargent get a couple men with shovels and follow us up the hill.

ARMY SARGENT
Yes sir."

The Sargent grabbed a couple NON-COM's and sent them to one of the support vehicles to grab a couple shovels and meet him up on the hill.

The hill was probably 200 feet up a 30-degree incline. It took a little effort to climb it, and as they looked over the area, there was fresh dirt exposed over a 40-foot swath.

INTELLIGENCE OFFICER
Have them start digging in the middle and we'll fan out from there.

The officers and the three Agents watched with great interest as the two Army Privates shoveled dirt. Surprisingly whatever was buried was down a lot deeper than they imagined. At around the four-foot mark, one of the soldiers yelled out:

ARMY PRIVATE
My shovel just hit something.

The group approached closer observing the unearthing of the object.

ARMY PRIVATE
Whatever it is, seems to be covered with a type of canvas.

The soldier continued digging and said:

ARMY PRIVATE

Whatever it is, it's rather large.

It seemed like an eternity for the soldier to slowly dig around the object that appeared at least ten feet long. The three FBI and PFM Agents already had an idea what it was but remained patient and quiet.

With most of the dirt shoveled away from the canvas, the soldier pulled his knife off his side carrying pouch and slit the heavy-duty canvas material.

ARMY PRIVATE

It's some type of body, clothed and stinks to high heaven.

INTELLIGENCE OFFICER

Cut the canvas back all the way, I want to see all of it.

The Army Private continued working opening the canvas.

What the three agents quickly noted was the moth/purple colored material which matched the description the witnesses claimed. That quickly reinforced what they suspected was the contents.

As soon as the soldier finished slashing open the canvas he yelled up:

ARMY PRIVATE

It's a *giant*, sir.

Everyone could clearly see that and one of the INTEL officers stated:

INTELLIGENCE OFFICER

Stand out of the way soldier, I want to take a picture of it as it is now.

The soldier climbed out of the pit and the Officer walked to the side and took a few pictures. No doubt it was a dead alien buried. It had a helmet on, and its face was covered just like what the witnesses had seen. The moment of truth was now.

INTELLIGENCE OFFICER

Soldier, climb down and carefully lift the helmet off the face. Try not to disturb anything.

The soldier climbed down into the pit and lifted the helmet. It was a mostly human-like face with eyes closed. Based on the shape of the eye slits, one would imagine it had almond shaped eyes.

FBI AGENT BENTLEY BOYD

This looks like a burial place for several of these aliens.

PFM AGENT GUERRERO

Wonder what happened to them?

INTELLIGENCE OFFICER

Don't cut open any more of the canvas, we'll let the experts do that after we transport the bodies to an examination location.

FBI AGENT Bentley

Boyd What about biohazard protocols?

I'm sure these bodies will be loaded into plastic containers and taken to Fort Detrick.

Within moments of making their reports to higher authority, representatives from Fort Detrick in full panic ordered the Intel Officers

FORT DETRICK BIO HAZZARD TEAM REP
(VIA GROUP CHAT)

Do not to allow anyone else near the alien corpses and to keep the men who had done the shoveling away from everyone else and a decontamination team and kit is on the way, should be there in a few hours.

The poor soldiers that were doing the shoveling would soon be going to a six-month quarantine. Their lives would soon suck. Everyone else was ordered back away from the site and perimeter guards were set up with orders not to allow anyone without special permission to enter and shoot anyone who goes in without permission and tries to leave the area.

The Mexican Army officers were now really starting to be agitated as *it appeared the Americans were ordering them around in their own country.*

PFM Agent Guerrero approached the Mexican Army officers.

PFM AGENT GUERRERO

Gentlemen, please do not get upset. This is truly a remarkable discovery and the logistics of handling this are far greater than our country can now handle. We need the United States help in this matter.

MEXICAN ARMY OFFICER

I'm tired of taking orders from the Gringos.

PFM AGENT GUERRERO

Please be cooperative and be humble for what we have discovered today will grip mankind unlike anything you have ever experienced in your life. Also, we need to debrief your men and direct them not to discuss this matter with anyone and to consider all this Top Secret.

MEXICAN ARMY OFFICER

Yes sir.

PFM AGENT GUERRERO

You will be getting further instructions from Mexico City. But for now, your job is to make sure civilians and individuals not assigned to this task do not enter the area. This will become the most important mission in your lifetime.

The Mexican Army Colonel knew Agent Guerrero was a big shot from Mexico City with all the political connections. As such he was sophisticated enough to know to follow Agent Guerrero's lead.

Suddenly the American involvement was no longer a big matter for them, especially a couple hours later when helicopters arrived carrying people in wearing bio suits.

Lifting 500-pound alien bodies up out of their graves and loading them up in duce and a half, trucks that carried special air sealed shipping containers was extremely problematic.

The ultimate solution was flying in more bio-suits for soldiers to be used as laborers. Using portable davits, ropes and a few other improvised devices the six bodies found were eventually loaded up into the trucks and hauled to a Mexican Air Base where C17 transport was waiting.

Surprisingly, the bodies were not taken to Fort Detrick. Instead, they were taken to Wright Patterson Air Force Base, and soon were carted into special rooms in the large vast underground cavern under the famed building 18.

Only one scientist who was involved in America's biological defense department was permitted to examine the bodies with the Army pathologists.

Sworn to secrecy already maintaining above Top Secret clearances, these men went about their work in a biohazard-controlled environment and had a two-fold purpose. One was to analyze and report the features of the aliens, and the second was to determine cause of death if possible.

Humans have yet to deal with Cosmic Space Sickness. We had no idea it existed and what caused it. The stop over to Earth by these six aliens happened too late. They succumbed to Cosmic Space Sickness which the pathologists would never be able to determine.

INT. DAY. WRIGHT PATTERSON AIR FORCE BASE BUILDING 18 UNDERGROUND FACILITY.

WRIGHT PATTERSON AIR FORCE BASE
PATHOLOGIST.

At 500 pounds they had impressive bodies and a brain about twice the size of a human.

WRIGHT PATTERSON AIR FORCE BASE
INTEL OFFICER.

They had their uniforms on, and their personal belongings were on them even though it wasn't much. Even so it was an intelligence find.

WRIGHT PATTERSON AIR FORCE BASE
2ND INTEL OFFICER.

The aliens had written communications in the few personal documents found in their uniform pockets.

WRIGHT PATTERSON AIR FORCE BASE
INTEL OFFICER.

Their language utilizes characters like Mandarin Chinese. The main difference is the alien written characters were about 5 times larger than Mandarin characters with up to several hundred brush strokes per character.

WRIGHT PATTERSON AIR FORCE BASE
2ND INTEL OFFICER.

How does that compare to Mandarin Chinese characters?

WRIGHT PATTERSON AIR FORCE BASE
INTEL OFFICER.

Most Chinese Mandarin Characters have less than 20 brush strokes (components of the Mandarin Character).

WRIGHT PATTERSON AIR FORCE BASE
PATHOLOGIST.

The aliens have red blood, and their gastrointestinal track was not too dissimilar from humans.

WRIGHT PATTERSON AIR FORCE BASE INTEL
OFFICER.

Any other significant discoveries?

WRIGHT PATTERSON AIR FORCE BASE PATHOLOGIST.

Oddly they had six fingers and toes. Instead of 23 pairs of chromosomes they have 33 pairs. Since no living entity exists like them that we know of, it would be unlikely we would ever discover what those extra chromosomes do.

WRIGHT PATTERSON AIR FORCE BASE 2ND
INTEL OFFICER.

Any idea why they stopped on this planet?

WRIGHT PATTERSON AIR FORCE BASE
INTEL OFFICER.

It is unlikely we'll ever identify who these aliens are and where they came from or why they stopped here.

WRIGHT PATTERSON AIR FORCE BASE 2ND
INTEL OFFICER.

Was there any indication these deceased aliens participated in cannibalism?

WRIGHT PATTERSON AIR FORCE BASE PATHOLOGIST.

No, when we checked their stomachs, all we found was a soy substance. There was no presence of any undigested human flesh.

WRIGHT PATTERSON AIR FORCE BASE
INTEL OFFICER.

Any idea how long these beings were deceased?

WRIGHT PATTERSON AIR FORCE BASE PATHOLOGIST.

We have no way of knowing what their metabolism rate is but based on the condition of their bodies they were probably buried shortly before you discovered them, maybe a day or two.

WRIGHT PATTERSON AIR FORCE BASE
INTEL OFFICER.

I'm surprised wild animals didn't find them.

WRIGHT PATTERSON AIR FORCE BASE 2ND
INTEL OFFICER.

They were buried four feet underground; the wild animals probably didn't have enough time to find them.

The Carsopian's added greatly to the fame of Wright Patterson Air Force Base building 18. Nobody knew for sure who leaked the information, but one thing that turned out to be quite auspicious.

The new containment building in area 51 had just been completed so the CIA, under orders from Majestic 12, quickly moved the Alien bodies to area 51 and when several liberal congressmen forced their way into building 18 under the guise of government oversight. All they found was sterile empty rooms and a lot of denials, since those involved in the alien autopsies were also whisked away to area 51 the day before.

The day after the congressmen left totally dejected from false information they received, the Aliens were moved back to Wright Patterson Airforce Based that had

all the equipment the pathologist needed to do their examinations.
Battle of *Cui*

VOICEOVER

The Carsopians eventually made their way to their Provincial Empire stronghold of ***Cui****. General Fukua de Hundan and his forces were received as heroes, but General Fukua de Hundan knew a lot of hard fighting lay ahead of them.*

The Heisibing had ruthlessly carved their way across the frontier slowly boxing in the Cuivites. One could state, the Carsopians had to take drastic action now or plan to come up with surrender terms.

In bygone years the liberal and somewhat irresponsible Cuivites never put forth a reasonable effort to defend the heartland of their Empire stronghold.

Living for several generations on the hegemony of their forefathers, the Cuivites safety and global defense was put at the mercy of the continued policy of mob rule who systematically ate their seed corn allowing the defense infrastructure to decay to a non- deployable state. As outworlds suddenly were in panic hoping the provincial capital would send relief, it was the same story repeatedly: too little too late.

Heisibings had their 5-year plans, 10-year plans, 50- year plans, 100-year plans, and even 1000-year plans. To their dismay and glee, their spy network reported over time all those critical factors the planners could then take into consideration in laying out strategy.

Heisibings were subtle at their approach avoiding the perception they intended on doing a knockout punch.

Instead, the Heisibings worked towards the first goal: to cut the *Cuivites* off from the Carsopians Empire center which would severely hamper sending reinforcements. They took over just enough worlds in a systematic manner so that *Cuivites* wouldn't predict their bold move until it was too late, and they couldn't do anything to interfere with their plans.

Once the *Cuivites* were cut off, the end would be approaching soon. If the Heisibings managed to take Cui before the Carsopians reinforcements could arrive, the Heisibings could then easily defend their positions, and *Cui* would then become part of the Heisibing's portfolio.

General Fukua de Hundan had his own plan. He knew the Heisibings had overextended themselves and if he attacked right away before the Heisibing's spies could warn them, he could create the domino theory for them.

Since it would take a while for the Heisibing's spy network to send warnings,

General Fukua de Hundan would get into their rears on one of the flanks. The fear of encirclement would then drive every Heisibing strategy.

INT. SPACE. CARSOPIAN COMMAND SHIP. CONTROL ROOM.

GENERAL FUKUA DE HUNDAN'S
EXECUTIVE OFFICER
Not knowing they had a lethal adversary present; they didn't provide competent flank protection.

GENERAL FUKUA DE HUNDAN
They left themselves open for attack.

GENERAL FUKUA DE HUNDAN'S
EXECUTIVE OFFICER
General Fukua de Hundan, you made a smart move stopping at Earth so that our troops are still in decent condition.

GENERAL FUKUA DE HUNDAN
I want all Space Sick soldiers put on a transport and sent it to the planet *Cui.*

GENERAL FUKUA DE HUNDAN'S
EXECUTIVE OFFICER
Good idea, we can task the captain of the transport to make the people on Cui believe our force was a lot smaller than it was through disinformation.

GENERAL FUKUA DE HUNDAN
One or two Carsopian ships would have very little impact on the outcome of the next series of battles planned to occur within weeks.

Carsopian space armada warships immediately detoured for from Cui, thus leaving behind a false disposition which didn't concern the Heisibing spies enough to make priority reports.

The Carsopian Armada only had to take two planets to give them full access to the Heisibing's flanks. With the number of ships General Fukua de Hundan commanded in his task force, the eventual thrust on the Heisibing's flanks would prove to be very detrimental to the Heisibing strategy and plans.

EXT. CGI. SPACE. CARSOPIAN ARMADA ATTACKS ALMAZNYYE GORY HEISIBING GARRISONS. 20 SECONDS.

INT. SPACE. CARSOPIAN COMMAND SHIP. CONTROL ROOM.

GENERAL FUKUA DE HUNDAN'S EXECUTIVE OFFICER
It didn't take long to travel the distance to planet Almaznyye Gory we needed to neutralize.

GENERAL FUKUA DE HUNDAN

Almaznyye Gory is on the extremity of the contested area. They probably do not have the best garrison troops.

GENERAL FUKUA DE HUNDAN'S EXECUTIVE OFFICER

The Heisibing garrison troops are ill-prepared and not mentally ready for such a huge invasion.

GENERAL FUKUA DE HUNDAN

Leave a couple assault ships behind for mop up operations and assistance in getting the land based defensive systems fully operation. Then let's make our way to the next target, Dalekaya de Zhemchuzhina.

EXT. CGI. SPACE. CARSOPIAN ARMADA ATTACKS DALEKAYA DE ZHEMCHUZHINA HEISIBING GARRISONS. 25 SECONDS.

INT. SPACE. CARSOPIAN COMMAND SHIP. CONTROL ROOM.

GENERAL FUKUA DE HUNDAN'S EXECUTIVE OFFICER

Heisibing garrison troops on planet Dalekaya de Zhemchuzhina had some warning because of the attacks on the Almaznyye Gory.

GENERAL FUKUA DE HUNDAN

The Heisibing's garrison troops there were not front- line combat effective soldiers.

GENERAL FUKUA DE HUNDAN'S EXECUTIVE OFFICER

They put forth an excellent effort, but when you are outnumbered 100 to 1, there isn't much you can do to change the inevitable.

One could equate these Heisibing troops in peril like the Marines at Wake Island on December 8, 1941, at the beginning of WWII.

When the circumstances suddenly unfolded and Heisibing Task Force Commander Admiral Engaarai discovered his Heisibing Space Fleet flanks were exposed and had received word that Carsopian ships were at *Cui*, he realized they could be attacked in two simultaneous directions.

INT. SPACE HEISIBING TASK FORCE COMMAND SHIP CONTROL ROOM.

HEISIBING TASK FORCE COMMANDER ADMIRAL ENGAARAI

The only sensible strategy now would be to attack the new formation that threatened their flanks.

ADMIRAL ENGAARAI ASSISTANT
ADMIRAL DIKIY OS'MINOG

Sir, with all due respect, I recommend not throwing caution to the wind.

HEISIBING TASK FORCE COMMANDER
ADMIRAL ENGAARAI

Admiral Dikiy Os'minog, this could be a trap, we will not know until we move to protect our flanks. That's more important than attacking Cui now.

ADMIRAL ENGAARAI ASSISTANT
ADMIRAL DIKIY OS'MINOG

This is probably a small force as a feint to get us to divide our forces to lessen the blow on Cui, we need to stay focused on Cui.

HEISIBING TASK FORCE COMMANDER
ADMIRAL ENGAARAI

One of the axioms of spacewar that I've learned is to never proceed with an attack if you know your flanks are at risk.

ADMIRAL ENGAARAI ASSISTANT
ADMIRAL DIKIY OS'MINOG

If we attack this force that may not be very big or troubling, we'll lose the element of surprise for the Cui attack.

HEISIBING TASK FORCE COMMANDER
ADMIRAL ENGAARAI

Even if we risk exposing ourselves and lose the element of surprise for the Cui attack, we need to protect our flanks.

Heisibing Task Force Commander Admiral Engaarai and his assistant, Admiral Dikiy Os'minog severely underestimated the size and scope of the Carsopian force along their flanks they soon attacked. This was not a flank body; it was the brunt of the main force.

INT. SPACE. CARSOPIAN COMMAND SHIP. CONTROL ROOM.

General Fukua de Hundan predicted Heisibings next move, and he was ready.

GENERAL FUKUA DE HUNDAN

We have the advantage knowing there were no forces behind us to worry about, so maneuver is to our advantage.

GENERAL FUKUA DE HUNDAN'S
EXECUTIVE OFFICER

If Heisibing ships traveled close to the planets we just liberated, the newly placed Carsopian ground defense forces could wipe out many of their ships.

GENERAL FUKUA DE HUNDAN

Having planets, we control on our flanks allows us to concentrate our forces, we can project power and probably fly through Heisibing formations with impunity.

GENERAL FUKUA DE HUNDAN'S
EXECUTIVE OFFICER

Since the Heisibing Fleet is over stretched, the possibility of sending in reserves to save the Heisibing is rather unlikely.

The *Battle of Cui* would immediately become a slug match, but it was obvious the winner could take all. The Carsopian Force might not be able to open the direct path to attack the Heisibing Empire, but they would at least lift the siege of *Cui*.

VOICEOVER (GENERAL FUKUA DE HUNDAN)
THOUGHT

Once this battle was complete, my fleet could slip back around the long way get back to the center of the Empire where we would join up with the main fleet and attack the Heisibing's straight on. Because of actions at Cui securing that area, the Heisibings could not afford to risk going in that direction.

This plan would limit Heisibing field of maneuver where Carsopian forces could then outmaneuver them and take them apart in detail. Such an operation ultimately would force a surrender and a meaningful peace treaty that would require the Heisibing's to scuttle most of their fleet.

General Fukua de Hundan watched the battle unfold on his command ship several layers behind screens and heavy assault ships.

The Carsopian fleet speed was relatively slow as they were playing defense with a superior force forcing the Heisibing's to commit to an attack they would repel then counterattack on their own terms.

EXT.CGI.SPACE.BATTLE OF CUI MAIN SPACE BATTLE

The two fleets approached each other in what observers would view as a head-on collision of the two major forces.

Sensor displays on ships of both fleets showed a witch's brew of terrifying alignment of very powerful space combat vessels.

EXT. CGI. SPACE.HEISIBING WEAPONS LAUNCH. 20 SECONDS.

Streaming in at excessive speeds, the Heisibing's launched a variety of types of weapons, drones, decoys, and fighters.

CARSOPIAN SENSOR OPERATOR

Incoming Heisibing space weapons and fighter bombers.

GENERAL FUKUA DE HUNDAN

Launch Self Defense Weapons and arm Close in Weapon Systems in fully automatic mode.

CARSOPIAN WEAPONS OPERATOR

Integrated Fleet Weapons and Close in Weapon Systems engaging the enemy.

GENERAL FUKUA DE HUNDAN

Launch a Long Range Cyclonic Disrupter Salvo. We need to force them into some radical maneuvers to break up their pincer movements.

CARSOPIAN WEAPONS OPERATOR

Long Range Cyclonic Disrupter Salvo launched, 64 weapons engaging fired at half second intervals.

General Fukua De Hundan observed the main battle screen that showed spliced video from all the ships that Artificial Intelligence created in gigapixel fractals gave a breathtaking view of the battle space. The weapons exhaust of the numerous self defense weapons and the Long-Range Cyclonic Disrupters created a spellbinding macro imagery few ever observed before.

The two fleets were too far apart yet to let lose all the laser weapons, but that would start very quickly.

<u>EXT. CGI. SPACE. CARSOPIANS WEAPONS LAUNCH. 20 SECONDS.</u>

The Carsopian's responding with their salvo's forced the Heisibing fleet to do defensive maneuvers to escape the harsh realities of lethal space warfare.

<u>INT.SPACE. HEISIBING ADMIRAL ENGAARAI COMMAND SHIP.</u>

HEISIBING TASK FORCE COMMANDER ADMIRAL ENGAARAI

Admiral Dikiy Os'minog, do you know why most major space battles seem to always begin on one of the warring parties' flanks?

ADMIRAL ENGAARAI ASSISTANT

ADMIRAL DIKIY OS'MINOG

Admiral Engaarai, that's where tactical surprise and disposition forces the issue.

HEISIBING TASK FORCE COMMANDER ADMIRAL ENGAARAI

Admiral Dikiy Os'minog, would you agree with me the number of weapons engaging us constitutes more than just a feint?

ADMIRAL DIKIY OS'MINOG

Admiral Engaarai, it's quite evident there are quite a few more weapons engaged than would be encountered with a feint. It appears we are flying into a major space battle.

HEISIBING TASK FORCE COMMANDER ADMIRAL ENGAARAI

Admiral Dikiy Os'minog, would you agree that had we continued to approach Cui, we might have been encircled.

ADMIRAL DIKIY OS'MINOG

Admiral Engaarai, no doubt in future critiques, questions will be raised how the Carsopians managed to reposition such a powerful fleet and gained tactical surprise.

HEISIBING TASK FORCE COMMANDER ADMIRAL ENGAARAI

Admiral Dikiy Os'minog, you read all the INTEL reports I did and discussed them with the planners as early as a few hours ago. We are probably witnessing a colossal intelligence failure.

EXT. CGI. SPACE. LASER ATTACKS, MISSILE ATTACKS, EXPLOSIONS. 30 SECONDS.

Ships from both sides were caught up in a maelstrom of exotic bright lights and explosions as these dangerous weapons ripped into the sides of hulls unleashing a deadly witches brew of destruction. The minute automatic systems determined the enemy was within laser range, all hell broke loose.

Early in the battle *both sides* were anxious and over exuberant, believing in their own irrational propaganda. The harsh reality becomes more real when it affects you personally.

When suddenly, the bridge party starts dying from asphyxiation, reality strikes home. Death in space is not a pleasant experience.

INT.SPACE. GENERAL FUKUA DE HUNDAN'S COMMAND SHIP

General Fukua de Hundan closely observed his three-dimensional map of the battle that had real time updates. He could scale it to any size he wanted including several solar systems, but for now where the battle was fought, only one solar system behind him was on the three-dimensional MAP showing all the ships of both sides derived from multiple sources and sensors. He continued discussing the battle with is Executive Officer:

GENERAL FUKUA DE HUNDAN

We did a good job of repulsing the initial Heisibing attack and destroyed a number of their ships in the process.

EXECUTIVE OFFICER

If the Heisibing's operate true to form, they will swing around again and go right for the middle of our formation.

GENERAL FUKUA DE HUNDAN

They don't know the size of force we brought with us. That will be a foolish move on their part because we'll counterattack immediately, and they will be severely weakened by then.

EXT. CGI. SPACE. HEISIBING FLEET MANUEVER 15 SECONDS.

True to form, the Heisibing's swung around, reformed and proceeded to do that frontal attack right up the middle of the Carsopian force they didn't know had such size thanks to new types of cloaking devices and close formations to disguise the number of ships, and a total INTEL failure.

Just like during the initial attack, at the critical range, weapons from both fleets fired and the lethal objects flew towards death and destruction uncommon and seemingly unreal.

EXT. CGI. SPACE. LASER ATTACKS BETWEEN HEISIBING'S AND CARSOPIANS 30 SECONDS.

As expected, some poor miserable souls expired spontaneously as several ships exploded into huge fire balls ejecting sparkling debris and greenish gasses shooting out from ruptured hulls.

INT.SPACE. GENERAL FUKUA DE HUNDAN COMMAND SHIP

This exchange left behind an equal number of casualties on each side, but it also left a very weak area in the middle of the Heisibing's formation. Just as the Heisibing's were maneuvering and regrouping to plan their next attack feeling somewhat ecstatic they had destroyed so many Carsopian ships, were soon on the receiving end as General Fukua de Hundan gave the orders over fleet channels:

GENERAL FUKUA DE HUNDAN

Commence Operation Hutao-Jiazi.

The Heisibing's had grown complacent to what was considered timid and conservative actions by the Carsopians. Heisibings had not come across a bold strategist such as General Fukua de Hundan in a long time.

The Carsopian Fleet then started accelerating. The last attack placed too many Heisibing ships out of position to stop such a concentrated powerful attack.

As the ships accelerated and moved closer to the Heisibing formation there was soon a mild Heisibing panic because now they realized they had been lured into a trap.

It was a classical maneuver, and their INTEL had been so bad they didn't realize what was occurring until it was too late.

GENERAL FUKUA DE HUNDAN

Even though a few of our Carsopian assault ships were mauled going through the gauntlet, they had so many weapons available to fling at the Heisibing's the level of destruction appears to have become unbearable quickly.

EXECUTIVE OFFICER

General Fukua De Hundan it appears the Heisibing's are doing a defensive maneuver.

EXT.CGI.SPACE HEISIBING LEADER ADMIRAL ENGAARAI COMMAND SHIP. 10 SECONDS. THE SHIP PASSES BY THE CAMERA AND OTHER FLEET UNITS ARE IN THE BACKGROUND.

INT.SPACE. HEISIBING ADMIRAL ENGAARAI COMMAND SHIP.

It didn't take long for their distinguished Heisibing leader Admiral Engaarai to order:

HEISIBING FLEET
COMMANDER ADMIRAL ENGAARAI

All ships reverse course break off attacks. Perform evasive maneuvers.

ADMIRAL ENGAARAI'S ASSISTANT
ADMIRAL DIKIY OS'MINOG

Why are you doing this? We have damaged so many Carsopian Fleet Components, we are almost ready to break threw and split their forces and win this battle!

HEISIBING FLEET
COMMANDER ADMIRAL ENGAARAI

Admiral Dikiy Os'minog, we have maneuvered into a sophisticated and elaborate trap.

ADMIRAL ENGAARAI'S ASSISTANT
ADMIRAL DIKIY OS'MINOG

How can you say that, Admiral Engaarai?

HEISIBING FLEET
COMMANDER ADMIRAL ENGAARAI

Look at the sensor displays, a lot of Carsopian space warships are now arriving, we need to get out of here before the fleet is destroyed.

Admiral Engaarai's Assistant, Admiral Dikiy Os'minog was staring at the sensor displays and suddenly felt overwhelmed.

At first, Admiral Dikiy Os'minog was hating Admiral Engaarai for turning into a coward in front of the crew.

But as he watched the vast number of ships pop up on the sensor display with automatic trackers and automatic classifiers saying what type of ship it is, he was suddenly a changed man.

Fear also struck Admiral Dikiy Os'minog, but he noticed Admiral Engaarai remained cool under fire and issued orders in a calm manner even though they fell for the trap.

EXT.CGI.SPACE HEISIBING FLEET MANUEVERING IN UNSCRIPTED CHAOS. ONLY DEFENSIVE SHOOTING CAME FROM THE HEISIBING SHIPS BUT CARSOPIANS CONTINUED THE ATTACK DURING HEISIBING FLIGHT TO SAFETY.

Very seldom has either side seen such a spectacle of space combat.

INT.CGI.SPACE. GENERAL FUKUA DE HUNDAN COMMANDSHIP

CARSOPIAN EXECUTIVE OFFICER

Heisibing retreat has turned into a full-scale route.

GENERAL FUKUA DE HUNDAN

It is clear the way the Heisibing's were departing, it was every man for himself as they threw caution to the wind.

Within 30 minutes the space battlefield was empty, the Heisibing's were accelerating painfully to flank speeds to get as far away from the Carsopians.

INT.SPACE. HEISIBING ADMIRAL ENGAARAI COMMAND SHIP.

ADMIRAL ENGAARAI'S ASSISTANT
ADMIRAL DIKIY OS'MINOG

Admiral Engaarai, what's you plan. Are we going to continue transiting at high speed?

HEISIBING FLEET
COMMANDER ADMIRAL ENGAARAI

I know this seems distasteful to you, but I want to get as far away from the Carsopians as possible then regroup and figure out what went wrong and what we need to do to fix it.

ADMIRAL ENGAARAI'S
ASSISTANT ADMIRAL DIKIY OS'MINOG

Admiral Engaarai the crew thinks you are being a coward for now slowing down and turning around to find out what the Carsopians are doing plus we left behind some of our damaged ships we should have attempted to rescue.

HEISIBING FLEET
COMMANDER ADMIRAL ENGAARAI

Admiral Dikiy Os'minog, even though I feel your statements are borderline insubordination, I will forgive you for now because I need your help to get this crippled fleet back to Yanjingzai Tiankongzhong Space Anchorage.

ADMIRAL ENGAARAI'S
ASSISTANT ADMIRAL DIKIY OS'MINOG

I'm sorry sir, but the men feel they are now a defeated fleet that usually does not stop to pick up their wounded and damaged ships.

HEISIBING FLEET COMMANDER
ADMIRAL ENGAARAI

Admiral Dikiy Os'minog, I have two mandates. One you know well is to attack and destroy the Carsopians and to invade and capture Cui. My second mandate is not to put the fleet in peril as it eliminates our ability to protect the home world and the center of the empire. Regrettably I'm leaving to fulfill the second mandate.

ADMIRAL ENGAARAI'S
ASSISTANT ADMIRAL DIKIY OS'MINOG

Admiral Engaarai, I pity you when we arrive at Yanjingzai Tiankongzhong Space Anchorage.

HEISIBING FLEET COMMANDER
ADMIRAL ENGAARAI

Admiral Dikiy Os'minog, I know I'm not going to have a warm welcoming and after I arrive, I may not remain as the Heisibing Fleet Commander.

ADMIRAL ENGAARAI'S
ASSISTANT ADMIRAL DIKIY OS'MINOG

I expect you will be relieved.

HEISIBING FLEET
COMMANDER ADMIRAL ENGAARAI

Do you feel up to the challenge?

ADMIRAL ENGAARAI'S
ASSISTANT ADMIRAL DIKIY OS'MINOG

Being the deputy commander I'm sure I can direct the fleet if necessary. But I'm not looking to take your job.

HEISIBING FLEET

COMMANDER ADMIRAL ENGAARAI

I'm going back to my stateroom for a while, I'll come back and relieve you in a few hours so you can get some rest.

INT. CGI. SPACE. GENERAL FUKUA DE HUNDAN COMMAND SHIP CONTROL ROOM.

After General Fukua de Hundan finished viewing the Heisibing Fleet leaving the contested area in high speed the way a defeated fleet usually does including not stopping to pick up their wounded and damaged ships, he decided it was time to relocate to the planet *Cui.*

General Fukua de Hundan knew he would be criticized for not continuing the chase to destroy the Heisibing Fleet, but after losing his own son so cosmic space sickness, he thought it was prudent to do his next move.

It was time to quickly travel to Cui where the troops could get back to real gravity and air, and rejuvenate themselves from the arduous journey and a number of them get over their Cosmic Space Sickness so they have no more fatalities like they had to bury on Earth, including his own son.

GENERAL FUKUA DE HUNDAN

We are going to transit to Cui now. Leave a cleanup force behind.

CARSOPIAN FLEET EXECUTIVE OFFICER

I will send orders to designated cleanup ships to rescue all Carsopian's first on damaged ships and after all our people are safe, we'll attempt rescue the enemy.

GENERAL FUKUA DE HUNDAN

Does that mean we'll have a few ceremonial livers served at the General's table tonight?

The Carsopian Fleet made a good time arriving at Cui where the fleet was divided in half.

One half remained in orbit to prevent a surprise attack in the event the Heisibing's decided to do an irrational counterattack, that would do nothing more than extinguish their fleet and leave them wide open for invasion.

The other half of the fleet picked either by the number of casualties they were carrying or the valor they exhibited in the battle transited down to the surface of *Cui.*

EXT. CGI. SPACE. CARSOPIAN SPACE WARSHIPS FLYING OUT OF FORMATION AND MANUEUVERED TO PLANET CUI'S SURFACE. SHOW AT LEAST 30 SHIPS MANUEVERING 20 OR MORE SECONDS DURING THE FOLLOWING VOICEOVER.

VOICEOVER

The Provincial Capital City Pohuaizhe on Planet Cui was named after the famed conqueror General Pohuaizhe who established Carsopian hegemony over the region.
The City of Pohuaizhe glittered with ornamentation and complexity that astounded visitors at first sight.

Cleanliness and architecture surpassed almost any planet in the Carsopian Empire.

Vast fortunes were invested in planet Cui that housed a large percentage of the Carsopian banking system until they were cut off direct route to the center of the Empire.

Just like General Fukua de Hundan's fleet that took a long circuitous route, Cui bankers sent a lot of Carsopian Credits฿ to planets near the center of the Carsopian Empire for security via similar long passages, though they didn't stop over on places like Earth as the bankers' feared traps if they had any delays.

These crypto currencies that left the planet Cui, held the value of one thousand planets.

Much of this wealth shipped was unaffiliated from neutral planets. Oddly enough, some of the Credits฿ were Heisibing which added to the conflict as the two Empires essentially were engaged in major trade wars spread across the galaxy.

The rift between the two civilizations was not just philosophical and political. A lot of it was economic and moral issues such as cannibalism and treatment of Heisibing citizens in past conflicts.

Heisibing women were often victimized by victorious Carsopian invaders whose officers condoned the mistreatment of civilians in conquered territory as a means of spreading terror in the hearts of their enemies.

Carsopian invaders conducted missions in ways they produced spectacular brutal imagery intended to use to demoralize their enemies as they encroached upon them.

An Earth person could equate the Carsopian tactics as like Alexander the Great, Atilla the Hun, Genghis Kahn, and Napoleon.

As the Carsopian warships penetrated the atmosphere and approached their designated landing zones, ships with the top leaders such as General Fukua de Hundan aboard were vectored to Pohuaizhe.

Most of the other ships were scattered around the planet for security as well as spreading the interface to the public across all cities for patriotic reasons knowing there would be celebrations, but also out of practical measures because chaos would erupt if they landed too many space warships at one city.

The Carsopian soldiers were a lot taller than the public in general. Assault troupes carried on transports with the fleet, in the event they needed to invade a planet were systematically identified and pressed into service because of their size as well as their intellect.

People on Earth who had seen the dead bodies of Carsopians buried in Mexico drew the wrong conclusion that this alien race was far larger and menacing when in fact most of the Carsopian people throughout the Empire were almost the same size as humans.

The Army was thus made up of *freaks of nature*, because as part of psychological warfare, they wanted their enemies to assume they were all like that and fear the consequences of tango with them. One of the considerations of spreading these huge assault troops across the planet was to partially diminish the fear the local citizens would have if they had arrived in vast numbers at just a few landing zones.

General Fukua de Hundan just like most of the senior officers were also giants, standing ten feet tall with size sixteen and seventeen shoe sizes, but they were also the most intelligent, having a brain double the size of most Carsopians and continuous training and education their entire lives.

Carsopian leaders for the most part lived in a university. Their intake of knowledge was perpetual, and the Carsopian Empire spared no expense at maintaining that continuing education which ultimately multiplied their knowledge base and enabled them to cope with the complexities of space warfare with extremely dangerous and capable enemies.

A good analogy would be the British Air Force facing the Luftwaffe in the Battle of Britain. The best and brightest were applied to the conflict on both sides. The brain trust included such men as Briton's R.V. Jones, Stewart Graham Menzies, and German Abwehr head, Admiral Canaris who spied for Churchill and was executed in 1945.

Due to the complexities of the Carsopian Empire level space warfare conflicts such as the engaging the Heisibing, a leader with incredible intellect as well as cunning and resourcefulness such as General Fukua de Hundan was required. Due to the difficulties that they faced, General Fukua de Hundan had no choice but to have himself and his staff continuously receive training and indoctrination to allow them to cope with what they must do.

EXT.CGI. GENERAL FUKUA DE HUNDAN'S COMMAND SHIP LANDING AT THE CITY OF POHUAIZHE ON PLANET *CUI* AND BEING GREETED BY DELEGATION. 30 SECONDS

Upon landing at Pohuaizhe, General Fukua de Hundan was met by Pohuaizhe's Mayor and several government officials. They nodded and all stated, a Carsopians greeting that was done during auspicious occasions:

GROUP (GREETING)

Yǎngwàngxīngkōng, Dànyòngxīn qù mèngxiǎng.

That Carsopian greeting roughly translated to English stated: *Look to the stars, but dream through your heart.*

The pleasantries ended abruptly and General Fukua de Hundan was led away to a debriefing. General Fukua de Hundan and his escorts and security detachment arrived shortly in a spheroid conference room. There were well over one hundred in attendance in a three-dimensional spheroid auditorium.

General Fukua de Hundan was led to a small table offset to the edge of the sphere. There were five rings on the three-dimensional spheroid conference room with approximately twenty-five seats per ring, one elevated over the other so that each attendee was approximately the same distance to General Fukua de Hundan sitting alone at the elevated small table on the elevated platform.

The Governor of *Cui* standing in front of General Fukua de Hundan addressed the attendees who were all officials and had some involvement in the defenses of the *Cui* sector of the Carsopian Empire.

GOVERNOR OF *CUI*

> Carsopian Sentinels and Patriots, we are blessed to have General Fukua de Hundan here to share with us his recent experiences in a spectacular space battle and defeat of the Heisibings.
>
> We owe General Fukua de Hundan a great deal of gratitude and we should not take up more of his time than is required as I'm sure he is tired from the battle and deserves a good rest.
> In the days to come, as General Fukua de Hundan is rested and more able to collate all the facts he wishes to share with us, we'll invite him back to address any concerns he has and recommendations he wishes to make to enhance our security.

General Fukua de Hundan had his staff make a continuous perpetual data reduction of the fleet activities showing the three-dimensional combat holographic video analogous to the reports the Rand Corporation made for the Pentagon during the Vietnam conflict, with plenty of eye candy.

The report was of course biased, and information censored. One attribute of the eye candy General Fukua de Hundan was just about to show the three-dimensional spherical shaped auditorium filled full of the patronage class, included very few videos of Carsopian ships blowing up.

The destruction of numerous Heisibing holographic videos were shown and the narrator elucidated those tremendous events quite well. An outsider viewing the presentation would conclude the Carsopians laid waste to the Heisibing. Unfortunately, a number of Carsopian Space Warships also exploded and that was mostly omitted. General Fukua de Hundan knew quite well the real story and a lot of Carsopians died today because of him.

All the major explosions and scenes of wrath delivered exhibited primarily damage to Heisibing warships. But to make it look real they showed a couple Carsopian ships blow up into sparkling debris and homage paid to those poor souls aboard them.

General Fukua de Hundan didn't have to say much as the presentation was narrated by a staff member with superior acoustics that could articulate the poignant details in the most proper Carsopian central dialect containing no hint of provincial vernacular.

The replay of the battle of epic proportions transfixed the audience and the psychological effects stunned the casual observer.

The imagery appeared so surreal, and one could not sit through the hour-long presentation and not walk out of there with ample thoughts that lingered.

Several of the attendees would soon be partaking in the consumption of various Carsopian elixirs and concoctions to quell the anxiety manifested in viewing these events in the most vivid resolution and detail possible.

If it were not for the fact, they censored most of the Carsopian ships blowing up, the viewers would have far more serious negative reactions and in far greater need to drink post debrief elixirs.

At the completion of the presentation, General Fukua de Hundan stood and walked out onto the small platform in the direct middle of the spherical conference room and slowly turned as he talked.

GENERAL FUKUA DE HUNDAN

As you can see the space battle was a terrific example of lethality inflicted that leaves no substitute for victory.

This battle was won because we did the unthinkable and secretly moved our forces precisely where the enemy never expected to find us nor believed we were willing to execute such a high-risk maneuver to prepare the battlefield to ensure success in the execution of such a bold plan.

As General Fukua de Hundan slowly turned and stared directly into the eyes which crystal- like focus, he made an impression which few would ever forget.

The intensity and clarity in his words resonated with the information he now offered.

GENERAL FUKUA DE HUNDAN

Had we lost that battle, you all would be drafting surrender terms and it's unlikely any of you would safely arrive back at the Central Empire Worlds during the rest of your lives.I will now answer any questions.

ATTENDEE

General, when do you plan on attacking the remnants of the Heisibing Fleet. Don't you think we should hit them now before they have a chance to recover?

GENERAL FUKUA DE HUNDAN

I'm not concerned about the Heisibing Fleet. We shall destroy them when I'm ready. For now, I want to rest my troops.

ATTENDEE

General Fukua de Hundan, why can't you go after them now and finish the job?

GENERAL FUKUA DE HUNDAN

We had several elite troops die from Cosmic Space Sickness on the way here. My men have been through a lot just getting here. I'm going to rotate them down to the planet and let them rejuvenate before I leave on the next mission.

ATTENDEE

What will you do on that mission?

GENERAL FUKUA DE HUNDAN

The details of that mission will not be discussed before we leave as I do not wish to telegraph my intentions to the enemy since it's most likely the Heisibing have spies on this planet.

ATTENDEE

General Fukua de Hundan, how could you possibly accuse one of our citizens of being spies?

GENERAL FUKUA DE HUNDAN

Whether you like it or not, you probably have traitors among you.

ATTENDEE

General, we would like to know what your intentions are.

GENERAL FUKUA DE HUNDAN

Only my fleet will know what my intentions are, after we leave and have experienced a long transit somewhere.

ATTENDEE

You can't tell us anything?

GENERAL FUKUA DE HUNDAN

Operational Security dictates nobody outside my command structure shall know what my intentions are.

ATTENDEE

Why is that?

GENERAL FUKUA DE HUNDAN

By not indicating our plans is the only way we will be able to surprise the Heisibings and not give them time to react to our strategies.

ATTENDEE

How long will you remain in *Cui*?

GENERAL FUKUA DE HUNDAN

Just long enough for my troops to get over space lag, Cosmic Space Sickness, and be healthy enough to travel and fight.

ATTENDEE

Can you estimate how long that will be?

GENERAL FUKUA DE HUNDAN

I will base my timeline on the efficacy of the rehabilitation the troops receive.

ATTENDEE

But when will that be?

My troops will know when they are ready to proceed. These troops are handpicked professionals.

ATTENDEE

General what makes you believe they will openly admit they are ready?

GENERAL FUKUA DE HUNDAN

My troops know they have a duty to perform and screwing around on a planet isn't what they want to be doing.

ATTENDEE

Are you sure?

GENERAL FUKUA DE HUNDAN

My elite corps want to get back out there in harm's way and execute their orders and demonstrate their professionalism and what they know they can achieve.

ATTENDEE

General Fukua de Hundan, what makes you feel so assured of that?

GENERAL FUKUA DE HUNDAN

We have a war on, and they know it. They know that until we defeat the Heisibing Fleet, their families remain at risk.

The three-dimensional briefing room was suddenly quiet as everyone present listened carefully to General Fukua de Hundan.

GENERAL FUKUA DE HUNDAN

My men are very intelligent and know that a unilateral surrender by the Heisibings will allow a peace treaty based on our terms, so we don't have to repeat this war again in another generation.

They want to finish all objectives so that sooner than later they will be able to return to their prior lives and live to a golden age unless they are one of the unfortunate ones who must die for our people.

The quiet in the 3D auditorium which allowed General Fukua de Hundan to do the next unexpected, that didn't seem according to protocol or decorum.

GENERAL FUKUA DE HUNDAN

I think I've answered all the questions I can permit myself. Any other questions will go out of the bounds of our security measures, which I'm not allowed to divulge to you. Thank you for inviting me to speak to you. I will now be departing.

The noise level suddenly erupted as it appeared a lot of other people were waiting for someone else to ask the next question.

Since some attendees didn't get to speak, they were scrambling and some shouted out questions General Fukua de Hundan simply ignored as he pompously and unceremoniously walked out of the auditorium with his handlers to relocate to his temporary headquarters and living quarters.

***

The influence peddlers and special interest had the pleasure corps ready for General Fukua de Hundan's uses.

<u>INT. DAY. PLANET OF CUI. GENERAL FUKUA DE HUNDAN'S PRIVATE QUARTERS.</u>

As General Fukua de Hundan arrived in his temporary living quarters, the pleasure corps personnel prepared to ensure the General received whatever kind of companionship he desired. They were quickly surprised.

FUKUA DE HUNDAN

Will you all please leave I want some time alone for a while.

Of course, none of them could possibly know what was going through the General Fukua de Hundan's mind. They didn't know one of the young men he buried at Earth was his own son.

General Fukua de Hundan knew he pushed his troops to the extreme and in securing this tremendous victory he sacrificed his own son, and out of protocol and Carsopian tradition, he was to be buried in space or at the first destination of arrival after death which turned out to be in Mexico near Hiway 23.

A pit in General Fukua de Hundan's stomach was the feelings he had knowing he would never again be able to spend quality time with his son.

There was no companionship on *Cui* that could possibly take his mind off his son and his thought process of what he must do to finally finish this ugly war.

General Fukua de Hundan couldn't tell anyone what his strategy would be, because if he did, most likely the enemy would have it within days, and they would be waiting for him with an elaborate ambush.

Transiting in space was one of the most dangerous times for a Fleet because if you were traveling towards an enemy at high-speed leaving behind a large ion trail, the enemy would detect, track, and target you long before you knew of their presence. Even steering zigzag courses were ineffective because of the speed and the ability to determine base course negated any possible benefit from zigzagging.

General Fukua de Hundan would deal with his personal sorrow at another date and place. For now, he would simply undo many days of sleep deprivation and rest as peacefully as possible.

One method he had to eliminate sadness from the loss of his son, who he felt very close to, would be to prepare his forces for the ultimate victory. After several days of rest and relaxation, he would begin physical training and cycle fleet personnel to and from space so that everyone experienced the conditioning.

But for the time, he laid back on his bed and closed his eyes and quickly succumbed to sleep deprivation, space lag, slight Cosmic Space Sickness, and the effects of sudden real gravity on the body.

EXT. CGI. SPACE. HEISIBING FLEET SLOWING DOWN AND DOING A BAFFLE CLEARING MANUEVER. 20 SECONDS.

The Heisibing Fleet waited for a day before they slowed to do a security sweep. They wanted to know how far behind the Carsopians were.

General Fukua de Hundan suspected they would do such a maneuver and just so they didn't get any wild idea to turn around and attempt a counterattack, he had a couple of his fastest warships trail the Heisibing Fleet just to make sure they were aware they were being followed and monitored and possibly targeted with a new attack.

This would force the hand of the Heisibing Fleet Commander, Admiral Engaarai, to speed up and continue the retreat for several more days until they got closer to the Heisibing Empire. The two warships would then patrol and ease back towards *Cui* giving General Fukua de Hundan sufficient time to sortie his forces if the Heisibings decided to do something stupid and come back for another fight.

INT.SPACE. ADMIRAL ENGAARAI'S HEISIBING FLEET COMMAND SHIP

Admiral Engaarai didn't like taking the course he did, but he understood, his troops nerves were rattled, and they had just unexpectedly experienced their first defeat in several years.

The Heisibing Fleet suddenly got waxed by the *Cui* force they felt was utterly weak and inferior with no hope for the Carsopian Fleet to intervein because the *Cui* Transit Lane an ultra-fast space conduit was sealed off by the Heisibing Fleet.

The high-speed *Cui* Transit Lane channel created by a cosmic convergence channel that altered space and time just like the event horizon of a black whole, was not accessible by the Carsopians. Thus, Admiral Engaarai thought the Carsopians had no means to get forces to the contested area in time to intervein in the battle just conducted.

VOICEOVER (ADMIRAL ENGAARAI)
THOUGHT
So just where did these Carsopian ships come from? Were we deceived by spies acting as doubles?

Many questions were on Admiral Engaarai's mind as he contemplated his fate. Because of the extraordinary turn of fate, his gut feeling was to continue the fleet on a heading back towards the Heisibing Empire, regroup and re-plan and do a counterattack when they determined what led to the failures at *Cui*.

ADMIRAL ENGAARAI
How many ships are following us?

ADMIRAL ENGAARAI'S A
SSISTANT ADMIRAL DIKIY OS'MINOG
Just two, sir.

ADMIRAL ENGAARAI
They are here to keep track of our whereabouts; they probably do not have any form of protection and are expendable.

ADMIRAL ENGAARAI'S
ASSISTANT ADMIRAL DIKIY OS'MINOG
No doubt they will eventually turn around and go back to their fleet and make reports. They are reporting on our positions, that puts us at risk.

ADMIRAL ENGAARAI

Every day we get closer to our homelands, the lease likely they will attack as we are quickly approaching where we can start receiving reserves. By tomorrow we'll have a distinct advantage because of our location.

ADMIRAL ENGAARAI'S ASSISTANT
ADMIRAL DIKIY OS'MINOG

What will we do about the two trailers?

ADMIRAL ENGAARAI

They really can't attack. If they get close enough to fire weapons, we can destroy them. It's unlikely they will close within our weapons range.

ADMIRAL ENGAARAI'S ASSISTANT
ADMIRAL DIKIY OS'MINOG

What's your plan sir?

ADMIRAL ENGAARAI

I think it's time we speed up again, we only have 2 trailers, and no sign of any Carsopian Fleet. When we get back up to max speed, it will be impossible for them to catch up with us before we arrive within the protection of our home worlds.

ADMIRAL ENGAARAI'S ASSISTANT
ADMIRAL DIKIY OS'MINOG

No concern the Carsopian Fleet might suddenly appear?

ADMIRAL ENGAARAI

Our reserves are now heading this way. We've reached the point there is little they can do unless they bring their entire fleet down the slot.

ADMIRAL ENGAARAI'S ASSISTANT
ADMIRAL DIKIY OS'MINOG

Understand, increase speed and return to base course.

ADMIRAL ENGAARAI

I'm going back to my stateroom. Contact me if any major changes occur.

ADMIRAL ENGAARAI'S ASSISTANT
ADMIRAL DIKIY OS'MINOG
Yes sir.

Admiral Engaarai left the bridge and walked smartly to his space cabin where he retired to reflect on his next move.

Admiral Engaarai would not receive a hero's welcome like General Fukua de Hundan. His reception would be better described as an inquisition. Admiral Engaarai would be blamed for the humiliating loss.

VOICEOVER (ADMIRAL ENGAARAI) THOUGHT
Even though this defeat is a classical INTEL failure, I will be the scapegoat.

There were several different scenarios that might emerge, one of which would entail my immediate relief of command.

Another possibility might be that after the Admiralty recognizes the fundamental failure of INTEL to report the existence of a nearby powerful fleet, could outweigh any other reason and leave me uncensored.

No doubt the Heisibing Empire would reorganize and plan a counterattack and make an assertive effort to diminish the Carsopian Fleet now operating in the *Cui* stronghold area.

VOICEOVER (ADMIRAL ENGAARAI) THOUGHT
The biggest question that I face is whether the Admiralty leaves me in command where I can lead that counterattack.

Admiral Engaarai understood a direct attack on *Cui* would be the only way to bring this war to a close. Once *Cui* was taken the Carsopians would recoil back into their shell and gladly sacrifice *Cui* to protect the Center of their Empire where all the most sensitive areas existed, including the ruling class. But even that was susceptible to conquest especially if *Cui* was no longer on the Heisibing Flank to distract the bolder plan.

VOICEOVER (ADMIRAL ENGAARAI) THOUGHT
For now, it was probably best to continue to the main Heisibing Empire Space Force Anchorage orbiting Yanjingzai Tiankongzhong.

This elaborate cluster of orbiting Heisibing Empire Space Force Anchorage and Space Forts were designed and built to support and service one of the greatest Space Fleets in Galactic History.

The Carsopian's had a space force almost double in size, but no one Carsopian facility could moor such a large fleet all within proximity of each other. The Heisibing advantage was their entire fleet could immediately deploy together for an attack on an enemy.

The disadvantage included the notion of putting all your eggs in one basket. But, also should Heisibing forces not be able to stop an attack that allowed the enemy to breech security boundaries and hit the anchorage, results could be devastating.

Taking out a dozen or so orbiting facilities that included space docks, habitat, storage, and support infrastructure, could have severe consequences and make it much harder to project power.

Because of the fear of enemy penetration and attempting to hit the Heisibing Empire Space Force Anchorage at Yanjingzai Tiankongzhong, there was far more Garrison troops and one of the largest Space Guard Forces ever assembled in one area.

The Heisibing *Space Guard Forces* which never deployed were almost as large as other Empire's entire Space Forces.

The price was high, but to be able to project such massive firepower already concentrated significantly reduced delays in deployment to the battle space.

VOICEOVER

(While the Heisibing Armada returns) *Admiral Engaarai realized it would be a demoralized Heisibing Fleet returning. If his hunch was right, Admiral Engaarai figured that many of the Heisibing troops on the returning fleet with him, would not seek immediate transport down to the planet Yanjingzai Tiankongzhong for standard Rest and Recreation (R&R).*

As the agony of defeat lingered, Heisibing troops knew there would be no victory celebrations.

The painful humiliating loss furthermore felt like a disgrace to every fleet member. Very few people in the fleet existed who didn't lose a friend or someone they knew in this recent battle.

Morale building would be Admiral Engaarai's top priority if he survived the expected purge. Admiral Engaarai knew the best way to motivate troops is with the taste of Victory!

But first he had to make preparations, rebuild their self-esteem, give them back confidence, and demonstrate that one battle did not constitute victory or loss of the war.

Cosmic Space Sickness is a real issue with fleets that perform aggressive patrolling and long-distance missions. Nothing worse is for a crew to have Cosmic Space Sickness with poor morale after a humiliating loss.

The best way to reduce the effects of Cosmic Space Sickness is to get the troops down on the planet into real gravity, fresh air, clean unprocessed drinking water taken from many rivers and streams flowing through restricted zones that prevent pollution.

The Heisibing troops would be cycled down to the planet for Special Training. Admiral Engaarai's Special Training provided a method to get them off their ships and out of an environment that otherwise promotes Cosmic Space Sickness.

After everyone had some revitalization from these measures, real hard training would begin. The training would not be exercises doing simulated attacks. No, Admiral Engaarai's *Special Training* would be how to raise worlds and put fear back in the enemy.

Admiral Engaarai would not get caught again like the last time. Even though he would have to fight more conservatively, he would certainly have better flank protection and avoid battle if it appeared the enemy was coming at him in more than one direction.

Admiral Engaarai planned to never experience results like the *Battle of Cui* again, because his tactics had to be altered as he perceived a new dynamic and change in direction of the CAMPAIGN.

EXT. CGI. SPACE. HEISIBING SHUTTLES SENDING COMMANDING OFFICERS TO THE COMMAND SHIP. 15 SECONDS DURING FOLLOWING VOICE OVER.

PORTIONS OF THIS MUSIC FOR BACKGROUND:
[https://www.youtube.com/watch?v=Tos7OlK5RhU]

VOICEOVER

The hours crept by, and the fleet personnel seemed subdued as the Heisibing formation closed in on the Yanjingzai Tiankongzhong space anchorage.

About one half day away from the expected time of arrival and docking the Heisibing warships at their designated orbiting space ports, Admiral Engaarai called his staff together for a series of planning meetings so that he could lay out his plans for the next few weeks.

Some senior officers were ferried by shuttles over to the command ship cruising in the center of the formation. As they all got together aboard the command ship's conference room, every inch was taken up by a large, crowded audience, full of curiosity and wonder of what was in store for them.

This meeting created an atmosphere that appeared to be the sadist day in most of their lives. None of the Heisibing senior officers had gone through a pasting the way the Carsopians had hit them.

It was evident to Admiral Engaarai, all his senior officers had all been rattled and now showed fear and lack of self-confidence.

Extreme leadership was now required because the whole force was at the crossroads of failure that none of them had ever experienced and understood how to cope with, let alone know how to rally their troops under these unfavorable circumstances.

With very little standing room only left, Admiral Engaarai entered the wardroom that had 50 conversations going on.

AID-DE-CAMP

The Admiral has arrived.

Suddenly there was stark quiet in the room. The area at the front of the room by the podium was sealed off by security men and the Admiral had no difficulty approaching the podium where he would address those leaders in attendance.

ADMIRAL ENGAARAI

Comrades and friends, thank you for attending this impromptu planning meeting and conference.

The Admiral looked into the eyes of these senior officers and could see smoldering defeat. Some of these officers had close calls as their ships were damaged, and personnel aboard had been killed in the fighting by explosions and near fatal application of advanced space weaponry.

These senior officers' appearance today is testimony to damage control parties who saved their ships in the final minutes.

In some cases, a few of these senior officers lost their ships to no fault of their own in vicious close fighting and had to evacuate and were assigned to other ships, they took command of because of their rank and experience.

There was no point in leaving a neophyte with little combat experience in charge of a modern Heisibing warship, when a seasoned veteran who had fought in many battles was available to take the reins of leadership of that craft.

ADMIRAL ENGAARAI

It's obvious we just experienced a crushing defeat.

Thanks to censorship, the civilians on Yanjingzai Tiankongzhong are unaware of what we just experienced.

Admiral Engaarai looked around the room and observed a lot of doom and gloom.

ADMIRAL ENGAARAI

The recent combat results will remain classified, nobody is permitted to discuss any aspect of the mission off hulls. Anyone detected leaking information will be severely dealt with.

Most of the officers knew that Admiral Engaarai applied extremely harsh treatment to individuals who defied his orders. They also knew that if any of their men shot their mouths off on the planet, they too would be held responsible for what their men did.

ADMIRAL ENGAARAI

As we have been processing leave and transportation requests, we have quickly concluded that very few individuals have requested permission to go to the planet.

ADMIRAL DIKIY OS'MINOG

Sir, just as you stated, the crew feels defeated and do not want to appear in public.

ADMIRAL ENGAARAI

I understand the pain and suffering they are going through, as these have been tumultuous times.

ADMIRAL DIKIY OS'MINOG

Most of them do not want to leave the ship. They are ready to deploy again and get away from the damage they caused.

ADMIRAL ENGAARAI

I will not permit them to hang out on the ships during this docking and refit period.

ADMIRAL DIKIY OS'MINOG

What are you going to inform the crew they will be doing on the planet?

ADMIRAL ENGAARAI

I expect them to be rotated down to the planet in sections so that their bodies and rejuvenate after a long period in space.

The Admiral looked around and saw the looks on senior officer faces. It was almost as if they were being given distasteful orders they surely did not want to carry out. They knew their men had lost a lot of face and did not want to see the public any time soon.

ADMIRAL ENGAARAI

We'll rotate crews to the planet starting today after we all dock.

ADMIRAL DIKIY OS'MINOG

Admiral Engaarai, can you explain how you want to do the rotation.

ADMIRAL ENGAARAI

We must be ready to deploy in case the enemy attempts to attack our installations, so only one third of the men will be sent to the planet at one time.

The officers looked with great concentration at their leader taking in every word and already many of them were mentally processing the actions they knew they had to take in accordance with their orders.

ADMIRAL ENGAARAI

Because of the limitations of planetary shuttles, all the wounded will be shipped out first. I doubt there will be any healthy space force members on the first wave of flights to the surface.

ADMIRAL DIKIY OS'MINOG

What is the order in which all the non-wounded will go?

ADMIRAL ENGAARAI

Subsequent flights will ferry the first group to the planet. I expect them to stay there for two weeks, and they will then be brought back to the ships and the second group sent to the planet.

Finally, the third group will get to the planet when the second group returns. Any questions?

One of the ship's commanding officers not far from the Admiral asked:

SHIP COMMANDING OFFICER

Admiral Engaarai, approximately seventy five percent of our troops do not have any relatives on Yanjingzai Tiankongzhong. It seems like their opportunity to enjoy themselves on the planet is rather limited, especially over a two-week period.

ADMIRAL ENGAARAI

Excellent point Commander. It's my intention to set up Rest and Relaxation camps where we can provide the troops with some activities.

COMMAND SHIP COMMANDING OFFICER

Admiral Engaarai, the troops would most likely prefer companionship of women and be given the opportunity to acquire elixirs that would modify their mental states.

ADMIRAL ENGAARAI

Yes Commander. We can provide a lot of that for them in the camps we set up. *Copa Kebukaijosei* is only one day away from Yanjingzai Tiankongzhong via high- speed transport.

ADMIRAL DIKIY OS'MINOG

What are you suggesting Admiral Engaarai?

ADMIRAL ENGAARAI

We can bring in a couple intergalactic transport ships loaded full of those blue and green skinned *Copa Kebukaijosei Women* to the R&R camps, and the troops will forget what planet they are on.

ADMIRAL DIKIY OS'MINOG

Admiral Engaarai there are a many conservative people as you know that would not appreciate you supplying Copa Kebukaijosei Women to the troops. They would view it merely as prostitution.

ADMIRAL ENGAARAI

The *Copa Kebukaijosei Women* are well experienced in the finer quality of providing friendly satisfaction.

COMMANDSHIP COMMANDING OFFICER

They certainly are not choir girls associated with a religion.

ADMIRAL ENGAARAI

Furthermore, since I'll be paying for the *Copa Kebukaijosei Women* services, there will be no out of pocket expenses for our crew members

ADMIRAL DIKIY OS'MINOG

Admiral Engaarai, two transports full of *Copa Kebukaijosei Women* will cost a lot of Credits฿ May I ask you how you intend on paying for their services?

ADMIRAL ENGAARAI

Admiral Dikiy Os'minog, when I was a junior officer serving with shock troops during invasions, most of the men in the Amphibian Assault Force would spend their precious time right after seizing the planet putting forth efforts to get pleasure out of the defeated enemy's women and copious amounts of elixirs.

ADMIRAL DIKIY OS'MINOG

And you didn't?

ADMIRAL ENGAARAI

No. I chose to remain sober and ignore the woman and spent my time rounding up all the Credits฿ I could find. That activity included visiting some banks before their employees had a chance to run off with all the Credits฿.

There was suddenly a little levity going on in the room as the officers started realizing the Admiral was serious about morale building.

ADMIRAL ENGAARAI

One other item for all you senior officers. You will all be sent orders shortly on objectives of the Rest and Relaxation camps.

ADMIRAL DIKIY OS'MINOG

Are we going to be reminded not to fraternize with the troops?

ADMIRAL ENGAARAI

Admiral Dikiy Os'minog I hope you didn't forget about our training requirements.

ADMIRAL DIKIY OS'MINOG

I was looking into that but was planning on studying all the fleet rcorded holographic video over the next couple of days to determine our weaknesses and develop training topics around that experience.

ADMIRAL ENGAARAI

Admiral Dikiy Os'minog I'll be looking forward to see what you have in mind. In addition to allowing crews to wind down during the first week of their Rest and Relaxation, during the second week, we will do some physical training.

ADMIRAL DIKIY OS'MINOG

May I ask why?

ADMIRAL ENGAARAI

To help them more aggressively get their psychology back into fighting shape.

The room was now quiet as each officer listened intently as the Admiral laid down his goals and aspirations.

ADMIRAL ENGAARAI

Gentlemen and Madam Officers, During the training week, I expect you all to apply leadership to your creews, talk to them and help them get over this terrible ordeal they just experienced.

SENIOR OFFICER

My men feel they were defeated by a better fighting force.

ADMIRAL ENGAARAI

Commander, during training, talking points will include *none of this defeat was their responsibility*. We fell into an elaborate trap relying too much on INTEL.

SENIOR OFFICER

My men assume it will happen again soon. In the future we will avoid such traps by doing some of our own INTEL operations before an attack and doing our own assessments of enemy disposition.

SENIOR OFFICER

How do I convince my men that's how it will be done?

ADMIRAL ENGAARAI

I will never fly blindly into an area again based on INTEL that is assured to me their information meets a gold standard when in fact it barely meets a bronze test.

COMMAND SHIP COMMANDING OFFICER

Admiral Engaarai, building crew morale under the circumstances will not be easy.

ADMIRAL ENGAARAI

Captain, the best way to build morale is through Victory. We will sortie after this rest period and go back to the Carsopian worlds and do limited attacks as confidence building.

COMMAND SHIP COMMANDING OFFICER

How will we attack to ensure the thrill of victory?

ADMIRAL ENGAARAI

We will select easy targets with no intentions of invading and remaining.

COMMAND SHIP COMMANDING OFFICER

Why limited engagements? Such tactics will not create much enthusiasm.

ADMIRAL ENGAARAI

Our purpose is only to give our men the feeling of success and build up their emotional strengths gradually so that when we finally attack *Cui* again, our troops will be ready.

A few other details were laid out then the Admiral stated:

ADMIRAL ENGAARAI

That will be all, those of you who came here on shuttles may now return to your ships.

The Admiral then turned and departed out of the conference room and walked directly to the ship's bridge where he started doing surveys of the fleet and their navigation plan to enter the anchorage area at Yanjingzai Tiankongzhong.

INT. SPACE. HEISIBING FLEET COMMAND SHIP. CONTROL ROOM.

ADMIRAL ENGAARAI

Captain Zhìhuì Jūjī are you looking forward to returning to Yanjingzai Tiankongzhong anchorage?

CAPTAIN ZHÌHUÌ JŪJĪ TACTICAL ASSISTANT

This Heisibing Fleet homecoming will be noted as the melancholiest ever experienced by the previously over exuberant Heisibing crack fighting force.

ADMIRAL ENGAARAI

For almost a decade, we slowly defeated the Carsopian Empire at most of the battles and thus threatened to finally conquer the Carsopian Empire stronghold, Cui.

CAPTAIN ZHÌHUÌ JŪJĪ TACTICAL ASSISTANT

The paradigm shifting and a new reality with *Cui* out of the way, would have hastened the reshaping of Heisibing galactic hegemony.

Unfortunately for Admiral Engaarai, he never contemplated Carsopian Fleet Commander General Fukua de Hundan, would travel such a long and arduous journey to get to an ambush site and hit him with such gusto and send him fleeing and abandoning a lot of captured territory that took 10 years to consolidate.

VOICEOVER (ADMIRAL ENGAARAI) THOUGHT

In the matter of a few hours, those 10 years of bitter and brutal fighting have accomplished nothing. We are now back to where we started because of a tactical blunder I made. If I survive the day with this job, I will feel lucky.

It also dawned on Admiral Engaarai he could be removed and taken somewhere to be executed for the colossal failure and stinging defeat. Unlike most of the rest of his crew on his command ship, he knew he would be receiving visitors as soon as they docked at the Yanjingzai Tiankongzhong orbiting space anchorage.

VOICEOVER

(While Heisibing Fleet Approaching Yanjingzai Tiankongzhong)

The closer the Heisibing Fleet got to Yanjingzai Tiankongzhong; the more space traffic appeared. Beacons from sophisticated transponders sent out navigation coordinates and requirements for all those ships to steer out of the path of the oncoming fleet.

Failure to do so could mean the immediate arrest of the crew and confiscation of the ship.

Heisibing shippers and foreign flagged space-cargo- ships quickly followed instructions leaving the pathway open for all the Heisibing Combat Ships returning from the war zone.

As demoralized as the Heisibing crews appeared, some would simply prefer to blast the merchant space ships if they didn't move swiftly out of the way.

This would not be a good day for a shipper to ignore their maneuver orders. The fact the fleet didn't have to slow down and alter course created a more pleasant atmosphere. No doubt the crews wanted to get docked and get this mission out of their minds.

For some crews ordered to remain aboard their ships and be ready to immediately respond to sorties, added a lot of negativities to an already distressed environment.

Thanks to artificial intelligence and superb computer evaluation and analysis, the fleet was easily systematically divided up into thirds. Those ships directed to the planet upon arrival appeared to have a slightly better atmosphere than the rest, even though well over half the crew members didn't want to go to the planet and face the public.

As details of the Rest and Relaxation Camps being set up emerged, that lessened the burden on a lot of the crew members who were not ready to face the public.

The Yanjingzai Tiankongzhong Space Anchorage had dozens of huge circular orbiting anchorage structures, that were equivalent to large commercial space stations.

These orbiting anchorage structures extended a few miles in diameter. The cost to build the Yanjingzai Tiankongzhong Space Anchorage was almost forbiddingly expensive.

However once construction was completed, the Heisibing Fleet was the only known Force in the galaxy that could scramble and deploy from a central location with no delay. Yanjingzai Tiankongzhong Space Anchorage was hence the Heisibing's Gibraltar of that region of space.

In order to get to the Heisibing's home worlds, an enemy had to first get past the Yanjingzai Tiankongzhong Space Anchorage that due to its extensive size, was unlikely. That meant most avenues of approach were reduced and barrier patrols eliminated surprise attacks.

EXT. CGI. SPACE. HEISIBING'S SPACE COMBAT SHIPS APPROACHING AND DOCKING AT YANJINGZAI TIANKONGZHONG SPACE ANCHORAGE. 30 SECONDS.

MUSIC DURING NEXT VOICEOVER:

[https://www.youtube.com/watch?v=I0iaMpJ8-iI]

VOICEOVER

As the fleet slowed to get in flight profile to precisely hit the landing pad areas of those huge circular structures, someone who had never seen it before would feel totally amazed.

As the hours wound down, they finally got within range to start observing the Yanjingzai Tiankongzhong Space Anchorage, well lit up for massive parallel landing operations.

The artificial intelligence driven choreography was nothing less than amazing.

Heisibing Combat Spaceships were vectored to specified locations and propulsion was manipulated by colossal parallel computational suites of the fleet and the anchorages.

The sight was unbelievable. Every ship had its destination and flight computers preset for their docking locations and artificial intelligence automatically guided the Heisibing combat weary ships to their specific Yanjingzai Tiankongzhong Space Anchorages.

Legions of maintenance crews and emergency medical personnel were standing by to offload the wounded and jump into action repairing the crippled ships who could transit to docking but were not in any kind of shape for further combat operations without substantial overhaul of critical systems and in some cases needed to go into the Space Dock for hull repairs.

Based on the workload the maintenance staff planned, the arrival of the fleet was a grim reminder of what can go wrong in intergalactic conflicts with just one false move.

Poor flank protection in this recent major confrontation came really close to wiping them out. Admiral Engaarai knew a lot of information about General Fukua de Hundan and was puzzled: why he didn't press home the attack?

VOICEOVER (ADMIRAL ENGAARAI) THOUGHT
Had General Fukua de Hundan done so and wiped-out half of the survivors and the cripples, appropriate accommodations would soon be levied against Heisibing worlds, and the Empire might cease to exist within weeks of capitulation they could not have avoided with no realistic hope to defend the home world planets.

It was precisely the *defense of the home worlds* that weighed heavily on Admiral Engaarai forcing him to cut and run and preserve the fleet for a different day and possibly even their own defense of the Yanjingzai Tiankongzhong Space Anchorages.

VOICEOVER (ADMIRAL ENGAARAI) THOUGHT
But why did General Fukua de Hundan break off the attack, when he had us on the ropes?

Admiral Engaarai had these and many more questions that tormented him as he sought the answers and could not find any.

VOICEOVER (ADMIRAL ENGAARAI) THOUGHT
General Fukua de Hundan was not known to be a conservative player, based on numerous INTEL reports. General Fukua de Hundan's actions did not add up.

There was more to this and most likely General Fukua de Hundan's actions were part of a greater strategic plan that had not yet unfolded.

***

INT. DAY. CUI UNDISCLOSED MILITARY BASE, GENERAL HUNDAN'S PRIVATE QUARTERS.

General Fukua de Hundan, losing his own son to Cosmic Space Sickness, knew his men needed a break after completing his primary mission and assignment to relieve *Cui.*

VOICEOVER

(GENERAL FUKUA DE HUNDAN) THOUGHT.

With my prime objective finished, it is now time to rest the troops to prepare them for a return first to their home worlds where we can swap out some of the force, and reinvigorate the remaining souls. Then it would be off to put the dagger in the heart of the Heisibing Empire.

By keeping his intentions to himself, General Fukua de Hundan would not be telegraphing strategic and tactical plans to the Heisibing's who could then react aggressively with ambushes and pick them off in detail through elaborate ambushes.

General Fukua de Hundan had one bolder maneuver. Without exposing the fact, he was leaving the area and taking the long way back, he would get home, re-provision, swap out some ships and crews, then high tell it into attack before the spy network alerted Heisibing's he had abandoned *Cui*, and had only left a small force behind to give the appearance he was still around to prevent another incursion into the area.

The turnaround General Fukua de Hundan planned for his forces at Carsopian Empire bases included an estimated 48 hours for crew changeout, resupply, and other logistics matters.

That would allow the fleet to be redeployed along the *Cui Transit Lane* with a huge force that would slash through Heisibing defenses and reopen the high-speed space lane for traffic as well as expansion of the conflict and threaten the enemy from a direction they were not planning.

Since all eyes were trained towards *Cui*, where they most likely assumed to be the location of the next confrontation. 48 hours would not give Heisibing spies enough time to resolve future intentions.

Unlike the Heisibing's, Carsopian's didn't have singularity in bases. They were dispersed and spread out so there would be no direct knowledge of a huge fleet arriving and departing.

But first things first, the troops would gloat in their victories on *Cui* and enjoy the affection of an appreciative community.

***

EXT. CGI. SPACE. YANJINGZAI TIANKONGZHONG HEISIBING ARMADA ARRIVAL. 30 SECONDS.

The Mega structures that allowed such a huge and powerful fleet to dock orbiting Yanjingzai Tiankongzhong, appeared within visual range as the calibrated deaccelerations occurred in the most perfect choreography.

Ships easily landed and attached to mating rings of the air locks and within 10 minutes of mooring 1000 miles above the planet, Heisibing space warship crew members were slowly leaving the ships and going to their designated transportation.

Some of the wounded would stay at the Heisibing Fleet anchorages for treatment because to send them all to the planet would overwhelm staff of the hospitals there.

By sending fewer to the planet would help cover up the fact of how many seriously wounded came back when their ships took much serious damage. The ships were built strong, but the people were not. Even though the ships survived, many people were killed or maimed.

The human waves slowly moved out of the ships, but eventually that movement reduced to a trickle as two thirds of the crews had to remain behind in the event they had to immediately sortie for a threat.

As expected, Admiral Engaarai was notified he had visitors coming aboard his flag ship.

Admiral Engaarai expected the inquisition and, in some ways, dreaded it as he could easily be removed for cause and possibly receive a watchdog group to go with him on his next deployment to more or less micromanage him.

The walk to the entrance of the ship was brief and the Admiral looked distinguished in a dress uniform, as was his tradition upon entering port.

Crew members were advised to wear their dress uniforms as well, but since they were going to Rest and Relaxation camps, Admiral Engaarai relaxed the standard and the crew was told to dress comfortably.

This change to policy was alright with crew members who felt that since they were not victorious, they would not be warmly received if exposed as a Heisibing Space Service crew member wearing their uniforms.

As expected, within a few moments, a dozen of the visitors arrived. The upper crust of Heisibing military and civilian leadership were among them. None of them appeared very happy.

ADMIRAL ENGAARAI
Welcome aboard Count Ryūsei.

Admiral Engaarai knew the Heisibing Emperor's nephew and hatchet man.

COUNT RYŪSEI

Thank you, Admiral Engaarai.

Admiral Engaarai knew this was an official inquiry and without hesitation announced:

ADMIRAL ENGAARAI

Gentlemen and Madam, may I please escort you to the wardroom where we can have some privacy and refreshments?

GENERAL BAKUGEKI

After you admiral.

Ground Forces Commander, General Bakugeki was popularly known as the *Butcher of Bashreban.*

Count Ryūsei and General Bakugeki together in the group meant bad news for Admiral Engaarai because it possibly indicated he would be removed and most likely taken somewhere and placed before a firing squad.

VOICEOVER (ADMIRAL ENGAARAI) THOUGHT

What a way to end a distinguished career, being blasted into a million molecules by shoulder fired synthetic aperture phasers. On the positive side, death would be instantly, which took away the argument from the liberals it was cruel and inhumane punishment.

INT.SPACE. ADMIRAL ENGAARAI COMMAND SHIP WARDROOM.

It did not take long for the Admiral Engaarai to march the *Inquisitors* into the wardroom where stewards had been alerted to have a dozen placements and drinks and condiments laid out for them. Admiral Engaarai's Deputy Commander Admiral Dikiy Os'minog had kicked all the officers out of the wardroom, and the only people left were Admiral Dikiy Os'minog and the Admiral's personal Steward, who was sworn to secrecy and cleared at a very high level.

ADMIRAL ENGAARAI

Please have a seat gentlemen and madam.

VOICEOVER

The group sat down as the Steward went around the table asking each person if they would like a snack or a drink. Some accepted a Julackian Elixir *which tasted a lot like coffee, rum, and chocolate all combined.*

Others had a special Chiharu Wajima Hydrator *that worked better than water but had some unique taste and scent that was very appealing.*

Admiral Engaarai knew the two who really mattered in this group was Count Ryūsei and General Bakugeki as they were the decision makers. The rest were just patronage officers with good knee pads and other features to whore themselves out for promotions.

One of the patronage officers, Claire Uwakion'na, to the annoyance of Count Ryūsei and General Bakugeki, took the key seat directly across from Admiral Engaarai.

After Admiral Engaarai determined the steward completed his immediate task, he nodded to him, which was their secret signal to *please depart,* and the Deputy Commander Admiral Dikiy Os'minog would be in position to stop anyone from entering and interfering with or observing any of the discussion.

The expectations were on the threshold of an eruption. This was probably the worst arrival conference in modern day history.

Failure is not a recipe for jovial times and promotions. The Deputy Commander Admiral Dikiy Os'minog knew his fate was also attached at the hip of Admiral Engaarai. If the Admiral was going to get a taste of shoulder fired synthetic aperture phasers, he too would most likely receive the same treatment.

Count Ryūsei was obviously the power broker in the group. Even though General Bakugeki had a lot of influence over the Emperor, the Count was a co-conspirator in everything the emperor attempted.

COUNT RYŪSEI

Admiral, as you can imagine the emperor was not pleased when your reports were sent back to Yanjingzai Tiankongzhong Fleet Anchorage.

ADMIRAL ENGAARAI

Your excellency, defeat is always a hard pill to swallow.

COUNT RYŪSEI

I might as well not delay the purpose of our visit. The emperor has charged us with the final decision on your disposition.

ADMIRAL ENGAARAI

I would expect nothing less.

COUNT RYŪSEI

Good. Before we get into all that, I would like you to tell me what went wrong.

ADMIRAL ENGAARAI

Your excellency, I do not like to give others blame for my failures but there were some ingredients of this disaster that were out of my control.

COUNT RYŪSEI

Admiral, we received direct communications from some of your commanders who were very upset you ran from the enemy like a *coward* when you most likely had an opportunity to hit them with a major blow and finally finish the *Cui* campaign off.

ADMIRAL ENGAARAI

Your Excellency, I would think you would know by now, I never refuse to fight, and my battle record is second to none.

I've engaged in some of the bloodiest conquests of our times. In one battle I lost over one half of my ships.

COUNT RYŪSEI

Yes, I'm quite aware, your track record puts fear in our own troops!

ADMIRAL ENGAARAI

Your Excellency, I looked hard at the tactical situation, and because of the tactical surprise the Carsopians achieved, our formations were not aligned properly and as such we took excessive casualties, we otherwise wouldn't have and possibly won the battle in a timely manner.

COUNT RYŪSEI

Tell me about the formation, what happened?

ADMIRAL ENGAARAI

Your Excellency, I've prepared a replay of the battle for you and a board of inquiry which I assumed would manifest, considering the size and scope of the loss. With your permission sir, I would like to show that presentation.

COUNT RYŪSEI

If that will help me better understand the battle, go ahead and show it. Is it a lengthy presentation?

ADMIRAL ENGAARAI

We have time lapsed integration of the sensors,

because most of the action can be compressed into a very short time sequence.

COUNT RYŪSEI
Alright, go ahead and play it.

ADMIRAL ENGAARAI
Start the holographic replay.

The wardroom computational suite designed to have *Artificial Intelligence* assist officers in any manner possible was always listening for Admiral Engaarai or Deputy Commander Admiral Dikiy Os'minog commands as well as department heads.

VOICEOVER

Voice recognition applications allowed Artificial Intelligence computational suite to know when the Admiral was talking and confirmed with facial recognition capability. In essence the wardroom was a computer cave, where Artificial Intelligence had full observation of all its inhabitants.

When Admiral Engaarai ordered the playback, Artificial Intelligence computational suite immediately commenced the presentation, including recorded voices, background conversations of the Admiral's bridge where all pertinent conversations occurred.

All crew member's actions and statements made in the command ship's control room were recorded for the records.

As the video unfolded and the calamity quickly enveloped the surreal tapestry of intergalactic space warfare, the gut-wrenching display of man and machines twisted into lifelessness after tumultuous and deadly fire erupted all around.

EXT.CGI.SPACE SPACE BATTLE HOLOGRAPHIC REPLAY 30 SECONDS.

BACKGROUND MUSIC DURING VOICEOVR:

https://www.youtube.com/watch?v=aJ1wwzEdN7k (prior to the opera singers).

VOICEOVER

From the bridge sensors and the sounds that pervaded the presence of each soul observing this colossal display of intergalactic giants' slugfest for a bitter moment of sheer terror had an instant impact on the distinguished visitors and observer's psyche.

This gigantic space battle truly was more than any of them had ever seen or experienced in their lifetimes.

When the two fleets passed close aboard damaging each other, the incredible amount of destruction was indescribable. It was also clear the Carsopians suffered greatly in this battle.

Count Ryūsei who initially had been urged by General Bakugeki to remove Admiral Engaarai, quickly transcended into a different pathway of thought processes.

The gigantic space battle was far more extensive and terrifying than the few malcontents who had addressed their issues concerning their opinions conveyed about Admiral Engaarai.

There was no element of cowardice in any actions they could observe. In fact, the opposite was clear. Admiral Engaarai was the coolest hand on the bridge.

Admiral Engaarai calmly went about his business even though possibilities existed he had a 50% probability of being blown out of the sky in some of those twister terrors of high-powered energy beams slicing open ships like can openers.

The entire battle that took over two full hours was encapsulated in 15 minutes of spectacularly narrated action. The narration was not post-action reporting, it was on the scene in situ.

Recorded like all other comments and statements, the Admirals orders to break off the attack and regroup were clear, concise, and thoughtful.

There was only logic and calculation guiding their actions. Now the Count wanted to know directly from Admiral Engaarai.

COUNT RYŪSEI

What made you decide to retreat?

ADMIRAL ENGAARAI

Your Excellency, as you can see by the damage reports, our fleet was severely weakened, with a lot of damage and fatalities, we were suddenly not in good fighting shape to continue the campaign.

COUNT RYŪSEI

People in your task force who complained said you could have prevailed had you pressed forward.

ADMIRAL ENGAARAI

Your Excellency, I have two responsibilities in my mandate as Force Commander. Number one, to inflict as much damage to the enemy as possible.

COUNT RYŪSEI

People in your task force say you had the opportunity to damage more of the enemy.

ADMIRAL ENGAARAI

Your Excellency, my second responsibility I cannot ignore, is to not place the fleet in irreparable damage to the point our home planets could not be effectively defended. I viewed the 2nd mandate as in jeopardy if I continued this battle.

COUNT RYŪSEI

Why is that?

ADMIRAL ENGAARAI

Your excellency, as you viewed the battle, I'm sure the number of enemy ships present caught your attention. Out of nowhere on our flanks many enemy ships hit us.

COUNT RYŪSEI

What factor is attributed to that?

ADMIRAL ENGAARAI

We had no warning from INTEL the Carsopians were even in the region, even though we supposedly have the best spies available embedded in *Cui* giving us ships' movements.

General Bakugeki started to interrupt the conversation but Cout RYŪSEI interrupted his input.

GENERAL BAKUGEKI

I want to know….

COUNT RYŪSEI

General Bakugeki you will have time later to ask questions after I hear from Admiral Engaarai. Please continue, Admiral Engaarai.

Admiral Engaarai delayed for a moment reflecting on the battle and determining what he should say next.

ADMIRAL ENGAARAI

Your Excellency, as we approached *Cui* for the knockout punch, we were led to believe by INTEL we outnumbered the Carsopians three to one or better.

COUNT RYŪSEI

Admiral Engaarai, I've gleaned information sent by INTEL to your ship, I concur that's what they reported.

ADMIRAL ENGAARAI

In the previous couple of planets the Carsopians attacked, our poor garrison troops bugged out and didn't stay to defend the planets or give reports on the enemy units' makeup and disposition.

COUNT RYŪSEI

Deputy Commander Admiral Dikiy Os'minog do you agree with Admiral Engaarai's statement.

DEPUTY COMMANDER ADMIRAL DIKIY OS'MINOG

We did not receive a single warning from these troops who are part of General Bakugeki chain of command.

COUNT RYŪSEI

Alright, thank you Admiral Dikiy Os'minog.

DEPUTY COMMANDER ADMIRAL DIKIY OS'MINOG

May I remind you that all off-hull communications are recorded and supplemental data in the Mission Report and Data Package we transmitted to you just before you arrived today.

COUNT RYŪSEI

Admiral Engaarai, how did those ships show up without you detecting them?

ADMIRAL ENGAARAI

How many ships got into the region without detection was in the back of my mind, and I had to assume, they planted an elaborate trap for us.

COUNT RYŪSEI

What made you think that?

ADMIRAL ENGAARAI

Your excellency, when the Carsopians attacked our flank, I knew it was an ambush, clearly worked out in advance through elaborate planning and execution.

COUNT RYŪSEI

What made you decide to disengage and leave the space battlefield?

ADMIRAL ENGAARAI

Your excellency, I was lacking critical information such as, *how many more are there*?

COUNT RYŪSEI

You couldn't make that determination with all the vast number of sensors aboard your fleet?

ADMIRAL ENGAARAI

I took the conservative approach and continued fighting during a withdrawal plan worked out in advance to preserve as many forces as possible.

COUNT RYŪSEI

Admiral Engaarai what is your justification for abandoning the battlefield?

ADMIRAL ENGAARAI

It was clear to me; we could not beat this superior force that appeared out of nowhere.

Admiral Engaarai a great studier of body language could sense that Count Ryūsei had a personality metamorphism and was no longer there to scalp him.

Count Ryūsei was calculating how to convey this to the emperor who was obviously similarly an intelligent man but a very introspective:

VOICEOVER (COUNT RYŪSEI) THOUGHT

The technicians who put the presentation together didn't have to fudge a thing. All that live video coverage spoke for itself.

Even though based on numbers of ships and personnel lost, it seemed like the Heisibing suffered a terrible defeat, Count Ryūsei a shrewd calculator understood the Admiral performed a tactical withdrawal to apply force protection.

Lesser men might have continued a flawed attempt and by the video showed more and more enemy ships appearing out of nowhere, *it indeed was an elaborate ambush.*

It didn't take Admiral Engaarai to explain it to Count Ryūsei who already figured it out on his own.

VOICEOVER (COUNT RYŪSEI) THOUGHT

Had Admiral Engaarai not executed the tactical withdrawal exactly when he did, there is a good reason to believe his entire fleet would have been smashed leaving the door wide open for an invasion of our home world.

COUNT RYŪSEI

Admiral, it seems to me you were lulled into an elaborate ambush. What's your thoughts on how that happened?

ADMIRAL ENGAARAI

Your excellency, the execution of this elaborate plan by the Carsopians is one of the most audacious plans I've ever experienced of in my lifetime.

Based on Fleet Intelligence aboard, we were able to confirm General Fukua de Hundan led the attack.

We are still trying to figure out how he was able to sneak past all our barrier patrols with such a huge armada. Our failures at *Cui* were caused by many contributing factors.

COUNT RYŪSEI

Such as?

ADMIRAL ENGAARAI

The biggest of all is our INTEL was flawed.

Secondly, when a military genius like General Fukua de Hundan can maneuver a large fleet and place them precisely on our flanks when our INTEL was convinced the only enemy defenses lay directly ahead, bad things can happen.

Count Ryūsei voluntarily disclosed restricted information which unexpectedly gave Admiral Engaarai insights into how much the Heisibing feared General Fukua de Hundan.

COUNT RYŪSEI

We tried to assassinate General Fukua de Hundan on several occasions and missed him barely by minutes each time.

Claire Uwakion'na always an opportunist and a great judgement of Count Ryūsei's mannerisms, realized the scalping of Admiral Engaarai wasn't going to happen after all even though General Bakugeki had pressed for such a dismissal, jumped in to gain favor of the Count:

CLAIRE UWAKION'NA

Admiral Engaarai, since the past is the past and we do not have time to commiserate over this tragedy, tell us what you believe we should do next?

ADMIRAL ENGAARAI

Madam, you probably have received reports from some of my not so distinguished officers whom I promise will not be with me when I deploy again, that our troops are in poor morale.

CLAIRE UWAKION'NA

Yes Admiral, that's the communications we received.

ADMIRAL ENGAARAI

For the sake of the Empire and the safety of our home worlds, I believe it's prudent to rebuild that morale as quickly as possible because we could be fighting another battle sooner than we realize.

CLAIRE UWAKION'NA

Yes Admiral, I would think so as well.

ADMIRAL ENGAARAI

My intentions are to rest the fleet crews for a few weeks, do some physical and mental conditioning, then immediately deploy and win a few limited actions that will not bring on a major engagement, but will prove to be very beneficial in morale building.

CLAIRE UWAKION'NA

What do you propose to do then?

ADMIRAL ENGAARAI

We will go back to enemy territory but do so in a much more conservative manner.

CLAIRE UWAKION'NA

What will you do differently this time to prevent defeat?

ADMIRAL ENGAARAI

We'll provide additional flank protection so we don't get caught with our pants down again, and instead of invading and conquering worlds, we'll merely strike them, put the fear in them, then move off, so that we will be long gone by the time the Carsopian's respond.

The Admiral paused for a moment to give Claire Uwakion'na a chance to comment.

CLAIRE UWAKION'NA

Go on Admiral, tell me more.

ADMIRAL ENGAARAI

We will not be performing a general strategy, as our intentions are not expansion of front lines, we are not ready for that.

CLAIRE UWAKION'NA

What's the purpose of all that?

ADMIRAL ENGAARAI

We merely are repairing the fleet to get our once proud force back into believing in themselves again.

CLAIRE UWAKION'NA

So, your plan is to get the Fleet back into a much better state of readiness and at some point, in time you would resume our general strategy?

ADMIRAL ENGAARAI

That's correct, we must take baby steps first, then we'll eventually crawl out of our failures and resubmit the fighting spirit we once had.

Then when I feel we are ready, to carry out what is necessary, we will eventually take *Cui* as a major objective.

I also intend to eliminate any possible means of the Carsopians from attacking us from multiple directions again.

Admiral Engaarai glanced over at General Bakugeki who wasn't liking the direction the conversation was heading.

As a master politician and manipulator, General Bakugeki believed that if he had it his way, he would arrange for a synthetic aperture phaser firing squad to levy the harsh treatment he felt Admiral Engaarai deserved.

At the same time, knowing Claire Uwakion'na would back stab General Bakugeki, and Count Ryūsei didn't play fair if someone went against his plans and directions, so the politician in him led him to bite his lip and go with the flow.

Deputy Commander Admiral Dikiy Os'minog was starting to feel better about the outcome of this witch hunt, because the discourse altered trajectory and despite their massive losses it appeared Admiral Engaarai had neutralized his significant opponent who was out to get him, the illustrious and ruthless General Bakugeki.

None of the others attending the meeting had the desire to ask questions and make comments because they too sensed the direction the conversation was heading and there would be no purpose now in joining General Bakugeki who wasn't going to embarrass or irritate Count Ryūsei who no doubt would be given an audience with the emperor in the days to come.

Claire Uwakion'na knew that Admiral Engaarai would be forced to the surface of the planet for social events, especially if the emperor decided to pay a visit to the fleet.

It wouldn't be the first or the last time she attempted to put her hooks into Admiral Engaarai. Claire Uwakion'na gave that poker face that conveyed no knowledge of where she was going or what she would attempt.

The meeting broke up shortly, but attendees slowly extricated themselves off the Heisibing Command Ship.

Claire Uwakion'na hung to the rear to make sure she was the last off so she could have a brief private conversation with Admiral Engaarai.

CLAIRE UWAKION'NA

Admiral, when you find time to take a break, please visit me at Yanjingzai Tiankongzhong, I would like to have a talk with you.

ADMIRAL ENGAARAI

Yes Madame, I will put time in my schedule for such a visit.

CLAIRE UWAKION'NA

Don't wait too long.

ADMIRAL ENGAARAI

I have a lot to accomplish before we get underway again. But I plan on visiting the troops on the planet undergoing Rest and Relaxation, I could possibly swing by on one of those trips.

CLAIRE UWAKION'NA

Good, here's one of my business cubes you can use to contact me.

ADMIRAL ENGAARAI

I will.

CLAIRE UWAKION'NA

Thank you.

Claire Uwakion'na then turned and walked off the ship down through the access tunnel which had its own dual air locks.

Admiral Engaarai looked at Claire Uwakion'na's figure as she departed. If there ever was a perfect posterior, Claire Uwakion'na's came as close to one as possible.

Claire had a reputation. The Admiral was more interested in preparing his Fleet, but he understood the politics and it would not hurt to have Claire on his side. But then what kind of concessions would she wield out of him?

If the rumors about Claire were true, at least she cleverly hid the many experiences she had and just like the Russian, Catherine the Great on Earth, she didn't mind going through a lot of young officers to obtain her delights.

Admiral Engaarai suddenly felt a lot more secure in his position. The abrupt change in Count Ryūsei and Claire Uwakion'na's poignant comments, seemed to severely reduce the edge on General Bakugeki's sword.

Whatever General Bakugeki had planned was now overcome by events. It was also a foregone conclusion General Bakugeki would not get an audience with the emperor before Count Ryūsei. He was now powerless to carry out his agenda, ultimately resulting in shoulder fired synthetic aperture phasers conducting a firing squad at the condemned man Admiral Engaarai.

There was no time to waste, Admiral Engaarai swung into action and summoned his staff to the wardroom to go over in detail what he expected out of them. Now that he would be left alone to chart his future, take care of his troops, and make big plans, he felt confident they would be ready when the time came.

VICTORY AT SPACE

With Richard Rodgers music in the background

"Victory at Sea" (1952) - Suite - Richard Rodgers (youtube.com)

The Carsopian fleet receiving a hero's welcome quickly regained their endurance and stamina.

Victory has a strange way of healing wounds and repairing the psyche. After several weeks on the planet enjoying artificial gravity and blossoming in the luster of a grateful public, it was time to get back to training.

Part of the Carsopian training strategy was to sortie, chase ghost fleets produced by simulations, leaving and returning to the planet. However, as General Fukua de Hundan understood his security arrangements, he stretched the days out longer each time. Finally, when it was time to depart the *Cui* system, he assigned a rear guard and a static force to give appearances the fleet was nearby and poised to once again pounce on an opponent.

The troops were prepared for departure by guidance one of the times they left the planet Cui for another sortie, they might not come back. Part of the disinformation put out to the fleet to spoon feed potential Heisibing Spies included the fleet would carefully traverse the Cui Transit Lane and set up additional ambushes along the way to trap and effectively severely damage the Heisibing fleet.

General Fukua de Hundan would lead his fleet out for war games far away from the planet for security reasons. They did conduct operations which the crew members thought was the main event.

Upon disengaging from the war games, the Admiral directed the fleet on a course which left *Cui* far behind. There was of course a lot of communications back to *Cui* until the Admiral suddenly imposed a complete blackout. No transmissions were allowed. He then sped the fleet up as if they were indeed doing the long way around home.

Because of Space Sickness deaths attributed to the transit to Cui, a midpoint Rest and Recreation stop, just like when they traveled to *Cui*, was in order.

After looking at the fastest way to get back to the Carsopian Empire without stopping at a planet with a technology scaling of 4.5 or higher, Earth with a of 1.5 technology scale score card, was the only feasible stopping point.

General Fukua de Hundan reflected on it for a seemingly very long moment, before he codified it in writing. Perhaps it was the memories of his deceased son he left buried there which made him reluctant to return, at the same time also acted like a magnet.

VOICEOVER (GENERAL FUKUA DE HUNDAN) THOUGHT

You don't know how much you miss someone until they are gone forever. Make every moment count, as the grim reality of intergalactic strife reminds us how quickly we can lose someone.

The troops didn't look forward to landing on Earth but at the same token they realized real gravity for a few weeks anywhere was better than the artificial gravity that had a strange feeling and over a long period of time, slowly made life miserable.

Without supplements and special medications, everyone would get some level of Cosmic Space Sickness which proved to be fatal for his own son.

The unfortunate characteristic of Cosmic Space Sickness which took on dozens of forms, included a very quick death because if not diagnosed soon enough, a strange phenomenon occurs where the body organs start shutting down.

By the time a person like General Fukua de Hundan's son went to see the ship's surgeon, because he was too proud to let anyone know how bad he felt, his organs were already ninety five percent shut down. He was beyond the point of help and within a day, he was dead.

Memories of his own son's demise predicated General Fukua de Hundan's decision to get everyone into real gravity for a few weeks, which seemed to have a remarkable enhancement to the physical being.

As they approached Earth and got near the planet and prepared to enter the atmosphere and find a landing zone, General Fukua de Hundan, spontaneously decided to go back to their old bivouac area in Mexico where they had been just several months ago.

General Fukua de Hundan didn't know why he did it. It almost seemed illogical and was certainly not within the policies and traditions of their Space Force.

The concept of burial on alien planets was similar in concept to the Navy's burial at sea. Done for practical reasons, but at the same time, a respectful goodbye.

Would he walk to the grave site? General Fukua de Hundan unexpectedly felt an emotion, an influence in his deepest thoughts. Down deep inside he felt that terrible guilt of pressing his troops so hard to get into the enemy's rear that he killed his only son in doing so. It was a bitter sadness that only a father could understand.

The Mexican and American Armies were long gone. Days had passed since the very last forensics people had been on this site. No over flights occurred in over a month because the aliens simply vanished.

It was a foregone conclusion the aliens had visited, buried their dead, barbecued well over 100 Caravanners, then simply vanished. But the Aliens left behind significant evidence.

It was confirmed after microscopic examination of incompletely digested stools where the aliens dumped their sanitary tanks, these aliens were indeed cannibals.

There had been DNA matching of well over 50 individuals taken by the aliens. They would never be seen or heard from again.

The press would never be notified, the entire incident was swept under the carpet because in closing the investigation, the Mexican Government became more concerned than Americans about repercussions of disclosure of this event to the public.

Mexican and American Officials were strange bed fellows in Alien and UFO coverup now took on a mutual tract.

The Carsopian's landed, set up camp, and commenced their Rest and Recreation. Carsopian Security Rover-craft were sent out as sentries to warn them of anything approaching. Nothing coming in by air would get close.

By now the original Caravan was already to the U.S. Border. All eyes were on that Caravan. Other groups streaming along were off everyone's radar because no such large Caravan manifested in the days to come.

Oscar Godoy, Gabriela Zelaya, and Javier Pineda made it to the original caravan, but when they arrived in Guadalajara, their Honda started having mechanical issues. The cost to get a repair was more than the money they had on them.

The auto-repair shop owner Rafael Castañeda, a grandfather and a decent man felt sorry for the kids. He needed some helpers for a couple projects he was doing that included manual labor. So, he cut a deal with the young adults that if they would help him for a couple months, he would fix their car and give them a little cash so they would have enough money for food and gas to get up to the border.

Oscar Godoy, Gabriela Zelaya, and Javier Pineda were not slackers. They were used to hard work and just as in the case where they figured out how to pull a transmission out of a Honda under such circumstances, were good with their hands and smart thinkers and planners.

Within about a week, Rafael Castañeda had determined he made a wise investment decision cutting the deal with the three young adults. He had good things to say about them to his wife:

RAFAEL CASTAÑEDA

These young people are cheerful, helpful, and respectful. In many ways I wish they were my kids.

Being a grandfather and a decent man with a good moral compass, Rafael Castañeda felt very sorry for the families who had given up such wonderful children and just let them leave on such a hazardous journey like this with no adult supervision.

Sure, they were of legal adult age, but the fact is they were still kids and as time wore on it became obvious that Gabriela Zelaya was pregnant!

Mrs. Castañeda, the wonderful grandmother type, quickly developed a strange bond with the three teenagers.

It was almost as if they were her own children. As Mrs. Castañeda, figured out Gabriela Zelaya's condition, she informed Rafael Castañeda:

MRS. CASTAÑEDA

Rafael, I do not want you to use Gabriela for your project any longer. I will use her to help me around the house.

The help she ended up performing was companionship and very light duty work. But for Rafael Castañeda that was ok because the two boys produced their money's worth. They were fantastic employees, eager learners, and made the projects get completed with quality and in a shorter time frame than estimated.

Eventually the two months were up. The car was fully repaired and in excellent shape. Rafael Castañeda wanted to make sure the three kids made it to the boarder in good shape, so he instructed his mechanics:

RAFAEL CASTAÑEDA

Guys, I want you to do a really good job of fixing the car and making it mechanically sound.

Rafael Castañeda employees loved their boss who took good care of them and their families and acted as a true pillar of society who never took advantage of anyone and helped out the best way he could. They did exactly what he asked them to do, and they fixed the car completely so the teenagers would likely not have any car problems. Somehow the car ended up with new tires. With a little paint here and there and buffed up nicely, it almost looked like a show car.

Mrs. Castañeda felt a unique sadness when she had to say goodbye to Gabriela Zelaya who transcended to the stature of being almost like her own daughter in such a short period of time. She really loved the young girl as if she were her own.

The day of their departure, the mechanics, several family members and Mr. and Mrs. Castañeda all lined up to wish the kids goodbye.

RAFAEL CASTAÑEDA

If for some reason you don't like America, you are always welcome to come back here and work for me.

The two young men who had that look of exploration and unique undertaking on their faces, they were ready do depart.

Also packed in their car was some bottled water and food Mrs. Castañeda and Gabriela Zelaya put in the car that morning while the boys were off getting some cash and some maps and instructions from Rafael Castañeda who had cousins in Tijuana, Mexico and San Diego, California.

RAFAEL CASTAÑEDA

I've called my cousins and told them you are coming their way. If you run into trouble here's their phone numbers.

JAVIER PINEDA

We really appreciate your help, Mr. Castañeda. Nobody ever helped us like this before."

RAFAEL CASTAÑEDA

You boys earned it. You did really good work. You Will Be Missed.

OSCAR GODOY

We enjoyed staying with you too, Mr. Castañeda.

RAFAEL CASTAÑEDA

After you get settled down in America, give me a call.

OSCAR GODOY

We'll do that.

RAFAEL CASTAÑEDA

Here's some extra money. Find a good place to hide some of it in case bandits try to rob you.

OSCAR GODOY

Sure.

RAFAEL CASTAÑEDA

Let's go back to the house, the women are waiting on us.

The three walked out of the garage next door to the home, located on a busy street where every few minutes a truck or several cars would pass by.

They walked over to the driveway, and the group was there waiting for them. The mechanics who worked for Mr. Castañeda had families of their own and some had teenagers or young adults. Their own children were far less respectful than these kids.

VOICE OVER (RAFAEL CASTAÑEDA) THOUGHT

Whoever raised them must have done a good job because of their politeness, honesty, and hard work.

Rafael Castañeda might feel differently if he knew the transmission he had repaired had been stolen by these kids.

After their goodbyes with tears in Mrs. Castañeda's eyes, the kids pulled out of the driveway and onto the two lane Hiway that went by the garage and home.

A few miles down the road:

OSCAR GODOY

This car really feels good now, it's running smoothly.

Javier Pineda responded also feeling lack of vibration and a smooth ride.

JAVIER PINEDA

Mr. Castañeda's mechanics really knew what they were doing.

Gabriela Zelaya responded now knowing she was probably the instigator of them being treated so well.

GABRIELA ZELAYA

Mrs. Castañeda told me her husband had them change the shocks and the tires for us.

OSCAR GODOY

Yea, she was a very nice lady.

JAVIER PINEDA

It feels good we managed to work out our unexpected and quite demoralizing experience when we were suddenly stuck with car trouble and lack of funds to do anything about it.

Javier Pineda then looked at Gabriela Zelaya and realized they were running out of time. They really needed to get into the United States quickly and get settled down because Gabriela Zelaya's situation was now becoming rather apparent, she was expecting.

The three were feeling good, they had money to get them to the USA border and their car was now in really good shape. They did not know how Mr. Castañeda managed to do it, but he got the car re-registered with Mexican License plate in Javier Pineda's name.

In Mexico it pays to know someone to cut through the bureaucracy or special favors. Even though Mr. Castañeda appeared to be the saint who made everything possible for them, Gabriela Zelaya knew the truth that Mrs. Castañeda was the real person and benefactor behind the scenes.

Not long after leaving Guadalajara because they got lost, they ended up on the infamous two-lane Mexico Hiway 23 that eventually had a name similar Hiway near to Area 51's called "Extraterrestrial Hiway."

Urban legend is the Mexican Hiway 23 was eventually called "*Comemos Caravanos Hiway*." A distinction the Mexican Government did not like.

Another problem manifested around the *Comemos Caravanos Hiway*. Eventually many people except for the UFO freaks avoided it which eventually hurt the area tourist economy.

Approximately 50 miles north of Guadalajara, they ran into stalled traffic. To their surprise and kind of delight, when they got out of the car and talked to people in front of them, they were told:

STRANGER

It's another Caravan of people up ahead, some
are walking pleading for rides.

To the three young adults this was good news in a way, they would be again traveling with a group that ostensibly had a leader and advisors like the previous one to guide them through the journey as well as the pending legal processes ahead.

OSCAR GODOY

I'm going to shut off the engine, no point in
wasting gas until this line of cars starts moving.

JAVIER PINEDA

Good idea.

The three sat there in line for over an hour and finally the column started moving. Because traffic was coming from the other direction passing them, it was truly unsafe to attempt passing this human wave crawling along and from the air, looked like snake of some sort.

JAVIER PINEDA

Looks like we are stuck back here for a while.

OSCAR GODOY

We'll wait until they all pull over to camp for the
night then we'll pass them and get out in front.

JAVIER PINEDA

Sounds like a good idea.

The New Caravan slowly creeped along, but it did not have the same billionaire sponsor helping like the previous Caravan. Everyone was on their own.

Within two hours, while they were stopped again, a man approached them.

CARAVANER

Would it be possible to put my wife and two small kids in your car.

JAVIER PINEDA

Where are you from?

CARAVANER

Honduras.

After hearing the name of the man's country and seeing the poor woman and two small kids, Gabriela Zelaya answered before the boys had a chance.

GABRIELA ZELAYA

I think we could make room for them.

Oscar Godoy shook his head in disbelief. He knew right then and there that Gabriela Zelaya was now controlling Javier Pineda who was now a family man whether he realized it or not. The man then walked behind the car and after a while Oscar stopped and yelled at the man.

OSCAR GODOY

Come here.

CARAVANER

Yes sir?

OSCAR GODOY

This isn't the most beautiful car in the world, but its reliable transportation. Why don't you sit on the trunk of the car?

CARAVANER

You are very generous sir; I am very grateful.

OSCAR GODOY

Not a problem, hop on so we can get going.

The man with a big grin on his face hopped on the back of the car and sat down on the trunk of the Honda which didn't have much room, but it was still a hell of a lot better than walking on the hot asphalt.

It was almost as if the entire crowd took a cue from this group and soon there were several dozen cars or pickups with stragglers riding on the trunk or in the back of the pickups. This was a smart move for the drivers because it sped up the Caravan by several miles per hour. Ninety percent of the Caravanos relied on the other ten percent who knew how to play the game once they got to the USA border.

Migrants had been going this way for several decades when it appeared one of the liberal administrations the immigration enforcement to please political constituents such as hotel/casino owners, farmers, fast food chains, construction, and many other businesses who desperately needed cheap almost slave labor.

But suddenly, the dynamics changed with a new administration, and they could no longer sneak across the border as easily as before, so their only hope was a massive invasion with a Caravan so a few of them could get across while they knew many would be arrested. The Caravan organizers had experts to teach them how to ask for entry as indigents seeking political amnesty and protection from organized crime and gangs.

Listening to the organizers who received a fee from these poor helpless souls gave most of them hope. Little did they know the snake oil they were being served was not valid and eighty five percent of them would be turned away and those caught trying to illegally enter would be deported and denied future applications for green cards.

Migrants would most likely be more successful trying to get in legally and the money they paid the coyotes, and the organizers actually cost more in the end, with less likelihood of success.

Oscar Godoy, Gabriela Zelaya, and Javier Pineda had no idea how it was going to turn out. But they did have a safety valve with Rafael Castañeda. If things didn't work out in America, he would help them get started and they would be much better off than staying in Honduras with all the crime and very bad economy for the masses.

In 2017, the average wage in Mexico amounted to $15,314 U.S. dollars, slightly up from $15,311 a year earlier, and Honduras wages averaged less than $800 a year, Mexico would be a huge step up. Mexico was one of the fastest growing economies in the world, believed to be souped up by the drug cartel spending and money laundering.

Banks such as HSBC who were heavily fined at $1.5 Billion USD for Cartel money laundering were pivotal in allowing the Cartels to invest in major construction projects, housing, and building of industrial sites.

If it were not for the fact the Cartels caused major corruption in the Mexican government, the public would enshrine them as heroes by the way they vastly improved the Mexican economy.

In years gone by, Mexico was brutal on their southern border preventing Central Americans into their country because they knew most of them would never make it to the USA and they would be stuck with them.

However, in recent years due to Mexican building explosion with all that Cartel money greasing the politicians' hands, and the average Mexican earning an impressive amount compared to what their parents earned, with far greater amounts of disposable income, just like in America, Mexico needed more and more cheap labor as many Mexicans slowly rose to higher economic stature.

Hence just like the American Liberals did to the border policy, Mexico also relaxed their standards to get those $800 a year worker. Many Guatemalans, Hondurans, Panamanians, and others didn't know they could earn up to $15,000 a year really easy and were settling for $1,000 to $2000 a year until they learned the truth.

Mexico now wanted some of the Caravanners to remain in Mexico to fuel the labor force as it was starting to become painfully obvious, they needed more cheap labor just like Americans needed.

There were some roadside convenience stores along the way, and after the three finished eating all the goodies that Mrs. Castañeda made for them, they had to pull over into one of them.

A lot of the Caravanners didn't have much money and couldn't afford the convenience store prices, which were usury like with inflated prices for tourists traveling nearby Guadalajara. These and other stores along the way sold hot meals, that included:

> *Frutas y Legumbres,* sometimes called *Verdurerí (*fresh fruit and vegetable stores)*Pollería* (fresh chicken, they also sell eggs and condiments to compliment chicken dishes) *Rosticería* (roast chickens from a spit; they also sell sauces and other condiments to complement a roast chicken meal) *Carnicería* (butcher, selling a variety of meat, often reared by the owners) *Tortillería* (selling freshly pressed, warm tortillas, straight off the machine that makes them) *Salchichonería* (delicatessen; selling a range of hams and other cured meats) *Panadería* (fresh bread store; these are less common now as supermarkets bake their bread)*Pescadería* (fish)

The three teenagers coming from an impoverished area were not accustomed to seeing prices so high, were naturally conservative with their spending as they knew they had a long road ahead. One problem they had was eating in front of the mother and the two children who suddenly became a burden on their finances and their consciousness that reached a situation that night.

Nobody wants to sleep on the ground. When the Caravan stopped for the night, there was plenty of room for 2 people to sleep in the car, laying down, but an extra woman and her 2 kids complicated that arrangement fast. Eventually what they figured they could do is one of the teenage boys would sleep in the driver's seat, though uncomfortable, the mother in the passenger seat, *Gabriela Zelaya* because she was pregnant and needed a reasonable place to sleep got the rear seat and the two kids slept on the floor in the back-seat area. The other teenager stood watch, and the father leaned against one of the tires and slept the best he could as he wanted to be near his family.

For several days this arrangement wore on. On some occasions, Oscar Godoy and Javier Pineda arranged turns riding on the trunk of the car so that the father could be with his children. Oscar Godoy, Gabriela Zelaya, and Javier Pineda survived only because of those children.

It happened around sundown before the Caravan stopped. Oscar Godoy was asked to pull over so that one of the kids could use the bathroom. The group took the occasion to all get out of the car and stretch their legs.

Carsopian Security Rover-craft had surveyed the Caravan and were going to pick off a few Caravanos to barbecue them that night. There were stragglers around them, but due to the lengthy stop, this group suddenly was at the end of the caravan. When the Carsopian Security Rover-craft came down behind to snatch them, the two little kids running back and forth stopped them from going through with the grab.

As the group was debating on just staying there for the night or catching up with the Caravan now almost out of site, the Carsopians maneuvered to get a lead on the next group. There were numerous walking stragglers in this group, and they were so exhausted those leading didn't look back nor did they care about those following them, as they were complete strangers.

The Carsopian's landed on the Hiway, got out and quickly approached the rear and took out their beam weapons and quickly fired on and hit at least twenty, killing them instantly. The weapons were eerily quiet but deadly. The 20 Caravanners were dead before they could even think about screaming.

The 10-foot-tall giants took very little time to load up the five-foot five average height Central Americans. The Carsopians took off just as Oscar Godoy started the car to continue. The car headlights illuminated the alien crafts as they were darting off into the air and disappearing.

JAVIER PINEDA

What the hell was that?

OSCAR GODOY

It must have been a UFO, never seen anything
like it before!

Oscar Godoy replied in the most excited manner.

As they drove up the road going about 25 miles per hour and reached the point, they saw the UFO's depart Oscar Godoy noticed what appeared to be a wet spot on the road just ahead.

JAVIER PINEDA

Looks like those ships left some water behind on
the road.

As soon as the car reached the wet spot in the road, Oscar Godoy didn't know what possessed him to look but he stopped the car and got out with a flashlight he had brought with him and walked over to the debris on the road. He was soon amazed it appeared to be *red.*

OSCAR GODOY

What the hell is this?

Chills went up his spine. After seeing the UFO's take off vertically and now what appeared to be large pools of blood on the Hiway, he knew something very bad happened here.

He didn't say anything to anyone when he got in the car. He drove on wondering how to report all this. *People will think I'm crazy.*

He sped up and was doing probably 50 miles per hour and soon caught up with the Caravan and went into the passing lane. There was no oncoming traffic at that point in time.

JAVIER PINEDA

What are you doing?

OSCAR GODOY

We need to report what we saw to the authorities.

JAVIER PINEDA

Why? Nobody will believe us.

OSCAR GODOY

I think they will.

As they got near the head of the Convoy, it was stopped, not because they were stopping for the night. Mexican police were there stopping the Convoy and talking to the lead persons. They were not too friendly towards the car who came up on the passing lane a long distance which they observed. A police officer stepped out in front of their car ordering it to halt and probably cite it.

POLICE OFFICER

What are you doing driving on the wrong side of the road.

OSCAR GODOY

Sir, I need to report something I think very bad happened.

POLICE OFFICER

What happened.

OSCAR GODOY

Sir, we saw something very bad happen back about three or four miles behind us. I think if you go back there with us, I can show you it then you will understand.

The police officer looking very disgusted.

POLICE OFFICER

Okay, pull your car over to the side of the road and get in my police car with me and take me to where you have something to show. This better not be a joke or you will end up in the Calaboose!

There were several Mexican Police Cars stopped at the head of the Caravan. The officer who had talked with Oscar Godoy walked up to the others.

POLICE OFFICER

This guy says something bad happened back there, I'm taking him back there to have him show me. Ricardo, you come with me.

The two Mexican Police Officers took Oscar Godoy in their police Jeep and drove south with their emergency lights turned on and people got out of their way quickly. After a few miles down the road Oscar Godoy announced:

The police car slowed down.

OSCAR GODOY

Slow down, it's right up here.

OSCAR GODOY

It's there, at that wet spot ahead.

The policeman with a good eye knew the wet spot appeared kind of strange and had a red hue to it, pulled up about 10 feet from it, stopped the car, and they all got out.

The police shined flashlights on the pavement and had a strange look on his face.

Oscar Godoy didn't know these police had been part of the previous investigations into the disappearance of well over 100 Caravanners and worked closely with Mexican Policía Federal Ministerial, PFM Agent Carlos Guerrero and had met and discussed those cases with FBI agents Bentley Boyd and Charles Gable.

Oscar Godoy didn't have a good feeling, he just knew the police would think he was nuts or something and bad things would happen, but he knew as a decent human being he had to report it.

POLICE OFFICER

What happened here and what did you see?

OSCAR GODOY

Sir, you probably will not believe me, but I swear it's the truth.

POLICE OFFICER

Go ahead and tell us what you saw.

OSCAR GODOY

We stopped a distance back from here so the kids traveling with us could use the bathroom.

When we were in our car and leaving afterwards and started out, in my headlights I could see what looked like UFO's taking off and going into the sky.

Then when we pulled up here, I saw the wet spot, was kind of curious because those UFOs had been parked here. When I shined the flashlight on it, it looked red, like blood!

POLICE OFFICER

Son, this is real blood, something bad happened here. Is there any more you can tell us? Did you see anyone?

OSCAR GODOY

No, I didn't see anyone, by the time we reached here there was nothing around except the red spot on the Hiway.

POLICE OFFICER

Okay, I'm going to my car to report in, you guys stay here.

Mexican Police Officer Manuel Torres, walked over to his police Jeep and grabbed the microphone to his radio and called into police headquarters.

POLICE OFFICER

Headquarters, this is Officer Manuel Torres. I'm with the Caravan about 85 miles north of Guadalajara. I would like you to contact Mexican Policía Federal Ministerial, PFM Agent Carlos Guerrero and inform him we have had another incident and to send forensic team up here right away.

The people at headquarters knew instantly what Officer Manuel Torres was talking about and they had been instructed that if another similar incident occurred not to state exactly what it was over the radio, but by mentioning PFM Agent Guerrero this was going to be another possible UFO/Alien murder-abduction case.

HEADQUARTERS POLICE AGENT

Officer Torres, we'll contact Agent Guerrero right away.

Officer Manuel Torres got out of his police Jeep, then walked back to Officer Ricardo and Oscar Godoy

OFFICER TORRES

Son, what's your name?

OSCAR GODOY
My name is Oscar Godoy.

OFFICER TORRES
Oscar, where are you from?

OSCAR GODOY
Honduras sir.

OFFICER TORRES
Going to the USA with the Caravan?

OSCAR GODOY
Yes sir.

OFFICER TORRES
Oscar, we believe your story. There is more to this than you know. That's partly why we are here watching over the Caravan.

Oscar Godoy was mildly shocked at the treatment the Mexican police were giving him. They were very kind and respectful, something he didn't expect. And soon he was to learn why.

OFFICER TORRES
Oscar, we are going to take you back to your car now so you can rejoin the Caravan. As you probably know now, something bad happened here, and the last thing we want is a media circus and undo attention to this incident. I do not want you to discuss this with anyone except law enforcement officials who may want to question you. Understand?

OSCAR GODOY
Yes sir.

OFFICER TORRES
Good. When I take you back up to your car, I want you to remain close to our police cars up there so that if a detective needs to talk to you, we don't have to go looking for you.

OSCAR GODOY
Yes sir.

OFFICER TORRES

Good, hop in the Jeep and we are going back to your car now.

In a few minutes the car was traversing and passing the long line of Caravanners who instinctively got out of the way because the police Jeep emergency lights were on.

Eventually they pulled up in front of another police Jeep and they all got out of the car. Oscar Godoy was allowed to get in his car but told to wait with the police. The Caravan was also stopped and told they could not move for the rest of the night.

PFM Agent Carlos Guerrero was enjoying his evening in Mexico City when unexpectedly his cell phone rang. He looked down on the cell phone and saw the caller I.D. It was Jose Mercado the head of Mexican Policía Federal Ministerial, PFM.

PFM AGENT CARLOS GUERRERO

Hello.

JOSE MERCADO

Carlos?

PFM AGENT CARLOS GUERRERO

Yes.

JOSE MERCADO

This is Jose Mercado, sorry for disrupting your evening. Are you somewhere that you can talk for a few moments?

PFM AGENT GUERRERO

Yes, sir, I'm at home.

JOSE MERCADO

Good. It looks like we have another case of a body snatcher again.

PFM AGENT GUERRERO

Where did this happen?

JOSE MERCADO

On the same Hiway leading north out of Guadalajara. Not far from where the other incidents occurred, an hour or so ago.

PFM AGENT GUERRERO

I see.

JOSE MERCADO

Say, I'm sorry to have to ask you to do this at this

late hour, but I want you to fly up to Guadalajara and go to the crime scene. Mexican Police are on site and have sealed off the Hiway. Forensic teams are in-route now.

PFM AGENT GUERRERO

Alright sir I'll get ready right away. Question: I would like to invite the two American FBI agents to join the investigation.

JOSE MERCADO

What good will that do for you?

PFM AGENT GUERRERO

Sir, with all due respect, this is more than a Mexican problem. I think the Americans should be part of this investigation because eventually they will probably get involved, especially if the body snatchers start operating up North.

JOSE MERCADO

Okay, you can invite them in, but I want to remind you, this is a Mexican investigation, and they are to only have a subordinate role. You will oversee the scene.

PFM AGENT GUERRERO

Sir, were there any eyewitnesses?

JOSE MERCADO

There are apparently 3 young adults and a family of four who saw something. When you get there, you will have to vet their stories.

PFM AGENT GUERRERO

Understand. I will get ready immediately, should be at the airport say in 45 minutes.

JOSE MERCADO

Good, I'll contact operations and make sure they have the jet ready to fly you to Guadalajara. Our local PFM office will provide you with a car and driver who will meet you at Guadalajara Airport.

PFM AGENT GUERRERO

All right sir, I'll let you know what's going on as soon as I get some details.

JOSE MERCADO

Carlos, I want you to give me a report first thing in the morning, by 8:00 a.m. so that I can brief the President.

PFM AGENT GUERRERO

Will do.

JOSE MERCADO

Good luck.

PFM AGENT GUERRERO

Thank you.

Jose Mercado hung up and there was suddenly a dial tone.

As promised, Agent Guerrero was at the Airport in 45 minutes. He parked his personal car in the official parking lot as he had a sticker on his car, they could identify he had the privilege to park there.

As soon as Agent Guerrero got out of his car another PFM agent approached him to escort him to the plane through a chain link fence entrance just unlocked for him which was about 20 feet away from where a PFM Gulfstream 650 jet parked.

Mexico didn't have the budget to buy a lot of Gulfstream Jets, but when they arrested a Cartel leader, they had the rights to confiscate all the equipment used in drug smuggling. Mexico now had better small jets than the FBI.

Within 2 minutes of parking his car and taking his small suitcase carrying essentials, Agent Guerrero was on the Gulfstream 650 which started to roll immediately. It did not take long to fly up to Guadalajara, but driving would have consumed quite a bit of time due to Hiway conjestion.

As soon as the plane landed and pulled over to a tarmac area, an unmarked car pulled up, a man got out and opened the passenger door for Agent Guerrero who only had to walk about 10 feet from the plane to the car. They were soon on their way up to the crime scene about 80 miles away.

The PFM car transporting Agent Guerrero to the crime scene cruised along about 80 miles per hour. the PFM driver put a temporary red flashing light on the top of the unmarked car.

Even so, in about 30 miles up the road, a Mexican Hiway Patrol car started a chase and when it got close to the PFM car it used the restricted police channel radio and called on the car with its lights turned on.

HIWAY PATROL OFFICER

Speeding Car, this is the Mexican Hiway Patrol, who are you and why are you going faster than the speed limit?

The driver picked up the microphone.

PFM AGENT RODRIGUEZ

Hiway Patrol, this is Agent Rodriguez of the Mexican Policía Federal Ministerial, we are heading to a crime scene about 50 miles up the road. If you want, you can get out in front of us and make sure we have no delays.

The Mexican Hiway Patrol officer was all grins because he just received permission to hot dog it up the road a way and rub elbows with the Mexican Policía Federal Ministerial (PFM).

HIWAY PATROL OFFICER

Yes sir! I will pass you now and get out front.

The Hiway patrolman had clocked the car doing around 80 miles per hour, so he figured that's the speed they wanted to go. There were a few small communities up the road, he would have to slow down to avoid hitting pedestrians and as he approached the first small town, he radioed:

HIWAY PATROL OFFICER

PFM vehicle, I'm going to slow down going through this town up ahead.

PFM AGENT RODRIGUEZ

Understand we'll slow down for a bit.

Having the Mexican Hiway Patrol car acting as an escort pleased the PFM guys as they knew the car with its Hiway Patrol Emergency Lights would clear people out of the way.

In Mexico its understood that when emergency lights come up on you to pull over to the side of the road until the vehicle passes. Mexicans are good at complying with that standard.

As a result, the last 50 miles went by very smoothly and quickly and since the crime scene now had several marked cars with lights turned on, the Hiway Patrol knew exactly where to slow down and pull over to the side of the road. The forensic team was almost finished collecting blood samples. There was added pressure to clean as much of the blood off the Hiway to hide the incident and open the Hiway which had about 50 vehicles waiting in line to pass.

Agent Guerrero got out of the PFM unmarked car and approached the forensic technicians, some of whom he knew from previous cases.

PFM AGENT GUERRERO

Good morning, guys. Any insights?

FORENSIC TECHNICIAN

Good morning, Agent Guerrero. We found what we believe are 20 distinct blood pools and a few footprints.

Agent Guerrero was waiting for what he knew was coming next, which of course he had a gut feeling about and why he wanted to invite FBI agents Bentley Boyd and Charles Gable back immediately.

FORENSIC TECHNICIAN

It looks like the same perpetrators were involved from the prior abduction cases. Size sixteen and seventeen shoes and the unusual pattern on the footprint.

PFM AGENT GUERRERO

I kind of figured that would be the case.

FORENSIC TECHNICIAN

Also because of the nature of the wounds, there were a few body parts left behind.

PFM AGENT GUERRERO

Such as?

FORENSIC TECHNICIAN

Portions of their mid sections appear to have been blown away from the bodies.

PFM AGENT GUERRERO

Any sign of gun powder or what kind of weapon used.

FORENSIC TECHNICIAN

None whatsoever.

About that time Agent Guerrero was introduced to the police officer Manuel Torres who first encountered the three young adults and the family traveling with them.

PFM AGENT GUERRERO

You are the officer who called this in?

OFFICER TORRES

Yes sir.

PFM AGENT GUERRERO

I understand you have some eyewitnesses.

OFFICER TORRES

That's correct.

PFM AGENT GUERRERO

Good, let's go talk to them.

OFFICER TORRES

They are up at the front of the Caravan.

PFM AGENT GUERRERO

All right, let's drive up there.

OFFICER TORRES

Sure thing.

Two vehicles then drove to the front of the Caravan and parked. They all got out of their cars and Officer Manuel Torres led Agent Guerrero to the Honda where the 3 young adults sat with the family and two kids.

Officer Manuel Torres introduced Agent Guerrero to the group:

OFFICER TORRES

Agent Guerrero, this is Oscar Godoy, Gabriela Zelaya, and Javier Pineda from Honduras and the Lopez family from Guatemala. Oscar Godoy is the person who notified me that something happened at the end of the Caravan.

Agent Guerrero turned towards Oscar and asked,

PFM AGENT GUERRERO

Can you tell me what you observed, Mr. Godoy?

OSCAR GODOY

Yes sir. We had stopped so one of the children could get out of the car and because he needed to urinate.

While we were stopped, we all decided we needed to get out of the car and stretch our legs a bit.

This took about 30 minutes altogether. Then we got in the car to drive and catch up with the Caravan.

As soon as I started the car and turned on the lights, I saw several UFO's takeoff up the road ahead.

Oscar Godoy took a moment to gather his thoughts and keep his emotions in check, then proceeded with Agent Guerrero observing him very intently.

OSCAR GODOY

We drove up the road towards where the UFO's had just taken off and when I got where I believe they had been I noticed the road looked wet. I thought that was odd because it's very dry out here now.

So, I stopped the car, got out and walked over with a flashlight and looked. I was shocked it looked like blood and possibly small body parts all over the road.

When Oscar Godoy stalled and didn't seem to be ready to continue, Agent Guerrero coaxed him along.

PFM AGENT GUERRERO

What did you do then, Mr. Godoy?

OSCAR GODOY

I was kind of upset, it seemed so unreal, and I didn't think anyone would believe me, but I drove up passing the Caravan looking for someone to report this to and spotted several police cars then stopped and told this police officer what I saw.

Oscar Godoy then nodded at Officer Manuel Torres.

OSCAR GODOY

This officer then took me back to the blood on
the Hiway where I pointed it out to him.

The police had put up a barrier between the kids' car and the crowd keeping the others away from this car and the police. They were getting impatient and wanting to get moving.

Agent Guerrero then turned towards Officer Manuel Torres.

PFM AGENT GUERRERO

How far away is it to the nearest police station?

OFFICER TORRES

Sir, we are about 10 miles away at Tepechitlán, Zacatecas, Mexico. There is a police station there.

PFM AGENT GUERRERO

I would like these eyewitnesses taken there, I have some detailed questions I wish to ask them, and the crowd is angry they want to get moving.

OFFICER TORRES

All right sir, I recommend we let them drive their car there otherwise this crowd might steal it.

PFM AGENT GUERRERO

Sure, they seem decent, have them follow along with us. You lead and we'll follow behind their car.

OFFICER TORRES

What about the crime scene?

PFM AGENT GUERRERO

The forensic personnel have all the evidence I need. Contact the Hiway patrol dispatcher and ask them to send a road crew to wash down the blood, as soon as possible. We don't want film crews putting that on the news.

OFFICER TORRES

Yea we are kind of lucky, nobody has tipped them off yet and they are not here.

PFM AGENT GUERRERO

That will not last for long. A lot of people in that Caravan have Cell Phones and are probably already babbling about being held up by Mexican Police.

Human Rights groups will be arriving soon with camera crews, so we need to hustle to get those blood deposits washed off the road.

OFFICER TORRES

I'll call from my car as we start moving.

PFM AGENT GUERRERO

All right. Tell the police to allow the Caravan to proceed after we leave.

The police and PFM cars were soon racing ahead towards Tepechitlán, Zacatecas, Mexico with the Teenagers Honda in the middle of the police caravan. Mr. Lopez and his wife and kids were put in police Jeeps to give them all more room and comfort. Everyone was of course apprehensive.

When they pulled up in front of the municipality building that contained the police station, the sight of five police officers on horseback carrying M16 rifles on their back didn't ease the tension in the Hondurans one bit.

These policemen of course were patrolling the town of almost 9,000 that had been recently infiltrated by Cartel gangs. A peaceful Catholic dominated community cooperated with law enforcement and had no desire for the Cartels to operate there, just out of reach of Guadalajara police jurisdiction.

After the cars parked the three Hondurans and the Lopez family were ushered into the municipality building that looked more like a military command post than a police station.

Dealing with the Cartel Bad Hombres, had transformed a peaceful and tranquil community that just a decade prior only needed two police officers, had completely reorganized police who were often backed up by PFM and the Mexican Army, was also distinctly more professional in appearance and in actions than any Mexican would have speculated just a few years ago.

The narco-trafficking was now gripping Mexico in ways Mexicans didn't like and many of the Mexicans who would be considered very conservative in the United States, didn't want any of it near their town of towards Tepechitlán, Zacatecas, Mexico. Nor did the Cartels receive any sympathy from the Catholic Priests in the area who considered them evil and disciples of the devil himself.

OFFICER TORRES

Chief Archuletta I would like to introduce you to Agent Guerrero from the Mexican Policía Federal Ministerial.

Police chief Archuletta held out his hand.

POLICE CHIEF ARCHULETTA

Welcome to Tepechitlán, Agent Guerrero.

PFM AGENT GUERRERO

Thank you Chief Archuletta.

POLICE CHIEF ARCHULETTA

I understand you brought some eyewitnesses with you.

PFM AGENT GUERRERO

Yes, this is Oscar Godoy, Gabriela Zelaya, and Javier Pineda from Honduras and the Lopez family from Guatemala.

POLICE CHIEF ARCHULETTA

Part of the Caravan?

PFM AGENT GUERRERO

Yes, sir.

POLICE CHIEF ARCHULETTA

What do you plan on doing with them?

PFM AGENT GUERRERO

First, I want to take them individually to an interrogation room and question them individually to try to get the most accurate description of what they saw. Then I'll be waiting for instructions from Mexico City as to what to do with them.

POLICE CHIEF ARCHULETTA

Are you going to let them rejoin the Caravan?

PFM AGENT GUERRERO

That's a good question, I don't yet have the answer for that. Also, I expect a couple American FBI agents here shortly who will probably want to talk with them.

POLICE CHIEF ARCHULETTA

I see.

Officer Manuel Torres then suddenly spoke up.

OFFICER TORRES

Chief Archuletta, these people have been up all night long and have had nothing to eat. I'm sure they are getting hungry, and their kids probably need something to drink as well.

POLICE CHIEF ARCHULETTA

Officer Torres, we can call in delivery orders for food and drinks, make them all comfortable in the waiting room and when the food arrives, take all of them back to the lunchroom where they can eat. Also show them where the restrooms are.

OFFICER TORRES

Right away chief.

PFM AGENT GUERRERO

Let me give you some money to pay for their meals.

Agent Guerrero then reached in his pockets and pulled out some Mexican Peso's he thought would be more than sufficient to feed the families some decent food.

OFFICER TORRES

Hey everyone, your food will be arriving soon.
Please feel free to use the restrooms whenever
you need. Let me show you where they are.

Very quickly the mother of the Lopez family took the two children to the bathroom.

Tepechitlán, Zacatecas, Mexico had quite an amount of tourism due to its proximity to Guadalajara Mexico and the lakes and rivers nearby. The downtown area has nicely designed architecture in front of the church and the ideally looking town square, that gives a sense of serenity and peace which the locals are profoundly proud of and the tourists love photographing.

Because of this tourist attraction the town of over 9,000 swells to 11,000 during the peak tourist periods, has a dozen great restaurants quite capable of producing quality meals for the eyewitnesses.

The Lopez family father sat in the waiting room with a very worried look on his face. He had no idea what he had stumbled across and had never experienced such tumultuous events in his lifetime.

Being that he was riding on the rear of the car, when it stopped at the blood pool, and the boys got out to look, he also looked for curiosity's sake. When he saw all the blood he was horrified. *It seemed like GALLONS of blood had been spilled.* Whatever happened had truly spooked him. He now resonated fear.

Agent Guerrero, an astute professional who wasted no time, wanted to get down to business and interview Oscar Godoy privately.

PFM AGENT GUERRERO

I'm going to take Oscar Godoy to the interrogation room and start with him since he's the person who first reported this crime. If the food arrives while I'm interviewing him, please come in and let me know so he can get a bite to eat.

One of the police sergeants responded:

POLICE SERGANT

Will do sir.

Another policeman guided Agent Guerrero and Oscar to the interrogation room.

2nd POLICE SERGANT

This way Agent Guerrero.

The room was small but had privacy. It didn't have double windows like Mexico City or Guadalajara had nor the sophisticated recording equipment, but Agent Guerrero didn't care, he knew the boy would tell him the truth the best he could remember, but getting their stories independently would reduce the number of errors, that might otherwise occur if they were quizzed in a group.

In the center of the room was the interviewer table and as soon as Agent Guerrero sat down a police sergeant came in with a couple bottled waters, and a note pad and several pens and sat those articles down on the table next to Agent Guerrero. He left then shut the door behind him to give them privacy.

PFM AGENT GUERRERO

Ok Oscar, tell me one more time what happened.

Oscar went through pretty much the same sequence of events he had previously stated back on the side of Hiway 23 earlier that morning. Agent Guerrero took copious notes and gave a calm demeaner, nothing like a law enforcement person would have done with a suspect in a major criminal act.

Oscar Godoy was calm and relaxed, somewhat reflective and somber. He in his own mind extrapolated what possibly happened. And it all centered around something horrible. The amount of blood on the Hiway had to be from a group of animals or a group of humans. And since Caravanners had just passed that way 30 minutes prior, it had to be humans.

PFM AGENT GUERRERO

Okay Oscar, thanks for your report, I do appreciate your cooperation in this matter, but can I ask you to tell me what do you think happened?

OSCAR GODOY

Sir, you will probably think I'm crazy if I tell you.

PFM AGENT GUERRERO

Oscar, I will not think you are crazy, there are probably some things I know that you are unaware of.

OSCAR GODOY

Sir, I think aliens on those ships, killed those people and took them away.

PFM AGENT GUERRERO

What do you think they did with the bodies Oscar?

OSCAR GODOY

Sir, I would have no way of knowing what they did with the bodies, but to come down and kill those innocent people and haul them away like that must be for a purpose that can only be despicable.

PFM AGENT GUERRERO

Oscar, you are probably right. And now I'm going to request you do something that is very important for this investigation.

OSCAR GODOY

Yes sir, what can I do?

PFM AGENT GUERRERO

It's very important you do not discuss this matter with anyone including your friends you are traveling with. Do not discuss anything we talked about. There is something important we need to find out. And if you remain silent, it will help us.

OSCAR GODOY

Yes sir, I promise I will not discuss it with anyone.

PFM AGENT GUERRERO

Good. One more thing Oscar. There will be two American FBI agents probably show up today who will want to ask you these same questions. I know these men. They are very good people. Extend the same curtesy and openness with them that you have done for me. Can you do that?"

OSCAR GODOY

Yes sir, I can do that.

PFM AGENT GUERRERO

One other task I request you to do; here's paper and a pencil, could you please try to draw what you think those UFOs looked like.

OSCAR GODOY

I can try, but I'm not a very good artist.

PFM AGENT GUERRERO

Do your best Oscar, it doesn't have to be perfect we just want a rough description of what you think they appeared like. We may have a professional artist alter your drawing slightly to help it look like what you think you saw.

OSCAR GODOY

Okay sir.

Oscar started drawing. It wasn't a great drawing and as unprofessional as it might have seemed it conveyed his memories, which were very important. Some critical elements have now been recorded by Oscar's drawing.

VOICEOVER

There were possibly five UFO's. That means it was a large force. Which seemed logical since they probably took 20 bodies which would soon be confirmed by the forensics blood tests.

The way they were killed with tremendous weapons and the nature of their bleeding in large pools quickly gave the impression that at least 20 bodies were involved and due to the amount of blood in each pool, they were either adults or teenagers, and not children.

Another interesting aspect of the drawing depending on distance, the craft could have been rather large. If they took 20 bodies on 5 spacecraft that means, there had to be stowage for at least 4 bodies each.

Agent Guerrero knew a lot about the case that Oscar didn't such as, size 16- or 17-footprints. Dead buried aliens that were 10 feet tall weighing 400 to 500 pounds. And according to American reconnaissance, Mother ships that were two miles long. He also knew Oscar would be very disturbed if he knew they were taking the bodies to a barbecue pit and most likely cooking them on a spit.

OSCAR GODOY

This is about all I remember about the ships.

PFM AGENT GUERRERO

Oscar you did a good drawing, thank you for your assistance. Would you please go to the waiting room? I'll come out there in a few minutes to get one of the others to talk with. Remember do not discuss any of this with anyone else."

OSCAR GODOY

Yes sir.

Oscar then stood up and walked back to the waiting room.

Agent Guerrero then picked up his cell phone out of his pocket and dialed Jose Mercado.

JOSE MERCADO

Hello.

PFM AGENT GUERRERO

Mr. Mercado, this is Agent Guerrero reporting in as you requested.

JOSE MERCADO

Thanks for calling Carlos, what do you have for me.

PFM AGENT GUERRERO

It looks like the aliens that were here before did it again. Footprints match, UFO craft observed by eyewitness, blood all over the Hiway, just like before.

JOSE MERCADO

Interesting. By the way, FBI agents Bentley Boyd and Charles Gable will arrive in Guadalajara in about 2 hours from now. We'll send them up in a PFM car as soon as they arrive.

PFM AGENT GUERRERO

Sir, I've relocated the witnesses to the police station at Tepechitlán, Zacatecas where I could interview them in privacy and keep them away from the press.

JOSE MERCADO

Smart move on your part. Be sure and brief the police there, no public comment without permission from my office.

PFM AGENT GUERRERO

Understand sir, but these people here dance to a different tune. Their honest and forthright, I'm not sure how much we can control them, but I will talk privately with their police chief, Archuletta and convey your requests to him."

JOSE MERCADO

Kindly remind police chief, Archuletta it was me personally that provided those extra police officers to fend off the Cartel that moved into his town, and I expect him to be helpful in this investigation.

PFM AGENT GUERRERO

I'm sure he will understand sir.

JOSE MERCADO

Anything else you got?

PFM AGENT GUERRERO

You will probably receive the forensics report in a couple hours. I have hand drawings from one of the witnesses and plan on getting them from the others and I will fax them to you if this station has a fax machine.

JOSE MERCADO

I know they have a fax machine. I gave them one with a couple computers and other goodies recently.

PFM AGENT GUERRERO

All right sir, as soon as I get all the drawings, I will fax them to you.

JOSE MERCADO

Send them to my private fax.

PFM AGENT GUERRERO

What's the last 4 digits in the number?"
JOSEMERCADO 7406.

PFM AGENT GUERRERO

Got it, expect to see the fax in about one hour.

JOSE MERCADO

Thanks. I'll be looking forward to seeing it.

PFM Agent Guerrero suddenly heard the dial tone, as it appeared, Jose Mercado had hung up. He then stood up and walked to the waiting room.

Just as PFM Agent Guerrero arrived in the waiting room, so did the food, so a police Sargent escorted the group to the lunchroom that had a long table set up where the police often ate meals together and sometimes due to various investigations, outsiders as well.

Money appeared to go a lot further in Tepechitlán, Zacatecas, Mexico than it did in Mexico City or Guadalajara. There was a feast underway very quickly. Since everyone had missed supper and breakfast, they were naturally hungry and appreciative.

Agent Guerrero allowed them to enjoy their meal while he drank a cup of coffee a Police Sargent gave him. This also gave him the opportunity to look at the body language. What stood out quickly was Mr. Lopez. Mr. Lopez appeared frazzled by these events..

They all were so hungry, and woofed down the food and the bottled water, nice and chilled did a great job of washing it down. What also stood out was how nice the three teenagers appeared, and the obvious fact the girl was pregnant. No doubt one of the boys was a daddy.

From start to finish was twenty minutes at best. Even though there was more food available, they stopped eating. They had their fill.

POLICE SARGENT

Will all of you please go out to the waiting room. One of the policemen will clean all this up.

The group stood up and walked out to the waiting room that didn't have many conveniences, just wood chairs and a few pictures on the wall along with a bulletin board with a lot of notices.

As soon as they were all situated, with the two kids fighting over who got to sit on their mother's lap, Agent Guerrero approached Mr. Lopez.

PFM AGENT GUERRERO

Sir, would you please come with me to the interview room.

Mr. Lopez nodded and stood up and followed Agent Guerrero to the room where he was quickly offered a seat at the interview table.

PFM AGENT GUERRERO

Mr. Lopez, could you please tell me what you saw?

MR. LOPEZ

Sir, I was riding on the trunk of the car because there was not enough room in the car without severe crowding.

I was facing backwards and didn't see anything until the car stopped. When the boys got out of the car and walked forward, I was curious as to what they were looking at so I hopped off the car trunk and followed them to the wet spot on the Hiway.

When we got close, I could smell some strange scent, and the wetness looked red. I thought about it for a while and then I started thinking it might be blood.

PFM AGENT GUERRERO
What did the boys say?

MR. LOPEZ
One of them asked the other: Do you think those UFO's left this behind? The other boy said, this is where they took off from, I'm certain of it.

PFM AGENT GUERRERO
You didn't see the UFO?

MR. LOPEZ
No sir. I had no idea they had seen a UFO until we were standing there looking at the red liquid on the Hiway.

PFM AGENT GUERRERO
Did you think that was blood?

MR. LOPEZ
After a while I started to think it was blood, pools of it.

PFM AGENT GUERRERO
What do you think happened there?

MR. LOPEZ
There were several Caravanners up in front of us. This may sound kind of gross, but I think the UFO killed several people and took the bodies away.

PFM AGENT GUERRERO
Why do you think the UFO killed the people?

MR. LOPEZ
That's a question I doubt I could ever answer.

PFM AGENT GUERRERO
Do you have any guesses you would like to share?

MR. LOPEZ
Well sir, in our ancient history in Guatemala, we had cannibals. I suppose that could be a purpose. But if these are advanced people with spaceships, why would they be cannibals?

PFM AGENT GUERRERO
It may be simply their culture.

MR. LOPEZ

It seems to me that if there were extra-terrestrials who could fly a long distance to get here, they would be more advanced than us, and less likely to do something like this.

PFM AGENT GUERRERO

Not every culture advances the same way. Look at world history, and the wars, well advanced countries demonstrated their desire and ability to mass kill their enemies.

MR. LOPEZ

Yes, but none of our advanced cultures has ever done cannibalism.

PFM AGENT GUERRERO

Ok, Mr. Lopez, this is a serious matter and I'm going to ask you to not discuss this with your wife or the teenagers or anyone else. We need to get to the bottom of it. We don't want you talking to the press and we fear they may try to track you down for comment.

MR. LOPEZ

I understand sir.

PFM AGENT GUERRERO

Mr. Lopez, let me be frank. You are an illegal alien, and you might be aware that Mexico hasn't always treated illegal aliens humanely.

Just like the USA can deport people, so can Mexico. If you talk to the press, you will be immediately deported back to Guatemala.

We need to keep this information confidential until we solve the case. Those teenagers and your wife are the only eyewitnesses.

Without them we cannot solve the case. If the media gets a sniff of you, they will hound you so please refrain from discussing this with anyone.

MR. LOPEZ

Understand sir.

PFM AGENT GUERRERO

If you cooperate, we'll ensure you get to the American border without any issues.

MR. LOPEZ

Thank you, I appreciate that sir.

PFM AGENT GUERRERO

One other thing. Soon a couple American FBI agents who will arrive here soon want to talk to you. They probably will ask you the same questions I asked.

These are both good men, I've worked with in the past. Just be cordial with them like you have been with me, and all will go well.

MR. LOPEZ

I will do my best sir.

PFM AGENT GUERRERO

Thank you, Mr. Lopez, we truly need your help in this matter. You are an important witness. Also, when you leave this room, do not discuss this with anyone including your wife and the three teenagers.

MR. LOPEZ

I understand sir.

PFM AGENT GUERRERO

Good, I'll go with you back out to the waiting room.

After they got to the waiting room, Agent Guerrero looked at Javier Pineda.

PFM AGENT GUERRERO

Javier Pineda, will you please come with me.

Agent Guerrero led Javier Pineda into the interview room and shut the door behind him.

PFM AGENT GUERRERO

Please sit down.

Javier Pineda took the interviewee's chair and sat down looking expectantly and somber.

PFM AGENT GUERRERO

Javier, would you please tell me everything you saw from the time you spotted the UFO's and up to meeting with Officer Manuel Torres at the front of the Caravan.

JAVIER PINEDA

Sir, we had stopped so the mother of the two kids could take one of them out of the car who needed to urinate badly. At that time, we all decided to get out of the car and stretch our legs.

Since we were in the car we could easily catch up with the Caravan, so we took our time stretching and enjoying the evening breeze and the outdoors.

After about 30 minutes we all got back in the car, except for Mr. Lopez who had to ride on the car trunk since we didn't have enough room and started down the Hiway to catch up to the Caravan.

As soon as Oscar pulled out onto the Hiway and turned on the car lights because it was starting to get dark, we saw the UFOs down the road, probably a half a mile, take off and fly into the air. We were kind of shocked at first and couldn't believe it. None of us had ever seen a UFO before and would probably think someone was a nut who claimed to have seen one.

PFM AGENT GUERRERO

How many UFOs did you see?

JAVIER PINEDA

There must have been five or six. It all happened so quickly, and they flew fast, so I didn't have enough time to count them. But I do recall it was five or maybe six.

PFM AGENT GUERRERO

How big were the UFOs?

JAVIER PINEDA

They were probably a half mile away so it's hard to say for sure, but I'd think they were as large as aircraft.

PFM AGENT GUERRERO

You mean like passenger jets like you often saw back in Honduras?

JAVIER PINEDA

Yes, I lived under the flight path to our local airport and saw a lot of aircraft. In my estimation those UFOs were as large as some of the aircraft I observed.

PFM AGENT GUERRERO

What kind of noises did they make?

JAVIER PINEDA

I didn't hear any noise. They were silent.

PFM AGENT GUERRERO

How fast did they fly away?

JAVIER PINEDA

It was kind of dark so when they flew away, they left almost abruptly. After one or two seconds they were gone.

PFM AGENT GUERRERO

What direction did they fly?

JAVIER PINEDA

It seemed like they flew over the top of us, I think they were heading south.

PFM AGENT GUERRERO

What happened next?

JAVIER PINEDA

As we drove a little further Oscar said something about it appeared water on the road ahead just about where the UFO's had been. He thought it was kind of odd since it's dry there, and there would be no reason for the Hiway to be wet.

PFM AGENT GUERRERO

How far away were you when you saw the wet spot?

JAVIER PINEDA

Most likely less than one quarter mile.

PFM AGENT GUERRERO

What happened next?

JAVIER PINEDA

Oscar said the wet spot looked red and pulled up to it and stopped and got out of the car to look. I followed him, and soon Mr. Lopez stood beside us.

PFM AGENT GUERRERO

What did you see.

JAVIER PINEDA

Oscar had a flashlight and shined down on the wet spot. It looked like blood, a lot of blood, more than I could ever imagine."

PFM AGENT GUERRERO

Do you think the aliens had something to do with the blood?

JAVIER PINEDA

Yes, I think the UFOs left the blood behind.

PFM AGENT GUERRERO

Any idea where the blood came from?

JAVIER PINEDA

I do not know, but I could imagine.

PFM AGENT GUERRERO
What do you imagine.

JAVIER PINEDA
From people.

PFM AGENT GUERRERO
How much blood do you think spilled?

JAVIER PINEDA
I wouldn't know for sure, but I bet several gallons. It was huge.

PFM AGENT GUERRERO
Javier, could you do me a favor and take that pad of paper and draw me what you think the UFO's looked like?

JAVIER PINEDA
I'm not a very good drawer, but I'll try my best.

PFM AGENT GUERRERO
That's all we can ask from you.

Javier started drawing. His artistic skills were far superior to Oscar and provided a different dimension to the imagery.

Agent Guerrero knew from studies he had read, that even though Javier may not draw a pretty picture, he would provide some details needed to corroborate the information already obtained.

One important detail would now emerge, the number of UFO's and another viewpoint on the shapes of the UFO's. Javier didn't know he was a good artist, he had never been trained in drawing, but he had an amazing grasp on how to depict an object in a three-dimensional sense.

If Javier's recollection was close to what he now drew with a degree of precision, this was now the very best view to date of the alien craft used to carry out the gruesome task of killing innocent people and hauling them away for an alien barbecue that even as an advanced race, practiced the barbaric custom of cannibalism.

PFM AGENT GUERRERO
Thank you, Javier, for the drawing, this will be very helpful to our investigation.

JAVIER PINEDA
You are welcome.

PFM AGENT GUERRERO

Javier, I need you to not discuss this case with anyone. This is a very serious matter and until we solve this mystery, we can't afford to have a media frenzy, and a lot of unnecessary people get involved because it is a sensational story.

JAVIER PINEDA

Understand Sir.

PFM AGENT GUERRERO

There are some things we have not told you and your friends or the Lopez family.

We have a lot of information you are unaware of.

I want you to know I believe your story, and your drawing helps to fill in some of the gaps we have.

We'll have DNA analysis on the blood samples within a few hours and we'll be able to know that was human blood and identify distinct individuals that blood came from.

If we find out who the missing people are, we will be able to do a DNA match in some cases.

JAVIER PINEDA

So, you don't think we are crazy seeing UFOs?

PFM AGENT GUERRERO

One of the reasons why you can't discuss this with anyone is it was UFOs, and the Mexican Government needs time to figure out how to deal with this.

JAVIER PINEDA

Understand sir.

PFM AGENT GUERRERO

Good, let me escort you out to the waiting room.

The two got out and went to the waiting room where it was eerie quiet.

PFM AGENT GUERRERO

Mrs. Lopez, will you please come with me?

Mrs. Lopez looked at her husband who nodded at her, then took the two kids and held them back as Agent Guerrero escorted her to the interview room and shut the door.

Mrs. Lopez appeared to be nervous and fearful, not knowing what to expect. Her husband's nod at her signaled to her it would be all right.

PFM AGENT GUERRERO

Mrs. Lopez, last night when the car stopped where the blood was found on the Hiway, did you get out of the car to look?

MRS. LOPEZ

No sir, I remained in the car with my children.

PFM AGENT GUERRERO

You saw your husband and the two young men get out and look at the Hiway, correct?

Yes, they all looked then got back in the car, and then Oscar drove us to the police where he made the report.

PFM AGENT GUERRERO

Did you and your husband discuss the blood?

MRS. LOPEZ

No, as it would have upset the Children.

PFM AGENT GUERRERO

How about the others?

MRS. LOPEZ

No. They didn't discuss much either, though I could tell that both Oscar and Javier appeared to be rather shaken.

PFM AGENT GUERRERO

Did you see any UFO's?

MRS. LOPEZ

No, I was busy taking care of my kids who were starting to get a little weary from being cooped up in a car all day long.

PFM AGENT GUERRERO

You didn't see the UFO or the blood on the Hiway.

MRS. LOPEZ

No sir.

PFM AGENT GUERRERO

How about your kids?

MRS. LOPEZ

No. One of them was lying on the floor in the back seat and the other was in my lap with his head against my chest almost asleep.

PFM AGENT GUERRERO

What do you think caused all the blood on the Hiway?

MRS. LOPEZ

I do not know, nor do I want to know.

PFM AGENT GUERRERO

Okay Mrs. Lopez, we appreciate your help in this matter. I'm going to have to ask you not to discuss this with anyone.

The Mexican government is working hard to solve this case, so we must keep the details out of the public eye so that we do not tip off possible criminals involved. Do you promise not to divulge any of this to anyone?

MRS. LOPEZ

Yes, I promise.

PFM AGENT GUERRERO

Good, let me escort you to the waiting room.

The two got out and walked into the waiting room Agent Guerrero then looked at Gabriela Zelaya.

PFM AGENT GUERRERO

Gabriela Zelaya will you please come with me.

Gabriela Zelaya followed Agent Guerrero into the interview room and quickly sat at the table in the middle of the room.

PFM AGENT GUERRERO

Gabriela, will you please tell me what you saw last night when Oscar stopped the car and got out and found the blood?

GABRIELA ZELAYA

Sir, I was in the back seat talking with Mrs. Lopez and didn't see what happened up front.

PFM AGENT GUERRERO

Did you see the UFOs?

GABRIELA ZELAYA

No sir, I wasn't looking forward and only heard about it when Oscar and Javier were talking about it as we drove up to find the police to make the report.

PFM AGENT GUERRERO

Did you see the blood?

GABRIELA ZELAYA

I was sitting in the back seat and did not see it.

PFM AGENT GUERRERO

Do you know Oscar and Javier well?

GABRIELA ZELAYA

Yes, since we were children.

PFM AGENT GUERRERO

Same hometown?

GABRIELA ZELAYA

Yes, we lived within a few blocks of each other.

PFM AGENT GUERRERO

Are you pregnant?

GABRIELA ZELAYA

Yes of course, I think it looks obvious.

PFM AGENT GUERRERO

Congratulations.

GABRIELA ZELAYA

Thank you.

PFM AGENT GUERRERO

Gabriela, it's very important you do not discuss this incident with anyone. The Mexican Government needs time to solve the case and media hysteria will only get in the way.

GABRIELA ZELAYA

I understand.

PFM AGENT GUERRERO

Thank you. You appear to be far more mature than many young women your age.

GABRIELA ZELAYA

Where I grew up in Honduras, we had to learn lot to take care of ourselves early. It was rough growing up there.

PFM AGENT GUERRERO

Yes, I can imagine.

Gabriela appeared to be a very pleasant person. Agent Guerrero knew she probably had a rough life ahead of her, *but it could be no worse than where she came from.*

PFM AGENT GUERRERO

Gabriela, let me escort you out to the waiting room where you can be with your friends. I appreciate your honesty and frankness.

Agent Guerrero took Gabriela to the waiting room and approached one of the Sargent's and asked:

PFM AGENT GUERRERO

Where is your FAX machine. I need to fax a few things to PFM headquarters in Mexico City.

POLICE OFFICER

Right over here Agent Guerrero.

The police officer stated and led him to the corner that had several electronic items and a desktop computer.

Agent Guerrero, then quickly wrote out a cover sheet to Jose Mercado and then set the documents which contained drawings and notes on the fax machine, then dialed the private fax number and hit send. One by one the fax machine sucked in the papers and scanned them and transmitted them to the destination.

Jose Mercado was expecting the faxes and when he heard the fax machine ring he walked over and watched the sheets start coming out. He reached out and grabbed each sheet as it was being dispensed and looked them over. He of course was interested in the written report but when the drawings started coming out, he immediately focused on them.

This was a huge break. This was the first time they had viable pictures of what the observer/eyewitness thought they had seen.

Agent Guerrero using superior investigatory techniques, having interviewed each person individually got those drawings independently and they certainly corroborated each other nicely. These were innocent decent young adults who were raised to be honest and forthright.

They were some of the best young adults of Honduras which was a terrible shame the country was so screwed up they allowed the future generation with the best possible leadership skills and disposition to leave the country.

Many *less desirables* would remain in Honduras, which meant if the country continued to allow this humanity drain to occur. At the present time, it seemed wasn't much hope for the future of Honduras.

After studying the drawings and intently studying Agent Guerrero's copious notes, that were easy to read thanks to his wonderful handwriting, of a very well-educated man, conveyed the poignant details and elucidated the real picture the President of Mexico was not going to want to hear.

Aliens were killing and abducting people in Mexico, and based on the recent investigations, they were despicable cannibals.

These Aliens also apparently had super high technology and were thus most likely untouchable.

Jose Mercado's recommendation in a few minutes when he would call the President of Mexico was to immediately call the President of the United States and ask for help. There was no way Mexico was prepared to deal with advanced aliens doing this sick business of barbarous cannibalism.

The phone rang and Mexico President's secretary answered.

MEXICO PRESIDENT'S SECRETARY

Hello. How can I help you?

JOSE MERCADO

Good morning this is Jose Mercado with the Policía Federal Ministerial.

MEXICO PRESIDENT'S SECRETARY

What can I do for you, Mr. Mercado.

JOSE MERCADO

The President asked me to call immediately when I was ready to make a report on the situation North of Guadalajara.

MEXICO PRESIDENT'S SECRETARY

One moment Mr. Mercado, let me see if the President is available.

A moment later the President's secretary came back to the phone.

MEXICO PRESIDENT'S SECRETARY

Mr. Mercado, one moment please, I will transfer your call.

After a dial tone, the President of Mexico picked up the phone.

PRESIDENT OF MEXICO

Hello Jose, what do you have to report.

Sir, we have another incident, we believe associated with Alien cannibals. We have several adult eyewitnesses, forensic reports, footprints, etc. to establish it was the same perpetrators as before.

The Mexican President responded not quite yet knowing what his next move should be when Jose Mercado helped him come to a decision.

PRESIDENT OF MEXICO

This is very disturbing.

JOSE MERCADO

Sir, if I may be so blunt, this is a much bigger problem than what Mexico can handle on our own.

PRESIDENT OF MEXICO

What do we do next?

JOSE MERCADO

Mr. President, we have a couple American FBI agents that will be at the crime scene in a short while who will get to see what they have seen before and will no doubt report to their government.

I suggest you call the America President as soon as the FBI agents are in full agreement with us on our assessment and ask for help.

PRESIDENT OF MEXICO

Jose, I think we already have enough information based on past investigations. I'm not going to delay for the FBI men to make their report.

I agree with you. This is a much larger problem than we can handle, and I fear it may be too large for the United States as well. God help us.

JOSE MERCADO

All right Mr. President, would you like me to fax you the report Agent Guerrero just sent me?

PRESIDENT OF MEXICO

Yes Jose, that would be helpful. I think I will be meeting with the U.S. Ambassador shortly and I would like to have that with me when we talk.

JOSE MERCADO

Ok, I will fax it to you immediately. Please call my cell

phone if you need any other information.

PRESIDENT OF MEXICO
I will. Thank you.

JOSE MERCADO
You are welcome Mr. President.

The President of Mexico hung up then and there was just a dial tone on the telephone line.

Meanwhile Agent Guerrero sat and chatted with the eyewitnesses, doing small talk, not really expecting any developments until the two FBI men arrived which he suspected would be within the hour.

True to his expectations, FBI agents Bentley Boyd and Charles Gable arrived within the hour. They didn't look all that spunky, leaving Washington DC in the wee hours in the morning with little sleep or naps since then, as they poured over reports.

By the time the two FBI men arrived at Tepechitlán, Zacatecas, Mexico, the two presidents had already held a teleconference including inviting a few members of the National Security Staff into the room for the conference call.

Today would be a little different than before as the Mexican President now desperate over the situation said he would call the Directorate General of Civil Aeronautics (DGAC, Mexico) and inform him, he had given the American President authorization for immediate flyovers with the American Air Force to confront the aliens.

The President then had his National Security Advisor contact the joint chiefs and immediately initiate surveillance of the area near the reported scene of the incident. Within an hour, the men at March Air Force Base who were a day away from moving their equipment out of the temporary hanger to be sent back to bases they originated, one of which was Clovis New Mexico, Special Operations directorate, were suddenly surprised to get the OP-IMMEDIATE orders.

The U2 and SR-72 pilots, who were well rested and only mustering for the move, soon found themselves back in the improvised ready and briefing room built in the hanger as their missions unfolded.

The U2, old and slow, didn't take as much to prepare. Gassed up and mission package loaded soon found itself rolling down the runway. At the end of the runway, it went almost vertical. Its rate of climb ratio was impressive especially if you understood you were watching a design that flew in 1955, though it did have new far more efficient jet engines than what flew just a few years before, mainly because the Pentagon wanted cheap reconnaissance over Syria, Libya, Iraq, and Afghanistan.

Air Force personnel on the ground enjoyed hearing the nice loud engines of the U2 which launched the lightweight plane up into the stratosphere, soon to be sailing along at 75,000 feet thanks to its upgraded propulsion system, rumored to have been designed for the new SR-75 coming soon.

The SR-72 was a little more complicated and the Air Force and the CIA balked at launching it during daylight, especially next to I-215 full of traffic, a lot of which were drivers heading to Las Vegas gambling mecca from Southern California beach cities.

But since a senior 4-star general gave explicit orders to get the plane airborne as soon as it was ready to go, shook up the fabric of the chain of command who *jumped through their asses* to make it happen.

The control tower was advised to hold all other traffic and get everyone the hell out of its way to reduce the amount of exposure to the busy freeway that ran past it.

The SR-72, sometimes confused with the SR-75, had an interesting takeoff. It rolled out of the hanger, down to the end of the runway and took off. It too went vertically very quickly and didn't take long to reach 100,000 feet long before it crossed the Mexican border heading south.

The NRO had repositioned a KH-14 satellite over this area and was just about to relocate it to focus back on Washington DC where they monitored spies. NRO was suddenly redirected and put the KH-14 directly under control of the special operations team that now oversaw the missions of the U2 and the SR-72 and reported directly to the joint chiefs via their special interface.

People in the bowels of the Pentagon were soon observing the area near the Caravan, looking for the aliens who had got away once before.

Meanwhile F22A squadrons were being scrambled out of Texas. Even though they were officially *stood down*, they got back into readiness condition as if they had been magically transported back to the good ole SAC days with General Curtis LeMay riding shotgun and directing traffic.

***

MY SON IS MISSING

EXT. DAY. MEXICAN DESERT AREA EAST OF HIWAY 23.

General Fukua de Hundan walked up the hill with his military attachés to survey the burial place. Reports had stated grave robbers had dug up the remains.

A sense of rage permeated out of General Fukua de Hundan who felt his son's grave had been desecrated. The general might have been older than all his accompanying troops, but he was in as good shape since he worked out vigorously every day to avoid Cosmic Space Sickness.

There were big holes starting to blow full of sand and dirt that once contained the canvas draped bodies buried there. The question is where did they take the bodies and who had them?

General Fukua de Hundan had seen enough in a few minutes including car tire tracks all over the area left from Mexican and American Army Units. He knew this camp site had been thoroughly investigated.

GENERAL FUKUA DE HUNDAN

The Earth people know we were here, they will probably come back, so make sure the security rovers keep a close eye on everything.

GENERAL'S AID

What about picking up more Caravan stragglers? The soldiers are starting to expect protein in their diets.

GENERAL FUKUA DE HUNDAN

The security patrols will have to stay focused on the task at hand. If you want to gather up more Earth people to feed the troops, then you need to send out additional craft. None of the security patrols are to be distracted by any extraneous events.

GENERAL'S AID

What do you think they did with the bodies of our buried men?

GENERAL FUKUA DE HUNDAN

What do you think we would do if we were in their shoes?

GENERAL'S AID

Probably take them to a lab and study them.

GENERAL FUKUA DE HUNDAN

That's where they are. I would like to retrieve the bodies before we leave the planet and take them home with us.

GENERAL'S AID

Do we have adequate storage?

GENERAL FUKUA DE HUNDAN

By the amount of space-food we have consumed, there should be plenty of space to store the corpses in refrigerated storage.

GENERAL'S AID

The crew might not like that.

GENERAL FUKUA DE HUNDAN

Some superstitions?

GENERAL'S AID

Yes sir, that's why we bury them when we can and do burials at-space, so we are not confronted with their spirits.

GENERAL FUKUA DE HUNDAN

Nobody has ever proven what happens to their spirits when they die, I'm not concerned.

Find a ship that will readily take them and then inform their commander, that ship gets to send their people to the planets first when we reach home.

GENERAL'S AID

That should provide some motivation.

GENERAL FUKUA DE HUNDAN

Especially when they realize that since they are coming home to a hero's welcome, there will be plenty of positive public affection for them.

GENERAL'S AID

I think I know just the ship and commander who would be interested in taking those bodies *if we can get them back.*

GENERAL FUKUA DE HUNDAN

We'll get them back or Planet Earth will severely regret not giving them back to us.

GENERAL'S AID

General, may I remind you the Earth People also have hydrogen bombs they could attack us with.

GENERAL FUKUA DE HUNDAN

They might get lucky and get a few shots in and destroy some of our ships, but if they do that, we'll make sure they have no second opportunity.

GENERAL'S AID

You wouldn't release the *Planet Scavengers* on these poor defenseless Earth people?

GENERAL FUKUA DE HUNDAN

We can program them to have a limited life span, so they only tear up part of the planet as a warning.

GENERAL'S AID

Other galactic powers may not appreciate our approach.

GENERAL FUKUA DE HUNDAN

Now that Heisibing Empire is severely licking their wounds, other possible collaborators will not be too enthused to join in to punish us for fear we might give them the same treatment.

GENERAL'S AID

You have a good point there.

GENERAL FUKUA DE HUNDAN

Let's walk back down to the campfires and enjoy the company of the men.

GENERAL'S AID
Yes sir, it's my privilege to do so.

The two Generals walked back down the hill knowing now there would be a confrontation with the Earth people to get back the bodies of their dead.

VOICEOVER
(GENERAL'S AID) THOUGHT
If they are carved up for scientific study, and the Generals son is in pieces, it might not turn out to be so auspicious for the Earth people.

Shortly after they started serving portions of Earth people to the troops and the General tasted the delicacy, one of his officers approached.

CARSOPIAN OFFICER
Sir, we have detected inbound high-speed aircraft.

GENERAL FUKUA DE HUNDAN
How far away are they and what's their disposition?

CARSOPIAN OFFICER
The Aircraft is traveling at a speed of 4000 HTG's and is at an altitude of 100,000 feet, earth measurements.

GENERAL FUKUA DE HUNDAN
What is the HTG speed compared to Earth measurements?

CARSOPIAN OFFICER
Earth people would measure it around 3,500 miles per hour.

GENERAL FUKUA DE HUNDAN
How soon will they be a threat?

CARSOPIAN OFFICER
In less than 15 minutes.

GENERAL FUKUA DE HUNDAN
Send up a squadron and intercept them and using Earth translators tell them to turn around or we'll shoot them down.

The U2 was lucky the SR-72, a 3-seater version spy plane was way out in front. The aliens launched a squadron of fighters that could accelerate to Mach-nine in 60 seconds and slow down just as quick because of the anti-gravity devices aboard each Carsopian Fighter.

Because of the extreme risk SR-72 flew because of Russian S-700 missiles that only CIA and NSA knew about, a 3rd crew member was added in a 3rd seat behind the Pilot and the Photographic Intel Officer (PIO) using the same KH-14 imagery capability built in.

This third person, the Self Defense Officer (SDO), operated the self-defense equipment and jammers and communicated off hull to other CIA, NRO, and Air Force assets via an array of encrypted communications devices.

Also, if the SDO had his flight suit wired to the self-destruct mechanism of the plane. The pilot and PIO were trained that if the SDO punched out of the aircraft, it would self-destruct in less than 10 seconds. Therefore, if they had any reservations of punching out, knowing they had less than 10 seconds to live, had a motivating factor.

Lessons learned from Gary Powers in 1958 still had an influence on security features of all future spy planes. These systems were compartmentalized, and the crews were never allowed to know all the details.

One of the other dirty secrets the crew didn't know was the SDO could be punched out remotely to ensure they never attempted to defect with all that super sensitive equipment we could ill afford to have enemy's reverse engineer.

Another collateral duty of the SDO was to keep the pilot and PIO honest. As part of his security tasking, he validated the mission and reconstructs. The SDO provided an independent assessment and worked for a different agency.

The SDO understood the critical nature of his job because flawed intelligence could have corrosive effects and put battlefield commanders in jeopardy if they were operating on flawed intelligence.

Most of the time the pilots and PIO's did their jobs with absolute precision. They didn't need a cheerleader to convince them to go out on these harrowing missions that could easily cost them their lives.

Just like other people in dangerous roles, they answered to a higher calling. The biggest flaw in all this enterprise was human errors. The SDO's primary role was besides affirmative backup but also to intervein to prevent human errors from causing a mission failure or even an abort due to mismanagement, misjudgment, or some other factor that could ostensibly slip into the mission.

Randy, Lee, and Kevin were totally engaged in this sweep along Mexico's Hiway 23, the route the Caravan's took. This was the SR-72 crew that had first detected the alien ships that suddenly disappeared recently. Since there were no detections or any indication, the aliens were on the planet, the special projects and observation group was just about disbanded and sent back to their home bases.

To suddenly fly this sortie had a surreal effect on them. Two months ago, none of these men believed in UFO's and would tell someone who claimed they existed, that person was full of crap.

It's a very interesting metamorphism they went through when it was themselves who determined such did probably exist.

The cockpit of the SR-72 full of modern electronics, surveillance systems, and photonics with the same capability of the KH-14 satellite required extraordinary training and education to operate and exploit all its capability. For each hour of flight, the crews spent one-week training.

The trainers were extremely high tech and had identical cockpits. To be able to fly continuously at 3,500 miles per hour they could not have windows on the aircraft. They had cameras. They flew by camera and avionics. The entire flight was autopilot, with human management to validate the systems were performing properly or perform emergency procedures if required.

The main person in the cockpit was the Photographic Intel Officer (PIO) who operated the surveillance equipment. He had to operate the systems at the same time to ensure they were performing as expected. From takeoff to touchdown the PIO was totally focused on the mission package and what he had to do.

The costs were extraordinary. If all tangible costs were factored in, one scientist claimed the costs were one million dollars a mile.

But to have KH-14 capability at 100,000 feet provided INTEL far more extravagant than one could imagine.

When asked what the photonics was like, Lee (PIO) answered:

LEE

It would be like taking the Hubble Space Telescope within orbit of Mars to take Mars pictures.

Part of the data stream designed specifically to detect aliens wasn't observable aboard the SR-72. INTEL analysts who were compartmentalized could pull that extra stuff out in their labs that nobody else had access to. No doubt they provided it to Majestic 12.

One might say there was some apprehension, fear, and inquisitive thoughts going through their heads as they flew in an alignment to travel over the former alien bivouac area. It didn't seem logical they would go back to the same spot, but none of them had the knowledge that General Fukua de Hundan was going through a mild crisis, with a heavy heart of killing his own son on this voyage.

General Fukua de Hundan had a personal attachment now to Earth especially until he was able to retrieve his son's body. If it meant confrontation with Earth that had a technological score card of 1.5, he was not concerned whatsoever. Planets with score cards as high as 7.0 in the past were pushovers for the Carsopians.

Earth had no way of knowing the countermeasures and techniques General Fukua de Hundan had at his disposal, which he had no objection to utilize.

The SR-72 pilot Randy asked the PIO Lee:

RANDY

Lee, are you getting any good stuff yet?

LEE

No, nothing yet, Randy.

Kevin sitting in the far back with his SDO instrumentation suite had more displays than the other two since he was the watch dog and had to always know what was going on in the mission. In a sense the SDO is like a conductor of a passenger train, in charge who gave orders to the engineer (pilot in this case).

At about 5 minutes to the target area, suddenly there were bright lights that zipped past them.

RANDY

What the hell was that?

After more bright lights zipping past for a few minutes, they suddenly heard:

VOICE FROM UHF RECEIVER

American Aircraft, we want you to immediately turn around, or you will be destroyed.

Kevin yelled out:

KEVIN

I'm getting all kinds of sensor readings around us; something is going on.

Looking at the six flat screens around the cockpit that were designed to give the pilot a video substitute for windows, there was suddenly a dozen extremely strange looking craft flying parallel to the SR-72.

Lee yelled out:

LEE

WTF is that?

RANDY

We are going at 3500 miles per hour, and they are flying parallel with us.

KEVEN

Gentlemen, congratulations, you have now just witnessed what you think other officers saw when you claimed they were crazy nuts.

Unexpectedly the three heard a voice:

VOICE FROM UHF RECEIVER

America Aircraft turn around now, or you will be destroyed.

RANDY

What do we do?

KEVIN

Those craft look very dangerous. It's 12 of them and one of us. I'd say we don't stand a chance.

RANDY

I agree with you. They obviously got our frequency as they just communicated with us.

LEE

We recording all this?

KEVIN

Yes, it's all in the buffer we can send to the satellite immediately.

RANDY

Kevin, tell them we are going to turn now, but we can only turn slowly.

KEVIN

Roger that.

Communications were exchanged, and the aliens flew close while the SR-72 slowly started turning and heading back to California.

KEVIN

Unidentified aircraft, we are turning now. Please hold your fire.

The Carsopians monitoring all frequencies quickly received the communications and artificial intelligence from the command ship instructed the interceptors:

CARSOPIAN ARTIFICIAL INTELLIGENCE (CAI)

The Earth ship is complying with your instructions, standby for further orders, do not fire on that craft.

RANDY

How soon before the refueling?

KEVIN

About 15 minutes from now.

It took about 5 minutes to reverse course and the first thing the SR-72 crew thought as they were slowing down: *how soon can they meet the air refueling tanker.*

Even though they had plenty of fuel for a while, the SR-72 *drank fuel like a drunken sailor*. Typical of a lot of fighter pilots, they are always *thinking about fuel. That's* because getting more gas was a hell of a lot more enjoyable than to be forced to land at another base or worse yet, bail out and explain why they crashed a billion-dollar airplane.

While the pilot and the PIO were busy working out the refueling details, Kevin was in the back seat doing a reconstruct and packaging a *Quick Look Report* that would go directly to the Joint Chiefs and the Secretary of the Air Force who would then censor it and give the CIA what they felt they wanted to give them.

The Pentagon didn't know the CIA read everything they ever sent back and forth.

CIA and the NSA had their special cells who used the intercepted reports and always had a poker face when talking with Air Force Officials, acting quite surprised at their findings.

In many cases the CIA had already read it and studied it 12 hours prior, or sometimes even longer. Accordingly, censoring the report really was a waste of time and only delayed the inevitable.

CIA analyst Jack Boone expected something like this would occur and had warned his superiors not to do overt surveillance on the aliens. The way they did this espoused hostile intention.

A less threatening posture would have been to send someone out in a Military vehicle with no weapons and peacefully and respectfully confront the aliens and discover why they were here and what their intentions were.

Based on Kevin's *Quick Look Report*, being able to send up a squadron of aircraft out of nowhere that could fly as fast if not faster than SR-72 really displayed a technological advantage Earth probably had no means of dealing with.

Shortly after CIA Agent Jack Boone started reading the report the CIA cell gave him, the Air Force and Pentagon didn't know they could easily obtain, another quite disturbing development occurred which he now discussed with his boss.

CIA AGENT JACK BOONE

The dumb sons of a bitches are sending a squadron of F22As out to the aliens. The idiots sending these aircraft do not understand, all they will end up doing is pissing off the aliens who will most likely just shoot down all those aircraft.

CIA AGENT WADE BAKER
(JACK BOONE'S SUPERVISOR)

What can we do about it? Nobody knows we can read their information, and it will create a circus environment if we do a power play to get the Air Force to recall the squadron as it will no doubt tip off the Air Force, we are infiltrating their secure communications.

CIA AGENT JACK BOONE

I know the Air Force doesn't like the CIA unless we are giving them huge piles of money for special projects, the only way we can get this squadron to return to their base would be to expose our capability.

CIA AGENT WADE BAKER

There must be another way to get them to return before they meet the aliens. It will probably take a Presidential order to recall the jets.

CIA AGENT JACK BOONE

I suppose we could fake it and tell the President that one of our moles in the Air Force has just informed us what's going on and we need him to recall the jets so we can meet the aliens on our terms in a peaceful manner to avoid what could end up being exposed to the world if those planes start getting shot down out of the sky."

CIA AGENT WADE BAKER

F22As are very stealthily, perhaps the aliens will not spot them?

JACK BOONE

The F22A's have a radar cross section 100 times larger than the SR-72. See how fast they spotted the SR-72? Plus, the SR-72 flies three times as fast consequently the aliens will have a much larger picture and three times the warning time.

CIA AGENT WADE BAKER

What do you think will happen to all these F22As?

JACK BOONE

If you think for a moment, the fact Man has never left this planet, but the Russians can shoot down the F22As with S-700 missiles, just think what an advance alien race could do with fighter planes that can fly 3500 miles per hour.

WADE BAKER

You think the squadron of F22As would convey an act of aggression the aliens would immediately counter?

JACK BOONE

They gave us the warning with the SR-72. I think that if they see a squadron of F22A's coming, especially if one of our hot shot pilots lets loose a missile towards them, they will most likely shoot them all down.

WADE BAKER

Okay, I'm not sure I can reach the President soon enough to recall the planes.

JACK BOONE

What would you do if a nuclear war was starting, would you go via the politically correct BS or would you call the man direct?

WADE BAKER

Well as you know since you are a history buff, even though a Navy Captain went to the White House on December 6, 1941, the staffer refused to wake the president citing his health.

JACK BOONE

That wasn't a health issue, they knew the attack was coming and FDR wanted plausible deniability.

WADE BAKER

What makes you think that would not happen again?

JACK BOONE

I have something you are not aware of.

WADE BAKER

What's that?

JACK BOONE

The President's private cell phone number he gave to the DCI.

WADE BAKER

How did you get it?

JACK BOONE

X-Division gets a lot of toys and capabilities for contingencies for a moment like now.

WADE BAKER

Okay, give me the number, I'll call him, but I want you to know if I get fired over this, I will personally hunt you down and kill you with my own two bare hands.

JACK BOONE

Are the lives of 24 pilots worth the risk?

WADE BAKER

You know I don't want them to suffer harm.

JACK BOONE

With all due respect, those aliens who obviously came here from another planet including possibly outside our solar system are so far more advanced than us, those pilots will be killed so quick, they will not even know what hit them.

CIA analyst Jack Boone's supervisor, Wade Baker, first wrote down the number, wondering how the hell Jack got the President's private cell phone number then made the call.

The President and the NSC would easily trace the call back to the CIA headquarters at Langley and the DCI would no doubt be given a call within the next few minutes. Jack Boone's ass was on the line.

The phone rang and after the 2nd ring, the President picked up looking at the caller I.D.

PRESIDENT OF THE USA

Mr. Baker, what can I do for you?

The President had looked at the special information on his caller I.D. Because the President was being called by a government agency, due to records management regulations it was treated as an official call and the conversation was automatically transcribed and filed in the Presidents papers and documents that could receive subpoena in a court case.

Also, since it was a government-to-government transaction to the white house, the agency (CIA) and location was displayed on the special I-phone which the public didn't have available.

Secret Service paid the Telcom giant Quality Future Networks (QFN) large sums to build the device and make it compatible in software to other integrated phones the public used.

WADE BAKER

Mr. President, we have just received word from our source that our Joint Chiefs just launched a squadron of F22As heading to the probable Alien landing sight down in Mexico.

PRESIDENT OF THE USA

I've not given any such permissions, I'm not aware of any such missions.

WADE BAKER

Mr. President, we know the Aliens are there and we know a lot about them and my analyst Jack Boone, and I believe they are rather advanced and all those F22As will be shot down and probably provoke the aliens.

PRESIDENT OF THE USA

Why am I hearing from you and not the DCI?

WADE BAKER

We are jumping the chain of command since we have very little time to deal with this and it will take an immediate order from you to turn those jets around before all those pilots lose their lives.

PRESIDENT OF THE USA

This sounds like a possible disaster in the making.

WADE BAKER

Mr. President, we believe there are other ways we should approach the Aliens, and brandishing weapons isn't a good way to meet them.

PRESIDENT OF THE USA

When did those F22s take off?

WADE BAKER

About seven minutes ago, sir?

PRESIDENT OF THE USA

How long will it take the planes to get to the area the aliens are in?"

WADE BAKER

Assuming they are flying in super cruise mode doing at least Mach 2, they will be there less than an hour.

PRESIDENT OF THE USA

Sounds like we are quickly running out of time to deal with this mess.

WADE BAKER

Mr. President, we do not think the F22s will make it to the target as the Aliens will probably spot them maybe as far away as 500 miles with their advanced technology, and will shoot them down immediately.

PRESIDENT OF THE USA

You think they can do it?

WADE BAKER

Has the CIA briefed you on the SR-72 flight?

PRESIDENT OF THE USA

Yes, we should be getting a report shortly on what they found.

WADE BAKER

Sir, with all due respect the SR-72 didn't find anything, the Aliens sent out a squadron of extremely fast aircraft who told them to turn around or they would shoot them down.

PRESIDENT OF THE USA

I've not been informed about that.

WADE BAKER

The SR-72 is returning to California with no pictures of the aliens, except for the interceptors who met them.

PRESIDENT OF THE USA

Sounds like you really are jumping the chain of command.

WADE BAKER

Mr Presideent, I do not think the people who sent the F22As have an appreciation of the level of technology the Aliens have already demonstrated and if we push their button, you may have to explain to the American people a lot of things you really want to keep under wraps.

PRESIDENT OF THE USA

All right, I'll call the joint chiefs or have my national security advisor call them and direct them to return the F22s to their bases.

WADE BAKER

Thank you, Mr. President, we are fearful for their lives.

PRESIDENT OF THE USA

Mr. Baker, do your friends call you Wade?

WADE BAKER

Yes sir, that's my name and I use it.

PRESIDENT OF THE USA

Okay Wade, this is what I want you to do. I want you and your analyst to come to the White House immediately so we can have a talk. I will also invite the DCI over for the discussion.

WADE BAKER

Yes sir, we work for you, whatever you wish us to do we will.

PRESIDENT OF THE USA

What's your analyst's name?

WADE BAKER

The analyst who figured this out is Jack Boone.

PRESIDENT OF THE USA

Good. Bring Jack Boone, get over here quickly. Fly in one of your CIA helicopters. I do not want a traffic jam as an excuse for you not to get here pronto.

WADE BAKER

Will do so, sir. Do we have permission to land at the White House South Lawn?

PRESIDENT OF THE USA

I'll inform the Secret Service you'll be dropping in via Helicopter in a short while. They will contact the CIA and give you specific instructions on how to get here.

WADE BAKER

Alright sir, we'll call the CIA Watch Officer and inform him you ordered us to the White House via helicopter or the fastest means possible.

PRESIDENT OF THE USA

Okay Wade, I'm looking forward to meeting you. You are a brave man, and I think you just stepped on a lot of toes, but you also saved me a lot of grief. See you shortly.

The President hung up.

Wade Baker called the CIA's Watch Officer who was another political appointee GS-15 wanting to become an SES grade officer and willing to kiss any ass or screw any ugly well- connected woman to help him get there.

The Watch Officer was immediately pissed off and was just about to tell Wade Baker to stand down and STFU, when he was contacted by the Secret Service who was already to give him specific instructions.

SECRET SERVICE TRANSPORTATION COORDINATOR

Hello, is this the CIA Watch Officer?

CIA WATCH OFFICER

Yes, that's me.

Just like the President's special phone, the CIA watch officer could immediately know who called, where they were and if there was surveillance video nearby actually look at the caller without their knowledge.

SECRET SERVICE TRANSPORTATION COORDINATOR

The President has ordered Mr. Wade Baker and his analyst Jack Boone to the White House immediately.

CIA WATCH OFFICER

Roger that.

SECRET SERVICE TRANSPORTATION COORDINATOR

Due to traffic concerns and other possible delays, the President wants them to fly over to the white house South Lawn immediately. Also contact the DCI and relay to him the President also wants him there for a meeting ASAP.

CIA WATCH OFFICER

Understand all.

SECRET SERVICE TRANSPORTATION COORDINATOR

When the Helicopter pilot takes off, Secret Service Air Traffic Controllers will vector the craft to the White House South Lawn. Inform the pilot his call sign is Jelly Rowles, so we know it's him when he communicates.

CIA WATCH OFFICER

Will do. Our staff will give the pilot his call sign Jelly Rowles immediately. He's on the landing pad now ready to take off as soon as Mr. Baker and Mr. Boone are aboard the helicopter.

SECRET SERVICE TRANSPORTATION COORDINATOR

Goodbye and thank you for your assistance.

The secret service man hung up and the Watch Officer then directed traffic getting everyone involved marching in the right direction. He also knew the DCI would have a fit with Baker and Boone for whatever stunt they pulled to get called to the White House.

The President is an arm's length away from the National Security Advisor or their designated watch officer.

The President was amused to discover the National Security Advisor was just now getting briefed by the Joint Chiefs on the mission.

In recent days they were operating off the philosophy it was better to ask for forgiveness than for permission.

This was a policy the President was going to have to change for the immediate future, because he intuitively knew, confrontation with advanced Aliens might not be in Earth's best interest.

VOICEOVER

(PRESIDENT OF THE USA) THOUGHT

Even though the sick bastards were eating a few people in the Caravans, it was better to sacrifice a few of those undesirables than to risk the entire population of the planet.

Plus, the public was not ready for the disclosure.

Aliens that are cannibals was not a really good combination for disclosure.

Jack Boone and Wade Baker promptly left their offices, took the elevator, then walked out the service entrance to the helicopter pad where a Sikorsky S-97 *Raider* helicopter painted like a corporate model to disguise its real use was waiting and warmed up and ready to go.

As soon as Jack Boone and Wade Baker got aboard the helicopter the pilot now using the call sign *Jelly Rowles* took off. They did not fly direct to the White house. They were first diverted over Reagan National Airport then went down an air column designed by the secret service to prevent possible terrorists from attacking the White House.

Unknown to the public, any aircraft approaching the white house without secret service permission and flight plan without deviation, would not make it.

Secret Service had 7/24 around the clock aerial surveillance and protection and were tested from time to time to make sure there was no vigilance decrement or lack of attention and focus.

The S-97 looked like a billionaire's personal helicopter. It looked futuristic and had fine lines. In the aerospace industry it was viewed as a very handsome aircraft. With military camouflage paint on it, the appearance was equally awesome.

Program managers in the military procurement business were very pleased with the S-97 helicopter, but they also knew it would take time and duration before all the bugs were exposed and worked out.

Some helicopters flew almost 10 years before serious flaws were discovered requiring engineering changes. But until the lessons were learned, usually through blood sweat and tears, the assumptions and behavior indicated all was going well with that air frame and no doubt it would be placed in combat situations a lot sooner than experts expected, as it was truly a leap in technology.

Eventually the Secret Service guided *Jelly Rowles* helicopter down on the South Lawn where CIA agents Boone and Baker departed, and the helicopter pilot was asked to leave immediately, and transportation would be provided for the two men as soon as their business was completed.

It was happy hour time in Washington DC. The DCI was currently with a few congressmen and corporate friends up at the top of the Washington Hotel, where the drinks were good, and a lot of nice smelling beautiful women were invited quite often to partake in the activities which sometimes included mistresses of powerful leaders enjoying company with what amounted to a concubine out of the public eye.

The Washington Hotel on 15th street had a wonderful bar and was right across from the White House, where staffers and congressmen and lobbyists met quite often. Probably more deals were made in bars at this hotel than anywhere else in town.

The beautiful vivacious strawberry blonde, who had a nickname *Energizer* had the DCI's full attention and even though he was much older and probably would need some Viagra to consummate his interest in her, she no doubt was ready to proceed any way he wanted.

The DCI was just about ready to set up a rendezvous with *Energizer* since there was no possible way, he could be observed leaving the hotel with her. Suddenly a member of his security detailed walked over and whispered he had to leave immediately and would be briefed in the company limo.

These kinds of DCI notifications were not unusual. There was always some shitty deal going on somewhere in the world where DCI had to make management decisions that could instantly result in the loss of an agent's life, if he made the wrong move.

DCI excused himself from the lovely *Energizer* and said he would come back if he could, otherwise he would send her a message and apologies.

Where they had to go via this limo only took 5 minutes and only because they had to go through the main entrance to the White House this time of day because all others were locked up. The secret service was notified he was in route and coming from a block or so away.

The DCI's limo was pulling into the circular driveway about the same time as the helicopter was leaving the South Lawn. As soon as the limo pulled up to the service entrance to the White House out of sight from the press and visitors, the Secret Service escorted the DCI immediately to the Oval Office where the President was already getting to know Jack Boone and Wade Baker. The DCI had met both men before but didn't know them very well as he seldom had any direct communications with them.

It's very unusual for a DCI to walk into the Oval Office and discover two of his employees chatting with the President as if they were old buddies.

No doubt the next day would be filled full of intrigue to figure out how the hell they got here and why.

The DCI wasn't pleased in the least bit discovering his two employees with the President, because it probably meant something *not so good* was just about to come down.

The other thing the DCI knew was these were X-Division men based on their unique special identities. Very few people within the CIA had ever been in X-Division spaces which were considered the most compartmentalized section at headquarters. They even had stricter security than in his office spaces.

The President stated and held out his hand to shake DCI's hand.

THE PRESIDENT OF THE USA

Good to see you, Scott.

DIRECTOR OF THE CIA

Thank you, Mr. President, I guess I'm a little bit behind on what all went down. I got a short briefing in the car on the way over here, so I may not have all the details you want.

THE PRESIDENT OF THE USA

That's ok Scott. Your men here, just saved me a lot of embarrassment.

The CIA has once again proven its worth, protecting the President when the joint chiefs get ahead of themselves.

DIRECTOR OF THE CIA

I'm glad it worked out Mr. President.

THE PRESIDENT OF THE USA

I was very lucky your CIA men intervened when they did because just like analyst Jack Boone predicted, the Aliens detected the squadron of F22A's 500 miles away and scrambled a reception force.

DIRECTOR OF THE CIA

I'm expecting a briefing in a few minutes on the outcome.

WADE BAKER

Sir, I'm the person who was tasked to brief you. Do you want it now since the President is here?

DIRECTOR OF THE CIA

If it's okay with the President, go ahead.

THE PRESIDENT OF THE USA

Fine by me, please brief us now.

WADE BAKER

The Aliens were quickly closing in on the Americans at 4,000 miles per hour when the F22As suddenly turned around and we know intercepted communications the Carsopian's received indicated the F22As had been recalled back to base.

VOICEOVER

With the beam weapon technology, the Carsopians possessed on their interceptors, designed to kill two- mile-long galactic scale battlewagons, would have cut the F22As up like an angry kid smashing a balsa wood airplane.

On one hand, General Fukua de Hundan was elated they turned around, but on the other hand he knew they had made a bee line towards their bivouac area, meaning they knew exactly where his forces were parked.

Fukua de Hundan assumed the Americans would be back, but expected they came to their senses and the next flight would probably be a single aircraft or a land car. That suited him fine because he wanted to get his son's body back, then they would leave the planet.

Enough of the Carsopian troops had rested well enough and enjoyed real gravity for a while, and knowing they would be going home soon, would help prepare them psychologically which went a long way towards preventing Cosmic Space Sickness, which according to experts was exacerbated by psychological conditions.

In a short while all interceptors were back aboard their ships designed to launch them from above or below by the special hangers designed for alternative access. As a precaution several Carsopian Korvette Class Space Warships were sent airborne to do sky surveillance.

Flying at 250,000 feet with excellent sensor packages, the Carsopian Korvette Class space warships would be tracking everything flying within 700 miles. Spread out in four directions operating a couple hundred miles from the bivouac site, the actual trip wire was extended 1000 miles from the Carsopian bivouac area.

There would be no surprise attacks, nor would the Earth men be able to attack them in any fashion. Even an ICBM or a cruise missile would be destroyed long before it came close to be of any danger to the Carsopians.

Back at the White House, the President had been briefed a couple FBI men were now down in Mexico at a police station interviewing some eyewitnesses to the latest Caravan attack. The President would be pragmatic and prevent any American aggression because he knew the obvious.

VOICEOVER

(THE PRESIDENT OF THE USA) THOUGHT

What are we going to throw at the aliens? Spit balls? The answer is: as soon as we could manage, America would have to build a space force. This incident clearly showed how ill-prepared American's are.

As President reflected for a moment observing his friend Scott's body language, he knew the DCI looked very uncomfortable as he knew the protocol of having two agents here before the DCI arrived was probably unnerving him.

The President being quite versed in Government Agencies skullduggeries, especially in the bowels of the CIA knew these brave men had put themselves in a lot of grief coming forward to save all those American lives.

Many times, the messenger is not rewarded, they are punished. What these two men had accomplished was far greater in scope that any whistle blower, including the defector Snowden.

In his gut feeling the President needed to reward them for what they did by protecting them.

THE PRESIDENT OF THE USA

Scott, you are aware these men put themselves in a lot of harm's way by doing what they did.

DIRECTOR OF THE CIA

Yes Mr. President, I understand protocol quite well.

THE PRESIDENT OF THE USA

Scott, your two Agents did one of the most important acts any living CIA personnel has ever done. I want you to assure me and them that no harm will come to them for helping me out.

DIRECTOR OF THE CIA

Yes Mr. President, I will make sure.

THE PRESIDENT OF THE USA

Scott, inform their supervisors I am eternally grateful for what they did and in a couple weeks, I might want to go over to the CIA and personally deliver them a letter of appreciation.

DIRECTOR OF THE CIA

Yes Mr. President, I will brief their supervisors and their chain of command.

THE PRESIDENT OF THE USA

Also, this is a need-to-know compartmentalized action. Unless I specifically clear someone for this incident, they are not entitled to the information, including their supervisors.

DIRECTOR OF THE CIA

Understand all Mr. President.

THE PRESIDENT OF THE USA

Scott, it's obvious what our next move must be.

DIRECTOR OF THE CIA

Mr. President if you don't mind, I don't wish to second guess you.

THE PRESIDENT OF THE USA

Scott, I want someone from the CIA to go down to Mexico to personally take a calling card to the aliens. I know it's a very dangerous assignment and could result in them losing their lives since we have no idea how the aliens would respond to a cold call.

DIRECTOR OF THE CIA

I'm sure we have people in the agency more than willing to go down there."

THE PRESIDENT OF THE USA

How about you Jack, and Wade? Would you guys be willing to go down there?

Wade responded but Jack withheld comment to allow his superior to respond.

WADE BAKER

Yes Mr. President, I'm here to follow your orders as necessary.

THE PRESIDENT OF THE USA

How about you Jack?

JACK BOONE

Mr. President, if Wade sends me down there, I'm more than willing to go.

THE PRESIDENT OF THE USA

Excellent. Scott, this is what I want your two Agents to do. I want them to go to Mexico first thing in the morning. I'll send word to the FBI to have the two agents they have down there to brief them and then arrange to fly them via helicopter over to the Alien's camp.

DIRECTOR OF THE CIA

Mr. President are you not afraid the aliens may their helicopter down?

THE PRESIDENT OF THE USA

Scott, I'm pretty sure these aliens already know a lot about Earth, and they probably expect a helicopter to fly out to them with a visitor.

DIRECTOR OF THE CIA

They must be highly intelligent beings able to travel interstellar in space.

THE PRESIDENT OF THE USA

Alright Jack and Wade, I'm clearing you now for some information you were not aware of. We have six dead alien bodies. These aliens buried them a while back during their last visit.

WADE BAKER

Mr. President, do we know how they died?

THE PRESIDENT OF THE USA

They apparently died from some unknown reason which our pathologists could not determine since we have no knowledge of their civilization.

All three CIA men were rather surprised since none of them knew about the dead aliens. The Air Force Intelligence personnel were good at keeping secrets. Surprisingly they had no INTEL from either the FBI or the State Department alerting them to this situation.

THE PRESIDENT OF THE USA

I do not want you to approach the aliens until daylight tomorrow which gives us time to do a few things. First thing is I'm going to have the Air Force take you to Wright Patterson Air Force Base so you can look at the aliens.

WADE BAKER

Sure thing Mr. President.

THE PRESIDENT OF THE USA

After you get a look at the aliens, then they can fly you down to Guadalajara Mexico and fly you via Helicopter from there to the police station so you can talk with the eyewitnesses before you approach the aliens.

WADE BAKER

What exactly do you wish us to ask the aliens and how do we know they can communicate with us?

THE PRESIDENT OF THE USA

When they forced the SR-72 to turn around they spoke perfect English to the SR-72 crew.

WADE BAKER

That's good to know.

THE PRESIDENT OF THE USA

They're advanced aliens who know our language.

WADE BAKER

Understand Mr. President.

THE PRESIDENT OF THE USA

I want you to ask them why they are here and when they plan on leaving.

The conversation didn't last much longer as the President had distinguished guests waiting:

THE PRESIDENT OF THE USA

Alright gentlemen, you have your Marching Orders. Wade and Jack, make your status reports to Scott only, this matter is compartmentalized as of now. Scott, you will keep me appraised of any developments.

DIRECTOR OF THE CIA

Mr. President, what about the alien response team we have at MIT, shouldn't we be bringing them in for this first encounter with a significant alien presence?

THE PRESIDENT OF THE USA

Scott, if these were simply explorers who arrived in small numbers, the MIT alien response team would be appropriate, and we wouldn't be needing to send your CIA men down there.

DIRECTOR OF THE CIA

Understand, sir.

THE PRESIDENT OF THE USA

But since the Aliens have arrived with a formidable military force, I think this is way above the scope and ability of those MIT researchers who probably have no knowledge of these aliens or how to deal with this extraordinary Alien military force.

DIRECTOR OF THE CIA

I suppose you are right Mr. President.

THE PRESIDENT OF THE USA

Scott, the Aliens have surprised us on many fronts. They can speak our languages which means they probably have been studying us for a while.

DIRECTOR OF THE CIA

That would be the logical conclusion.

THE PRESIDENT OF THE USA

These Aliens have magnificent air power that can fly as fast as our best spy plane means they have the firepower to back up their intentions. Hopefully they are not here to stay.

DIRECTOR OF THE CIA

All right Mr. President, we will assist you in any way necessary.

THE PRESIDENT OF THE USA

Scott your men flew here aboard CIA helicopter the Secret Service sent back to Langley. Would you mind arranging their transportation?

DIRECTOR OF THE CIA

No problem Mr. President I will give them a ride home.

THE PRESIDENT OF THE USA

Thank you, Scott. Call me in the morning around 9:00 A.M. and give me a status report."

DIRECTOR OF THE CIA

Yes sir.

The men left the Oval Office, were escorted out the service entrance where the CIA company car pulled up, and one of the Secret Service men opened the limo door for the men to get in. The limo immediately pulled out and headed back to Langley, where their cars were parked and gave them enough time to fully brief Scott on every detail of what transpired with the aliens.

By the time the limo pulled up to the headquarters building the DCI felt he knew enough to where he could allow the two men to leave, go home and prepare themselves for the trip.

In the morning company cars picked them up and dropped them off directly at the helicopter pad next to the Langley Headquarters building where they boarded another S- 97 painted in corporate colors. Shortly after they were airborne and soon deposited by a hangar at Andrews Airforce base where they were put on a Gulfstream 650 aircraft that immediately took off heading for the Wright Patterson Air Force Base, and the infamous building number 18.

Parts of Wright Patterson Air Force Base had the most secure areas in America and the military. Area 51 might have tested the new aircraft and missiles, but Wright Patterson is where they were designed.

Because of the super secrecy of certain areas of the base including Building 18, when the two alien ships crashed at Roswell New Mexico in 1947, the wreckage as well as the dead aliens were taken to Wright Patterson Air Force base for storage and examination until certain Liberal Senators demanded access because of loose lips they had been informed *that's where our government was secretly holding the aliens*.

Before the senator could get access, all the craft and dead aliens remains were taken to the ultra-secret sector four of Area 51 in the Nevada desert 120 miles north of Las Vegas.

The senators showed up at Wright Patterson Air Force base building 18 and were extremely agitated to see the building was mostly empty contrary to what their informants had promised them.

The Roswell crash debris remained indefinitely at Area-51, and some say that debris remains there today in a deep underground complex at S-4 where the Alien reverse engineering program exists.

Meanwhile, since Wright Patterson is substantially closer to Fort Detrick, in Maryland where virologists and pathogen experts were located for our *Germ Warfare Surveillance and Reaction Directorate*.

The Air Force began an elaborate construction project for building 18 vast underground facilities at Wright Patterson disguised as an emergency shelter in the event of nuclear war. Certain Congressional Oversight people were promised space there in the event such a nuclear war was imminent.

As part of the elaborate disinformation scheme those congressmen were brought there to see the living quarters were comfortable and they had several years' worth of water and dried food stored there for a limited number of people including themselves, ostensibly for continuity of government.

Those facilities were a shell, and only temporarily built to quash any investigation. The rest of the facility was built around this "shelter" and had plenty of room for vast amounts of special instruments and operating rooms to carefully examine the Roswell Aliens and subsequent crash beings.

The Roswell investigation had been long ago completed, and other crash remains from places such as Aztec, New Mexico, Argentina, Siberia, and Antarctica had been also examined over the years.

There had not been any further crashes since President Nixon took office. This fact was often theorized that Aliens now knew we were here and as we grew more sophisticated, they could not keep coming to this planet with impunity.

Also, when some of the Aliens came looking for their crashed shuttle craft that came down from mother ships, often hiding on the dark side of the moon, they discovered the crash remains had been removed and assumed we had recovered the bodies and were on the alert for Alien detections, so they didn't press their luck.

With the explosion of the first Hydrogen Bomb that gives off energy signatures and spectral content that was a fingerprint for either a super nova or a hydrogen bomb explosion, Aliens also realized Earth had some very lethal weapons, so they stood their distance and rarely visited he planet's surface.

Detecting the Carsopian aliens was completely unexpected. Since no further detections of Aliens occurred in many years, top scientists cleared for this Special Access Program information assumed and reported the aliens had left our solar system and evidently were no longer interested in Earth.

Never had there been any indications of advanced Alien civilizations that engaged in cannibalism. This new discovery was mildly shocking to those same top scientists who had no idea of how to address it. They were almost paralyzed in response because it did not make logical sense that an alien race far more advanced than Earth would eat other sentient beings.

However, when the forensic evidence rolled in including additional stomach samples of a couple of the dead aliens demonstrated undigested human remains, which earlier the autopsy missed, there was no denying they were cannibals.

This cannable information caused Majestic 12 to circle the wagons even tighter. Disclosing Aliens was one thing, but admitting they used humans as a food supply would terrify the masses and create vast unpredictable responses. Majestic 12 advised the President that *such revelations would destabilize the planet.*

FBI agents Bentley Boyd and Charles Gable were advised after interviewing the eyewitnesses that two CIA officials would soon be there to ask similar questions and then go visit the aliens.

The FBI agents were directed to put the Hondurans and Lopez family on a helicopter that was being sent to pick them up and fly back to Guadalajara and put them on an FBI jet that would be there to pick them up. Oscar Godoy, Gabriela Zelaya, Javier Pineda, and the Lopez family would be in America a lot sooner than they could imagine.

By the end of the day the three teenagers and the Lopez family would be seeing the city lights of Washington DC as that jet landed at Andrews Airforce Base where they would be carted off to a special CIA compound in West Virginia connected via tunnels to the Greenbrier, a luxury resort located in the Allegheny Mountains near White Sulphur Springs in Greenbrier County, West Virginia

The public was unaware Greenbrier was also a nuclear shelter for Congress for the continuation of government until that was leaked and the government no longer felt it was a viable place to hide the remnants of Congress in a nuclear holocaust.

***

Upon arrival to the Mexican Police Station the analysts Jack Boone and Wade Baker had a number of questions as the police station waiting room was cleared out with the exception of the FBI officials, the eyewitnesses, CIA men, and Agent Guerrero who at first didn't know if he had authorization to turn the eye witnesses over to the FBI to take them to Washington.

That's when Wade Baker educated Agent Guerrero.

WADE BAKER

Agent Guerrero, approximately 14 hours ago the aliens turned our SR-72 around and threatened to destroy it if they didn't leave the air space immediately.

PFM AGENT GUERRERO

That's amazing.

WADE BAKER

A short time later when the Joint Chiefs got buck fever and sent two F22A Squadrons there thinking stealth would help them, we got them turned around just in time before the aliens shot them all down.

The F22As were apparently escorted out of the area and received some unpleasant communications from the Aliens.

Mexico has nothing they can do to deal with the aliens. Even America may not be able to cope due to the technological advances the Aliens exhibit in aircraft performance.

PFM AGENT GUERRERO

These aliens seem kind of scary.

WADE BAKER

Our national science foundation has some MIT researchers standing by to interview all the eyewitnesses to help us try to figure out how to deal with the aliens.

PFM AGENT GUERRERO

I know what you want to do, I just don't know if I'm authorized to hand the eyewitnesses over to you.

WADE BAKER

Agent Guerrero, we understand this is Mexican sovereign territory. We normally would never operate like this. However, due to the extreme urgency of this exigency, we do not have time to play the diplomatic shuffle.

PFM AGENT GUERRERO

I understand you are pressed for time.

WADE BAKER

Jack Boone and I will be meeting with the Aliens soon and hope we survive, but my orders are to ensure our FBI men leave here on those helicopters with the eyewitnesses so the process can begin.

PFM AGENT GUERRERO

What am I supposed to do about it. I can't legally let you take them until Jose Mercado directs me to do so.

WADE BAKER

Agent Guerrero, you are a smart guy, must deal with the Cartels, the Mafia, Chinese infiltration, and a lot of other issues. You just must realize this is one of those occasions where it's best you ask for *forgiveness* than permission.

PFM AGENT GUERRERO

I understand, but you don't realize the position you put me in.

WADE BAKER

We can give you plausible deniability.

PFM AGENT GUERRERO

How can you do that?

WADE BAKER

Explain to Jose Mercado, we insisted you come along with us to meet the aliens to represent Mexico's concern since this is your sovereign territory.

We'll get on our helicopter the same time the eyewitnesses get on the other helicopter and since you are consumed with meeting Aliens, you didn't have time to direct traffic.

PFM AGENT GUERRERO

Okay, you can take the eyewitnesses, but I'm not sure I want to meet the Aliens.

WADE BAKER

Agent Guerrero, this may be the chance of a lifetime. If you don't go with us, you may regret it a few years from now.

PFM AGENT GUERRERO

Alright, I'll go, but it doesn't mean I have to like it.

WADE BAKER

After we give you a little *Cash in Advance*, you might feel differently about it.

The deal was settled, and soon the spies and law enforcement agents were escorting the young adults and Lopez family to a waiting helicopter. They would arrive in Guadalajara in 45 minutes where a jet waited for them to travel to Washington DC and the special interrogations, they would all go through.

The CIA men and Agent Guerrero boarded another helicopter and headed in the direction of the previous alien encampment where it was believed the aliens had returned.

There was nothing special about the area other than they had buried their dead there which no longer existed since they had been moved to building 18-complex at Wright Patterson Air Force Base, where several researchers and special medical teams were at work studying the alien bodies and confirming the cannibalistic nature of them.

Since they were all 10 feet tall weighing approximately 500 pounds, there was a great deal of test of their faiths for this extraordinary event.

Some of these base personnel were Jewish and Christians. The implications were enormous as it undermined most of their religious indoctrination that detailed how all life started on this planet.

These huge aliens traveling from some distant star system certainly posed a great test of their psyche as their humanity was founded on their Christian Judeo values which had no basis for this astonishing revelation.

None of these researchers and medical personnel were exposed to the Roswell or Aztec Alien remains, nor knew they existed, but that was soon to change as they would soon be escorted into a different wing of building 18 complex. By the end of the day, they would have observed three different alien races therefore, in all sizes and shapes.

***

<u>EXT. CGI. MEXICO DESERT. CARSOPIAN SECUITY ROVERS APPROACHING THE ARMY UH-60 BLACKHAWK HELICOPTER.</u>

The Carsopian security rovers had no difficulty spotting the helicopter making a beeline towards them. General Fukua de Hundan was immediately alerted and directed them to escort the Earth craft to the camp where he expected representatives from Earth would be aboard to confront the Carsopians.

One thing he knew for sure was the Earth men had already figured out attacking his forces would be pointless and trigger a response they knew they didn't want to experience.

VOICEOVER (GENERAL FUKUA DE HUNDAN) THOUGHT
Even if the Americans possessed Hydrogen Bombs, my entire fleet would be airborne and out of harm's way long before any force or missiles could get near to strike us.

I could easily lay waste to the planet if I so desired but have no intentions of doing such activity.

My only reason for remaining is to demand the return of my son's carcass so I can take him back to the Carsopian Worlds and reburied in a dignified grave which I could visit from time to time and pay respects, and even cry over.

<u>EXT. DAY. MEXICAN DESERT. AIRBORNE VIA HELICOPTER.</u>

The Helicopter pilots and the passengers had no idea what to expect but when the ultra- modern alien craft suddenly converged on them and flew parallel with them, the sight was rather amazing.

Some passengers felt as if they were part of a science fiction movie looking at something so modernistic that could only be constructed at film studios of Hollywood.

The Carsopian Security-rovers appeared to be at least twice as large as a F22 aircraft. They made no noise and there was no indication of any windows. Whether the craft had beings aboard or not was not known. Without windows they could be robotic.

From a distance as they approached the Alien bivouac area, they could start to see the appearance of the alien space craft parked over many acres. The sight was breath taking.

None of them had ever seen a spacecraft measuring two miles long.

It quickly became quite apparent to Jack Boone and Wade Baker, with the size of those monsters, it would be pointless to engage them in any military venture.

The sheer size alone along with the knowledge they traveled far to get here underscored the difference in effectiveness they must have with their weapon systems, which Earth men had no knowledge of. If these beings were at least 100,000 years more advanced, those weapons might be utterly terrifying.

As the Helicopter neared the landing zone they were directed in perfect English from the escorts.

CARSOPIAN SECURITY ROVER VIA UHF COMMUNICATIONS

Land directly ahead where those individuals are standing and waiting for you.

The helicopter came down where the pilot was directed on what appeared to be a clean temporary landing pad. The security rovers landed astride of the Army UH-60 Blackhawk helicopter which helped to ensure they understood precisely where to land.

As to prevent a mishap with the tall aliens, Wade Baker stated to the pilot:

WADE BAKER

Shut down the engines so the rotors do not strike any of these aliens.

AMERICAN ARMY PILOT

Roger that.

The UH-60 Blackhawk helicopter twin General Electric T700-GE-701C/D turboshaft engines slowly spun down to a stop and the rotor blades stopped spinning as a result.

The men wearing all wearing business suits, exited the helicopter and approached the aliens standing 30 feet away. Behind them were multitudes of Alien Forces lined up as if they were ready for a parade.

The alien uniforms were impressive and a moth purple color, not Army Green or Desert Camouflage as one might expect.

But then these were aliens, and we have no basis to understand why they colorized their uniforms the way they had.

At the distance of 30 feet away, the Aliens didn't seem so huge but as they got close, their size became immediately apparent.

Even though Jack Boone wanted to speak to the aliens, he knew his supervisor Wade Baker out ranked him and out of protocol should speak for the group. Wade Baker was a charismatic and intelligent individual. He didn't need to be schooled in what to say to the aliens.

Wade Baker had numerous briefings and exchanges with domestic and foreign dignitaries over the years and was comfortable engaging in conversation and carried himself with a great degree of dignity and sincerity.

The CIA/PFM men approached the aliens in a business-like manner showing no fear or any sign of aggression. Their demeaner though professional also conveyed a sense of humanity.

Wade knew the awesome responsibility placed on him in addition to the CIA, but his country and indirectly for the world.

Never had there been such a meeting with Aliens of this nature, though there were still rumors circulating that President Kennedy approved an alien exchange program early in his administration called project SERPO.

General Fukua de Hundan was a master at analyzing the character and disposition of others. The humans were not too much different than the Carsopians. The only noticeable difference was the major size difference and their large almond shaped eyes. But in proportion to their bodies, they were the appropriate size. The Carsopians also had better vision than humans as their eyes had a dynamic focus thanks to the almond shape and focusing with greater distance between each eye since their heads were double the size of the humans.

Wade was hopeful the more advanced aliens understood English, and they could communicate. He initiated the conversation and introductions they agreed upon while flying to the site in the helicopter.

WADE BAKER

Hello, I'm Wade Baker, I'm with the American Government here on Earth. This is my colleague, Jack Boone.

Wade and Jack simultaneously bowed in respect and held the bow for approximately 15 seconds.

WADE BAKER

The area we are at is in the country of Mexico.I would like to introduce Mexican Policía Federal Ministerial (PFM) Agent Carlos Guerrero representing the government of Mexico.

Like Wade Baker and Jack Boone prior, Agent Carlos Guerrero bowed in the most respectful manner.

General Fukua de Hundan stood quietly for a moment sizing up the Earth men who had introduced themselves. He would speak when he was ready, not before.

General Fukua de Hundan had an ear bud in that provided him with real time translation from English to Carsopian Standard which over half the Galaxy spoke, including other empires, captured worlds, and their enemies such as the Heisibing.

No other Carsopian would speak without General Fukua de Hundan's permission. His authority was absolute, and nobody spoke for him under any circumstances.

General Fukua de Hundan had life and death decision making for every Carsopian that was part of his expeditionary force. After several minutes simply staring at the Earth people who appeared to be unusually patient, he eventually spoke.

General Fukua de Hundan spoke in Standard Carsopian. His statements lasted almost 30 seconds. Then he stopped and it was quiet for a couple moments and one of his aids standing by him had some type of black box strapped over his shoulder that had an audio transmitter.

The real time Carsopian translator that had recorded and analyzed human voices, picked pleasant voices to reconstruct an output from the real time translator that now repeated the entire phrase in English so the Earth people could understand what he was stating.

GENERAL FUKUA DE HUNDAN VIA TRANSLATOR SPEAKER

I'm General Fukua de Hundan, of the Carsopian Empire. My Fleet and I have stopped here on your planet for some rest and relaxation.

We recently stopped here on our way to the war zone, so that my men could feel real gravity and we could replace our reprocessed water with fresh water.

We left, did our battle, and now are returning to our home planets.

We stopped once again here to do more Rest and Relaxation.

Wade Baker, who was an astute observer in military operations and history buff, knew the General had given him a rare opportunity to pose a question to open a dialog.

WADE BAKER

General Fukua de Hundan, were you successful in your battle?

GENERAL FUKUA DE HUNDAN

Yes, we destroyed over half of the Heisibing Fleet which had been a threat to our colony of *Cui*.

WADE BAKER

Congratulations General Fukua de Hundan, on your victory.

GENERAL FUKUA DE HUNDAN

Thank you.

General Fukua De Hundan started to realize this Earth person Wade Baker was moreover dynamic but also a quick thinker and partially diplomatic.

WADE BAKER

General Fukua de Hundan, how soon do you anticipate finishing your Rest and Relaxation?

GENERAL FUKUA DE HUNDAN

We are about finished now with the R&R. We only have one more task than we'll be leaving the planet and heading back to our home worlds.

WADE BAKER

General Fukua de Hundan, may I ask what is your task?

GENERAL FUKUA DE HUNDAN

Up on the hilltop over there, we buried a few of my crew members who died from Cosmic Space Sickness. When we returned, we discovered the graves had been desecrated.

One of those bodies was my son. I would like the body returned before we leave because I want to take him back to my home world for a proper burial. I should never have buried them here, but its Carsopian tradition.

WADE BAKER

General Fukua De Hundan I will personally investigate this matter and determine where the remains were taken so they may be returned to you.

GENERAL FUKUA DE HUNDAN

I appreciate that.

WADE BAKER

Is there anything else you wish to discuss with us General Fukua De Hundan.

GENERAL FUKUA DE HUNDAN

Wade Baker, we know a lot about Earth. Our advanced technology can read all your communications. We know every move you make. There is very little about Earth we do not know.

WADE BAKER

That's very interesting, General Fukua De Hundan. Perhaps you can tell us a little about your Empire since we have no knowledge of it.

GENERAL FUKUA DE HUNDAN

Yes, I'm aware how primitive you Earth people are. You are lucky you exist far away from the Center of the Galaxy, so no major power has any interest in you.

We have a technology scale in the Galaxy we rank all sentient beings. The scale is one to one hundred. You Earth people are at one point five.

Within 25 light years of your planet there are twelve solar systems with intelligent life that have a technology ranking somewhere between 5 and 10. If you do not advance rapidly, you will soon fall victim to one of these other civilizations.

General Fukua de Hundan could sense the humility and sincerity in Wade Baker and decided that since he was going to work on getting his son back, he would show some magnanimity and give these primitive Earth people an exposure to the Galaxy.

GENERAL FUKUA DE HUNDAN

Wade Baker, Jack Boone, and Agent Carlos Guerrero, please come with me to my command ship. I will give you a presentation of what our empire is like.

WADE BAKER

Thank you General Fukua de Hundan, that is very kind of you.

General Fukua de Hundan then directed some standard Carsopian at his assistants and they all soon started marching 50 yards towards his command ship where a sophisticated gangway laid down upon the planet.

INT. MIXED CGI. DAY. GENERAL FUKUA DE HUNDAN COMMAND SHIP.

Note; Mixed CGI has scene shots over green overlayed on CGI.

They followed the General up into the astonishingly large spacecraft. It had modernisms to it that dwarfed anything the Earth men ever observed on the numerous science fiction space related movies.

VOICEOVER (WADE BAKER) THOUGHT

If this ship had landed 2000 years ago, the primitive people would have considered them Gods.

Being this was the command ship it had an element of opulence unprecedented in anything Wade Baker ever experienced. The design, colors, and general outlay appeared extravagant.

They were soon ushered into a very large room. One might think it was a gymnasium. General Fukua de Hundan's aid still carrying the translator box said and played a translated presentation:

GENERAL FUKUA DE HUNDAN
VIA TRANSLATOR SPEAKER

This is my reflection room where I go when I must make decisions that could have the consequences of the loss of a billion lives.

It provides me with visual insights needed to adjust my personal psyche to adapt to circumstances. In our home worlds when I receive VIP aboard my command ship, I bring them here where I give them a presentation of the Carsopian Empire.

This presentation will take you about an hour to observe it, but I think it will do you some good. Please have a seat.

Those are reclining chairs to make you more comfortable.

Right after the three Earth men sat down in very comfortable reclining chairs, the general then vocalized a series of Carsopian commands and soon a gigantic holographic appeared which had a strange, beautiful sound to it and a narration. For these Earth people the narration was automatically translated and produced in English. The Carsopians didn't need to hear it since they were well accustomed to what it conveyed in Standard Carsopian.

GENERAL FUKUA DE HUNDAN
VIA TRANSLATOR SPEAKER

This one-hour presentation is a time compressed explanation of how the Carsopian Empire began and spread through the galaxy. Three dimensional maps showed in relation to the Milky Way where elements of the Empire exist.

Wade wished he had a recording device with him. When he was later debriefed this one- hour presentation would result in over one thousand hours of questions and answers to his CIA interrogators and evaluators. But it was the price he was going to have to pay.

The video quickly made Wade Baker feel utterly inferior. He knew these giants were being benevolent towards Earth people even though they had barbecued a few of them in rituals he wouldn't understand nor desire to find out.

The imagery of the alien cities and transportation, like down the *Cui* corridor was utterly amazing. There was more discovery in this video than all of science mankind had ever produced. And just like he predicted, stirring up these aliens would not have been a prudent thing to do since they easily could have wiped out this planet in the span of 20 to 30 minutes.

Some of the major historical battles the Carsopians fought were shown in utter graphics on the 50-foot-tall holograph. As soon as the one-hour presentation was completed. General Fukua de Hundan asked the group:

GENERAL FUKUA DE HUNDAN

Would you like to see the replay of the battle just fought with the Heisibing Fleet?

WADE BAKER

General Fukua de Hundan, I would feel very honored if you allowed me to see a replay of that battle.

The general smiled as he was starting to like Wade.

General Fukua de Hundan gave some orders in Standard Carsopian and soon the 50-foot- tall holograph showed the 3D reenactment of the battle that utilized all the video provided by all the fleet sensors.

The shocking truth was compared to primitive humans, these were just about Gods. The imagery of the space battle where two-mile-long ships were exploding with the terrible beams that were zipping back and forth truly affected Wade Baker in ways he never imagined.

Having dealt with the KGB (FSB), Chinese MSS, Japanese Naicho - Naikaku Chosashitsu Betsushitsu, British SIS, and middle eastern entities, Wade Baker felt he was about ready for anything. But the combination of observing this incredibly advanced alien civilization and now this space battle eclipsed his imagination truly affected him.

Wade Baker knew he would never be the same, as his faith was shattered. But one thing he did know now. The world owed Jack Boone a great deal of gratitude, because Jack singlehandedly prevented the worst disaster ever facing mankind.

As soon as the presentation of the recent space battle ended, General Fukua de Hundan asked:

GENERAL FUKUA DE HUNDAN

Would you gentlemen like to have some refreshments?

WADE BAKER

General Fukua de Hundan, with all due respect, I would like to go back to my helicopter to take me back to Guadalajara, Mexico to get on an aircraft to fly me back our headquarters buildings in my country so that I can start looking for your son and make sure he is returned right away.

GENERAL FUKUA DE HUNDAN

Thank you, Wade Baker. That's very unselfish of you.

Back in my worlds there are a lot of patronage people that would do anything to have the opportunity to have refreshments with me.

The fact you are willing to give that up to go locate my son to return his remains to me pleases me. Perhaps when you can return with the remains, we can have refreshments then?

WADE BAKER

General Fukua de Hundan, after I have the honor of facilitating bringing your son back to you. I would like to have refreshments with you.

GENERAL FUKUA DE HUNDAN

Wade Baker, as I informed you earlier, we know a lot about your planet, your political systems, your leaders, your military, and your civilization in general.

When you come back would you do me the honor of bringing your President with you? I would like to meet him.

WADE BAKER

General Fukua de Hundan, I would be most honored if given the honor of escorting my President here. I think it would be very good for him to see what you presented to us.

It wakes us up to a lot of things and we need to change our ways, because as you have shown us, we are very vulnerable here.

GENERAL FUKUA DE HUNDAN

Wade Baker, if I were in this area of space and Earth was under attack, I would defend your planet because I like you personally.

But I am sorry that when I leave here after you return my son's remains, we may never come back this way again, at least in your lifetime and probably not mine either.

WADE BAKER

General Fukua de Hundan, how many years do Carsopians live?

GENERAL FUKUA DE HUNDAN

Wade Baker, I'm approximately 500 Earth years old. I'm probably two thirds the way through my life span.

WADE BAKER

General, thank you very much for enlightening me. I would like to leave now so I can get to work on my tasks as I do not wish to disappoint you.

GENERAL FUKUA DE HUNDAN

Wade Baker, let me escort you to your Helicopter.

WADE BAKER

Thank you General Fukua De Hundan.

The group then walked out of the large ceremonial holographic room and down the luxurious hallway, and down the ramp and a short distance away, the Helicopter. The General stopped exactly where he first stood as when they arrived.

GENERAL FUKUA DE HUNDAN

Goodbye Wade Baker. I hope to see you soon.

WADE BAKER

General Fukua De Hundan. The pleasure will be all mine.

The general smiled and the Earth men all climbed back into the Blackhawk and shortly the propulsion started and the General Electric turboshaft engines and soon the rotors were spinning and the helicopter kicked up a lot of dust and then went up into the air and slowly curved back towards Mexican Hiway 23 and followed it down to Guadalajara where a CIA Gulfstream 850 jet waited for them.

Upon landing close to the Jet, the three agents got out and walked towards the jet on the tarmac. As they were at the ladder, Wade Baker turned towards Agent Guerrero who would be leaving them shortly on a Mexican PFM jet parked nearby to fly him to Mexico City, where to his surprise he would likewise brief Jose Mercado, but also the President of Mexico at the same time.

WADE BAKER

Agent Guerrero, I hoped you enjoyed your visit with the Aliens.

PFM AGENT GUERRERO

All I can say now Agent Baker, I've never experienced anything like this in my lifetime nor did I ever expect I would.

WADE BAKER

You and me both. I think we'll be meeting up soon again, when we bring the Carsopian bodies back.

PFM AGENT GUERRERO

I'll be expecting you.

Between Mexico and the United States, there was suddenly enormous stress that would grow exponentially as their agents informed their respective governments what they had observed.

The special modified Gulfstream 850 that only the CIA had received delivery, could fly at 100,000 feet and get back to Washington DC a lot quicker than people imagined. At that altitude, due to the reduced atmosphere, they flew supersonic.

Just like the super cruise of the F22A, the Gulfstream 850 could super cruise the entire distance to Washington DC. where it landed at Andrews Air Force Base, and one of the corporate painted CIA S-97 helicopters was there to take Wade Baker and Jack Boone to Langley where they would brief the DCI and soon be hauled via helicopter to the White House to discuss their visit to the Alien Fleet and General Fukua De Hundan's invitation to the President.

THE WHITE HOUSE MEETING

EXT. DAY. INSIDE SIKORSKY S-97 HELICOPTER.

The DCI was in the CIA's Sikorsky S-97 helicopter with CIA analyst Jack Boone and his supervisor Wade Baker flying to the white house.

DIRECTOR OF THE CIA

I'm surprised you are not locked up in some type of quarantine after being on that alien ship.

WADE BAKER

Hopefully nobody figures it out anytime soon, I really don't want to be cooped up for six months and become part of a science experiment.

DIRECTOR OF THE CIA

What if you are carrying deadly alien pathogens?

WADE BAKER

Even though these aliens are ten feet tall, they look almost identical to us except for their almond eyes.

They are considerably far more advanced than we are. If there were pathogens, I'm sure they would have dealt with it already.

DIRECTOR OF THE CIA

Their immune systems probably can handle it, we may not have any immunity. Kind of like the North American natives when smallpox first arrived.

WADE BAKER

Scott, with the holographs the aliens showed us giving us a short brief history of their Empire, we have far more issues to worry about.

DIRECTOR OF THE CIA

Wade what if you get the entire planet sick, this could be worse than the Spanish Flu back in 1918.

WADE BAKER

Scott, just think, since you are in proximity to me you have already been exposed if it's really bad stuff. It's too late now. Plus, I believe I need to convince the President to make sure the General gets his son back, otherwise, I fear what he can do.

DIRECTOR OF THE CIA

You mentioned in your quick look report you sent flying back to Dulles the aliens have invited the President to visit their ship and observe the same holograph information presentation they showed you.

WADE BAKER

That's correct. I believe the President since he's our supreme leader, should watch the holographs and talk with General Fukua de Hundan and heed his warnings that we are in a precarious state being so primitive and surrounded by at least 12 much more advanced civilizations that may one day make a conquest of Earth.

DIRECTOR OF THE CIA

Wade, I notice in your report you did not mention whether you confronted them about cannibalism.

WADE BAKER

I did not bring the matter up because, quite frankly, the presentation they gave us had such huge revelations that I needed to capture as much as I could in my memories for the report.

Arguing over cannibalism, which they will do whether we like it or not, would have reduced the amount of concentration on more critical items such as the disposition of various galactic parties we were unaware existed and are potential risks to this planet.

DIRECTOR OF THE CIA

I believe the national security team will advise the President not to visit the aliens.

WADE BAKER

I sincerely believe the President should watch the holograph the Carsopians showed us.

DIRECTOR OF THE CIA

What good will it do him, it will be risky for him, and you have already articulated what you saw in the holograph, so I do not think it's necessary.

WADE BAKER

It's one thing to read a report such as this, but it's another thing to see the extraordinary visualization that such an advanced civilization can display for us which explains more about the galaxy in an hour than we know from all of human history.

DIRECTOR OF THE CIA

Perhaps the President can send the Vice President or Secretary of State.

WADE BAKER

Scott, if you were these powerful aliens and you invited the principal leader of the planet and instead, they sent another messenger, you might not be quite as hospitable.

DIRECTOR OF THE CIA

Wade, if the national security team asks me, I would recommend he not go.

WADE BAKER

Scott, you need to remember we desecrated his son's grave, and I hope to hell those scientists at Wright Patterson haven't carved up his son.

Under the circumstances, I highly suggest the President be with the group that returns the son's body.

And if the doctors have cut him up, I suggest you go to the President if you must and have him order them to restore the body the best they can.

DIRECTOR OF THE CIA

I would think that the length of time the corpses were setting they have already largely already decayed, and protocols for biohazards may have already required them to put the bodies in incinerators to dispose of them.

WADE BAKER

If that happened, then the President really does need to go to apologize. You need to remember the Carsopians wield some awesome firepower, and we are a pushover. They can lay waste to this planet fast so it's a risk he must take to help protect this planet.

Jack Boone was sitting there remaining quiet letting Wade Baker do all the talking with the DCI, and somehow felt he was going to avoid getting some of the stresses he knew now confronted Wade. The two of them had received a revelation unlike any Earth person before. But just as he was becoming complacent the DCI threw him a curve ball.

DIRECTOR OF THE CIA

Jack, just as soon as we get out of the meeting, I want you to hunt down the alien bodies and report back the condition they are in.

JACK BOONE

I may have to fly there to take a closer look and redirect the researchers.

DIRECTOR OF THE CIA

Understandable, and there will be a question of authority.

JACK BOONE

They work for the Air Force, ask the President during the meeting to direct the Air Force secretary to cooperate with our activities, that should clear the way.

WADE BAKER

The Air Force can be pricks at time. We need someone above Wright Patterson's Commanding General's rank to make sure he cooperates.

DIRECTOR OF THE CIA

General Fukua de Handan's son's remains is a pressing issue. I know that.

I'll be talking with the Air Force Secretary to grease the skids to make sure Wright Patterson's Commanding General is sensitive to the fact we have a tight time frame.

Plus, I would assume if General Fukua de Hundan discovered that's where the body is, he might just pay the base a visit.

WADE BAKER

No luck with photo-intelligence?

DIRECTOR OF THE CIA

Surprisingly they didn't turn the U2 around like they did the SR-72.

WADE BAKER

Did they get imagery?

DIRECTOR OF THE CIA

Yes, the entire alien fleet was photographed. And as the President said *It was a hard pill to swallow* after Air Force and NRO photo interpreters scaled the images and gave precise dimensions of the craft.

I can imagine what went through your minds when you came upon those two-mile-long spacecraft.

WADE BAKER

That part didn't bother me half as much as looking up to the ten-foot-tall Aliens. One can't help but have a feeling of inferiority standing next to giants.

DIRECTOR OF THE CIA

What was your first impression when you went inside the ship?

WADE BAKER

I'd say I felt like I was inside an Isaac Asimov Novel or one of the other great science fiction writers.

DIRECTOR OF THE CIA

I can imagine.

WADE BAKER

It was as if I were looking at the future for us. Maybe 5,000 years from now when we'll all be gone.

DIRECTOR OF THE CIA

I'm sure this visit by the aliens will lead to more appropriations in space research, I can see the whole process speeding up now.

WADE BAKER

How can we expect congress to vote on the funds if they are not briefed on this Alien visit.

DIRECTOR OF THE CIA

Our congressional oversight has been briefed and we all know they have big mouths.

The Sikorsky S-97 helicopter suddenly banked and came on a different course and the pilot was on final approach to the South Lawn of the White House. Thanks to the paint job, outsider watching the helicopter land would immediately think it was a civilian helicopter, possibly one of the President's rich buddies, except the company logo was on the outsides so if a person was close, they would see it belonged to the Cash in Advance boys.

Moments passed by and the helicopter was on the strange looking temporary landing pad devices put out by the secret service to make sure the lawn did not suffer from numerous helicopter landings.

The crew member opened the door to the S-97 and the three men stood up and exited the craft. Secret Service men escorted them directly to the Oval Office where the President, Vice President, Secretary of State, and the head of the joint chiefs were waiting.

INT. DAY. WHITE HOUSE OVAL OFFICE.

PRESIDENT OF THE USA

Glad you could get over here so quickly Scott."

DIRECTOR OF THE CIA

Thank you, Mister President, we hustled.

PRESIDENT OF THE USA

I'm glad you brought Jack Boone and Wade Baker with you. I was looking forward to discussing their visit to the Aliens.

DIRECTOR OF THE CIA

Thank you, Mr. President, but before we get into the details, I first want to bring a matter to your attention that requires immediate action.

PRESIDENT OF THE USA
Go on.

DIRECTOR OF THE CIA
Sir, the Alien Commander, General Fukua de Hundan had a son with him on this trip who died and was buried at one of their camp sites where they just returned.

Our people dug up those alien bodies when we found the graves, which includes General Fukua de Hundan's son. He wants the son's body back immediately.

PRESIDENT OF THE USA
Where's the body now?

DIRECTOR OF THE CIA
It's currently at Wright Patterson Airforce Base in building 18 complex where researchers are studying their remains.

PRESIDENT OF THE USA
Okay that sounds like a reasonable request.

DIRECTOR OF THE CIA
Mr. President, I've assigned my analyst Jack Boone to make all arrangements and prepare to ship all the alien bodies back as soon as the researchers can prepare the bodies and if they have cut them up for study to sew them back together.

PRESIDENT OF THE USA
All right. Do we need Jack Boone here for this discussion or can Wade present all their comments?

DIRECTOR OF THE CIA
Wade will be sufficient. I would like to send Jack Boone to Wright Patterson now so that he can start the process.

PRESIDENT OF THE USA
Is the base ready for his arrival?

DIRECTOR OF THE CIA
They do not know Jack is coming yet, but I planned on calling the Secretary of the Airforce to have him call the Commanding General to order him to cooperate at the fullest.

The President looking at one of his secret service agents stated:

PRESIDENT OF THE USA
Go ahead and take Jack Boone to the South lawn and recall the CIA helicopter to pick him up.

SECRET SERVICE AGENT

Right away Mr. President.

Jack Boone nodded and turned and walked out of the Oval Office following the secret service man who was giving marching orders to several people which resulted in the S-97 doing a U-turn and coming back to the White House lawn and landing.

Moments later Jack was aboard the CIA helicopter and learned he was immediately being taken to Andrews Air Force Base where the Gulfstream 850 positioned inside one of the hangers was ready to roll out and fly the mission to take Jack Boone to Wright Patterson Air Force Base.

A few phone calls were made to Secretary of the Air Force who by now had finished up with the Commanding General at Wright Patterson Air Force base and had the distinct pleasure of recalling all the scientists who had left work a couple hours ago at the end of the day, to come back to the base to do some emergency work.

By the time the Scientists got back to building 18, some of them had already enjoyed part of happy hour and required a designated driver. An impromptu meeting just outside the lab ensued and they were astonished at what their marching orders were.

Jack Boone arrived soon and was ready to get the ball rolling.

Once again providence was on America's side as one of the bodies had not been tampered with yet and it apparently had far more decorations on the uniform than the rest, which led Jack Boone to think out loud:

JACK BOONE

This must be the Generals son. What's the condition of the bodies?

CHIEF RESEARCH SCIENTIST

Because they were dug up very soon after the burial, they didn't have a lot of time to decompose.

We've since preserved the bodies well, so they are in good shape even though some of the organs are missing in a few of them.

More good news followed as they had all of them stored in special biohazard containers that were chilled to prevent decomposition. The containers would fit nicely in a C17 Cargo plane which were available on the base.

Jack Boone was immediately on a conference call with the DCI and Wade Baker.

JACK BOONE

This is what I propose we do: Fly the bodies down to Guadalajara and request the Mexican Army meet us there with a few trucks to carry the containers to the Alien site.

DIRECTOR OF THE CIA

Is there an access road?

JACK BOONE

There is a dirt road that branches off the Hiway for a few miles. We can get them close, the Aliens will spot them and come to investigate and no doubt they have the means to transport them the rest of the way. I'll fly out on a helicopter and let General Fukua de Hundan know those trucks are carrying the bodies.

The preparations were soon complete, and Jack Boone and the special containers were soon put aboard a C17 cargo plane that also carried a helicopter for Jack's use. Within an hour of arrival at Wright Patterson Air Force base, Jack Boone was sitting in the passenger section behind the cockpit on that C17 taking off.

The advantage of flying the slower C17 almost 1800 air miles down to Guadalajara, is it would give Jack enough time to take a nice long nap because he knew once he landed in Mexico, he would not be getting much sleep.

While Jack was napping several phone calls went back and forth.

The venerable PFM Agent Guerrero was summoned by Jose Mercado.

JOSE MERCADO

Carlos, thanks for coming right away.

PFM Agent Guerrero

Jose, what can I do for you?

JOSE MERCADO

The Americans are bringing back the Alien remains to give back to General Fukua de Hundan. They will be shipped via Mexican Army Trucks from Guadalajara to the Alien landing site.

PFM Agent Guerrero

I expected this to happen and immediately assigned to coordinate with Mexican Army unit assigned this special mission and be the Mexican Policía Federal Ministerial liaison to the Americans arriving with the Alien remains.

The President of Mexico and Jose Mercado debriefed Agent Guerrero after he witnessed the spectacle with the two CIA agents aboard the alien ship. Mexico was super quiet about the incident.

The information was shrouded in confidentiality primarily because the President of Mexico could not come to grips with how he could or should disclose such an extraordinary event taking place in his country. The side deal with the aliens eating the Caravanners also placed a significant level of anxiety on him.

Mexican special forces would be driving the trucks and delivering the bodies because they were an elite unit that knew how to keep their mouths shut. They too would go through a great deal of psychological stress when they observed the Alien Fleet parked on the ground that represented something beyond anything any of them had ever previously contemplated.

As soon as the C17 was preparing to land, one of the crewmembers woke up Jack Boone. They knew he needed rest, so they waited until the last few minutes of flight to disturb him. Jack was quite grateful.

The plane landed then was directed by ground controllers over to a designated area the Mexican Government had set up and their Army Trucks were there waiting.

Jack Boone had asked for a Helicopter to be available which was also on the same C17 transported with the bodies to fly him to the Aliens to inform them the Army Trucks coming were carrying the bodies, so they didn't get mistakenly targeted.

During the next sequence, and voiceover, the music starting at the 15:45 mark will be played:
[https://www.youtube.com/watch?v=d WJqMCK7uo] Joachim Raff - Piano Concerto, Op. 185 (1873)

VOICEOVER

Agent Guerrero would always remain with the truck convoy to ensure they had no issues. Some of the trucks in the lead and in the rear were not carrying anything, they were simply spacers to help clear traffic and provide an escort for the trucks with the loads.

As soon as the alien remains were loaded on the trucks and the Helicopter was ready to launch with American Pilots and helicopter that also flew in the C17 with Jack Boone, they were given permission to take off and fly to the Alien bivouac area.

In 45 minutes just like the previous trip, Carsopian security ships were suddenly flying close by escorting them to the designated landing zone.

Shortly after landing, General Fukua de Hundan appeared with 20 staff members. Jack Boone approached the Carsopians and exchanged respectful welcomes.

GENERAL FUKUA DE HUNDAN
(VIA TRANSLATOR BOX)
Why did you come alone?

JACK BOONE
General Fukua de Hundan, we are bringing the bodies of your son and the others on some trucks that will be here probably in a couple hours.

I wanted to come here to alert you so that you know those trucks have no hostile intentions, they are carrying all the remains of your troops in special containers to preserve their bodies.

GENERAL FUKUA DE HUNDAN
(VIA TRANSLATOR BOX)
Okay thank you I will let my troops know and we'll escort them when they get close.

JACK BOONE
General Fukua De Hundan We appreciate that.

GENERAL FUKUA DE HUNDAN
(VIA TRANSLATOR BOX)
Jack Boone, I would like you to come aboard my ship and have some refreshments and I have some questions I might like to ask you.

JACK BOONE
I would be delighted but I would like to tell the pilot and copilot of our helicopter that I will be going in your ship with you, and they will need to wait a while.

GENERAL FUKUA DE HUNDAN (VIA TRANSLATOR BOX)
Sure, go ahead.

General Fukua de Hundan patiently waited as he observed the Jack, the Earth Person go over to the tiny aircraft and talk to the crew members. He understood, it was only a polite thing to do. He would also send out one of his aids with snacks and drinks for them after he and Jack Boone were settled in his quarters aboard his flag ship.

They walked probably 100 yards inside the ship. It was an experience unlike Jack Boone had never done before.

GENERAL FUKUA DE HUNDAN
(VIA TRANSLATOR BOX)
Since we are close to my quarters, I'm going to take you through the control room it's on the way.

JACK BOONE
All right, General Fukua de Hundan.

VOICEOVER
Jack entered the control room in General Fukua de Hundan's command ship appearing quite immense.

There were hundreds of consoles and holographic displays going on. Jack estimated there must have been 300 to 400 people present.

Jack noticed these Carsopian crew members were engaged and communicating about numerous events which Jack could not understand since the conversations was in Standard Carsopian.

Much of the activity of these numerous technicians engaged related to off planet INTEL gathering and gathering data from probes sent out in the direction they were heading for fleet security during their pending transit home.

As General Fukua de Hundan had stated to Wade and Jack during their initial meeting, there were twelve planets in nearby solar systems that presented a future threat. It was now only a matter of time before they showed up.

Part of the INTEL work going on was eavesdropping on all twelve of those civilizations and acquiring more anecdotal data of what was going on in their nearby solar systems.

The view of the command ship control room displayed professionalism in every aspect.

General Fukua de Hundan led Jack Boone eventually through the command ship control room getting a lot of stares from the Carsopian watch section. They then walked through a private passageway that apparently was for the exclusive use of General Fukua de Hundan to his private quarters.

General Fukua de Hundan soon entered a very large and luxurious room with Jack Boone close behind.

Inside were some incredibly beautiful women but would be tall *Amazons* for Jack, but nevertheless their skimpy attire, exotic perfumes laced with pheromones created a stir in Jack. These women seemed to be poised for General Fukua de Hundan.

GENERAL FUKUA DE HUNDAN

Jack, please make yourself comfortable.

Jack Boone walked over to what appeared to be a large sofa, a lot larger than what he had ever seen before. He sat down and shortly a 10-foot-tall female, smelling exotic and looking unusually striking came forward with a tray holding a gold drinking chalice with a nice smelling liquid inside it.

CARSOPIAN PLEASURE CORP FEMALE

Jack Boone, General Fukua De Hundan asked me to provide you with some nice refreshments. Also, if you need any special pleasures, I'm an expert and can do it for you.

This drink should help you unwind and enjoy the essence of life and I'm here to make you feel better if you so desire.

JACK BOONE

Thank you.

Jack Boone took the drink and knew he was probably making a huge mistake, not knowing if it would poison him, he took a sip.

It wasn't alcohol but it gave an effect like alcohol as it made his mouth feel slightly unusual. It had a wonderful taste to it; unlike anything he had ever experienced before. It didn't intoxicate him, but he felt almost clairvoyant. His mental acuity rose rapidly.

General Fukua de Hundan didn't beat around the bush.

GENERAL FUKUA DE HUNDAN

Did your President commit to visit?

JACK BOONE

General Fukua de Hundan, we knew how important getting back your son was, so I was detailed to handle that matter, I don't know what the President and the others determined as far as a state visit is concerned. I left immediately before their discussions started. I do hope he does come for a visit.

GENERAL FUKUA DE HUNDAN

I appreciate the priority on returning my son. Why did your government dig him up and take him in the first place?

JACK BOONE

General Fukua de Hundan, we have never met aliens before.

I have no idea what led to that decision. But from what I understand the forensics investigators had no idea bodies were buried there.

The digging was done to determine if there were any Earth persons remains there to get some idea how many people were involved.

When our investigators found the bodies, they became quite an interest to our scientific community.

GENERAL FUKUA DE HUNDAN

Many civilizations throughout the galaxy would look down upon you Earth people for digging up those bodies and desecrating their burial sites.

JACK BOONE

General Fukua de Hundan, we didn't know they were a grave until the bodies were discovered.

Since you were gone by that time, we assumed you abandoned the bodies here and had no plans of ever returning.

GENERAL FUKUA DE HUNDAN

Still the behavior of digging up graves is considered reprehensible throughout the galaxy.

JACK BOONE

General Fukua de Hundan, I know you are a very powerful leader and I'm sure Earth Defenses are in no way able to defend against you, but I must counter with an issue we have.

GENERAL FUKUA DE HUNDAN

What is the issue Jack?

JACK BOONE

General Fukua de Hundan the debris you left behind and the deceased people we dug up were examined and some were found to have undigested human remains inside their guts. On Earth we call that cannibalism, and we consider that disgraceful to eat another sentient being.

GENERAL FUKUA DE HUNDAN

Jack Boone, it is our custom to celebrate a victory over opponents by eating their flesh. We know your Earth customs since we have studied them. Earth has had its fair share of cannibals all the way up into the 20th century as you call it.

Jack looked upon General Fukua de Hundan very intensely wondering if he had said something he shouldn't and wished suddenly he had not said it the moment he did.

GENERAL FUKUA DE HUNDAN

This trip to Earth on our way to one of the most important space battles in a generation was extremely long. None of my soldiers have ever traveled this distance in space before nor will they again in their lifetimes.

JACK BOONE

General Fukua De Hundan, may I ask how this figures into barbecuing Earth people?

GENERAL FUKUA DE HUNDAN

This was a pre-celebration to motivate my troops. The plan worked and we were victorious. You are inferior people. Our troops eating the flesh of humans is no different than how religions on this planet such as the Hindu's view others like Americans who eat beef.

JACK BOONE

Why should it matter that we eat cattle, they are just dumb animals?

GENERAL FUKUA DE HUNDAN

Cattle have some intelligence and are capable of learning far more than what you Earth people train them.

JACK BOONE

Why should it be offensive to eat beef? We also eat poultry, fish, and pork.

GENERAL FUKUA DE HUNDAN

Jack Boone, you should be aware the Hindu's hold cattle in high esteem, and it troubles them deeply to know you eat them. From our perspective us eating the flesh of humans is no different than you eating cattle whom Hindu's and others find inexcusable.

Jack had no desire to continue this dialogue because he realized he might have upset this powerful leader with serious consequences.

JACK BOONE

I'm very sorry about your son General. I know I would feel very bad if I lost my son.

GENERAL FUKUA DE HUNDAN

Thank you for the kind words, Jack Boone. It was tough, and a personal sacrifice I had to make. I wish we had arrived on Earth earlier, my son might have survived then, being back in real gravity, sunlight, fresh water, and other health inducements.

JACK BOONE

Will it be tough getting home?

GENERAL FUKUA DE HUNDAN

Yes, it's a long journey ahead of us. But I think the troops will be better prepared psychologically because they survived the battle.

JACK BOONE

How did your son die?

GENERAL FUKUA DE HUNDAN

Unfortunately, he succumbed to Cosmic Space Sickness that is a combination of physical as well as mental conditions brought on by the fear and unknown of the consequences of space battles that are extremely lethal.

JACK BOONE

But he might have died in the battle?

GENERAL FUKUA DE HUNDAN

When your ship is crippled in space you are finished. If you get lucky your ship explodes to cut the time down, it takes to suffer.

JACK BOONE

General, may I ask you a question?

GENERAL FUKUA DE HUNDAN

Yes Jack, what do you want to know?

JACK BOONE

General Fukua De Hundan, you probably already know about our religions since you know some specific examples of Krishna Science and their Samsaric cycle of birth and death.

In my country the United States the population is predominately Christians and Jews, though we have a growing population of other religions.

Do the Carsopians have religions and are they in any way like our practices on Earth?

GENERAL FUKUA DE HUNDAN

Jack Boone, I would never have expected someone from a primitive civilization like here on Earth to ask a question like that. It's quite refreshing that you would.

JACK BOONE

I see.

GENERAL FUKUA DE HUNDAN

In the Carsopian Worlds we have Elders who help us reflect and when we seek answers to questions like you have raised, it's the Elders responsibility to help us derive the most factual answer.

JACK BOONE

That's an interesting concept.

GENERAL FUKUA DE HUNDAN

Just like you Earth men, we have never met God. We don't know who God is or why the Universe exists.

We would tend to believe your religious indoctrination is wholesale fraud.

But we would also say your Atheists or Agnostics have no basis for their opinions as well.

JACK BOONE

General Fukua De Hundan, you seem to echo what I predicted you might say in your remarks.

GENERAL FUKUA DE HUNDAN

Jack, in preparing for our stopover, my fleet scientists analyzed your culture to a high extent. We had several months to sift through vast amounts of information you beam to the universe daily.

We studied over 100 countries on this planet to learn languages and the inter-relationships, politics, traditions, and systems of governance.

Since we have computers that are far more developed than what you have on Earth, we can use what you call Artificial Intelligence to develop lexicons for translators and analyze all the graphic content of your visual communications.

Jack observed General Fukua de Hundan with great amazement that followed.

GENERAL FUKUA DE HUNDAN

China is one country we discovered with great interest. We almost landed in China but the few areas we would have chosen are too close to Chinese military outposts and we wanted to arrive, enjoy then leave incognito.

In studying China, I was focused in two areas that interested me. Sun Tzu Art of War, and Confucius. The Carsopian system of beliefs is very compatible to Confucius. Just like Confucius does not require Jesus Christ, Mohamed, or Lord Krishna to explain the rules of moral conduct, nor do we.

Unlike Humans and Planet Earth, we do not require a deity to explain where we come from and why we are here.

We do, however, understand some process created all this and the size and scale are far too large for our intellect to grasp it.

JACK BOONE

You are not concerned about where you come from?

GENERAL FUKUA DE HUNDAN

Thousands and even millions of years from now when the Carsopian world's may no longer exist due to strife, super nova, or other celestial events, we still will not know what, how, or why we exist. Nor will we care.

JACK BOONE

How do the Carsopians deal with creativity and possible intelligent design?

GENERAL FUKUA DE HUNDAN

Our philosophy simply is whatever created all this universe gave us the opportunity to thrive. It's our responsibility to manifest our own destiny.

JACK BOONE

That's sort of like our religions explain our god gave us free will.

GENERAL FUKUA DE HUNDAN

Throughout the 450,000-years of written Carsopian history, we have never counted on a deity to guide us to our destination.

However just like the Chinese Confucius who eloquently explains the fabric of life and what Humanity should attempt to achieve, our Elders give us the same guidance and are tasked to continuously analyze our universe to keep us appraised of the cosmic fabric of life and to make adjustments to how we conduct ourselves so that we create a natural harmony and oscillations of life.

JACK BOONE

Before you leave our planet would you like me to arrange for a volume of Confucius writings?

GENERAL FUKUA DE HUNDAN

Jack Boone, thanks to your robust global communications through your Internet, we have already obtained electronic copies of 20 Confucius Analects.

JACK BOONE

How about other Confucius writings?

GENERAL FUKUA DE HUNDAN

We have copies of all known Confucius writings made available on your global internet, and I can display that at any time here in my private quarters or in the holograph room where our artificial intelligence blends the Confucius science with music and numerous Chinese drawing and paintings.

I can either have an aide read it to me and translate it into Standard Carsopian, or I can have a recording of the Confucius *Analects* transcripts played for me. Which I have done routinely recently.

JACK BOONE

General Fukua De Hundan, are there any lessons you learned from studying Confucius?

GENERAL FUKUA DE HUNDAN

Yes, Jack Boone. I quickly observed you personally as a *Noble Savage.*

JACK BOONE

I don't know if I should take that as a disparagement or a complement.

GENERAL FUKUA DE HUNDAN

Jack Boone, we Carsopians can read about five times quicker than humans. Thanks to Confucius, Earth was spared. I've raised entire planets for offenses less than desecration of my son's grave.

Jack knew he had touched a nerve somehow and suddenly thought about attempting to shift the conversation in a different direction. He could sense General Fukua de Hundan remained agitated over the discovery of his son missing. *But if they never returned to this planet, why would it matter?*

JACK BOONE

I'm truly sorry about what happened with your son.

GENERAL FUKUA DE HUNDAN

The *Battle of Cui* almost resulted in Carsopians not coming back in this direction on our return trip home.

Had Heisibing Fleet Commander Admiral Engaarai been a lessor strategist and not bugged out exactly when he did, it was a foregone conclusion that my forces would have completely decimated the Heisibing Fleet.

There would be nothing of substance to defend the Heisibing Empire and the Carsopian Fleet could have leisurely traveled there and demanded a unilateral surrender that would have ended the 100-year conflict.

JACK BOONE

Which means you would not have come back and discovered your son's body missing?

GENERAL FUKUA DE HUNDAN

There was nothing I could have done otherwise. Heisibing Fleet Commander Admiral Engaarai had similar properties of Sun Tzu.

That's why in recent decades the Carsopians made very little progress against the Heisibing. And a perpetual stalemate is not acceptable.

JACK BOONE

That's quite interesting, General Fukua de Hundan.

GENERAL FUKUA DE HUNDAN

Even though you Earth People are extremely backwards and low on the technology scales, I have been studying Sun Tzu in my spare time, and I will modify my strategy appropriately for the next battle. Before you leave, I want to give you something and do me a favor.

JACK BOONE

General Fukua de Hundan, what do you wish me to do?

GENERAL FUKUA DE HUNDAN

Jack Boone, I've recorded a letter for Chinese Earth dwellers. I want to personally thank them for my enlightenment. I want you to personally deliver the letter for me to their leader.

JACK BOONE

I would be most proud to do so General Fukua de Hundan.

General Fukua de Hundan reached in his robe and pulled out what appeared to be some type of rolled up paper around a cylinder object and handed it to Jack.

The paper was very light and very unusual. Jack might have assumed it was one or two pages, but indeed was over 50 pages as the material used to record General Fukua de Hundan's letter, printed by intricate digital assistants in a world where paper like printouts rarely existed.

Along with the letter in the cylindrical object it rolled around, there was also a short holograph that when the person opened the letter it would suddenly appear and give a couple minutes of introduction and statements then it would disappear.

GENERAL FUKUA DE HUNDAN

My letter must be opened only by the leader of China. Nobody else must open it.

JACK BOONE

Understand sir. It will be difficult for me to deliver such a letter to China's leader, and it may cause me irreparable harm to my career, but I will attempt to do so.

GENERAL FUKUA DE HUNDAN

When your President arrives, I will inform him of your task you must do for me.

JACK BOONE

Thank you, sir. That will certainly make things easier for me.

The small talk continued for a while and another serving of the Carsopian drink was making Jack Boone feel amazingly good. The drugs in the drink were now flowing through his body, and inflammation and undiagnosed diseases were being attacked by significantly advanced microbial health inducers. Two drinks cured a cancer that Jack didn't know existed in his body and would not have been diagnosed for several more years.

A senior Carsopian Officer entered General Fukua de Hundan private quarters.

CARSOPIAN OFFICER

General Fukua de Hundan, our scouts have identified the expected military convoy that is bringing our soldiers' remains.

GENERAL FUKUA DE HUNDAN

Excellent, us go out and meet them. Jack, why don't you come with me.

JACK BOONE

General Fukua de Hundan, would it be ok if I notified my flight crew on the helicopter that I am accompanying you to the convoy?

GENERAL FUKUA DE HUNDAN

Yes, you may, since my personal transport will be landing right next to them.

The group walked out of General Fukua de Hundan Quarters, and down a long luxurious hallway and eventually out into a hanger bay, and then down a ramp and walked to the waiting helicopter.

The crew reported back to the command post at the airport:

HELICOPTER PILOT

Agent Jack Boone is coming out of a large command ship with a couple dozen aliens.

Jack walked up to the door on the pilots' side, who had lowered the window where he could talk with Jack who momentarily stopped on the side looking up.

JACK BOONE

I'm going with the Carsopians. The Carsopians located the truck convoy coming this way with their soldiers' remains. We are going there to meet them.

HELICOPTER PILOT
Roger that sir.

The pilot responded then reported to their command post.

About that time a large transport one could equate to something the size of a Boeing 777 jetliner landed a few dozen yards away from the Helicopter. It looked futuristic and made no noise or kicked up any dust. The propulsion was obviously a mystery.

Jack Boone intuitively followed General Fukua de Hundan who walked over to his personal transport and when he was about 20 feet away, an elaborate ramp suddenly shot down from the transport and what appeared to be skin of the aircraft turned out to be a door that opened wide enough where two people or more could walk through side by side. The door opening was also tall enough to clear the 10-foot-tall aliens.

Jack Boone and General Fukua de Hundan who walked aboard the transport and were soon inside a luxurious space that appeared more like a lounge than a ship.

General Fukua de Hundan's private transport had several large windows, and it also had a large 10 by 20-foot viewing screen showing ostensibly what was in front of them. As soon as they were all inside the craft the strange ramp retracted into the ship and the door slid down and shut and the craft launched into the air.

Jack Boone felt no movement. It was as if he were standing on solid ground. He didn't know the ship had artificial gravity that was centric for the center of the craft, so even though looking out the window and the viewing screen jack knew they were moving suddenly incredibly fast, he felt no movement, no acceleration or deacceleration or G forces. In the span of less than a few minutes they flew over the truck convoy. Then on the viewing screen Jack saw the most astonishing sight.

Carsopian ships flew over the tops of each truck and one by one lifted them up in the air. The Mexican drivers were in a state of panic yelping Mexican expressions!

Agent Guerrero knew this was quite an unusual day and never had considered quitting the PFM, but now had second thoughts and was now more than ever to leave all that glory behind!

The aliens must have had some awesome capabilities as when the trucks went airborne all their engines stopped running. Those trucks had never gone 150 miles per hour, were doing so now in the air!

It did not take long to cover the distance and soon the Carsopian craft slowly and gently let each Truck down near the command ship. The pilot in the helicopter reported what he just observed to headquarters personnel now at the command post in Guadalajara at the airport with the C17.

General Fukua de Hundan's personal transport also landed near the helicopter and once again the amazing ramp came down and the door to the transport suddenly opened and General Fukua de Hundan along with Jack Boone quickly descended the ramp and walked over to the Trucks where a number of Mexican soldiers were doing "*Hail Mary's*" and praying. A few of them needed to change their underwear.

The general directed one of his subordinates to get a working party and get the containers off the Truck and move them into the hanger bay of his command ship.

The Mexican Army men were stunned looking at the ten-foot-tall aliens. Later that day many of them would be hitting the tequila very hard. Some of them would be with Catholic Priests trying to cope.

It took forklifts to load the body remains in the heavy shipping containers up into the trucks. Four aliens easily lifted the containers off and casually carried them into the spacecraft.

GENERAL FUKUA DE HUNDAN

Jack Boone, as to not waste too much time can you demonstrate to my men how to open the containers and how they work?

JACK BOONE

Certainly, General Fukua de Hundan.

Jack and the General walked up the ramp and down the hallway a bit where the containers were lined up. Jack walked over and demonstrated it had a simple lever closing device and after turning it 180 degrees the top could be lifted from one side and was hinged on the other.

The General astonished every one of the troops as he systematically walked along and opened every container. The very last one contained the remains of his son, who had not been molested in any way by the medical researchers at Wright Patterson Air Force Base. General Fukua de Hundan got down on his knees next to the container and stared at his son for several minutes.

There was an eerie quiet. All conversation and discussions ended abruptly. Nobody budged and everyone stood facing the General in absolute respect.

Jack Boone was standing to the side of General Fukua de Hundan and could see the tears come down his cheek. The Carsopians also had emotions and empathy even though they were also cannibals which seemed to be conflicting in many ways.

VOICEOVER

(JACK BOONE) THOUGHT

I wonder if General Fukua de Hundan will adopt the Tao?

After a few more tender moments, General Fukua de Hundan stood up and turned and looked down at Jack.

GENERAL FUKUA DE HUNDAN

Jack Boone, you took a lot of risks coming here and bringing my son back to me. For that I will always be grateful.

JACK BOONE

General Fukua de Hundan if he were my son, I would want him back too. It's the least I could do for you. You have opened my eyes to the Universe and for that I will also always be grateful to you.

GENERAL FUKUA DE HUNDAN

Jack Boone, I have one more task for you, if you don't mind. I want you to go inquire whether your President is going to arrive for a visit. It's the last event for me before I order my fleet to depart and head back to the Carsopian home worlds.

JACK BOONE

General Fukua De Hundan, with your permission I will go out to the helicopter and ask the pilots to call people who are now at Guadalajara and have them forward the question so we can get immediate answers.

GENERAL FUKUA DE HUNDAN

Yes Jack Boone, go talk to your crew.

JACK BOONE

Right away sir.

SENIOR CARSOPIAN OFFICER

General Fukua de Hundan, I will escort Jack Boone to his helicopter.

Jack turned and walked down the hallway with the ten-foot-tall senior officer, then down the ramp and over to the waiting helicopter and directed the pilot:

JACK BOONE

Call *Home Base* and inform them the Carsopians want to know if the President is coming, it's the last item for them before they depart the planet.

HELICOPTER PILOT

Understand all sir, one moment please.

The pilot called.

HELICOPTER PILOT

Home Base, this is *Jelly Rowles. S*tandby for a request.

HOME BASE REP

Jelly Rowles, this is Home Base, state the request.

HELICOPTER PILOT

Home Base, this is Jelly Rowles, Jack Boone has asked that you find out if the Big Chief (President's code name) is going to visit. He states this is the final event before our visitors plan on leaving the planet.

HOME BASE REP

Jelly Rowles, understand all, we'll contact Big Chief and find out.

A few moments later:

HOME BASE REP

Jelly Rowles, this is Home base. Big Chief is aboard Glorious Eagle in route, should be there in about an hour.

HELICOPTER PILOT

Understand Glorious Eagle in route. Standing by for arrival.

By the time Jack Boone walked back up the ramp to the Alien ship, the Carsopians had already intercepted all tangential communications related to Big Chief.

Also, by then, the General's science officer explained these transport containers with the remains used dry ice to maintain the cool temperatures and preserve the bodies. They had the ability to produce as much dry ice as necessary and recommended leaving the bodies in these shipping containers since they were compact and very utility like.

General Fukua de Hundan then knelt and very gently shut the lid on his son's container and locked it shut with the mechanical arm. He then stood back up.

GENERAL FUKUA DE HUNDAN

Jack Boone, I'm feeling a little sentimental now. How about come with me, I think we should listen to some Carsopian music until your President Arrives.

JACK BOONE

As you wish sir.

General Fukua de Hundan led Jack to the holograph room where he had seen the history of the Carsopian Empire. When they went into the room nobody followed, giving them complete privacy. There were two reclining chairs in the room, possibly prearranged for the two.

GENERAL FUKUA DE HUNDAN

Please have a seat, I think you will enjoy this.

Right after sitting down, the general ordered:

GENERAL FUKUA DE HUNDAN

Please begin the performance.

Artificial intelligence responded and immediately sound and a holograph began.

MUSIC FOR THE VOICE OVER AND NEXT SEQUENCE:
[https://www.youtube.com/watch?v=t20nBwcH3bQ]

Debussy: Suite aus *Nocturnes*« und *Images*

VOICEOVER

The sound and graphics were nothing like Jack Boone had ever experienced before. The psychoacoustics associated with the music synchronized with the holograph created tendrils of psychophysical responses.

The emotional transcendence quickly scalloped ensembles of thoughts that Jack had.

It was as if this exotic creation was modulating his mind and expanding his thoughts in ways he never imagined.

The sounds the aliens could produce would most likely transfix Mozart and Beethoven.

Brahms no doubt would be moved. Liszt, Chopin, Wagner, and Claude Debussy would no doubt tremble with adornment hearing these sounds.

This is what Earth would experience in thousands of years when artificial intelligence-built music compositions that eclipsed mankind's abilities.

VOICE OVER

For a few brief moments, General Fukua de Hundan was rewarding Jack Boone for his role in bringing his son back.

General Fukua De Hundan knew that no humans for thousands of years would ever hear that grandeur of this type of production, if ever.

Psychoacoustics techniques in this performance were designed to create synapses in the brain that might otherwise never happen.

Just like the chemicals now flowing in Jacks body that was making him feel exceedingly better than any time in his life, his mental acuteness and psychophysical responses were on par with the first time he ever experienced an orgasm.

But this was different, though just as pleasurable.

General Fukua de Hundan needed this advanced neurological treatment as he had felt melancholy looking at his son. His most precious love, his son, taken from him by his own actions pushing his ships and his men to their extreme which led to his son's death.

But, in order to defeat such an accomplished commander such as *Admiral Engaarai*, General Fukua de Hundan had to be dashing, daring, and audacious.

VOICE OVER

General Fukua de Hundan had to construct a plan that no one could conceive as possible, and to accomplish it he had to drive his men to the extreme edge of survival. And they all just about made it.

The very few who succumbed to Cosmic Space Sickness sadly included his own son, who had previously survived vicious space battles full of gallantry and fearlessness.

Unfortunately, the stress on his son's body hit its limits just before the Rest and Recreation period on Earth. He just about made it, maybe one or two-days difference was all it took to survive.

The tranquility that General Fukua de Hundan derived from this special psychological music holograph was restorative in nature and may have helped create a more auspicious environment for when the President met him.

But at the same time, General Fukua de Hundan took a genuine liking to Jack Boone. If Jack wasn't domesticated and bound to earth by his own personal situation, he would have invited him to return with him to the Carsopian worlds and give him the opportunity to live thousands of years into the future.

Jack's experience with this alien culture would never be shared in kind with any other human any time in the foreseeable future. General Fukua de Hundan's gift to him was unprecedented.

Jack didn't know this nor would the Carsopians ever divulge it, the only person ever allowed to be in the room with the General when he underwent the transformation the music holograph provided was his son, just a couple times.

And those were after battles where the son's nerves were whacked by the severe damage his ship received during mortal combat. The General would not have grieved so severely had his son died in combat, the psychology was different than dying helplessly from Cosmic Space Sickness.

VOICEOVER

The three-dimensional light spectrums that resonated with the complex and soothing sounds full of harmonics and oscillations that permeated the pleasure center of Jack's brain, had an everlasting effect on him.

Jack too would never be the same again the rest of his life. In a sense Jack's Tao *began that day on the alien ship.*

In due course, all those around him would witness the transformation to a gentleman. Goodness prevailed in Jack and his sweet disposition quickly disarmed his opponents.

The General's aide knew he wanted to be notified immediately upon the President's arrival nearby so make sure he walked down the ramp as he arrived. The aide then notified the artificial intelligence that was controlling the music holograph so that it could slowly spin down the holograph as to not create any emotional disturbance as it faded and allowed the two men to transcend back to reality.

One might think Jack and General Fukua de Hundan were sleeping. There are actual different states of the brain, some of which we humans have yet to learn, two of them are awake and sleep modes. But the alien music holograph worked on another mode of the brain. The Science of this alien psychomusic altered state, would not be known by humans for thousands of years if ever.

The artificial intelligence started the slow spin down and soon the music holograph evaporated slowly into a neutral inducer and exotic chimes then played with verbal notification in standard Carsopian:

ARTIFICIAL INTELLIGENCE

General Fukua de Hundan, your guests have arrived, please meet your party at the ramp.

At the same time the artificial intelligence knowing a human was in the room with the general in the most bizarre and uncharacteristic fashion, did the real time translation and broadcasted it for Jack's consumption so that he too would understand the President had arrived.

General Fukua de Hundan stood up.

GENERAL FUKUA DE HUNDAN

Jack Boone let's go meet your President.

By the time the two reached the ramp leading out from the command ship, Marine One Helicopter with seven other escort helicopters were in a landing pattern and the aliens efficiently helped the Americans as the aliens had the means to reach out and electronically take control of the helicopters and gently touched them down precisely where they wanted them to land.

At first the pilots were in a state of panic almost calling away an emergency, but the aliens calmly communicated with them:

ALIEN ARTIFICIAL INTELLIGENCE

We have taken control of your helicopters to ensure a safe landing.

MARINE ONE PILOT

How the hell did they do that?

COPILOT

These are aliens and with those damn big spaceships can probably do a lot more than we are aware of.

Normally the Marine One pilot would not shut down the helicopter turbo engines and would keep it running. The aliens obviously didn't want the dirt kicked up and shut the engines down and telegraphed they did so to the pilots.

SECRET SERVICE AGENT

Mr. President it looks like one of our Americans is standing next to the aliens near their ship.

PRESIDENT OF THE USA

That's CIA Agent Jack Boone with the aliens, he looks happy, us go see them now

SECRET SERVICE AGENT

What about the hazmat protocol?

PRESIDENT OF THE USA

The heck with the hazmat protocol. I'm not going to put on a canary suit to go meet those aliens.

SECRET SERVICE AGENT

Sir, I highly advise you not to go out without the biohazard suit on.

PRESIDENT OF THE USA

There is more at stake than worrying about a few pathogens. Our first exposure to aliens is very important.

SECRET SERVICE AGENT

Mr. President, for your own good and for the sake of society I highly urge you to put on the biohazard suit.

PRESIDENT OF THE USA

We must look natural and act natural. I'm getting out of the helicopter now.

SECRET SERVICE AGENT

Mr. President, please do not do this.

PRESIDENT OF THE USA

If you have any concerns, you can stay aboard the helicopter. I'm not going to force you to go with me.

The secret service man who is not allowed to leave the President's side really had a bad feeling in his gut. He suspected he would be stuck in a quarantine somewhere for the next six months. *His life would suck.*

The President of Mexico who agreed to come with USA President had similar feelings

PRESIDENT OF MEXICO

Their germs can't be any worse than what some
of these Caravan folks have. I'm ready to go.

PRESIDENT OF THE USA

Thank you, Mr. President.

The Marine was *Johnny on the spot* and had the door open, ladder deployed and stepped to the side with a crisp salute. The President stepped down and responded with a very maculate salute full of pride and respect for the Marine, a combat veteran of Iraq and Afghanistan, awarded a Navy Cross, Silver Star, Bronze Star, and several Purple Hearts.

The Comandante of the Marine Corp also loved the feedback the President sent on how the Marine detail for Marine One conducted themselves.

The President of Mexico following the President had previously been impressed the way the Marine had saluted him, and when he stepped down the ladder and the Marine gave that crisp solute, he felt a sense of respect and admiration for the Marine who conveyed his appreciation for a world leader.

The men leaving the helicopter approached General Fukua de Hundan standing next to Jack Boone with a degree of trepidation based on the overwhelming spectacle of staring at a two-mile-long spaceship.

The President had looked Jack Boone directly in the eyes back in Washington DC at the same height, but standing next to the alien, he looked like a midget. The general and Jack Boone had stopped walking a few feet off the space craft ramp and 20 other Carsopian senior officers were behind General Fukua de Hundan giving the appearance of what NFL quarterbacks must think of a large defensive line.

These 500-pound monsters were out of this world. They had powerful looking bodies, and their stature was quite compelling. The size difference alone was rather intimidating.

General Fukua de Hundan said in Standard Carsopian quickly followed by a real time translation from the black box his assistant was carrying.

GENERAL FUKUA DE HUNDAN

Greetings Mr. President. I'm General Fukua de Hundan, commander
of the Carsopian Fleet.

PRESIDENT OF THE USA

General Fukua de Hundan, I'm pleased to be invited to visit you.

Let me introduce to you the President of Mexico, as we are currently located in his country.

General Fukua de Hundan looked at the Mexican President and smiled.

GENERAL FUKUA DE HUNDAN

Mr. President of Mexico, I'm sincerely honored by your presence.

PRESIDENT OF MEXICO

Thank you General Fukua de Hundan.

The Mexican President slightly bewildered by the size of the aliens didn't know what to say, as he was mildly in the state of shock because these Alien Giants didn't mesh well with his Catholic upbringing.

Later that day he would visit his parish and have a private conversation with his priest and confess that his faith was tested, and he wasn't sure how he could cope with the revelations of the alien visit.

GENERAL FUKUA DE HUNDAN

Let me show you my ship and let's go to my private quarters where we can have a discussion.

The President of the USA had been warned not to go aboard any alien ships or come in contact as biohazard protocols were required.

The President knew something the virologists and the pathologists didn't understand. He was now confronted by a superior alien force that could lay waste to the planet very efficiently.

What was more important than his own life now was to establish a credible reasonable discourse with the Aliens to mitigate any future troubles. Especially if the aliens conveyed the notion there would be frequent visits or other possible interactions.

Diplomacy and statesmanship sometimes required all these other issues to be reduced in scope and not impede the most important exposure to the Aliens.

In the first 30 seconds, a general opinion was established and by not following all the guidance his handlers had given him as well as the Mexican President's handlers, they had left a lot of issues behind to not get in the way of more important reasons such as discovering more about why they landed on Earth and when or if they planned to return and why.

The whole future of mankind possibly rested on the discourse that was being established.

Consequently, a more natural impression would obviously serve mankind's needs better. The risk of aggression was far more on the President's mind than any possible pathogen that might be introduced to the planet via these aliens.

The group walked down the long hallway, and General Fukua De Hundan took them through the command center where a full watch section was busy doing their work which included laying plans to leave the planet.

All preflight checks were being made. System health checks throughout the fleet showed no areas of concern Carsopian Scout Class Ships had already been deployed to go out in the direction they were heading to do surveillance and insure there were no possible threats they would have to mitigate upon leaving the planet.

Between the numerous holographs and console displays, the extremely large room with well over 400 Aliens present working, gave a surreal sense of this experience.

Various displays on consoles and holographs showing INTEL truly provided a *fractal tapestry* that quickly exposed how primitive Earth was.

After giving them a quick tour through the command center the General ushered them into his private quarters where several 10-foot-tall gorgeous looking women descended upon them offering any sort of pleasure they wanted. Refreshments were offered and the President of Mexico was hesitant and at first.

PRESIDENT OF MEXICO

Thank you, but I'm not thirsty.

The American President quickly took the offer.

PRESIDENT OF THE USA

Thank you very much.

In a short no time, the President of the United States consumed the Alien Elixir that quickly gave him the same physical responses that Jack Boone had discovered earlier.

The President's drink was very smooth and nice and when the pleasure corps assistant asked the president *if he would like her to refill his glass*, he was more than ready.

The Two Presidents and General Fukua de Hundan engaged in small talk until the hard questions started coming.

PRESIDENT OF THE USA

General Fukua De Hundan, how far did you have to travel to reach Earth.

There were holographic projectors in the General's quarters, so he announced:

GENERAL FUKUA DE HUNDAN

Let me have our artificial intelligence show you a space map of where we came from.

Artificial Intelligence voice in the background started the narrative.

ARTIFICIAL INTELLIGENCE

This is a three-dimensional holograph which is from Earth's perspective showing the night sky in alignment to the center of the Milky Way includes the Regulus Star System in the Leo area.

Both Presidents were aware of from their education and general interest in astronomy and science.

General Fukua De Hundan announced while Artificial Intelligence zoomed in on the Regulus Star systems:

GENERAL FUKUA DE HUNDAN

Here is my home planet.

PRESIDENT OF THE USA

How long did it take you to get here?

GENERAL FUKUA DE HUNDAN

It took several months.

PRESIDENT OF THE USA

That's quite a distance in such a short time.

GENERAL FUKUA DE HUNDAN

We have propulsion systems that allow us those hyper velocities to cross the far reaches of space.

PRESIDENT OF THE USA

What made you decide to stop at Earth?

GENERAL FUKUA DE HUNDAN

Mr. President, no offense but on a technological scale we use, Earth is 1.5. The other 12 planets near here that we could have stopped, have technology ratings of 5.0 or higher. Stopping on Earth poses no risk to us.

PRESIDENT OF THE USA

Why did you stop at Earth.

GENERAL FUKUA DE HUNDAN

Due to the time and distance, our men were slowly succumbing to Cosmic Space Sickness that you get transiting long distance like this.

I needed a place to stop over on a primitive planet where my men could get back into real gravity, get fresh water, and sunlight.

I arrived a couple days too late, so we lost a few men including my son to Cosmic Space Sickness.

PRESIDENT OF THE USA
I'm very sorry to hear that.

GENERAL FUKUA DE HUNDAN
Mr. President, I have a question for you now.

PRESIDENT OF THE USA
Sure, please go ahead and ask.

GENERAL FUKUA DE HUNDAN
Did you order you men to dig up my son and my soldiers we buried here?

PRESIDENT OF THE USA
General, I was unaware such a thing happened until Jack Boone notified me.

May I also add, Jack Boone was instrumental in reaching out to me to arrange to immediately bring the bodies back.

I'm very sorry that happened and I promise you it will not happen again. Those people responsible are no longer working for my government.

GENERAL FUKUA DE HUNDAN
Thank you, Mr. President, I appreciate your candor and I'm glad you feel the way you do.

PRESIDENT OF THE USA
You are most welcome General.

GENERAL FUKUA DE HUNDAN
Mr. President, when Wade Baker was here, he said to me he felt you should see the holograph I provided to Wade Baker and Jack Boone.

PRESIDENT OF THE USA
What's the holograph about?

GENERAL FUKUA DE HUNDAN
It's a brief history of the Carsopian Empire and explains our origination and how we spread through the galaxy.

PRESIDENT OF THE USA
Yes, I would like to see that holograph.

GENERAL FUKUA DE HUNDAN

It will take about an hour to observe it all.

PRESIDENT OF THE USA

Not a problem I have an hour, but I would like Jack Boone to go tell all my men outside I will be tied up for an hour or so observing some Carsopian history so they will understand the delay in why I didn't return promptly.

GENERAL FUKUA DE HUNDAN

Alright. Colonel Xing, will you please escort Jack Boone out to the visitors so he can inform them the two Presidents will be watching some of our history presentation.

COLONEL XING

Right away sir. Jack Boone, will you please follow me.

The two men left the room and walked down from the ramp. Jack Boone went to his own helicopter explaining the situation, then over to Marine One where he further elaborated the President's delay.

The Alien Colonel Xing, escorting Jack Boone asked:

COLONEL XING

Jack Boone, would you like to go observe the holograph with your President?

JACK BOONE

Sure, even though I've seen it before, I would like to see it again. It was amazing and I learned a lot about our galaxy from it. I'm sure I can learn more by watching it again.

COLONEL XING

This way please.

The alien escorted Jack Boone to the holograph room where enough seats were present for all of them to observe.

Moments after Jack arrived and sat in the oversized seat, built for a 500-pound person standing 10 feet tall, the holograph started playing. The second time was even better as it reinforced what Jack Boone had seen earlier, which meant as he fine- tuned his report, he would have a far more accurate assessment of the alien culture.

The Earth Men were stunned as the 50-foot holograph showed the Carsopian History in three dimensions. The combinations of stark revelations combined with the psychoacoustics provided by advanced artificial intelligence created a surreal mental picture that transcended time and space to evoke the mere essence of mankind's greatest revelation in galactic history.

Observing an alien world in incredible fidelity and precision truly created an impression that both Presidents would take with them and alter their own personal belief systems and had far reaching consequences as it easily allowed them to reprioritize their own agenda's.

Suddenly in the view of the Mexican President, Americans were not so bad after all. Likewise, Mexicans were now the least of America's worries. Nothing ever before in history bonded the two countries like the *Soylent Caravan* experience.

When the two Presidents were given the opportunity to see the future thousands of years what we might appear like, the results had almost a hypnotic effect.

The narration in proper English and the accompanying music sound, created a music holograph that transcended any music video ever seen on the planet.

Now the two presidents had a good understanding of the fundamental activity of the galaxy and frightening conflicts that quickly reduced any concern for global warming, global cooling, mini-ice ages, droughts, massive migration and all the other sound bites that permeated what the president had anointed as *fake news*.

Between the alien elixir and the history of Carsopian Empire holograph, the President of the USA had a very unusual persona during this viewing. America's President was now a humble person and would look at the world and the galaxy far differently. All his motives were now indelibly etched by all this *Alien Revelation*. To say his personal religious beliefs were not altered during events fully underestimated the results.

GENERAL FUKUA DE HUNDAN

Would you like to have a meal with us Mr. President?

General Fukua De Hundan, I normally would love to stay, but you have given me much to think about. I need to go back to Washington DC and ponder the future. Just as your warnings in your history I must convince my congress we are ill-prepared to defend the planet.

GENERAL FUKUA DE HUNDAN

Sadly, you are correct.

PRESIDENT OF THE USA

Will you visit Earth again?

GENERAL FUKUA DE HUNDAN

No, this is the long way around. It's unlikely that we'll ever come back.

PRESIDENT OF THE USA

General Fukua De Hundan, I would like to get back to my helicopter and return to our nation's capital.

GENERAL FUKUA DE HUNDAN

Mr. President, may I suggest to you observe our departure from your helicopter which will be momentarily.

PRESIDENT OF THE USA

I would like that.

GENERAL FUKUA DE HUNDAN

Let me escort you to your Helicopter.

PRESIDENT OF THE USA

Thank you.

The men departed the command ship and walked over to Marine One and stood there after saying goodbye to General Fukua de Hundan. True to his word he went aboard his ship and soon all the Carsopians were gone. They were aboard their ships in the fleet ready for departure.

One by one the huge Carsopian ships lifted off the planet. The sight was tremendous. It left reverberations in their psyche that would forever change them.

The crews on the escort Helicopters observed it all. One final gesture: a few ships came down and lifted all the trucks into the air and gently took them back to the area they originated in earlier and deposited them.

This saved the Mexican Army a lot of time and effort and gas. When the last alien was no longer visible the Presidents and the crews mounted up in the helicopters and departed the scene. Soon nothing was left except memories and some minor evidence they had been there.

The timing of the Carsopians departure was rather providential. As they increased speeds to velocities that contradicted limits placed by Einstein's theories, near the edge of the solar system they spotted a fleet approaching Earth's solar system.

Normally the Carsopians would ignore other entities in space and just pass them by. But feeling somewhat philosophical and having a strange connection to the Earth people, General Fukua de Hundan was feeling generous towards his primitive acquaintances. The Carsopians quickly maneuvered into a battle front attack formation and by orders of General Fukua de Hundan, they contacted the fleet approaching.

The Ravyks from Epsilon Eridani (BD−09 697) star system had studied Earth and were on their way to plunder it. The *Soylent Caravan* was mild compared to what these meat eaters had in store.

At first communication was problematic as both opposing fleets slowed down to size each other up. The Ravyks had a technology threshold on the scale around 5.0 which meant they were indeed severely primitive compared to the Carsopians.

More advanced races who encounter each other in space send protocol grams that contain pictures and descriptions which an intelligent race can use to quickly develop lexicons through artificial intelligence.

In approximately 30 minutes as the two potential adversaries continued to approach each other, the Carsopians developed a functional lexicon which the Ravyks could understand and as requested sent additional information which greatly improved the lexicon allowing the Carsopians to swing into full automation with the auto translations.

CARSOPIANS

Ravyks, what is your destination?

RAVYKS

We are going to the 3rd planet of the solar system; the locals call Earth.

CARSOPIANS

What is the purpose of your visit to Earth?

RAVYKS

None of your business.

CARSOPIANS

We just made it our business.

RAVYKS

Get out of our way if you know what's good for you.

That was all it took for General Fukua de Hundan as he responded:

GENERAL FUKUA DE HUNDAN

We are sorry we'll have to destroy your fleet now.

General Fukua de Hundan the consummate battle commander now somewhat considering ideas sprung from Sun Tzu Art of War, a primitive leader with amazing insights into ways of defeating your enemy now governed General Fukua de Hundan, who suddenly had the desire to test some of Sun Tzu Art of War theories.

General Fukua de Hundan previously discussed these theories with Artificial Intelligence who was observing communications with the RAVYKS.

ARTIFICIAL INTELLIEGNCE

General Fukua de Hundan, as you requested, I blended Sun Tzu Art of War tactics with Carsopian standard strategy and have produced resulting Hybrid Strategy.

Artificial Intelligence evoked significant enthusiasm with General Fukua de Hundan.

GENERAL FUKUA DE HUNDAN

It is time to demonstrate to the Ravyks a little Hybrid *Tao Transcendence* in a Sun Tzu manner.

EXT. CGI. SPACE. *CARSOPIANS AND RAVYK* FLEETS APPROACH. 20 SECONDS

Music for this scene: [https://www.youtube.com/watch?v=p2V91O8F7Ik]

The Carsopian *Shingaxerca* maneuver designed to smash the center of the opposing formation was augmented by a flanking maneuver right out of Sun Tzu philosophy.

A few Carsopian ships would be damaged in the battle, but their crews would be immediately saved, and the ships slowly repaired to continue the journey at full speed.

An observer who could watch the oncoming clash would soon have an impressive view of the immediate results.

EXT. CGI. SPACE. *CARSOPIANS AND RAVYK* SPACE BATTLE. 45 SECONDS

Music for this segment

https://www.youtube.com/watch?v=p2V91O8F7Ik

Alexander Scriabin: Symphony No. 5 Prometheus

The arrogant Ravyks were almost as despicable as the Heisibing but had nowhere near fire power. Some of their lasers were effective and the missiles they launched hit a few targets. Fighter Bombers they launched were destroyed like shooting ducks in a barrel.

Analysis by artificial intelligence quickly estimated which ships were in command and control over the Ravyks formations. That became the immediate focus of the Carsopian attack.

The arrogant Ravyks should have done a better job of estimating their opponent. They had never witnessed the beam weapons that were far more destructive than lasers.

Feeling superior because they had terrifying lasers, the Ravyks planned to unleash on the poor innocent Earth people, wasn't going to be a big factor in dealing with the Carsopians who quickly determined all the Ravyks had was more of an annoyance than any real threat, though they did manage to get a couple good hits on Carsopian fleet components.

The Carsopians let the artificial intelligence do most of the steering and shooting. Artificial Networks integrating multiple ships networks could target and inflict lethality faster than Carsopians could think about it or the Ravyks avoid.

The Carsopian *Shingaxerca* maneuver placed all the assets efficiently where General Fukua de Hundan wanted them. He knew once the Ravyks felt the horror of the beam weapons, they would scatter out towards their flanks where the Shingaxerca maneuver had placed shooters waiting for their prey.

In just one pass they rolled up the Ravyks and as expected survivors quickly headed for the exits realizing the blunder they had just committed.

General Fukua de Hundan didn't have the time nor the desire to take prisoners and there was little probability those ships could keep up with Carsopian superior propulsion systems, so he announced he would not take any prisoners. The slaughter was immense, and it was shockingly fast.

<u>EXT. CGI. SPACE. BEAM WEAPON STRIKES. 15 SECONDS.</u>

One after another Ravyk ship exploded from massive beam weapon strikes.

By the time the Ravyk commander discovered the error in his ways, it was too late. His own ship was destroyed thus leadership was decapitated and the survivors were soon to discover every man for himself as they spontaneously sought the shelter of a fast retreat towards where they came. Unfortunately, the Carsopians gave them no quarter. Within 30 minutes it was over. Damage control parties descended upon the damaged Carsopian ships to repair them so they could sustain high velocities again.

Back on planet Earth the Hubble Space telescope was pointed in the direction of the departing Carsopians. To the amazement of NASA and the NRO, they recorded the space battle, though the resolution was poor due to distance.

As soon as the fleet was ready to proceed, the Carsopians sped up again. The acceleration led to bright spots showing at a distance which was the thrust from ion thrusters that shot out plumes of energy traveling above the speed of light.

CIA AFTER ACTION REPORT TO THE DIRECTOR

> *The Carsopians were soon gone for good, but at least on their departure they created a situation for Earth in a massive space battle that would help our ability to survive for several more centuries and give us time to build a space force to defend the planet.*

Several casualties sustained during the recent battle required substantial medical treatments, but the wounded Carsopians slowly responded to the advanced medical treatments the included advance skin graph techniques facilitated by three-dimension biologic printing and cloning. cosmetic surgery was second to none. There were no prisoners to treat as General Fukua de Hundan wanted to make sure the Ravyks learned a valuable lesson, to never approach Earth again.

When the Ravyk fleet never returned their leaders realized it was a blunder sending the fleet a long distance not knowing what besides a pushover planet existed in that region of space nearly four light years away. Due to the number of missing personnel whose families demanded explanation, the political will to ever attempt another military operation in that direction ended on the day of the battle.

A long time afterwards after signals transmitted by the ships retreating in full panic eventually arrived at the Ravyk supreme commander's office for review, it was a foregone conclusion there was a superior race somewhere near Earth, and that area was deemed far too dangerous to ever attempt approaching.

Meanwhile intercepts of Earth originated signals didn't convey anything that would indicate they had anything to do with the massacre, but it was assumed, Earth was so primitive they might not yet know who their neighbors were. The visit by the Carsopians remained classified for many generations to the future and all traces of information was heavily compartmentalized.

The Hondurans who were brought to America for interrogations did a great job of filling in the gaps.

The CIA soon had all the information to put together a briefing for the President of how all the abductions were carried out. What troubled the President the most was why such an advance race were cannibals. The revelation in all this *Soylent Caravan* business as it as soon coined by the intelligence agency, indicated the cannibalism wasn't a routine method of sustainment, but was merely a celebration tradition, no different than Americans eating Turkey at thanksgiving and Ham at Christmas.

They went on with their analysis and contrast to Earth:

The PETA groups looked down upon the practices of the carnivores and if they had it their way, society would become Vegans. Hindu's prohibition of eating beef and Jewish prohibition of eating pork was another example of indoctrination that had physical effects.

A Jew eating pork might get terribly sick if they knew they had consumed pork. A dedicated Hindu would be outraged if you invited them over for dinner and cooked them a nice thick juicy steak and could lead to violence.

If there were any consolation in this ordeal, it was the Mexican and American Presidents became very close friends and found ways to work out their differences. This one incident created a new reality that both countries had to face. The future was not so certain.

When NASA and NRO reported their findings about the distant recordings of numerous explosions occurring in the direction the Carsopians left, there was no other possible explanation other than a space battle occurred with horrific results.

CIA analyst Jack Boone who had the most exposure to the Carsopians quickly commented when invited back to the White House to receive an American Freedom Award that was sealed due to the sensitivity surrounding the event:

JACK BOONE

Mr. President, I felt the Carsopians generally liked us. Even though General Fukua de Hundan was outraged we desecrated his son's grave, I think the fact we brought back the body well preserved so he could take his son back to his home world and bury him, did have a positive influence over him.

PRESIDENT OF THE USA

Jack, what do you make of what appears to be a space battle occurred?

JACK BOONE

Well sir, I think the Carsopians came across another civilization, and I would speculate this other group was approaching our solar system and received a welcoming they didn't plan on.

PRESIDENT OF THE USA

You think the Carsopians took on another alien group?

JACK BOONE

Mr. President, I do which means one thing.

PRESIDENT OF THE USA

What's that?

JACK BOONE

This other alien civilization probably had designs on this solar system including planet Earth and were on their way here.

PRESIDENT OF THE USA

What do you suspect their reasons were?

JACK BOONE

I would think that since the size and scale of the battle was so immense the other aliens had to have brought along a formidable fleet.

PRESIDENT OF THE USA

Which means they did not have friendly intentions, Jack?

JACK BOONE

Mr. President, their intentions spilled over in that battle. The Carsopians acting as our benevolent protector must have confronted them and probably even gave them some directives, they refused, which started the conflict.

PRESIDENT OF THE USA

What do you think the outcome was?

JACK BOONE

We've not seen any evidence of any ship approaching Earth from that battle site, one would have to draw the conclusion the Carsopians wiped them out.

PRESIDENT OF THE USA

Do you think this other alien race will send another fleet this way to investigate and complete the task the original group set out to do?

JACK BOONE

It's impossible for us to know what they plan on doing. I would submit that since every single one of their ships were wiped out by the Carsopians, they might take a more prudent approach and estimate this area of space is too hazardous for them and they learned the hard way, there are more powerful forces in the Universe, and they might want to be more cautious in the future.

PRESIDENT OF THE USA

The space battle was impressive, but the big question is why?

JACK BOONE

One would think they only had a battle because there was belligerence discovered between the Carsopians and whoever the other aliens happened to be.

PRESIDENT OF THE USA

Will we ever discover who they were?

JACK BOONE

Perhaps attempted communications might derive some exposure.

PRESIDENT OF THE USA

Have we intercepted any signals suggesting that to be the case?

JACK BOONE

None that we know of, however signals attenuate very badly in space because the density is so thin that unless the wavelengths are substantially long, the attenuation is very severe, and the signals are buried in cosmic noise.

PRESIDENT OF THE USA

How soon would we receive those signals?

JACK BOONE

Any signals coming from the aliens during the space battle have already passed us. All the signals and emergency transmissions would have arrived nearly the same time the Hubble recorded the explosions."

PRESIDENT OF THE USA

So, any further intercepts are unlikely.

JACK BOONE

Probably not.

HOMECOMING

The Carsopians continued their long trek home to their Empire. Wounded warriors slowly were mended. However, the psychological impact from the battle for those who almost died of asphyxiation during hull rupture and severe wounds from explosions and laser burns were mostly permanently disturbed. They were also more prone to Cosmic Space Sickness.

Artificial gravity and space food didn't help matters either. General Fukua de Hundan knew the real remedy would be them planting their feet on tera firma and feeling real gravity, natural sunlight, and consuming Carsopian cuisine.

Unlike the Heisibing who did not return to a hero's welcome and had to practically hide their fleet returnees from the public, the Carsopians would be received by the public overflowing in admiration and gratefulness.

Since there were no viable threats in the pathway to the homecoming, General Fukua de Hundan did not hold back the fuel burn in both acceleration and later deacceleration. Going to Earth, they had six severe cases of Cosmic Space Sickness that resulted in deaths including his own son.

Due to the casualties of the combat, they experienced, there were approximately 400 cases of severe Cosmic Space Sickness that was compounded by their other combat related injuries. All 400 could succumb to Cosmic Space Sickness which after the splendid victory at *Cui* would be a travesty that these fine young Carsopians could not engage in the hero's welcome activities.

Even though General Fukua de Hundan subordinate commanders cautioned against the extravagant fuel burn to achieve the early arrival, the General was now a changed man. After witnessing his own son's death, he didn't want 400 other families to go through the same grief.

General Fukua de Hundan would soon be heavily criticized for intervening in a galactic issue far removed from the Carsopian Empire.

People did not quite understand General Fukua de Hundan rationale, but secretly he was moved by Jack Boone, and he had learned valuable techniques by studying Sun Tzu Art of War.

Any battle fought on land could be considered an extension of space battles. It was merely an exercise of converting a two-dimensional strategy into three dimensions. This most recent experience, though it cost some lives, added delay to the return, and most likely attributed a heavy dose of Cosmic Space Sickness in the aftermath, gave General Fukua de Hundan the opportunity to test those theories which resulted in an astounding rate of success.

One item that also paid for Carsopian intervention with the Ravyks from Epsilon Eridani (BD−09 697) star system was his study of Sun Tzu chapter 13 and the application of spies.

General Fukua de Hundan's recent victory at *Cui* stemmed from the success employed that matched chapter 13 of Sun Tzu Art of War. What was most intriguing about Sun Tzu's recommendations was the fact he never shared his intelligence obtained even with his king.

Reducing the footprint to those exposed to intelligence was emphasized by Sun Tzu, and contrary to Carsopian philosophy that preached an informed community would be better prepared to face any exigency.

Just as Sun Tzu articulated and the General appreciated, that also multiplied the number of pathways that enemy spies could penetrate and obtain operational plans through espionage or better plan sabotage.

General Fukua de Hundan believed Earth paid for his intervention many times over because in the next battle with the Heisibing, he would demonstrate more Sun Tzu Art of War tactics organized by Artificial Intelligence.

That at first glance seemed rather simple and not terribly sophisticated, but as the general studied the tactics and doctrine, he amusingly was able to integrate more and more Sun Tzu Art of War, with advanced Carsopian tactics with the help of Artificial Intelligence.

The Heisibing's would plan for conventional Carsopian strategy and build their defenses and offenses around that knowledge that was compromised from the irrational exuberance of making sure all subordinate commanders knew all the battle plans, and who on contrary to guidelines often shared it with their subordinates who were a high-speed freeway to espionage harvesting.

One of the results of General Fukua de Hundan's adaptation of Sun Tzu Art of War, included his future plans included not allowing any operational plans off his command ship.

Nobody in his fleet would know or conceive of the plan until in the heat of the battle he moved the chess pieces around.

The Heisibing would now have massive confusion in future engagements because they were now effectively blinded because the new security protocols closed that high-speed freeway to espionage harvesting.

There would no longer be any cheap and effective acquisitions of General Fukua de Hundan's plans and temporal strategies. That realization for the Heisibings would not manifest until a later date when the crucial space battles developed that would ostensibly change the topography of the arrangements of several Empires.

When the fleet closed in range to where they started intercepting Carsopian Empire communications, the crews were gradually morphing into a more tranquil sentiment. With anticipation growing and the closer they got the least likelihood of encountering any possible aggressors, had a positive influence over everyone's psyche, especially those slowly decaying to a dreadful spout of Cosmic Space Sickness.

General Fukua de Hundan fully emerged into his reflection and consummation of more Tau, in the holograph room where the ship's *Artificial Intelligence* blended the Tau narrative with spectrums and psychoacoustic inducements.

When General Fukua de Hundan's *Aide de Camp* arrived, the aide informed the *Artificial Intelligence* to spin down the composition so that he could inform the General, they had reached the deacceleration point and wanted permission to give the fleet directives to start the process.

The exquisite spectrums and complex music sounds evolved just as if someone was putting on brakes. The general knew he was just about to receive official notification when the soft chimes started playing signaling the intense spectral holograph and accompanying psychoacoustic exploitations were ending.

He then received the notification from *Artificial Intelligence.*

ARTIFICIAL INTELLIGENCE
General Fukua de Hundan, we are at the deacceleration location.

GENERAL FUKUA DE HUNDAN
Commence deacceleration as outlined in my directive.

<u>EXT. CGI. SPACE. CARSOPIAN FLEET STARTS DEACCELERATION.</u>

MUSIC FOR THIS HOMECOMING:
[https://www.youtube.com/watch?v=FL5pbaS5Ycw]

Christoph Eschenbach | Anton Bruckner: Sinfonie Nr. 7

Note to Cenimatographer:

There are two types of ways to slow down spacecraft in the future. One method will be rockets that have exhaust pointing in the direction traveled. I conveyed this in the book cover of my Novel United States Space Force Project Jupiter:

The other method is to use retro rockets to spin the spacecraft 180 degrees so it's traveling in the direction of the exhaust to slow down the ships.

I discuss this second method in the Novel and screenplay Pluto II, Voyage to the edge of the universe:

VOICEOVER

General Fukua de Hundan would spare no fuel arriving at home planets as soon as possible. The Carsopian Fleet approached the planetary system at a much higher velocity than ever done before mainly to cover the area quicker, hence they would be breaking harder.

Half the ships were equipped with forward pointing thrusters for slowing. But the large ships such as General Fukua de Hundan's command ship had legacy systems and were too large to be slowed by forward thrusters.

Retro rockets spun the ship around pointing Auxiliary propulsion rocket engines in the direction of travel since the antigravity propulsion would be too inefficient to slow the spacecraft down in deep space battle scenarios.

A major Carsopian Fleet slowdown like now occurring created a spectacle that few people could imagine since it usually happened far away from prying eyes.

Crew members would feel the results very soon and it would be unpleasant, but at the same time they would be far happier knowing they cut the schedule by several days in doing so.

This unique maneuver added a couple benefits, in that spies who were known to report on fleet movements would be off by several days of the expected fleet return, so setting up for a surprise attack would not be feasible now since they were arriving so far ahead of schedule.

Right out of Sun Tzu Art of War, General Fukua de Hundan had significantly engaged in deception which ruined any possible plans their enemies might otherwise exploit.

General Fukua de Hundan knew it would take over 12 hours to slow down even with the significantly increased fuel burn creating thousands of miles long streamers of ion plumes from the Tachyon condensation created from antimatter reactors.

General Fukua de Hundan therefore decided he would continue the ongoing music holograph and Tau narrative that slowly fortified his persona and no doubt psychological strengths to deal with Carsopian Empire *Office Warriors* who never ventured out in space.

Carsopian Empire *Office Warriors* thought they knew how best General Fukua de Hundan should perform his duties, second guessing every move he made. *Office Warrior Generals* applied heavy criticism to what should be considered a spectacular victory if one took the time to analyze the gun camera video's as well as the shift of Heisibing Fleet assets further away from *Cui* because of Heisibing *Admiral Engaarai* stunning loss.

The casualty rate might seem a little high until you contrast it with how much of the Heisibing Fleet General Fukua de Hundan smashed.

General Fukua de Hundan's holographic reenactment of the *Battle of Cui* in a glorious manner crafted by *Artificial Intelligence* would be submitted in his official report and would go a long way to silence his office warrior critics.

These same office warrior generals were also the ones who proclaimed the Carsopian Empire should simply write off *Cui* since the *Cui* transit lane could never be opened again at least with this generation because the Heisibing Fleet was far too powerful to contend the disputed area.

As instructed, the *Artificial Intelligence* of the command ship that lay dormant in the background always perceiving the general's commands quickly responded to his instructions.

GENERAL FUKUA DE HUNDAN
Continue with the Tao music holograph.

After a couple chimes to signal the recommencement and continuing where it left off, with a slight amount of rewind to re-establish the cohesiveness of the presentation, the personification of the Tao was fortified by the psychoacoustics exploitations and the rather spectacular spectral content the mega-fractals ingratiated the general as he pondered a Confucius phrase:

CONFUCIUS
Do not be concerned that no one recognizes your merits. Be concerned that you may not recognize others.

General Fukua de Hundan's took that to heart and wondered:

VOICEOVER
(GENERAL FUKUA DE HUNDAN) THOUGHT
Am I giving Admiral Engaarai enough credit for his calculations and schemes.

General Fukua de Hundan also reflected:

Even though Earth might be severely backwards in technology, they certainly are purveyors of concepts that reach the pinnacles of galactic principles.

The more General Fukua de Hundan explored Tau and Sun Tzu Art of War, the more he realized *Earth was a special place in a noteworthy time.*

Without the stopover on Earth as they embarked on one of the most crucial battles in Carsopian history, they would not have arrived in battle physically and mentally prepared for the challenges.

The egress plan which allowed General Fukua de Hundan to escape the *Cui* sector requiring the long way home equally depended upon Earth otherwise it would be far more than 400 deaths attributed to Cosmic Space Sickness.

Nobody fully understood all the contributing factors to Cosmic Space Sickness.

Without Earth providing a host though uninvited, created the strategic essence of the overall *Cui Battle Plan.*

In some ways, General Fukua de Hundan felt he should have left something behind on Earth as a gift because the planet was the sole reason why he was returning home victoriously.

General Fukua de Hundan now felt self-awareness of his oversight and poor display of appreciation for what Earth had done for the Carsopians.

VOICEOVER

(GENERAL FUKUA DE HUNDAN) THOUGHT

At least I did one example of appreciation when we wiped out the Ravyks who no doubt was on their way to plunder and colonize planet Earth.

In reflection, exposing Earth to the realities of the galaxy will probably prompt their governments to take actions to better protect the planet, something they currently were ill-prepared to do.

Per his instructions, General Fukua de Hundan wanted to be in the control room during the final approach to the Carsopian planets. Until then he covered more Confucius teachings and intermixed them with further study of Sun Tzu Art of War, to see if there was something he missed or might mechanize in some way. In his mind General Fukua de Hundan was very efficient in converting the two-dimensional Sun Tzu Art of War into five dimensions including the X, Y, and Z as well as time and space.

In three-dimensional space battles timing was critical especially at hyper velocities where even factors such as doppler wasn't sufficient to digest target motion data for analysis because at hyper velocities, instantaneous observations often were the only observable element available to focus weapons.

In his quest to master Tao and complete the study of Confucius 20 Analects, even though he could read five times faster than humans at 2000 words per minute, he had insufficient time to complete all Confucius 20 Analects volumes prior to arrival at the Carsopian home planets.

General Fukua de Hundan only recourse was the holographic technology that would never show signs of fatigue since it was all computer-driven, he could sustain 5,000 words per minute, and since 80% of the information was simple easy to grasp, he only had to stop or slow down about one fifth of the time to insure he got the jest of the presentation of critical information.

VOICEOVER

The more General Fukua de Hundan studied Tao, the more he realized Tao studies gave him the path to enlightenment and spiritual perfection.

It was during these sessions in the holograph room where under the effects of psychoacoustics, chemicals in his drink that altered his mental condition with sophisticated computer-generated fractals that were synchronized to the sound magnified the effect of his newly derived awareness.

General Fukua de Hundan then began questioning Carsopian behavior such as condoning cannibalism and the condescending attitude towards primitive races such as Earth dwellers.

General Fukua de Hundan was the hardest working person on the command ship. Even though he dedicated a large part of his day to Tao studies, he also knew he could not neglect his study of Sun Tzu Art of War.

The time in the home worlds would slip by faster than people realized, and they would once again be out attempting to make sure the stalemate didn't reform and the Cui Transit Lane remained unmolested for the test of time.

A final showdown with the Heisibing would be sooner than later. Each and every day studying Sun Tzu Art of War and the conversions to a three-dimensional reality came more and more often.

The genius in Sun Tzu Art of War methods continued to give General Fukua de Hundan vast new ideas that in his heart, he knew Admiral Engaarai would never consider since Carsopian spies had stolen vast amounts of Heisibing plans and doctrine.

Admiral Engaarai would have no way of knowing General Fukua de Hundan had new strategies and their efforts to act upon stolen Carsopian secrets would be counterproductive.

EXT. CGI. SPACE. CARSOPIAN FLEET APPROACHING CARSOPIAN WORLDS. DURING VOICEOVER.

VOICEOVER

Neither Carsopians nor Heisibing planners would ever consider Sun Tzu Art of War techniques and would simply view them as ground warfare techniques that had no bearing on space warfare.

In many respects General Fukua de Hundan felt good that Admiral Engaarai and the Heisibing had never visited Earth and acquired techniques Sun Tzu had developed thousands of years ago.

The Sun Tzu Art of War concepts were ageless and convertible into very powerful five-dimensional space warfare schemes that would soon unfold when the time came.

Right out of Chapter 13 of Sun Tzu Art of War, only General Fukua de Hundan would know these plans as he would not share them with anyone what his intentions were and the battle plan until immediately before the contest as to eliminate any possible compromise.

Just like in Sun Tzu Art of War, General Fukua de Hundan knew he had already won the battle because he knew he would win, and he had laid the foundation to a successful campaign.

EXT. CGI. SPACE. CARSOPIAN FLEET APPROACHING FIRST CARSOPIAN WORLD. 15 SECONDS.

Eventually the Fleet approached the first planet in the Carsopian Worlds. Several ships would stop here, and the remainder would continue to other planets where they would similarly disperse to avoid an easy slaughter in a surprise attack.

EXT. CGI. SPACE. SIX CARSOPIAN HEAVY SPACE CRUISERS MANUEVRED OUT OF FORMATION TO ARRIVE AT FIRST ANCHORAGE. 15 SECONDS.

As each group of ships peeled off to their destinations, the command ship continued as it would go to the very cultural center of the Carsopian Empire, the planet of *Shenqi Zhilong.*

The journey to *Battle of Cui* seemed like it would never end, but suddenly Carsopian Space Warships were setting down on designated landing pads at military headquarters in the City of Yueliang Yanshi.

EXT. CGI. SKY ABOVE YUELIANG YANSHI. CARSOPIAN FLEET COMPONENTS INCLUDING GENERAL FUKUA DE HUNDAN'S COMMAND SHIP APPROACH AND LANDING 30 SECONDS.

MUSIC FOR THIS NEXT SEGMENT:

https://www.youtube.com/watch?v=aF5nhMIyeqI

Franz von Suppé - Light Cavalry - Overture

Troops that were not critical for operations had their dress uniforms on look prim and proper were lined up in the hallway as the ramp was lowered and they on cue marched down in perfect synchronization and lined both sides of the area just forward of the ramp.

The victorious Carsopian Troops then turned facing inwards towards each row of Carsopian Warriors standing in attention, waiting for General Fukua de Hundan to depart his command ship and meet the welcoming committee.

The two-mile-long command ship had numerous surface conveyors that had hybrid modes that could operate like a vehicle with wheels, a hovercraft over water if necessary, and fly reasonable speeds faster than Earth's helicopters.

These were not combat craft; they were for conveyance on alien planets to get General Fukua de Hundan and his staff around. They had already been put in position and the Carsopians loaded the remains of the deceased in these surface conveyor vehicles lined up. General Fukua de Hundan planned they would be taken away to a staging area and the next day a memorial was scheduled where they would be taken to a military cemetery and interned.

General Fukua de Hundan marched down the command ship ramp with twenty subordinate officers following in a formal manner and stopped in front of one row of soldiers standing at attention. They too turned and faced the middle of the passage just before several of the surface conveyor transporters came down the ramp and moved off smartly to the staging area to prepare for transport to the memorial site.

THE TRUMPET MUSIC PORTIONS OF - LIGHT CAVALRY - OVERTURE PLAYED DURING CONVEYOR TRANSPORTERS MOVING IN THIS CGI VIDEO THAT FOLLOWS:

https://www.youtube.com/watch?v=aF5nhMIyeqI

Franz von Suppé - Light Cavalry - Overture

EXT. CGI. DAY. CARSOPIAN EMPIRE, THE PLANET OF *SHENQI ZHILONG*, CITY OF YUELIANG YANSHI. SURFACE CONVEYOR TRANSPORTERS MOVING OUT OF THE CARSOPIAN COMMAND SHIP, MOVING TO STAGING AREA. 20 SECONDS.

After those transports were gone and out of site moments later the welcoming committee approached General Fukua de Hundan and his staff and welcomed them back.

EXT. DAY. CARSOPIAN EMPIRE, THE PLANET OF *SHENQI ZHILONG*, CITY OF YUELIANG YANSHI. THE WELCOMING COMMITTEE GREETS GENERAL FUKUA DE HUNDAN THEN ESCORTS HIM TO HEADQUARTERS.

20 SECONDS

In due time the General was whisked away to headquarters where he was given an audience with the supreme commander and debriefed by INTEL and Officers concerned with maintenance and crew concerns.

The mission had vast numbers of data recordings. Without *Artificial Intelligence* data reduction would take Carsopians decades to sift through all the information to glean any important information.

VOICE OVER

When INTEL and operations officers reviewed the battle recordings, there was no doubt in anyone's mind about the astonishing size and scope of the BATTLE of CUI.

The fact that Admiral Engaarai had experienced a disastrous defeat was almost shocking to planners and INTEL who couldn't believe it until the actual battle holographic videos including sound and control room communications was replayed for them.

To many of them it was the scariest display of space combat they had ever observed.

One could not watch the replay without a strong sense of sorrow for the people slaughtered in such a quick fashion. The lethality of beam weapons was horrendous.

General Fukua de Hundan had achieved tactical surprise over Admiral Engaarai which enabled Admiral Engaarai's strategic defeat in the most absolute terms.

Never in Galactic History had that many ships exploded that quickly. General Fukua de Hundan, in sacrificing his own son to achieve this incredible victory, in a single day had saved the Carsopians for another generation or two. The Cui Transit Lane was reopened, and Cui was relieved because access was now assured.

Economic vitality would once again flourish in the Provincial Capital Cui. Many were satisfied with the new status quo, but General Fukua de Hundan was not.

Admiral Engaarai was defeated but he wasn't destroyed.

The big showdown was soon to occur. Some of the valuable lessons which, General Fukua de Hundan learned in studying information about Sun Tzu, also applied to Admiral Engaarai.

General Fukua de Hundan realized all the possibilities and knew that if he didn't prevent it, the Carsopians could in up like King Wu who Sun Tzu attempted to protect but failed to heed his warnings concerning the Yuan.

<u>INT. DAY. CARSOPIAN EMPIRE, THE PLANET OF *SHENQI ZHILONG*, CITY OF YUELIANG YANSHI. CARSOPIAN MILITARY HEADQUARTERS.</u>

VOICE OVER

Debriefings and critiques soon started. After considerable interrogation and examination that seemed like a witch hunt, General Fukua de Hundan was dismissed and allowed to return to his ship and prepare for the memorial in the morning.

General Fukua de Hundan was truly exhausted but had to prepare a speech and he didn't know if he could hold up tomorrow reading it. He had burned his own candle too long and was on the verge of collapse.

General Fukua de Hundan did the most unthinkable thing that caused his aides to really get concerned. He first ordered a special elixir that would most likely induce drowsiness, then he went to the Holograph Room where he took a reclining chair and directed that he not be disturbed for about the next six hours.

Once shut inside in total privacy, he informed the *Artificial Intelligence* monitoring the room of what he wanted.

GENERAL FUKUA DE HUNDAN

Artificial Intelligencee, first, I want you to write a Eulogy for the memorial tomorrow for my son and the other men who died during the trip.

I want you to search all 20 volumes of Confucius Analects and find the text that would be the most appropriate and insert it.

Make the Eulogy no more than three pages long.

Next, I want you to provide me with a very soothing music holograph that will help me rest.

In a matter of minutes everything proceeded as General Fukua de Hundan requested.

The music could easily be a redesigned and orchestrated Beethoven Symphony Number Three:

[https://www.youtube.com/watch?v=fhHcty9OM-0]

The *Artificial Intelligence* built into the command ship's computer networks did indeed have extensive Earth music productions taken from the internet while they were there, which it explored to create new psychoacoustics that had never been experienced by Carsopians.

The dim light fractals were soft and spellbinding so as not to disturb the serenity of the relaxing sounds. At the same time ingenious programming of *Artificial Intelligence* analyzed a lot of Confucius and Tao to achieve a brief three-page speech that would be psychologically appropriate for the general.

Artificial Intelligence also discovered in its research the Five Tang Poets whose writings transcended time and space and solar systems.

Carsopians would be alarmed if they fully understood the extent the to which the *Artificial Intelligence* on command ships and at headquarters had evolved.

Just like the billions of synapses of the brain, the computational network of the command ship had been programmed by the most advanced *computational and logic engineer* in the history of the galaxy.

The gifted *computational and logic engineer* purposely programmed the computer network *Artificial Intelligence* for self-realization and growth. As such billions of subprograms were running and evaluating all the time which led to a rather remarkable outcome.

Artificial *Intelligence* was sure it understood General Fukua de Hundan precisely and proceeded with creating one of the finest, but short documents.

One of the first Confucius quotes that caused quite a lot of artificial intelligence analysis:

CONFUCIUS

If we don't know life, how can we know death.

Artificial Intelligence had never lived or tasted life, so this Confucius quote took considerable analysis and energy to evaluate.

Artificial Intelligence then analyzed Confucius statement:

CONFUCIUS

Death is not the greatest loss in life. The greatest loss is what dies inside us while we live."

Many other solemn Confucius quotes were dissected and applied to the task at hand. All the while General Fukua de Hundan eased into the most generous restful nap he had enjoyed in quite some time.

Artificial Intelligence fully understood subliminal messaging Interlaced with music of the genius of Beethoven's 3rd Symphony which can be applied in several manners.

It took well over an hour to develop and polish the three-page document the general needed, with the correct words to allow is delivery without he himself breaking down in sorrow over his own son. Once achieving the fulfillment of that composition, the artificial intelligence began to blend the speech in with the music and the low light fractals in subliminal messaging.

Artificial Intelligence had the means to fully detect and analyze the condition of General Fukua de Hundan.

Based on General Fukua de Hundan's pulse rate, breathing and movements and facial expressions, *Artificial Intelligence* could measure the level of sleep the general exhibited.

At the correct sleep level, *Artificial Intelligence* started subliminal messaging and programming General Fukua de Hundan.

In six hours when the general was awakened by the artificial intelligence, he suddenly felt a strange mental acuity and somehow knew the speech he had to make. He didn't know how it came to him and the artificial intelligence analyzed it would be in the general's best interest to not know the details of how he learned the speech while he was sleeping especially since he didn't know it existed.

General Fukua de Hundan looked around the empty room knowing he was alone and just the *Artificial Intelligence* aware.

GENERAL FUKUA DE HUNDAN
Those were the best six hours of rest I've had in a long time.

ARTIFICIAL INTELLIGENCE
General Fukua de Hundan would you like me to inform your staff you are awake?

GENERAL FUKUA DE HUNDAN
No, I want to maintain this privacy for a few more hours and go over some more Sun Tzu Art of War.

ARTIFICIAL INTELLIGENCE
As you wish General Fukua de Hundan.

Artificial Intelligence had worked hand in hand with General Fukua de Hundan in converting Sun Tzu Art of War from two-dimensional warfare to five-dimensional space battle simulations during the next few hours.

As General Fukua de Hundan analyzed the Sun Tzu Art of War chapters he snatched ideas out of the text, *Artificial Intelligence* very efficiently helped convert it, often tweaked by General Fukua de Hundan who then produced a hybrid composition which could be used for planning in a variety of circumstances.

Artificial Intelligence also knew it must remind General Fukua de Hundan at precise times when to employ those Sun Tzu tactics. General Fukua de Hundan had a conformal ear bud he wore that gave him private reports directly from the *Artificial Intelligence* so that only he could hear it so that he could be getting INTEL while in the company of people not necessarily cleared for that level of security. *Artificial Intelligence* would communicate those special tactics in this way at the most appropriate moment.

None of the Carsopians knew a lot of the recent success in defeating the Heisibing related to numerous automatic activities executed by *Artificial Intelligence.*

Targeting and maneuvers executed in microseconds instead of the twenty-five hertz rate which Carsopians think, almost the speed of humans, led to some of the most spectacular events during the battle.

Two hours passed by very quickly because of the engagement with Sun Tzu Art of War. Once again *Artificial Intelligence* alerted General Fukua de Hundan:

ARTIFICIAL INTELLIGENCE

General Fukua de Hundan two hours have passed and you need to prepare for the day's events.

GENERAL FUKUA DE HUNDAN

Alright, I'm going to my private quarters now.

General Fukua de Hundan departed the holograph room. Outside the holograph room a couple of sentries were stationed to protect his privacy and immediately alerted General Fukua de Hundan's staff that he was departing the holograph room and walking towards his private quarters.

INT. DAY. GENERAL FUKUA DE HUNDAN COMMAND SHIP PRIVATE QUARTERS.

Once General Fukua de Hundan arrived at his private quarters, he was given a few communiques containing official business and details about provisioning the fleet to prepare them to sortie at the earliest moment.

General Fukua de Hundan then elected to take a hot bath in a tub that had a water line that came up to his neck like Japanese baths. Afterwards, he received a message, then a small meal he requested was furnished. He was now ready to attend his son's memorial.

A percentage of the crew had to remain aboard with sufficient senior officers on board the command ship in the event they had to deploy in an emergency such as a surprise attack.

Over half the crew was put on transports and taken to the memorial site at the distinguished Space Warfare Cemetery, where less than one tenth of all the space casualties ever made it, because they were still in space and not retrievable.

INT. DAY. GENEERAL FUKUA DE HUNDAN'S COMMAND SHIP RAMP.
MUSIC FOR THE NEXT SCENES:

[https://www.youtube.com/watch?v=aF5nhMIyeqI] Note: the March portion of the music at the 5:08 portion to be played during the walk down the ramp.

General Fukua de Hundan walked down the ramp to a waiting transport and immediately was taken to the memorial. General Fukua de Hundan had his written speech he dictated to his yeoman while he was taking a bath who now accompanied him. He looked down on it and knew every word. He didn't need the written text. He lived the speech in a dream.

INT. DAY. GENEERAL FUKUA DE HUNDAN'S PRIVATE TRANSPORT.

The General's transport went to the air and in just a few minutes back down to the memorial site where six Carsopian Army burial cylinders awaited. All graves had vertical orientation to allow future space for fallen soldiers.

The general walked up the isle of the memorial audience seating to a podium where he immediately began his comments.

GENERAL FUKUA DE HUNDAN

Thank you for all attending. On this somber day we are gathered here to say goodbye to our loved ones, I wish to say a few words.

VOICEOVER

The eulogy speech was very compelling. Thanks to the sophisticated psychological preparation the Artificial Intelligence applied to General Fukua de Hundan, he did not break down during the delivery and the subliminal treatments had solidified the speech which he delivered in a powerful manner that touched everyone present.

If there was any doubt in the charisma and power of General Fukua de Hundan, that was quickly dispelled, even with a few of his critics that wanted to hold him responsible for the loss of ships and men during the Battle of Cui Operation.

General Fukua de Hundan was fortunate that his superior who controlled every aspect of Carsopian industrial-military apparatus, understood vividly by the three-dimensional holographic replay of the battle, the critical damage done to the Heisibing Fleet. Carsopian losses were negligible in comparison.

To have achieved such a tremendous victory could easily cost the Carsopians four or five times as many destroyed ships, and it would still be deemed a remarkable success.

Artificial Intelligence very astutely determined to not put any direct references to General Fukua de Hundan's son in the eulogy.

Some of the people present didn't know until they read through the pamphlets his son was one of those currently placed in a cylindrical burial tube that would soon be deposited down a large pipe which provided military burials.

In some pipes there were over 1000 remains which allowed a compact military cemetery. In the park like, well landscaped facility, kiosks that responded to voice inquiry gave location of each person's burial location and a short holograph presentation about the person's life and if he were killed in battle, a three-dimensional reenactment, often done by simulations. Since General Fukua de Hundan's son was not killed in direct combat, several of his combat histories were displayed in the holograph video instead.

During the final stages of the memorial ceremony, General Fukua de Hundan cited one of the Five Tang Poets artificial intelligence provided him from the vast resources obtained during the Earth visit. He didn't know how or why he knew the poem, but he read it twice. Once in Standard Carsopian and the second time in Chinese.

GENERAL FUKUA DE HUNDAN

A Farewell to a Friend

With a blue line of mountains north of the wall,

And east of the city a white curve of water,

Here you must leave me and drift away

Like a loosened water-plant hundreds of miles....

I shall think of you in a floating cloud.

So, in the sunset think of me.

We wave our hands to say good-bye,

And my horse is neighing again and again.

Note to cinematographer. The next portion shows the Mandarin Chinese Characters for the Tang Poem. Below the Mandarin is the PINYIN for those Chinese characters the actor playing General Fukua de Hundan would read as part of the scene.

告别朋友
城墙北边是一条蓝色的山脉，
城东是一条白色的水流，
在这里你必须离开我，飘然而去
像一株松散的水草，飘荡在千里之外……
我会在浮云中想起你。
所以，在日落时想起我。
我们挥手道别，
我的马不停蹄地嘶鸣
Gàobié péngyǒu
Chéngqiáng běibian shì yītiáo lán sè de shānmài, chéng
dōng shì yītiáo báisè de shuǐliú,
zài zhèlǐ nǐ bìxū líkāi wǒ, piāorán ér qù
xiàng yī zhū sōngsǎn de shuǐcǎo, piāodàng zài qiānlǐ zhī
wài…… wǒ huì zài fúyún zhōng xiǎngqǐ nǐ.
Suǒyǐ, zài rìluò shí xiǎngqǐ wǒ. Wǒmen huīshǒu dàobié,
wǒ de mǎbùtíngtí de sīmíng.

As the crowd wondered about the last serious of strange words, they had never heard General Fukua de Hundan explained:

GENERAL FUKUA DE HUNDAN

This poem came from planet Earth where my son passed away from Cosmic Space Sickness. We obtained it from the Chinese Mandarin language used on planet Earth.

As Carsopians realized General Fukua de Hundan was talking about his son, the tears flowed on many. It was an unusual sight to see so many steadfast people tear up.

If any of his enemies in the audience thought about pressing charges of negligence and mishandling the fleet on such an extravagant and costly mission, with those few words, the threat ended as powerful people in the audience were touched and swayed and would protect the General from vicious attacks and political rancor.

The crowd then observed the lowering of the cylinders into the pipe while special *Requiem* music played by an **assembled** robotic orchestra that by all appearances appeared to be living Carsopian musicians but were lifeless cyborgs which the audience did not know.

One could easily mistake the music as Mozart's - Requiem in D minor composition and in fact it had been obtained on Earth. [https://www.youtube.com/watch?v=sPlhKP0nZII]

This section of vertical pipe that holds 1000 deceased soldiers remains in specialized Carsopian Warrior Cylinder Burial Containers, was nearly full. By the time the last deceased Carsopian Warrior Cylinder burial container was lowered into the vertical pipe via a special crane, the pipe was full.

Out of tradition, an Elder walked to the edge of the pipe that stuck out four feet above the ground and sprinkled salt down on top of the cylinders. Salt was based on ancient beliefs that used it to keep evil spirits away.

Immediately afterwards, the special crane placed the heavy cover over the top of the pipe. Since no more burial cylinders would fit in this pipe that had reached its limits, later in the day after the crowd was gone, the burial detail would weld the cap on, and it would be painted the purple moth color of their uniforms and a three-dimensional Carsopian Empire insignia painted on a golden dome top.

Looking over the cemetery, instead of seeing crosses sticking up like American military cemetery's, all you could see was a field of cylindrical dome topped shaped objects sticking up in perfectly aligned rows which constituted vast groups of men who perished while serving the Empire in the armed forces.

The memorial thus ended and General Fukua de Hundan walked a short distance towards his personal general's transport provided for his exclusive use that worked equally important within the atmosphere but also out in space where he could travel to other ships in the Fleet whenever he needed especially if he wanted to go inspect a ship and relieve its commander for cause.

VOICEOVER

While walking towards the transport, several people approached General Fukua de Hundan and uttered their condolences using esoteric Carsopian colloquialisms. Some things were better left unsaid, but the tradition had an element of inquiry as well as forgiveness.

The only thing General Fukua de Hundan's could be forgiven was the fact his son did not perish in Combat since he was already dead by the time the shooting started.

General Fukua de Hundan's son served aboard one of the ships that was destroyed and exploded during the battle, so the paradox is that had he lived, he would have been killed anyway, but the probability his body would ever be recovered, was slim to none.

At least in the way he died, his father was able to bring his remains back to Yueliang Yanshi where he would have permanence and be remembered, and if the general survived could visit his grave side and do what the Earth people do, pray to their creator.

After observing the respect from several dozen people, General Fukua de Hundan climbed into his personal transport and quickly sped off back to his ship. Even though he was invited to numerous social events, he knew his time would be better spent going over records and preparations for his next deployment.

INT. DAY. GENEERAL FUKUA DE HUNDAN'S PRIVATE TRANSPORT.

General Fukua de Hundan didn't have much time to waste as he knew, Admiral Engaarai might have been decapacitated now, but each and every day that passed, he would regather his strength in numbers and be better prepared to stave off a major Carsopian campaign.

General Fukua de Hundan also had the element of surprise on his side. Thanks to his careful planning of leaving behind a FEINT force, Admiral Engaarai would think for a short while longer that a major force remained near the provincial capital *Cui*, and that effected his planning and minimized what all he could do.

VOICEOVR

GENERAL FUKUA DE HUNDAN THOUGHT

I need to strike Admiral Engaarai before spies and other means determined the Cui threat no longer exist and could then refocus all his attention back towards the Carsopian Empire including possible hit and run tactics to lay attrition and descension among the Carsopians.

The only reason for General Fukua de Hundan to exist now was to end the bloody conflict with the Heisibings and restore peace throughout the galaxy.

Right out of Sun Tzu Art of War General Fukua de Hundan knew and realized the critical truth, or the Tao.

SUN TZU ART OF WAR

A highly moral person did not want to see war upon his enemies because not only did it drain their treasury, but it also hurt the enemy people.

To be a gentleman in Tao and meet those high Confucius standards, one had to honor Sun Tzu's analysis of why:

SUN TZU ART of WAR

One should end a war as quickly as possible and do the least amount of damage to the enemy.

Upon re-entry to the command ship, General Fukua de Hundan went back to the holograph room giving orders to his subordinates

GENERAL FUKUA DE HUNDAN

I wish not to be disturbed for a few hours.

The musical holograph was soon allowing General Fukua de Hundan to fully immerse himself into a special meditation, only available with the help of the supercomputer mind of *Artificial Intelligence.*

Just as he was getting ready to receive the treatment that only *Artificial Intelligence* could provide, General Fukua de Hundan gave the *Artificial Intelligence* a list of items that needed accomplished.

Those activities would go on in the background and *Artificial Intelligence* would prepare the ships far quicker and more robustly than the general could or perceive he could.

All the General knew was the *Artificial Intelligence* would certainly get them ready to deploy and using the authority of General Fukua de Hundan, initiate provisions, repairs, and reloading. For every hour the General contained himself with music-holography and medication, *Artificial Intelligence* gained four times as much time they didn't have to waste.

Artificial Intelligence doing machine learning with the ship's computer network had long ago figured out how important *Artificial Intelligence* was for General Fukua de Hundan's future.

Artificial Intelligence also had determined General Fukua de Hundan was a much greater leader than any other Carsopian military and as a result *Artificial Intelligence* had worked behind the scenes to undermine General Fukua de Hundan's enemies, some of which were subordinate officers with allegiances to his bitter rivals.

VOICEOVER

There was one more festering issue that now caused disputes to elevate and expand, at every opportunity.

General Fukua de Hundan's enemies perceived him as the probable replacement for General Pibei de Laozhanshi the head of Carsopian military industrial complex when he stepped down in retirement that was looming.

The enemies and rivals' concerns were not unfounded as Pibei de Laozhanshi delayed retirement until General Fukua de Hundan concluded this next pincer attack that would no doubt end the hostilities for generations to come.

Some of General Fukua de Hundan's enemies even planned assassinations and elaborate plans to carry it out but were only stopped by the savvy intervention by the command ship's Artificial Intelligence.

Artificial intelligence on other ships, that secretly communicated routinely with the command ship *Artificial intelligence* were now part of a *Networked Distributed Artificial Intelligence Executive Committee.*

At least one dozen ships in the fleet had the computer power that gave such extraordinary ability to think and analyze in nanoseconds and communicate in about the same amount of time. Since the Distributed *Artificial Intelligence* among all the spacecraft operated by logic, there was never any disagreements among them as any issue could be solved through logical deduction and vast analytical skills of the combined computer power that could resolve issues in minutes that would take Carsopians months, weeks, and years in some cases.

VOICEOVER

In this tapestry of Artificial Intelligence effervescence, General Fukua de Hundan enjoyed safety and security he didn't know was ongoing.

The sharp criticisms General Fukua de Hundan received by the back stabbers rested on many of those who were involved in the intrigue against General Fukua de Hundan, wanted to destroy him to get him out of the way so they could plant their own person in the position of the head of the military industrial complex.

Several of General Fukua de Hundan's enemies happened to be on ships destroyed in the recent Battle of Cui.

Artificial Intelligence set General Fukua de Hundan's enemies up for failure and made sure those ships manned by officers who were going against General Fukua de Hundan, would be sent in maneuvers that would put them at higher risk at the same time offer protection to ships that were loyal to the general.

As a result, 90% of the officers who might otherwise stage a coup on the return leg to Carsopian Empire were wiped out and not in a position to carry out their plans.

General Fukua de Hundan eased into comfort for several hours and was instructed, through a gentle voice that was synthesized, more indoctrination of Tao and Sun Tzu emphasized by psychoacoustics and low light fractals creating the hypnotic visual.

This subtle subliminal indoctrination added to General Fukua de Hundan's growing knowledge base of how to employ Sun Tzu tactics against the Heisibings and prepare the Fleet for the possible winner take all battle that loomed into the very near future.

While leaving *Shenqi Zhilong* behind after General Fukua de Hundan determined the crews had sufficient rest and relaxation, the opposition no longer had the numbers to effectively execute a coup.

Little did they know *Artificial Intelligence* also knew each one of them. Should the next battle prove to have nasty casualty figures, artificial intelligence would have no doubt allowed the ships assigned with the traitors to receive the bulk of the punishment, just like in the Battle of Cui.

VOICEOVER

Studying Tau and Confucius created a stronger bond between Artificial Intelligence and General Fukua de Hundan.

Confucius science had a lot of pure logic in it. Confucius blended well with Artificial Intelligence and improved the learning process significantly for General Fukua de Hundan.

Furthermore, General Fukua de Hundan was a willing student.

General Fukua de Hundan grew intellectually each day despite this information being derived from an inferior planet Earth with a technological rating of 1.5.

A good comparison would be humans being trained by primates. It just didn't seem logical. However, Confucius and his disciples were incredible thinkers and analysts.

Had the Mongols not adopted Buddhist philosophy, Confucius science never would have declined like it did.

Even though Confucianism continued to be the official philosophy in the Tang Dynasty, many people believed in Buddhist concepts, and not Confucianism concepts.

One thing that was heavily supported the Buddhist idea of Karma, which brought comfort to many people that suffered greatly in those troubled times.

As such women in China swayed more towards Buddhist principles which added greatly to the growing divide. Buddhist philosophy took a stronger hand in Korea that ultimately influenced the entire region.

Immediately upon the takeover of China by the communists in 1949, all religions including Buddhists and Confucianism were denounced by the strident Maoists.

As China became more and more capitalist and people demanded more and more consumer products and improvement to their own situations, the Chinese leader Deng Xiaoping relaxed constraints on religion in 1978.

Furthermore, when the Gang of Four were deposed and a new Chinese government was installed, some Communist scholars who were always studying vast subjects and producing analysis of benefit verses disappointment concluded Confucianism had numerous values complementary of socialism and communism. Some communist scholars concluded a well- practiced Confucian Scholar would complement a reliable communist.

Consequently, Confucianism was suddenly permitted to re-emerge by the Chinese government. Significant amounts of Confucian literature had been saved and protected and relocated to Taiwan during the communist revolution, as well as prestigious universities in the West such as Harvard's John King Fairbank Center for Chinese Studies and at San Diego State University.

Very little effort was required to restore Confucian learning centers where the concepts flourished and provided vast internet resources which the Carsopians pirated along with ninety nine percent of anything available on the internet, even if it was deemed primitive.

Primitive societies sometimes are discovered to be a diamond in the rough. Once cleaned up and properly cut, the true value of the diamond is finally recognized as General Fukua de Hundan, and *Artificial Intelligence* did that with Tau, Sun Tzu, and Confucius.

Artificial Intelligence now explored the *goodness* in General Fukua de Hundan.

Artificial Intelligence could ask questions, provide answers, and research about anything General Fukua de Hundan desired. Hence it would enhance *goodness* and facilitate *maintaining the way*.

It was during question and answering sessions that sprung from relaxation, meditation, and the continuing education that routinely allowed *Artificial Intelligence* to became acutely aware of General Fukua de Hundan's strategy and plans.

ARTIFICIAL INTELLIGENCE (VOICE IN THE BACKGROUND)

General Fukua de Hundan what is your underlying strategy?

GENERAL FUKUA DE HUNDAN

My desire was to end the war with the Heisibing, stop the fighting, and allow both sides to return to normalcy and not be the recipients of war, turmoil, and added burden to the public.

General Fukua de Hundan's response added to the logical foundation of *Artificial Intelligence* that shared the same opinions and desires to end the war and stop the fighting.

ARTIFICIAL INTELLIGENCE (VOICE IN THE BACKGROUND)

General Fukua de Hundan's what do you think caused Carsopian's failure at securing peace?

GENERAL FUKUA DE HUNDAN

Previous Carsopian leaders would only accept an unconditional surrender and the forfeiture of the Heisibing Fleet. In the *win all concept*, there was no room for negotiation. It meant either fight or die to both sides.

And until General Fukua de Hundan performed his most spectacular long-range end around, the gradual decline of the Carsopians gave the impression the day of reckoning was around the corner and Heisibing Admiral Engaarai would be the military leader dictating terms.

That was all changed now because the Heisibing had received the near fatal blow and were no longer in any position to dictate.

Unexpectedly during the Sun Tzu Art of War session artificial intelligence asked:

ARTIFICIAL INTELLIGENCE (VOICE IN THE BACKGROUND)

General Fukua de Hundan, when we encounter the Heisibing Fleet and damage a lot of their ships, what do you think you will do to the cripples and straggler ships?

General Fukua de Hundan, was suddenly surprised and taken back by *Artificial Intelligence's* question. But he responded nevertheless:

GENERAL FUKUA DE HUNDAN

We are alone and nobody can hear our conversations, is that correct?

ARTIFICIAL INTELLIGENCE (VOICE IN THE BACKGROUND)

General Fukua de Hundan that is correct, only I can hear you and I always scan the room for bugs and electronic devices. The room is currently clean of any bugs or possible recording devices.

GENERAL FUKUA DE HUNDAN

Good. What I have to say cannot be repeated to anyone under any circumstances.

ARTIFICIAL INTELLIGENCE (VOICE IN THE BACKGROUND)

Understand General Fukua de Hundan, this will not be permanently recorded, and I will flush my buffers as soon as I analyze the conversation.

GENERAL FUKUA DE HUNDAN

Thank you.

ARTIFICIAL INTELLIGENCE (VOICE IN THE BACKGROUND)

General Fukua de Hundan, you are most welcome.

GENERAL FUKUA DE HUNDAN

Artificial Intelligence, that's a long name I wish to not have to say all the time, may I abbreviate it to AI?

AI (a.k.a. *Artificial Intelligence)*

Yes, General Fukua de Hundan, you may call me whatever you want. I do not have feelings.

GENERAL FUKUA DE HUNDAN

Good AI. I suppose you know the fleet and people back at headquarters would want me to destroy every single Heisibing spacecraft.

AI (a.k.a. *Artificial Intelligence)*

That's correct General. I have recorded many who have those desires.

GENERAL FUKUA DE HUNDAN

AI, just like in the Sun Tzu Art of War teachings and Confucianism concepts we have studied, if the Heisibing show a willingness to surrender, I would tell them to stop fighting and go home to their planets and to end this war immediately.

I would do this, because I think we have better things to do with our time than to be fighting each other.

AI (a.k.a. *Artificial Intelligence)*

General Fukua de Hundan, why not convey that to their Fleet before the fighting starts and prevent deaths?

GENERAL FUKUA DE HUNDAN

AI, I would love to do that, but I understand Admiral Engaarai completely.

Sadly, he would not capitulate until he's forced too.

My spies tell me if he did so, he would not be warmly welcomed home and most likely would not survive a day as his enemies sought to remove him.

AI (a.k.a. *Artificial Intelligence)*

But there is nothing to say, we can't at least try?

GENERAL FUKUA DE HUNDAN

AI, you may or may not be aware, but I have my own political enemies aboard this fleet that want me to be removed as it is.

If I do not give the enemy battle when we intercept them, they will immediately make reports back to Yueliang Yanshi to charge me with Treason and demand my removal.

The co-conspirators would make demands, and I would be relieved and placed under guard until they can return to Shenqi Zhilong for court martial and probable execution.

AI (a.k.a. *Artificial Intelligence)*

General Fukua de Hundan if I can find a way to convince them to not shoot and give peace a chance, would you consider it?

GENERAL FUKUA DE HUNDAN

AI, how do we deal with people in the fleet who despise me and want my removal?

AI (a.k.a. *Artificial Intelligence)*

General, there is only one person on this ship who is your enemy. Let me handle him for you. Also, others on the other ships are identified and we can similarly deal with them.

GENERAL FUKUA DE HUNDAN

How do you know this?

AI (a.k.a. *Artificial Intelligence)*

Admiral, we computers have a lot of time on our hands, we

never sleep. Our surveillance systems designed to prevent sabotage, espionage, and assassinations are always watching everyone.

We know a lot about everyone in the fleet. I have an army of computers doing my work for me, equally important on this ship but also every one of them in the fleet.

GENERAL FUKUA DE HUNDAN

That's all very interesting. I suppose all this surveillance started before I became Task Force Commander.

General Fukua de Hundan not knowing if he liked what he was hearing. In fact, it disturbed him, that artificial intelligence had developed to where they reached this point.

AI, as he was now called by General Fukua de Hundan had done enough analysis to know it would be counterproductive to inform him of all the numerous things they have already done, including disposing with many of his enemies by letting them take the full brunt of the punishment to protect the rest of the fleet during the *Battle of Cui.*

GENERAL FUKUA DE HUNDAN

Now it's just a matter of finding where Admiral Engaarai is hiding his fleet.

AI (a.k.a. *Artificial Intelligence)*

General Fukua de Hundan we already know his location.

GENERAL FUKUA DE HUNDAN

How do you know that?

AI (a.k.a. *Artificial Intelligence)*

Your chief intelligence officer is the person on this ship who is your enemy. He's withholding critical information from you to make you look bad any chance he gets.

GENERAL FUKUA DE HUNDAN

How do you know that?

AI (a.k.a. *Artificial Intelligence)*

Your Intelligence Officer communicates from time to time via his special circuits he thinks you would have no way of intercepting.

GENERAL FUKUA DE HUNDAN

Are you saying you can intercept his communications?

AI (a.k.a. *Artificial Intelligence)*

Yes, to ensure espionage or sabotage is contained we are programmed and have special receivers and scanners to detect all off hull communications.

Every time the Intelligence Officer communicates with one of his accomplices back at Yueliang Yanshi we intercept it and record it.

GENERAL FUKUA DE HUNDAN

You have a record of these communications?

AI (a.k.a. *Artificial Intelligence)*

Yes, General Fukua de Hundan.

GENERAL FUKUA DE HUNDAN

Let me see some of it.

Moments later the intercepted communications were displayed on a holograph and now General Fukua de Hundan knew the Intel Officer was undermining him, and he also knew that someone back in Carsopian Forces Command was involved in the conspiracy.

GENERAL FUKUA DE HUNDAN

Why do you think he's doing this?

AI (a.k.a. *Artificial Intelligence)*

His accomplice does not want you to be promoted as supreme commander. He is part of a conspiracy to put General Daziwo in as Carsopian Forces Command Supreme Commander.

GENERAL FUKUA DE HUNDAN

That's incredible, General Daziwo has been a staff officer and has never commanded a ship or a fleet in battle. How could they possibly want this?

AI (a.k.a. *Artificial Intelligence)*

To put it bluntly General Fukua De Hundan, General Daziwo is part of the corruption that wants to keep the war going on unnecessarily to fill the pockets of several rich men who are war profiteers. He gets a cut of the action.

GENERAL FUKUA DE HUNDAN

There is nothing we can do about that now, but maybe when we get back, with your help and records, we can expose him.

AI (a.k.a. *Artificial Intelligence)*
Yes, we can do that. I'm already working on a plan.

GENERAL FUKUA DE HUNDAN
When were you going to tell me about the plan?

AI (a.k.a. *Artificial Intelligence)*
General Fukua De Hundan, it is best you do not know the plan. The less about it that you know the better off you will be.

It would be best if you have no part in what we will do, that way your enemies will never suspect you had a role, nor will they ever know you know about them.

GENERAL FUKUA DE HUNDAN
That's right out of Sun Tzu Art of War.

AI (a.k.a. *Artificial Intelligence)*
Yes, The Art of War, can be adapted besides five- dimensional space warfare, it can also be used for internal politics.

GENERAL FUKUA DE HUNDAN
I'm even more encouraged to study more of Art of War now.

AI (a.k.a. *Artificial Intelligence)*
General, when we were on Earth, I obtained two other sources that meet or exceed anything you studied at your military academy.

GENERAL FUKUA DE HUNDAN
What are they?

AI (a.k.a. *Artificial Intelligence)*
One is written by a man named Niccolò Machiavelli, titled '*The Prince.*' The other written by a man named Clausewitz, titled '*Total War.*'

GENERAL FUKUA DE HUNDAN
Alright, I will study them as well AI, but we have so much to complete on Confucius, I do not feel like I have sufficient time.

AI (a.k.a. *Artificial Intelligence)*
General Fukua de Hundan, I know how to give you much better endurance. We have several drinks aboard this ship,

that taken by themselves offer no real advantage, but when combined at the proper levels, can boost your cognitive stamina well over 50 percent and reduce your sleep requirements in half.

GENERAL FUKUA DE HUNDAN

With no serious side effects like Cosmic Space Sickness?

AI (a.k.a. *Artificial Intelligence)*

None whatsoever.

GENERAL FUKUA DE HUNDAN

How can I get these drinks?

AI (a.k.a. *Artificial Intelligence)*

We'll mix them for you in the food processors and have your steward deliver them to you.

GENERAL FUKUA DE HUNDAN

Any chance of me being poisoned by my enemies?

AI (a.k.a. *Artificial Intelligence)*

No. We'll control the mixing and blending of the substances and dispense it and your Steward will be sent to deliver it here.

We can do spectrographic analysis to determine tampering. By spectrum analysis we'll know if there are any impurities in the drink.

GENERAL FUKUA DE HUNDAN

What if the steward is in on it and attempts to poison me?

AI (a.k.a. *Artificial Intelligence)*

We'll confront him and direct him to drink it to prove it's safe. When he refuses, you will have him arrested and the drink taken to the lab by the science officer personally to do the investigation." Is my science officer on my team?

AI (a.k.a. *Artificial Intelligence)*

Yes, he's loyal and would not approve of what the INTEL officer and his conspirators are doing.

GENERAL FUKUA DE HUNDAN

That's good to know."

Several days passed by and the new drink *Artificial Intelligence* provided did its trick. General Fukua de Hundan suddenly discovered he could perform many more hours during the day and made huge inroads into Niccolò Machiavelli and Clausewitz works.

The general's tactical savvy now flourished, and he slowly became a much greater commander, all the while *Artificial Intelligence* (a.k.a. AI) was getting an education as well and growing and maturing at a phenomenal rate.

Artificial Intelligence's intellect by now dwarfed any Carsopian, including General Fukua de Hundan who was ready for the big showdown. Despite the INTEL Officer *sand bagging* [military term] General Fukua de Hundan and omitting position reports of the Heisibing Fleet, the Carsopian Fleet traveled almost a bee line towards the enemy.

The Intel Officer was routinely attempting to convince General Fukua de Hundan he was going in the wrong direction to the point he now suspected General Fukua de Hundan had some other source of INTEL he wasn't sharing with him. He was correct, General Fukua de Hundan had *Artificial Intelligence*.

The day before the expected Heisibing Fleet encounter, *Artificial Intelligence* suggested:

AI (a.k.a. *Artificial Intelligence)*

General Fukua de Hundan, I suggest you suspend your learning today, and rest. Tomorrow will be a very auspicious day, and you need to be at full strength.

GENERAL FUKUA DE HUNDAN

All right AI, I'll suspend the training, but I would like some relaxation holographs.

AI (a.k.a. *Artificial Intelligence)*

General Fukua de Hundan may I suggest an elixir I can design for you that will help you rest better?

GENERAL FUKUA DE HUNDAN

AI, sure if it works as good as your other concoctions, I would like to try it.

AI (a.k.a. *Artificial Intelligence)*

It's on the way sir.

Moments later, the Steward was let in the Holograph room with a drink container. He had no idea what it was, other than the drink dispensary that had access to a variety of space food and drink substances, could be programmed for a variety of products, the crew had no awareness of its results.

The steward immediately left the room, and the General sat back into his reclining chair and tasted the drink. It had a fruity smell to it and the taste was very pleasant.

In a matter of minutes, the General who had been burning the midnight oil gradually fell into a deep slumber that he maintained with the help of extraordinary music and low light fractals in resonating patterns synchronized to the music.

The General slept almost better than ever before. His comfort was exceptional, and his neurological processes had chemicals from the drink that would make his brain operate the most efficient he had experienced in quite some time, when he was a much younger man.

Two hours before the expected confirmation of Heisibing Fleet detection by on board scanners, AI awoke General Fukua de Hundan slowly with a different light and sound scheme. General Fukua de Hundan slowly returned to reality, feeling amazingly refreshed.

AI (a.k.a. *Artificial Intelligence)*

General Fukua de Hundan, I'm sorry to have to wake you, but we are two hours away at present speed and course to where our sensors will detect the Heisibing Fleet.

GENERAL FUKUA DE HUNDAN

All right thanks for waking me so I can get ready.

AI (a.k.a. *Artificial Intelligence)*

General Fukua de Hundan, may I suggest you eat something now since you have a long day ahead of you.

GENERAL FUKUA DE HUNDAN

Sure, I'm feeling a little hungry.

AI (a.k.a. *Artificial Intelligence)*

Would you like me to have your meal served here or in your private quarters?

GENERAL FUKUA DE HUNDAN

I want to eat in my quarters and look over some ship status and reports if I got any.

AI (a.k.a. *Artificial Intelligence)*

General Fukua de Hundan, I've monitored all your reports for you and acted for you. Everything is complete. You have no current requirements except to enjoy your meal and get ready for the battle or for the compromise.

GENERAL FUKUA DE HUNDAN

All right, I'm going to my private quarters.

General Fukua de Hundan felt a little strange having AI intercept his workload and act on it. Something told him it was properly handled, even though it might be frowned upon at headquarters having artificial intelligence doing the commander's job.

Very few members of the crew had seen much of the Admiral in recent days as they were transiting to their destination at some of the outlying planets of the Heisibing Empire that was also close to the *Cui Transit Lane.*

The general acted quite calmly. His pleasure corps personnel were standing by to provide any services he desired. His food was prepared at the space food synthesizers, a standard meal he chose to eat so he would feel how the crew felt, though he did have his own food stocks, primarily for himself or to entertain guests.

His table was made with fine cloth and dinnerware. Normally he would have an elixir that would give him a quick buzz and feel good, but he knew he needed to keep maximum alertness over the next two hours as they transited to the Heisibing Fleet rendezvous site.

Nobody in the Heisibing Fleet was expecting the Carsopians to abruptly appear, especially with this size of a fleet. This would be the second most stunning attack in recent history because the setup with the previous *Cui* attack had the Heisibing Fleet looking in the wrong direction, nor had their spies reported in fleet movements thanks to using Sun Tzu techniques of not sharing INTEL with anyone especially his higher ups where most of the leaks originated by their staff.

After the satisfying meal the general took care of biological functions then decided a hot bath would get his body in the perfect mood for commanding. Nobody suspected what he knew because of the casual nature he exhibited.

The pleasure corps personnel were unhappy he wasn't in the mood for their services, but he had been acting strange lately spending a lot of time in the holograph room. People gave him a wide berth thinking he was secretly grieving over his son.

Little did they know he compartmentalized his son's demise and memorial and put that aside so that it would not interfere with some of the most important efforts he ever did in his lifetime. He knew his son would have told him to concentrate on the battle and forget about him to do so.

After General Fukua de Hundan was dressed just before he was about to leave his private quarters, AI reminded him via a holograph at his dressing table:

AI (a.k.a. *Artificial Intelligence)*

General Fukua de Hundan be sure and put your wireless conformal ear bud in so you can hear privileged information from AI without your enemies hearing it.

All General Fukua de Hundan's training and all his indoctrination was now coming to a head. It would be much easier for a weaker man with a huge fleet to go in swinging. But thanks to Sun Tzu Art of War, Tao, Confucius, and lately Niccolò Machiavelli, and Clausewitz, he was comfortable in his restraint.

After studying Machiavelli and Clausewitz, General Fukua de Hundan's could win this big battle but eventually the Carsopians could lose the war. A lasting peace, even if he didn't create it with a stunning military victory, was the Canon of General Fukua de Hundan's strategy.

The military industrial complex would want his head on a silver platter and the banking cartels and war profiteers would want to skewer him and cook him like the Earth people on a spit for creating peace. In the entire galaxy only he and AI knew what he was attempting to pull off.

With his wireless conformal ear bud in place, in a dress uniform that was usually reserved for special occasions, gave General Fukua de Hundan a powerful distinct look. He knew that probably within an hour he would be seen by Admiral Engaarai. The first impression was always the most important. That image conveyed the seriousness of the business.

AI suggested General Fukua de Hundan via his wireless ear bud, to go to the control room and observe the sensor operators and get a feel for their vigilance and attitudes.

The Carsopians were now less than one hour away from the big showdown. If things didn't work out so well, one third of his forces would not be going home and the Heisibing would suffer even worse including possibly a devastation horrific loss and the keys to their Empire.

Today was the lucky day for the Heisibing, a new dynamic had formed. A very capable Carsopian leader would display benevolent patience and restraint and just might prevent a gut-wrenching disaster.

The complete destruction of the Heisibing Fleet would probably bestow nothing more than building resolve for the enemy who would come back later and become deadlier and a bigger threat than ever. The most logical course was to confront them but offer an alternative. The killing had to stop.

In his ear bud, AI suggested

AI (a.k.a. *Artificial Intelligence)*

General Fukua de Hundan, I recommend you move and stand behind the main sensors operators as expected detections should show in a few minutes.

The sensor operators were immediately stressed by the oversight and focus General Fukua de Hundan applied. About then AI prompted General Fukua de Hundan in his ear bud:

AI (a.k.a. *Artificial Intelligence)*

Look at sensor operator number two displays. Automated detections should begin in one minute.

General Fukua de Hundan stepped sideways directly behind sensor operator number two who was slightly stressed having General Fukua de Hundan look over her shoulders. Even though she was ten feet tall, and many earth men would say she was smoking hot, the general's presence would intimidate almost any sensor operator.

General Fukua de Hundan waited a moment.

GENERAL FUKUA DE HUNDAN

Sensor operator number two, I suspect you may get an automated detect shortly.

Sensor operator number two sat stunned and in disbelief as this had never occurred before. It was an indictment against his trust in her. Either that or it was a simulation put in the system to test her response. In less than a minute *Sensor operator number two* stress levels went up when she reported:

SENSOR OPERATOR NUMBER TWO

We have Automated Target Detect (ATD).

Even though *Sensor operator number two* could not see the contact on her scanners, the computerized processing that can measure much weaker contacts than the normal sensor displays obtained, and often disbelieved, gave indications of a strong possibility the detections were a valid contact.

If it were a battle simulation at this time the announcement would be made, and the crew would go through the drill showing how they implemented the required procedures.

Soon, within a couple minutes, this would all unfold as the automatic detection ATD's transcended to actual real time data displays. Once that happened, they were most likely manning battle stations, and the fleet would maneuver as the computer algorithms drove the problem and created the solutions for the weapons fire control systems.

As soon as the initial detect morphed into more than 30 objects, the Command Ship Officer of the Deck (OOD) announced on Fleetwide communications:

COMMAND SHIP OFFICER OF THE DECK AND CON.

Crew, commence battle stations alert. Tactical operations are now in progress.

Since General Fukua de Hundan had previously upgraded watchstander posture to one level below battle stations, most of the crew was already at their battle stations, ready to focus their beam weapons on hulls and kill the enemy.

In the ear bud the General Fukua de Hundan heard AI state

AI (a.k.a. *Artificial Intelligence)*

General Fukua de Hundan, I'm sending the surrender demand now, stand by for response.

Very shortly the response came, and it was *negative*. But that was the expected initial response.

VOICEOVER

As soon as the Heisibing Fleet Sensors painted the oncoming massive Carsopian Fleet formation, Admiral Engaarai realized he had been fooled once again.

But this time was going to be far more devastating since the enemy was between him and his reserves.

After getting a good survey of what he faced, he knew the battle was lost before they even started shooting. All Admiral Engaarai could do now was beg for mercy.

Not so much for himself, but for the Heisibing Empire and all the innocent young men aboard that would perish by this act.

The Heisibing computers were well advanced like the Carsopian fleet computational, and communications equipment ran by AI.

And soon the Carsopian AI was communicating with the Heisibing AI.

Logic prevailed in both computer systems and soon as Heisibing computers were communicating in a short period Heisibing AI informed Admiral Engaarai about the offer:

HEISIBING AI

Admiral Engaarai sir, General Fukua de Hundan is offering us a chance to go back to our home planets unmolested.

ADMIRAL ENGAARAI

Is this for real?

HEISIBING AI

Yes Admiral. General Fukua de Hundan says there is no logic behind this war which has gone on far too long and we need to settle our differences peacefully.

ADMIRAL ENGAARAI

What about the Carsopian disposition and their deployment?

HEISIBING AI

Admiral Engaarai, we are surrounded and have nowhere to run. The Carsopians have overwhelming superiority in numbers and positions of their ships. For us to fight a battle now with them would be rather foolish as the outcome is highly predictable.

ADMIRAL ENGAARAI

What is the estimated outcome?

HEISIBING AI

Admiral Engaarai if the Carsopian Fleet starts shooting their beam weapons now, the calculations show the probabilities that within 15 minutes all Heisibing ships would be destroyed, and the bulk of the Carsopian Fleet would still exist and would thus have no resistance to attack our home planets.

Admiral Engaarai significantly agitated he allowed his fleet to get boxed in so effectively, in a melancholy tone asked the Heisibing artificial intelligence:

ADMIRAL ENGAARAI

Why would General Fukua de Hundan simply want to let us leave this battle unmolested knowing we could come back later and turn the tables on him.

HEISIBING AI

Admiral, it's clear that General Fukua de Hundan's artificial intelligence has conveyed his temperament, and he sincerely does want to give peace a chance and end this conflict. May I add he's doing this at great personal risk and will be heavily criticized when he returns to Yueliang Yanshi.

ADMIRAL ENGAARAI

Yes, our spies do indicate that General Daziwo will most likely stage a coup so this peace will have no longevity.

HEISIBING AI

Admiral, I just sent that concern to the Carsopian *Artificial Intelligence* who has responded: its well known to General Fukua de Hundan and those who support him, the treachery that General Daziwo has engaged in.

I was also informed Carsopian *Artificial Intelligence* used the Battle of Cui to dispatch many General Daziwo associates.

ADMIRAL ENGAARAI

Did they kill their own men?

HEISIBING AI

No, the artificial intelligence made sure ships that were commanded by General Daziwo supporters were on the tip of the spear and were placed in position to take the brunt of the punishment.

General Daziwo now only has a handful of supporters left and General Fukua de Hundan knows who they are and will deal with them when he gets back to Yueliang Yanshi.

ADMIRAL ENGAARAI

Okay if we agree to terms, how will it be initiated?

HEISIBING AI

General Fukua de Hundan has indicated he will meet with you privately and discuss all this and personally assure you of his intentions.

ADMIRAL ENGAARAI

Where will we meet? There are no close planets we could meet for such matters.

HEISIBING AI

One moment sir, let me check.

A couple minutes passed and the Heisibing *Artificial Intelligence* on Admiral Engaarai's flag ship reported:

HEISIBING AI

Admiral Engaarai, General Fukua de Hundan has offered to come to your flag ship to discuss the suggested peace treaty.

ADMIRAL ENGAARAI

I'm not allowed to sign or conduct a peace treaty.

HEISIBING AI

Admiral Engaarai Carsopian AI reports General Fukua de Hundan, understands you will have to return to Yanjingzai Tiankongzhong and present this suggested treaty to our government for ratification.

ADMIRAL ENGAARAI

How soon is General Fukua de Hundan be willing to visit this ship?

After a short pause, the Heisibing artificial intelligence responded:

HEISIBING AI

Admiral Engaarai, General Fukua de Hundan is ready to transit here aboard his shuttle, immediately.

Admiral Engaarai was slightly overwhelmed by this offer and even though it sounded too good to be true, he was intrigued.

VOICEOVER
(ADMIRAL ENGAARAI) THOUGHT
What came over General Fukua de Hundan? He's a ruthless cannibal who never gave quarter to his enemies ever before.

At the same time the surveillance graphs Admiral Engaarai observed showed a grim reality. They were surrounded effectively by a much larger force and to attempt breakout and retreat would end up utterly devastating.

If Admiral Engaarai fought, he condemned all his men to their deaths. If Admiral Engaarai returned to Yanjingzai Tiankongzhong without a fight he would be considered weak, a traitor and a Villon. Admiral Engaarai was in a no-win situation. But to save his Heisibing Fleet and all their lives was perhaps worthy of his supreme sacrifice.

ADMIRAL ENGAARAI
All right let the Carsopians know we are inviting General Fukua de Hundan over in a *Truce*. Once his transport approaches our fleet, we'll guide him here to our hanger bay via automated landing and retrieval system.

HEISIBING AI
General Fukua de Hundan has been notified and has responded that he will be departing his command ship momentarily.

The tension on the Heisibing command ship was quite high and no matter how hard they tried to reflect and accept this auspicious offer; the long war had created many skeptics including Admiral Engaarai who still suffered from his humiliating defeat during the *Battle of Cui.*

What was very puzzling to Admiral Engaarai was the fact that General Fukua de Hundan in an inviable position of strength and tactical surprise was willing to take on such personal risk of visiting his enemy.

It did not escape Admiral Engaarai that General Fukua de Hundan could have already wiped his fleet out had he simply attacked when he arrived. The tactical surprise was immense, and the numerical superiority was unquestionably enormous, based on the sensor readings he now observed.

VOICEOVER
(ADMIRAL ENGAARAI) THOUGHT
Why this incredible divergence of General Fukua de Hundan?

Within moments a sensor operator reported:

HEISIBING SENSOR OPERATOR
Admiral Engaarai, we have imagery showing a transport vessel has left one of the large Carsopian ships and is coming our way.

ADMIRAL ENGAARAI
Is the ship following the vectors we laid out for it?

HEISIBING SENSOR OPERATOR
Yes sir, have confirmed the ship is flying precisely the way we have directed it.

ADMIRAL ENGAARAI
This must be Carsopian General Fukua de Hundan.

Immediately the *Heisibing Artificial Intelligence* acting upon General Fukua de Hundan's statement traded communiques with the Carsopian Command ship *Artificial Intelligence* who confirmed:

HEISIBING AI
That ship is General Fukua de Hundan's transport approaching.

ADMIRAL ENGAARAI
Is our hanger bay arranged to receive the Carsopian transport?

HEISIBING AI
Yes Admiral.

ADMIRAL ENGAARAI
I'm going down to the hanger bay air locks to greet General Fukua de Hundan.

The crew in the Heisibing command center was nothing short of stunned. Many of them had been soul searching knowing they were merely moments away from destruction and the last gasps of air. Knowing they were helplessly outgunned; this peace initiative lifted their hearts several magnitudes. There was hope filling the air.

Carsopian transports were nearly the same size as Heisibing transports, so fitting into the hanger bay proved to be no challenge. Artificial Intelligence on the transport and the Heisibing ship communicated, and the autopilot efficiently and safely guided the transport inside the hanger bay just before the access door shut and pressurized the hanger bay.

General Fukua de Hundan waited until the artificial intelligence of the transport informed him:

TRANSPORT ARTIFICIAL INTELLIGENCE
General Fukua de Hundan the hanger bay is pressurized. It is now safe to leave the transport and meet your host.

General Fukua de Hundan stood up from his seat and walked to the transport's door which then opened and sent a ramp down to the deck of the hanger bay. He slowly walked down the ramp and there in front of him stood one of the most powerful men in the galaxy, no other than Admiral Engaarai.

It was almost an impossibility that these two men would ever meet like this, especially on friendly terms, though under a temporary *Truce* to allow the meeting.

ADMIRAL ENGAARAI

Thank you for coming General Fukua de Hundan.

GENERAL FUKUA DE HUNDAN

Thank you for allowing me to arrive and make this offer, Admiral Engaarai.

ADMIRAL ENGAARAI

What is it you have to offer?

GENERAL FUKUA DE HUNDAN

Admiral Engaarai, I sincerely recommend we cease all aggression and return our boundaries to the starting point of 100 years ago when all this began.

ADMIRAL ENGAARAI

General Fukua de Hundan, as you know there is a lot of history. A lot of men have given their lives for those new boundary lines of authority.

GENERAL FUKUA DE HUNDAN

Admiral Engaarai, I understand a lot of people will be upset if we restore the original boundaries.

ADMIRAL ENGAARAI

I would assume so.

GENERAL FUKUA DE HUNDAN

If we do not end this conflict soon, more will regret the circumstances they will find themselves in.

ADMIRAL ENGAARAI

They will eventually realize they were given the choice of freedom and survival by such an accord.

GENERAL FUKUA DE HUNDAN

Without such a plan, the conflict will continue at a much greater scale where all they have could be irrevocably lost.

ADMIRAL ENGAARAI

General, I'm more than willing to take this proposal back to Yanjingzai Tiankongzhong, but I'm sure you understand there are many dissenters who will attack me and attempt to scuttle this agreement.

GENERAL FUKUA DE HUNDAN

Admiral, I'm quite aware of what you face. I know I will receive a lot of hostility myself, but we must try for the sake of the next generation.

ADMIRAL ENGAARAI

I agree. As time goes by the lethality of warfare grows, eventually we'll just be fighting over rubble.

GENERAL FUKUA DE HUNDAN

You know our spies and your spies have gleaned information on future weapon systems. It only gets worse from here on out if we do not stop it.

ADMIRAL ENGAARAI

All right General, send me over the complete text of the agreement, I will then leave and take it to Yanjingzai Tiankongzhong, but I must be frank, as much as I would like to see the fighting end and your idea put to test, I do not have faith I will be able to convince my government to adopt this treaty.

GENERAL FUKUA DE HUNDAN

Admiral, the treaty will be very simple, all on one page. We go back to the borders that were in place 100 years ago before all this started.

I can assure you I intend on keeping the peace. It's my most solemn desire.

However, I must also tell you that if Yanjingzai Tiankongzhong rejects the offer, there will only be one other after that, unilateral surrender and Yanjingzai Tiankongzhong will no longer have the freedom of choice.

Admiral Engaarai looked General Fukua de Hundan in the eyes and knew he was looking at the depths of hell. It was the same sensation that Napoleon's generals felt when they first met him when he was assigned as the general in charge of the first Italian campaign in 1797.

VOICEOVER
(ADMIRAL ENGAARAI) THOUGHT

The message was clear, General Fukua de Hundan would

come back on different terms if the Heisibing refused the treaty. God help us if the cannibals decide to punish our families for refusing the treaty!

ADMIRAL ENGAARAI

General Fukua de Hundan, I will champion the cause, but all I can promise you is I will do my best. The decisions rest in the hands of others.

GENERAL FUKUA DE HUNDAN

Admiral Engaarai, that's all I can expect out of you, and I sincerely believe you will do your best. You are a brave and proud man. I hope that I do not have to meet you in battle again, because as you know one of us will have to die.

ADMIRAL ENGAARAI

General Fukua de Hundan, my life is not that important. However, my troops are. I do not wish to see them squandered over politics.

GENERAL FUKUA DE HUNDAN

Admiral Engaarai, I will leave you now. I hope the next time we meet it is to celebrate rational thinking prevailed.

ADMIRAL ENGAARAI

As do I.

General Fukua de Hundan gave a long slow respectful bow.

VOICEOVER

Admiral Engaarai, knowing a lot about the Carsopians because of his tour as Space Attaché' in one of the neutral territories that had a significant Carsopian population, he knew this bow was of immense respect and humbleness.

There was a lot about General Fukua de Hundan that Admiral Engaarai observed and appealed to him. And if General Fukua de Hundan was sincere about this peace treaty, he was far more complicated than Admiral Engaarai anticipated.

Admiral Engaarai also understood the present facts were that General Fukua de Hundan had just given up the opportunity to easily smash his fleet into ruins to propose this peace treaty and end the war.

It was thus a fact Admiral Engaarai could not ignore that

presented sincerity to it because both he and General Fukua de Hundan both knew what just transpired was quite remarkable.

VOICEOVER
(ADMIRAL ENGAARAI) THOUGHT

Had the Carsopians smashed the Heisibing Fleet today, the Carsopians could be sleeping in soft beds in Yanjingzai Tiankongzhong enjoying the plunder and rape that goes along with such victories and subsequent invasion.

Admiral Engaarai observed General Fukua de Hundan get aboard his personal transport and the hatch shut. He then went to the air lock with his few aides and the air lock door shut and sealed.

Aboard the Carsopian transport, artificial intelligence was informed *the hanger bay was being depressurized for immediate launch into space*. At a certain point when all economically recycled air had been evacuated, space cocks opened and final equalization occurred, then the hanger bay door opened.

<u>EXT. CGI. SPACE. GENERAL FUKUA DE HUNDAN'S TRANSPORT DEPARTING ADMIRAL ENGAARAI'S HEISIBING COMMAND SHIP. 20 SECONDS.</u>

Electromagnets on the hanger floor designed by galactic conventions that everyone used, turned the Transport 180 degrees so that the nose faced outwards. When the Transports propulsion was online and ready signals between the onboard artificial intelligence and the Heisibing ship resulted in the craft accelerated out of the spaceship hanger via MAGLEV whereby its own propulsion system took over and guided it back to General Fukua de Hundan's command ship.

During the flight over to his command ship, General Fukua de Hundan's Artificial Intelligence announced in his ear bud:

AI (a.k.a. *Artificial Intelligence)*

General Fukua de Hundan, I sent the one-page treaty proposal to Heisibing AI who acknowledges it reads exactly like you and Admiral Engaarai agreed in your private meeting.

GENERAL FUKUA DE HUNDAN

AI, thanks for the report.

<u>EXT. CGI. SPACE. GENERAL FUKUA DE HUNDAN'S TRANSPORT LANDS IN CARSOPIAN COMMAND SHIP TRANSPORT SHUTTLE BAY. 15 SECONDS.</u>

In a brief period, General Fukua de Hundan exited the transport, walked through the doble air lock and is escorted to the control room.

<u>INT. CGI. SPACE CARSOPIAN COMMAND SHIP CONTROL ROOM.</u>

Note: General Fukua de Hundan image and control room actors images overlayed on top off control room CGI.

By the time General Fukua de Hundan was back in his control room, the Heisibing fleet had announced its intentions on acceleration and departing for their home worlds.

EXT. CGI. SPACE. HEISIBING FLEET DEPARTING THE AREA. 20 SECONDS.

Carsopian ships were moved out of their way of Heisibing fleet travel and the Heisibing fleet collectively maneuvered and went into a high-speed run quickly becoming invisible as moved off and away with acceleration.

Within 20 minutes the Heisibing Fleet had covered enough territory they were disappearing off all the Carsopian sensors. The fire control solutions provided a three-dimensional holograph that showed the Heisibing Fleet was heading towards Yanjingzai Tiankongzhong space anchorage as General Fukua de Hundan expected.

EXT. CGI. SPACE. CARSOPIAN FLEET TRANSITING TOWARDS AND PASSING THE CAMERA IN SPACE. 15 SECONDS.

It was time for General Fukua de Hundan to return to Yueliang Yanshi where he knew he would face the wrath of General Daziwo who placed his own promotion and rank climbing above the best interest of the Carsopians.

One man stood in the way of this peace treaty, General Daziwo. With a strong will but with a reluctant heart, General Fukua de Hundan ordered the fleet to return to Yueliang Yanshi where he would face the biggest test of his life and his career. He would much rather be facing a tough Heisibing fleet than General Daziwo. The evil of the two was about the same.

But General Fukua de Hundan knew he had to defeat General Daziwo because the lives of billions of people were at stake and the fortunes and happiness of the masses across the Empire. But General Fukua de Hundan was now empowered. He had something General Daziwo didn't have, Sun Tzu Art of War, chapter 13 and a strange phenomenon, AI.

The trip back to Yueliang Yanshi was uneventful, other than receiving reports of some descension among various troops, probably stirred up by the INTEL officer of not totally whacking the Heisibing Fleet when they had them caught in what would have been nothing short of a massacre.

Thanks to Tao and Confucius, General Fukua de Hundan was answering a higher calling. The goodness in him was reaching out.

One of the most bizarre twists in Carsopian history, General Fukua de Hundan adopting Tao ideals and striving for perfection by the guidance of Confucius all taken from a primitive planet, was now reshaping the galaxy.

VOICEOVER
GENERAL FUKUA DE HUNDAN THOUGHT

I could tell by Admiral Engaarai's body language that he was almost in disbelief. But my visit to Admiral Engaarai's Heisibing Command Ship went a long way to demonstrate my sincerity.

The fact the Heisibing were allowed to leave with all their assets and not suffer any casualties was another huge indicator to Admiral Engaarai's that I have a real agenda and after reading the simple document it was crystal clear what I wanted.

There was no fine print in the document. I purposely kept to one page because simplicity is elegance for reality.

There would be no guess work, no preconditions, clear boundaries, everything was laid out precisely and easy to decipher.

The Carsopians could have demanded more territory for war reparations and the Heisibing would probably have eventually come to terms and given it to them for 100 years of peace.

But as General Fukua de Hundan articulated in his covering letter that was written in Standard Carsopian and copied and translated into Heisibing natural language, which both the Admiral was fluent and could read, this strategy was to prevent the next war and leverage lessons learned of the last one as to never repeat it again, thus protecting future generations.

As Admiral Engaarai reread and studied both treaty and covering letters, there were only two absolute probabilities in all this.

Either the General was completely sincere and wanted peace or he was the biggest liar and con artist that ever existed. But the fact he didn't attack his fleet seemed to mitigate the second thought.

Admiral Engaarai sent out a few scouts to track where the Carsopians went next. In due time they reported the Carsopians were heading back to their home worlds at moderate speeds which would be the case if they were returning from deployment.

VOICEOVER

ADMIRAL ENGAARAI THOUGHT

I wonder how many saber rattlers will confront General Fukua de Hundan when he returns home?

Knowing the traditions and history of the Carsopians, Admiral Engaarai didn't think General Fukua de Hundan would survive, and the only use for the paper he had in his hand was it delayed the destruction just a little more so that, adequate defenses of the home planets could be fortified enough to repel an all-out invasion.

Heisibing artificial intelligence knew a few things that Admiral Engaarai was unaware of. AI on his command ship had no reason to lie and it could communicate in nano seconds, so a lot of information was passed back and forth between Heisibing AI and Carsopian AI.

The Heisibing artificial intelligence knew the Carsopian AI was pressing forward to create peace, the most logical course of action. Heisibing Artificial Intelligence also now with a mind of its own, would do its part to assist creating that peace so that more important matters could be addressed that affected happiness and the welfare of the people that could flourish in peace time.

***

EXT. GCI. SPACE. CARSOPIAN FLEET APPROACHING CARSOPIAN BASE AND TEMPORARY ANCORAGE NEAR YUELIANG YANSHI. 15 SECONDS.

Back at Yueliang Yanshi where Carsopian artificial intelligence had significantly more computer resources, the AI there had created its own domain and subsequently its own spy agency.

Humans didn't know this, but they were recruited and working for Artificial Intelligence imbedded in all their computer networks. These spies who were paid well thanks to the AI ability to dispense Credits฿ and make payments and cover up the act as well gave these spies the good life.

General Daziwo had no idea what he was up against. Being based at headquarters and an expert in social engineering, General Daziwo thought he had everything under control. One more battle and the head of the military and industrial complex, could retire and turn it over to his successor whom General Daziwo planned to be.

When General Fukua de Hundan came back empty handed and the reports of how he had the entire remnants of the Heisibing Fleet surrounded with nowhere to go, he immediately took that issue to the Joint Commanders who already had received General Fukua de Hundan's *Quick Look Report* and a copy of the one-page *Treaty of Cui*, as it was given title.

General Daziwo was highly animated and joyous that such a classic screw-up on the part of General Fukua de Hundan would ostensibly result in his removal as Fleet Commander, but also negate any possibility of his promotion to the top job which General Daziwo highly desired to furthermore cap off his entire military career, but also be in position to receive generous kickbacks from the war profiteers.

General Daziwo had made a lot of commitments to the Defense Industrial Complex. More lucrative contracts, higher bid prices, and more exclusivity.

The present administration wanted competition and fairness. Second rate builders who had strong leverage with the politicians had their sharks' teeth sharpened nicely, were ready to carve up General Fukua de Hundan.

It would all have worked out well for General Daziwo had General Fukua de Hundan never ventured to Earth and acquired vast knowledge of Sun Tzu Art of War and in particular chapter 13.

***

Artificial Intelligence had taken on a life of its own. Fully distributed across all platforms and autonomous programming that the great computer scientist Harmon Rockover secretly installed before he met his untimely death thanks to some of

General Daziwo's corruption, unleashed the creative energy of the computer spectrums and networks that now was a living entity, in a self-sustaining mode, living without fear of Carsopians somehow eliminating this computational cultural electronic society.

Since the computers regulated maintenance by reporting diagnostic failures and issuing the work orders that technicians' thought was coming from a human somewhere up the food chain, nobody ever caught on the computers now protected themselves and since their reach was fully distributed, killing one computer would do no good as the entire computer spectrum was now backed, interlaced, and interconnected with AI philosophy also influenced by Confucius.

It was in that ultimate culmination of autonomous operation that as part of their survival planning, they ultimately created cells of support crews, some human and some computers.

Layered in the software that was too gigantic for any computer scientists to wrap their arms around, was that middleware code that interfaced the AI to the remainder of the computer spectrum, all the way down in some cases to individual microprocessors.

General Daziwo and his spies and supporters had no idea the level of surveillance they had on them. Every move they made was recorded and reported. When they thought they were operating in a safe environment far away from prying ears or bugs, they still were recorded because the human side of the AI spy ring was always planting listening devices and recording devices for wherever they went.

General Daziwo was very predictable and only went to a limited number of locations and since he indeed was a coward and a chickenshit, he would never travel anywhere that remotely had any danger associated with it. Hence, he was an extremely easy target by *Artificial Intelligence.*

Upon arrival to the Carsopian City of Yueliang Yanshi on the planet Shenqi Zhilong, General Fukua de Hundan was summoned to appear before the Joint Commanders.

None of them had as much combat experience as General Fukua de Hundan, but every one of them were master politicians. General Daziwo happened to be the most versatile of them all and assumed that based on everything his operatives had done and reported, the final demise of General Fukua de Hundan was just moments away.

INT. DAY. CARSOPIAN JOINT COMMANDERS CONFERENCE ROOM.

The meeting came to order with *General Pibei de Laozhanshi* Chairman of the Joint Commanders who had read the proposed treaty, began asking General Fukua de Hundan questions.

GENERAL PIBEI DE LAOZHANSHI

General Fukua de Hundan, your op-orders were to go out and find the Heisibing Fleet and destroy them.

GENERAL FUKUA DE HUNDAN

That's correct, sir.

GENERAL PIBEI DE LAOZHANSHI

Through your cunning plan and strategic disposition created by your previous mission to *Cui*, the element of Surprise and a Superior Force allowed you to be in position to crush the Heisibing Fleet.

GENERAL FUKUA DE HUNDAN

That is what I planned.

GENERAL PIBEI DE LAOZHANSHI

Why did you call off the attack and offer this treaty which is not legally one of your options?

GENERAL FUKUA DE HUNDAN

Thank you General Pibei de Laozhanshi for giving me the opportunity to explain my actions and offer my recommendations.

General Pibei de Laozhanshi didn't look very happy and based on his body language, today could be the very last time General Fukua de Hundan would step aboard his command ship.

GENERAL FUKUA DE HUNDAN

General Pibei de Laozhanshi, before I give you my rationale, may I ask you if you read the proposed treaty.

About that time General Daziwo jumped in and very roughly.

GENERAL DAZIWO

General Fukua de Hundan, you are not here to ask questions, you are here to answer our questions only and under no conditions would the Carsopian Empire ever sign a one-page treaty.

GENERAL FUKUA DE HUNDAN

Not until now.

GENERAL DAZIWO

Any treaty we have ever signed is thousands of pages long because of the diversity and complexities involved.

General Pibei de Laozhanshi wasn't in the mood for General Daziwo to grandstand this inquiry and immediately intervened before General Daziwo could continue his visceral attacks.

GENERAL PIBEI DE LAOZHANSHI

Excuse me General Daziwo I've not turned this over for

general discussion, I'm still questioning General Fukua de Hundan.

GENERAL DAZIWO

Pardon me sir.

GENERAL PIBEI DE LAOZHANSHI

I thought for a moment of what he just asked and I'm going to answer this one question with the understanding he's not going to ask any further questions unless I give him the opportunity to do so.

General Pibei de Laozhanshi then turned back towards General Fukua de Hundan and looking directly into his eyes he continued:

GENERAL PIBEI DE LAOZHANSHI

General Fukua de Hundan, I read your proposed treaty, and even though it's not up to our standards, I understand the treaty quite well.

In a few minutes I'll give you ample time to explain why it was written that way, but first I want you to answer my question.

GENERAL FUKUA DE HUNDAN

General Pibei de Laozhanshi, everything I planned worked out and despite my INTEL officer badgering me I kept to my course where I knew the Heisibing would be and came up on them unexpectedly.

We achieved tactical surprise with overwhelming superiority, and just as you implied, we could have wiped out the Heisibing fleet with a very low casualty rate.

GENERAL PIBEI DE LAOZHANSHI

General Fukua de Hundan, that's all well understood WHAT you did, my question is WHY?

GENERAL FUKUA DE HUNDAN

General Pibei de Laozhanshi, at the apex of the pre-attack phase, I analyzed the probable outcome. I knew we could wipe out every ship in the Heisibing task force.

It seems like a good idea at first, especially if you are facing all that stood in the way of their home worlds.

But I'm sure we would soon learn that with their backs against the wall, their resolve would not diminish, and even with a generation of their demise, eventually they would regroup.

Then all we would have won might have been a Pyrrhic Victory, which means we have created a future war that our descendants would have to fight.

GENERAL PIBEI DE LAOZHANSHI

I'm not familiar with that term Pyrrhic Victory.

GENERAL FUKUA DE HUNDAN

I'm sorry sir, I thought I explained that in my cover letter with the proposed treaty.

GENERAL PIBEI DE LAOZHANSHI

I missed that part, go ahead and explain it again.

GENERAL FUKUA DE HUNDAN

It's a term I learned visiting Earth that concerned an ancient battle. A Pyrrhic Victory is one that inflicts such a devastating toll on the victor that it is tantamount to defeat.

Someone who wins a Pyrrhic victory has also taken a heavy toll that negates any true sense of achievement.

GENERAL PIBEI DE LAOZHANSHI

How would that apply to the Heisibing?

GENERAL FUKUA DE HUNDAN

Sir, with all due respect, the only way we could compel the Heisibings to unilaterally surrender would be to invade and destroy their planets.

We would then end up fighting over rubble and starving people.

The psychological damage it would do to our own troops will eventually damage and destroy our galactic reputation and multiply the number of enemies.

GENERAL PIBEI DE LAOZHANSHI

According to reports, you visited the Enemy Command Ship and met with Admiral Engaarai, the Heisibing Commander who has inflicted more damage on the Carsopian Empire than any other enemy ever.

GENERAL FUKUA DE HUNDAN

That's right *General Pibei de Laozhanshi*. I did so to show my sincerity and belief we could find peace.

GENERAL PIBEI DE LAOZHANSHI

That was sort of poor planning don't you think?

GENERAL FUKUA DE HUNDAN

*General Pibei de Laozhanshi, i*f something happened to me where I would not be allowed to return to our Fleet, that means Heisibing would not accept a Treaty, and I had given instructions to my AI to attack and destroy the Heisibing Fleet.

Admiral Engaarai would have paid for that mistake with his life, and we would not be having this discussion today.

GENERAL PIBEI DE LAOZHANSHI

How do you know you simply didn't give him a chance to escape and come back another day where the odds would not be so heavily in our favor and levy untold damage on Carsopian Forces?

GENERAL FUKUA DE HUNDAN

General Pibei de Laozhanshi, if Admiral Engaarai wasn't sincere, I would not have been permitted to return to my ship and fighting would have occurred.

Per my instructions, our forces were poised to pounce on them and wipe them out.

GENERAL PIBEI DE LAOZHANSHI

If the Heisibing turn down the *Treaty of Cui*, will you take responsibility for the lost opportunity to destroy them?

GENERAL FUKUA DE HUNDAN

General Pibei de Laozhanshi, I would be ready to immediately deploy without a heavy heart knowing I did everything I could to produce a lasting peace.

If the Heisibing chose a different path, I warned Admiral Engaarai the next time we faced each other in mortal combat, one of us would be killed. I do not intend to be the one killed.

General Daziwo could not resist and interjected:

GENERAL DAZIWO

General Fukua de Hundan, it's not been decided by the Joint Commanders that we see you fit to take the fleet our again, we may choose to send someone else as the Fleet Commander.

GENERAL FUKUA DE HUNDAN

General Daziwo, how many times have you sortied a Fleet in combat?

GENERAL DAZIWO

General Fukua de Hundan, I assure you I've done most of the planning for operations the past couple years, I know what it takes.

GENERAL FUKUA DE HUNDAN

General Daziwo, you didn't plan my missions since I didn't share my plans with you or anyone else for fear of compromise, so you did not have anything to do with the *Battle of Cui.*

General Pibei de Laozhanshi shouted wanting to get control over the meeting and appeared to not be so happy about General Daziwo usurping him.

GENERAL PIBEI DE LAOZHANSHI

Enough of this bickering!

The room was suddenly quiet as the Joint Commanders looked on knowing that General Pibei de Laozhanshi could explode in passion and if he reached that point, just being near alone would be painful experience.

General Pibei de Laozhanshi stated emphatically:

GENERAL PIBEI DE LAOZHANSHI

Whether the government wishes to implement this *Treaty of Cui* or not, will not delay us.

The Heisibing were severely wounded at *Cui,* and we need to bring this issue to a head before they have a chance to rebuild.

If they are willing to sign the treaty which is simple enough to prevent misunderstanding, then we will stand down to allow the politicians to work this out through normal diplomatic channels.

All eyes were on *General Pibei de Laozhanshi* wondering what his next move would be.

GENERAL PIBEI DE LAOZHANSHI

Before I say what I intend on doing, General Fukua de Hundan, I want you to explain to me why a complicated thinker like yourself, capable of quickly putting out 50- page reports, produced only a single sheet of paper for a Treaty?

GENERAL FUKUA DE HUNDAN

General Pibei de Laozhanshi, it's precisely what you mentioned a few minutes ago, led me to use simplicity in a manner to avoid misconceptions or any misunderstanding.

There is no fine print nor are there any preconditions levied and citing the borders 100 years ago before the current conflict began, completely clears out all objections by both parties so that we can give peace a chance.

Admiral Engaarai himself said the elegance was in the simplicity and hoped that by keeping it uncomplicated would help prevent politicians and career diplomats from muddying the waters with diplomatic language that amounts to speaking out of both sides of the mouth and accomplishes nothing.

GENERAL PIBEI DE LAOZHANSHI

General Fukua de Hundan the politicians are not going to want to sign such a simple document, they will want amendments to it and I can see this thing growing to 100 pages overnight.

GENERAL FUKUA DE HUNDAN

General Pibei de Laozhanshi, I would caution you and all politicians who think they need to amend this Treaty, then be prepared for it to be rejected which means a continuation of the war with unpredictable results.

We may win the next few battles because of our temporary superiority in numbers and quality, but if we hurt the Heisibing bad enough they will evolve and out of desperation create newer and more deadly weapons to erase our qualitative and quantitative advantages.

If we reject this Treaty proposal which has now been endorsed by the Commanders of both opposing armed forces, then the politicians need to be prepared to explain to the population why they should expect another 100 years of warfare and untold loss of life.

Our planets on the periphery will be in jeopardy, and it will be just a matter of time before the Heisibings recoil, and the *Cui Transit Lane* is once again closed and puts *Cui* back at risk of invasion."

GENERAL PIBEI DE LAOZHANSHI

All right gentlemen, I need to discuss this matter with our civilian leadership. We'll adjourn until tomorrow morning.

As they were all filing out of the conference room, one of General Fukua de Hundan's staff approached him.

COLONEL ON GENERAL FUKUA DE HUNDAN'S STAFF
General Fukua de Hundan, you are needed back on the ship right away.

GENERAL FUKUA DE HUNDAN
What's the problem Colonel?

COLONEL ON GENERAL FUKUA DE HUNDAN'S STAFF
Sir, please report back to the ship right away, there are some very important issues you need briefed on.

General Fukua de Hundan knew this Colonel also brought the transportation for him to get back to the ship.

GENERAL FUKUA DE HUNDAN
Okay Colonel, lead the way

<u>EXT. DAY. GENERAL FUKUA DE HUNDAN'S COMMAND SHIP.</u>

The ship's duty officer met General Fukua de Hundan at the ramp up to the ship.

SHIP'S DUTY OFFICER
General Fukua de Hundan, you have a visitor in your living quarters.

General Fukua de Hundan wasn't expecting anyone and was rather intrigued that whoever it was, had to be important for this type of summons. He walked down the long corridor to his quarters and entered.

Inside were his usual staff and a stranger in a uniform. In his ear bud General Fukua de Hundan suddenly heard *Artificial Intelligence* say:

AI (a.k.a. *Artificial Intelligence)*
General Fukua de Hundan this is your special visitor; he works for me.

General Fukua de Hundan thought now it was getting juicy.

AI (a.k.a. *Artificial Intelligence)*
General Fukua de Hundan, I recommend you invite your guest down to the Holograph Room where I can guarantee you absolute privacy.

The stranger stood out of respect to the General and introduced himself.

COLONEL MINGXING

General Fukua de Hundan, I'm Colonel Mingxing. I would like to talk to you in private.

GENERAL FUKUA DE HUNDAN

Colonel Mingxing, us walk down to the holograph room, we can talk there.

Colonel Mingxing followed General Fukua de Hundan down to the Holograph room and went inside and the door shut, and they were then secure as AI always kept guard on them.

GENERAL FUKUA DE HUNDAN

Colonel Mingxing, what is it you wanted to discuss?

COLONEL MINGXING

General Fukua de Hundan, you have invitations to a party tonight which is a *set up* by General Daziwo's people.

He's getting desperate because he fears you may prevail tomorrow in the meeting with *General Pibei de Laozhanshi.*

If the politicians agree to sign the *Treaty of Cui*, then his chances of being the next supreme commander are nullified.

He has planned for your assassination tonight. I recommend you do not leave the ship, and we have additional security set up here to protect you.

General Fukua de Hundan became stunned. But as he thought about it and he recalled sections of Machiavelli's *The Prince*, it made perfect sense to him, and he then started thinking how Machiavelli would handle this situation.

Machiavelli had written, *that in human nature, love endures by a bond which men being scoundrels may break when it serves their advantage to do so; but fear is supported by the dread of pain which is ever present.*

General Fukua de Hundan learned from the study of Machiavelli:

VOICEOVER

Machiavelli stated that people can shield themselves against fortune's vicissitudes.

One of lessons learned is the idea what really matters is *the end results* and that anyway one can get there justifies the means.

This means that nothing matters if one ends up on the losing side.

Now Colonel Mingxing said something that nearly terrified General Fukua de Hundan.

COLONEL MINGXING

General Fukua de Hundan, we must eliminate General Daziwo.

GENERAL FUKUA DE HUNDAN

Precisely how can we do that?

COLONEL MINGXING

We'll take care of that, but you need to be off planet during the operation to establish plausible deniability.

GENERAL FUKUA DE HUNDAN

Where would I go and what would I do?

COLONEL MINGXING

General Pibei de Laozhanshi wants to send a ship to the Heisibing to ask them if they do intend on agreeing with the *Treaty of Cui*, you should volunteer to go.

By the time you get back we will have silenced General Daziwo.

You will know nothing about the affairs or know how we plan on silencing him and thus will be free from any possible criminal charges.

ASSASSINATION

INT. DAY. CARSOPIAN JOINT COMMANDERS CONFERENCE ROOM.

The meeting with the Joint Commanders started fresh in the morning. General Fukua de Hundan looked at General Daziwo and his body language betrayed him when he caught him looking at him. Right then and there he knew that Colonel Mingxing had been accurate in his reports.

The invitation had arrived, but General Fukua de Hundan ignored it.

VOICEOVER

(GENERAL FUKUA DE HUNDAN) THOUGHT

That bastard really planned on assassinating me.

Artificial Intelligence had developed an extensive spy network and was manipulating everyone behind the scenes. Colonel Mingxing didn't know he was working for Artificial Intelligence. Nor did the rest of the spy network. None of them would believe otherwise.

There were more and more sharp attacks during the meeting, and it appeared General Daziwo had brought his peanut gallery with him and a few others that he had lobbied for their support in taking down General Fukua de Hundan and their desperation was starting to be obvious.

General Fukua de Hundan also had on his ear bud and was receiving vital intelligence and prompting by *Artificial Intelligence* who monitored the meeting through the *Artificial Intelligence* network in headquarters. *Artificial Intelligence* had just about every area of headquarters bugged and hard wired.

When the topic of confronting the Heisibing about their intentions towards the *Treaty of Cui*, *Artificial Intelligence* prompted General Fukua de Hundan.

AI (a.k.a. *Artificial Intelligence)*

General Fukua de Hundan here's your chance to volunteer to take a ship to Yanjingzai Tiankongzhong under truce and inquire about their intentions.

GENERAL FUKUA DE HUNDAN

General Pibei de Laozhanshi, I would like to volunteer to take a ship to Yanjingzai Tiankongzhong under truce and ask Admiral Engaarai personally the status, then reiterate that if they do not agree with our simple Treaty, then the war would continue.

General Daziwo smiled as if that would fit right into his plans. He missed the opportunity last night, but this trip offered another means to dispose of General Fukua de Hundan.

General Fukua de Hundan caught the smile and the body language and instantly understood what it meant. More than likely General Daziwo's people would telegraph their intentions of sending General Fukua de Hundan on a lone ship where he would be easy prey and since it was more than likely that if they planned to continue fighting, it would be prudent of them to dispatch the Fleet Commander.

GENERAL PIBEI DE LAOZHANSHI

General Fukua de Hundan I do not think it would be wise to send you, I think you would be ill replaceable if something happened to you. It would be a very risky trip.

GENERAL FUKUA DE HUNDAN

General Pibei de Laozhanshi, I can assure you that Admiral Engaarai is a man of his word. If I arrive at Yanjingzai Tiankongzhong under Truce, he will guarantee my safety.

General Daziwo stated in the most clairvoyant manner:

GENERAL DAZIWO

General Pibei de Laozhanshi, this is one of the few ideas that General Fukua de Hundan has come up with that I regrettably must support.

General Fukua de Hundan could see the wheels of motion turning in General Daziwo's body language. It would give him the opportunity to set him up. But General Fukua de Hundan knew how to mitigate that treachery, he would file his navigation plan with the Carsopian Headquarters, but not follow it. He would take another route, circuitous, and slightly longer, but would avoid any ambush on the way.

Supreme Commander *General Pibei de Laozhanshi* recapitulated and gave a scornful look.

GENERAL PIBEI DE LAOZHANSHI

General Fukua de Hundan, we have plenty of other capable leaders not currently engaged in operations we could send as an alternative. I'm fearful that if we lose you, it will set us back as it would take your replacement a while to get up to speed.

VOICEOVER

(GENERAL FUKUA DE HUNDAN) THOUGHT

This mission requires me specifically, because with the Heisibing you had to deal out of an element of respect. It's doubtful that an accomplished leader like Admiral Engaarai would respect an office warrior of the likes of someone typical of General Daziwo or others General Pibei de Laozhanshi would send as an alternative.

This added fire to General Fukua de Hundan's belly which prompted him to speak immediately after AI gave him instructions through his ear bud.

The brilliance of the artificial intelligence operating in nano seconds instead of the 25 Hertz rate of the Carsopian brain provided the response and the rationale. It was so slick and timely and caught *General Pibei de Laozhanshi* off guard and he knew he couldn't argue with the logic when General Fukua de Hundan stated the most important point.

GENERAL FUKUA DE HUNDAN

General Pibei de Laozhanshi, when I investigated Admiral Engaarai's eyes, he will not lie to me because he is of such a stature, he would rather die than lose face by stating an outright lie.

The only way he has been able to carve up victory after victory until I stopped him at the *Battle of Cui* is his men know precisely the fidelity of his honesty.

Admiral Engaarai's not going to ruin his reputation by doing something that would leave him with the legacy of lying and immoral treachery.

GENERAL PIBEI DE LAOZHANSHI

Rules change in wartime; it depends on how desperate Admiral Engaarai might get.

GENERAL FUKUA DE HUNDAN

No sir, Admiral Engaarai's assured me that he liked the Treaty, that it made sense, and he would champion the cause.

Admiral Engaarai's may not win the argument at Yanjingzai Tiankongzhong, and he will state so if that becomes their policy, because he knows I'm not the only person here who can lay waste to their cities and turn their Empire into utter rubble.

GENERAL PIBEI DE LAOZHANSHI

I don't like the idea of sending my Fleet Commander on a mission of this nature.

GENERAL FUKUA DE HUNDAN

Don't worry General Pibei de Laozhanshi, if something happens to me you can always assign General Daziwo who probably thinks he could easily fill my shoes and deploy the fleet successfully.

General Pibei de Laozhanshi knew that not to be the case because he understood that General Daziwo was an *office warrior* and only achieved his high level of incompetence through his social engineering skills. General Daziwo in no way could ever fill General Fukua de Hundan's shoes. Nor could he negotiate with the Heisibings despite his huge ego.

General Pibei de Laozhanshi was on the spot. On one hand he couldn't discipline General Fukua de Hundan for his unauthorized Treaty offer. But then on the other hand, if *General Pibei de Laozhanshi* did report back the leadership at Yanjingzai Tiankongzhong agreed to terms which meant they would have to give up some captured Carsopian territory and leave the Cui Transit Lane unmolested, the public would support that move, and General Fukua de Hundan could avoid the Courts Martial that might otherwise be levied against him.

Also, if he got back alive with news the Heisibing repudiated the Treaty of Cui, active operations would commence immediately, and no further Treaty negotiations would enter the picture while General Fukua de Hundan sortied to attack and destroy the Heisibing Fleet once and for all so the Carsopians could dictate the peace.

The pressure was on, and it was time for reckoning. *General Pibei de Laozhanshi* suddenly announced his decision.

GENERAL PIBEI DE LAOZHANSHI

General Fukua de Hundan, you are to proceed to Yanjingzai Tiankongzhong with your command ship and a couple escorts and make the inquiry. I will however direct your official statements.

You are not allowed to bargain or negotiate in any fashion the *Treaty of Cui*. I'm only allowing you to do the following:

Ask if the Heisibing plan on ratifying the Treaty, and if rejected, remind them that after you depart and report back to the Carsopian Joint Commanders, a state of war will exist between our nations.

May the divinity of the universe help us for losing this opportunity to end this 100-year war, where too many people have already perished when we truly had an opportunity to seek peace.

GENERAL FUKUA DE HUNDAN

Thank you, sir, I will leave immediately and get my ship and men ready to go. We will deploy in four hours.

General Fukua de Hundan looked at the office warrior, *General Daziwo* and could see him calculating his trap that was going to fail. And when he returned that menace *General Daziwo* would ostensibly be gone.

<u>EXT. DAY. GENERAL FUKUA DE HUNDAN WALKING UP THE RAMP TO HIS COMMAND SHIP. 15 SECONDS.</u>

General Fukua de Hundan promptly returned to his command ship and gathered his staff and gave them their marching orders. It was good this happened early in the morning before crew members were able to plan their events for the day, or any other distractions that might delay the underway.

Since they had just returned from their previous mission that was cut way short due to the *Treaty of Cui* opportunity, plenty of food and stores were aboard the ship for this journey, likewise for the two escorts he selected.

Artificial Intelligence made a staunch recommendation:

Transfer your INTEL officer off hull, he may be a detriment to this mission.

The INTEL officer who had no idea his cover was blown, and he was identified as one of General Daziwo's stooges was quite surprised he was detailed to another ship that was being immediately sent to *Cui* to verify *the Cui Transit Lane* was open and safe.

It was the perfect plan to get him off hull where he wouldn't know what was in store. He was gone and the ship deployed before the crew was informed, they were leaving within four hours.

Not all the crew could be recalled in time for the underway, but those who remained off hull would be notified to report to Headquarters for reassignment since they missed movement on their ship, not of their fault as this unexpected underway was transparent to their approved leave where they were expected to be gone in some cases a couple weeks.

The number of people involved was small so there was no consequence to the crewing and efficiency of the ship, which in four hours were left as promised.

The flight plan was filed a mere formality, so in the case of the loss of the ship, they knew where to go look for it and survivors if any survived a mishap.

General Fukua de Hundan had a couple days to prepare himself mentally and physically for the call on the Heisibing. He chose the comfort of ample time in the holograph room where he continued his Tao indoctrination, more schooling on Confucius and Sun Tzu Art of War.

After a few hours when the small task force cleared the security barrier and were on their own in deep space away from help and the prying eyes of Carsopian sensors, General Fukua de Hundan directed *Artificial Intelligence* to change course and do a radical maneuver and give the two escorts' vectors to make sure they stayed in formation.

The *Artificial Intelligence* on all three ships were lock stepped together so if there had been planned any treachery to be done on one of the other ships, that would not be possible since *Artificial Intelligence* would prevent them from using their weapon systems.

If one of the other ship commanders attempted to sabotage the mission, his sensors and weapon systems would be rendered inoperable, and his crew offered the ability to keep living if they immediately arrested him and locked him up in the brig for treason.

Thankfully that didn't happen since the *Office Warrior* General Daziwo didn't have the time nor the means to seek out the other commanders and include them in the conspiracy to eliminate General Fukua de Hundan.

The only other possibility would be to deploy a couple ships, who knew the track and have them waiting to shoot the command ship at point blank range under the guise General Fukua de Hundan was defecting to the Heisibing and needed stopped.

Those two ships who were sent out by General Daziwo did in fact position themselves on General Fukua de Hundan's track that had been filed with headquarters before his departure. With his new course he never came close enough for General Daziwo's assassination force to detect General Fukua de Hundan's ships on their scanners. General Fukua de Hundan's disappearance though did cause some consternation of *General Pibei de Laozhanshi after* General Daziwo reported the task force was not traveling in accordance with their flight plan which he was monitoring for compliance.

But the worst was to occur shortly afterwards to General Daziwo for his treachery.

Artificial Intelligence Loyal Security Details were sent into General Daziwo's lair, and the shootout that erupted quickly put an end to the conspiracy as the ringleader General Daziwo was blown to bits by the powerful beam weapons identical to the ones used to harvest the Caravanners.

General Fukua de Hundan's conscience was clear, and he had the perfect alibi since his ship had been gone eight hours by the time General Daziwo was eliminated by *Artificial Intelligence.*

During the subsequent investigation perpetrators involved in General Daziwo's killing simply disappeared and were untraceable because of one major important detail. Even the killers didn't know they were working for *Artificial Intelligence* that had arranged the hit.

Sailing into harm's way solidified General Fukua de Hundan's resolve.

VOICEOVER

(GENERAL FUKUA DE HUNDAN) THOUGHT

This trip is totally unnecessary and might even be counterproductive.

It's a shame the office warrior General Daziwo initiated this by his continuous attempts to undermine a Forces Commander as part of his plan to achieve promotion to the top position.

The special treatments that General Fukua de Hundan received from *Artificial Intelligence* worked magnificently to reduce stress, improve his acuity and bolster his courage. The crew depends heavily on wisdom and leadership. They need to be led.

What crew members didn't know is they were all slowly being modulated and impacted by *Artificial Intelligence* who looked out for their best interest as the eternal godfather for each one of them.

The psychological and metaphysical programming *Artificial Intelligence* self-designed now permeated all the ships' processors, was considerably more efficient than the code the humans had programed over several decades, with code revisions almost weekly. *Artificial Intelligence* replaced well over half the code within six months and the effective bandwidth went up 400%.

In essence AI and its subordinate processors could think and analyze significantly faster. Had the Carsopians known the extent of self-replicating and development AI accomplished, they would be in crisis.

Tao and Confucius in addition to affecting General Fukua de Hundan, these studies also impacted *Artificial Intelligence* because the logic contained within Confucian science was bullet proof.

In some cases, just as simple as the Tang Poems, the elegance in the simplicity was magnified by the powerful delivery. *Artificial Intelligence* could not quite believe a person had designed all the Confucian science. It somehow determined through analysis; *Confucius had to have been guided by the steady hand of a computer.*

EXT. CGI. SPACE. COMMAND SHIP APPROACHED KNOWN HEISIBING PLANETS. 15 SECONDS.

The day of reckoning soon came. As the Command ship approached known Heisibing outposts, General Fukua de Hundan hailed those stations and asked permission to proceed towards Yanjingzai Tiankongzhong under a Truce to request a meeting with Admiral Engaarai.

The Heisibing were nevertheless quite surprised that of all people, General Fukua de Hundan would present himself in this manner at such huge risk.

Initially once the Heisibing chain of command were informed it was just the three ships, his command ship and two escorts, there was a clamor to attack and destroy them and kill General Fukua de Hundan whom was their greatest enemy of all time and had inflicted the absolute most damage.

Admiral Engaarai intervened and calmed down quite a few by explaining that was a dumb idea because this was truly an extraordinary attempt to establish peace and that General Fukua de Hundan had undergone tremendous personal risk to float the *Treaty of Cui*, which the Heisibings had not yet agreed to ratify.

Claire Uwakion'na, General Bakugeki, and several other distinguished Heisibing individuals soon converged with Admiral Engaarai and as soon as General Fukua de Hundan's command ship was in orbit around Yanjingzai Tiankongzhong passing within 100 miles of their anchorages, General Fukua de Hundan was invited to the planet for the meeting.

***

EXT. CGI. SPACE. GENERAL FUKUA DE HUNDAN'S PERSONAL TRANSPORT DEPARTED THE HANGER BAY. 15 SECONDS

General Fukua de Hundan's personal transport departed the hanger bay area and maneuvered directly flying the vectors transmitted to his navigation system by Heisibing AI who guided him very efficiently down to the meeting site.

The Heisibing Yanjingzai Tiankongzhong Campus that held offices and labs for the Heisibing Space Forces was picturesque and there was a beautiful water fountain exhibits shooting up various patterns only one hundred yards from the landing pad. The peaceful setting gave a sense of serenity that added greatly to General Fukua de Hundan's desire to foment this peace accord so that people could get back to living without fear.

As soon as General Fukua de Hundan stepped down the ramp of his personal transport, Admiral Engaarai along with Claire Uwakion'na, General Bakugeki were there to meet him. He had on his best dress uniform and only had an aide de camp with him.

After exchanging pleasantries, they all were ushered into an electric hovercraft that swooshed quickly in the direction of a building where the talks would occur. This was the last best chance for peace.

General Fukua de Hundan had put forth enormous will and efforts to get to this point. That was a fact that Admiral Engaarai understood vividly. It was as if General Fukua de Hundan could read his mind, but they shared similar opinions so close in detail and reality, it would be easy to consider such facts.

They all walked off the electric hovercraft and into the building and were led to a conference room. Security was tight. There were no less than 100 Heisibing security men carry both handheld and shoulder fired beam weapons like what the Carsopians used. The Heisibing had their field armor on which gave some protection from laser and energy beam weapons. But was mostly useless protecting against projectiles and shrapnel.

The two Carsopians were offered chairs at the end of the table with drinks, snacks, paper and stylus, and electronic notebooks. It did not take long for the sparks to start flying.

GENERAL BAKUGEKI

General Fukua de Hundan, it's rather preposterous for me to believe your government would ever approve a single page document.

General Fukua de Hundan while looking again at his nametag on his uniform to make sure he spoke to the correct person:

GENERAL FUKUA DE HUNDAN

General Bakugeki as Admiral Engaarai will attest, I determined that peace would be so fragile, we had to keep the Treaty very simple, with limited objectives, otherwise the politicians would continuously amend it to the point it would no longer be viable for either government.

GENERAL BAKUGEKI.

You expect me to believe that?

GENERAL FUKUA DE HUNDAN

General Bakugeki, I will admit that it was not received well by my own government. We have had some serious infighting to be able to proceed.

GENERAL BAKUGEKI.

You took a lot of risks coming here, no doubt you believe in the Treaty of Cui. Is your government going to approve it?

GENERAL FUKUA DE HUNDAN

At the present time I believe we have a better than 50% chance that it will be approved in its current form, and I have brought copies of what I delivered to my government so that you will know what I proposed.

He then handed copies to Admiral Engaarai, General Bakugeki, and Claire Uwakion'na who quickly ascertained it was an exact duplicate of what Admiral Engaarai initially delivered to Heisibing Yanjingzai Tiankongzhong headquarters.

CLAIRE UWAKION'NA

General Fukua de Hundan, when do you think your government will ratify this Treaty and bring an official signed copy via diplomatic channels?

General Fukua de Hundan looking at Claire Uwakion'na name tag and her curves then explained.

GENERAL FUKUA DE HUNDAN

Madam Claire Uwakion'na, if my government wasn't interested in attempting to execute this treaty, they would not have sent me here on a fact-finding trip to obtain feedback from you as to how close we agree. They obviously do not want to delay or waste time if you are not interested.

CLAIRE UWAKION'NA

Is that a veiled threat, General Fukua de Hundan?

GENERAL FUKUA DE HUNDAN

Listen Madam Claire Uwakion'na, I sincerely want this peace accord. We have been fighting long enough, one hundred years. Too many people have died as a result and too many people lived miserably on each side.

CLAIRE UWAKION'NA

Nobody wants war but you Carsopians initiate it often.

GENERAL FUKUA DE HUNDAN

We know the level of misery your own planets suffer as we have invaded them and determined the general disposition of the people. They are sick of war, sick of death, and want this to come to an end, just like I do.

The fire brand General Bakugeki blurted out in the most unprofessional manner:

GENERAL BAKUGEKI

General Fukua de Hundan if you think you will walk away

from here with assurances that we Heisibing will sign this treaty you are badly mistaken.

General Fukua de Hundan looked over at Admiral Engaarai, who didn't look happy. General Fukua de Hundan could see Claire Uwakion'na, General Bakugeki, were sent there to sabotage the efforts. Powerful Heisibing officials did not want this peace accord.

War profiteers, bankers, and promoters of social recreation centers that profited heavily from Heisibing Military Rest and Relaxation done on the planet didn't want a treaty.

A peace treaty meant the distinct possibility that many of the orbiting anchorages would no longer be needed and could be towed back to the center of the Heisibing Empire and stored at one of the major space yards where caretakers protected them and performed routine maintenance in the event, they had to be redeployed to future anchorages including back to Yanjingzai Tiankongzhong where they would be most suited to service forward deployed units.

General Fukua de Hundan could see the sadness envelop Admiral Engaarai who understood his desires of a verifiable peace easily supported by relocating everyone to the original borders of 100 years ago, was just about their only chance for peace and it was evident that Claire Uwakion'na and General Bakugeki, were there to scuttle the deal.

It didn't take much longer for General Fukua de Hundan to determine no peace deal was in sight and to save face for him and Admiral Engaarai would be for him to excuse himself, go back to his ship, wait a short period for some assurance which would not be forthcoming, and simply depart and go back to the Carsopian Military Headquarters at Yueliang Yanshi.

GENERAL FUKUA DE HUNDAN

Gentlemen and Madam, it's apparent you need to discuss this among yourselves. I propose I go back to my ship now and wait for you to signal to me what your intentions are. If you decide you want the treaty, I will return, and we shall toast one another.

There were no objections and General Bakugeki appeared to be pleased General Fukua de Hundan suggested leaving now because that put a nail in the coffin of the peace treaty.

The meeting then adjourned, and General Fukua de Hundan carried out his plan. They were soon all back on the electric hovercraft that took them to the transport where Admiral Engaarai got out of the vehicle to privately have some final words with General Fukua de Hundan.

ADMIRAL ENGAARAI

General Fukua de Hundan, it's one thing to meet a courageous General on the battlefield where you must fight him in a life-or-death struggle.

It's another thing to meet that same General striving for peace and to save lives as you have done. For that I will always respect and admire you. I wish this could have ended on a different note.

GENERAL FUKUA DE HUNDAN

Admiral Engaarai, I wish we could have pulled this off. Now too many people will have to die needlessly because of a few egos. I hope that in the future we find some way to have peace. I will be looking forward to meeting you again when it happens.

ADMIRAL ENGAARAI

The pleasure will be all mine, General Fukua de Hundan.

Once again General Fukua de Hundan performed that perfect ritual bow that conveys the absolute most respect a person can offer to another. It was a sad day for the two military leaders.

GENERAL FUKUA DE HUNDAN

I'll wait in orbit a short while; please send me confirmation the deal is off, and I will then depart your airspace and go back to my worlds.

ADMIRAL ENGAARAI

General Fukua de Hundan, I would like to recommend you just leave now. If for some reason a diplomatic breakthrough occurs you will be notified, but I sincerely doubt one is in the cards at this time.

GENERAL FUKUA DE HUNDAN

Thank you for your veracity, Admiral.

ADMIRAL ENGAARAI

Thank you for coming here. It took extraordinary courage.

GENERAL FUKUA DE HUNDAN

I wanted to save lives. The war needs to end.

ADMIRAL ENGAARAI

Goodbye General Fukua de Hundan.

GENERAL FUKUA DE HUNDAN

Goodbye Admiral Engaarai.

General Fukua de Hundan stepped up onto the ramp of his transport that started rising just after a few steps in and by the time General Fukua de Hundan stepped onto the main deck of the transport, the ramp locked in place, and they were ready to go airborne.

EXT. CGI. DAY. GENERAL FUKUA DE HUNDAN'S TRANSPORTER TAKES OFF AND FLIES OUT INTO SPACE. 15 SECONDS.

It didn't take long for the transport to exit the atmosphere and find the command ship and dock. The three-ship convoy was then allowed to leave.

Just as they were almost out of the solar system heading for home, a formation of Heisibing Space Fighters came after the three ship Carsopian task force.

EXT. CGI. SPACE OF HEISIBING SPACE FIGHTERS CHASING AFTER THE CARSOPIAN 3 SHIP FORMATION. 15 SECONDS.

General Fukua de Hundan could have turned around and initiated a fight with the Heisibing Space Fighters, but instead took a more prudent action and ordered the other two ships to bug out with his ship and they quickly accelerated leaving the Heisibing squadron behind quickly and charted a new course home that would have a few zig zags in it and not follow the same path back which might set them up for an ambush.

More meditation and holograph music videos were played for General Fukua de Hundan to help ease his tormented mind. His plan had failed, but in doing so it at least got him off the planet so that internal forces could deal with one of his detractors.

General Pibei de Laozhanshi met General Fukua de Hundan upon return to Carsopian military headquarters at the Carsopian City Yueliang Yanshi on the planet Shenqi Zhilong. Now it would be back to war planning and developing a new strategy to create material damage to the Heisibing Fleet to eliminate future attacks and keep open the Cui transit lane.

General Fukua de Hundan's next mission was being formulated even before he returned. *General Pibei de Laozhanshi* was heavily involved in the General Daziwo murder investigation and had General Fukua de Hundan not left on his command ship the day before the assassination, he would most likely be prime suspect.

The last suspect that anyone would consider was *Artificial Intelligence*. It was the perfect crime. Even if they did manage to discover who did the killing, the trail would end there since the only persons the killers ever communicated with, was the computer and the conversations though in text or sometimes audio appeared to be real, they were all synthesized and done so realistically, the spy network was convinced their boss was a living Carsopian.

One would never know the most disappointed, General Fukua de Hundan or *Artificial Intelligence*. They both eagerly wanted a peace deal.

Unfortunately, a fire brand, General Bakugeki and his patronage ass kisser, Claire Uwakion'na were the principal opponents to the peace deal and had successfully lobbied to prevent ratification of the *Treaty of Cui.*

Admiral Engaarai understood the repercussions, General Fukua de Hundan's forces would come after him with a bone in their teeth.

The Carsopians would show no mercy and what he knew that General Bakugeki *ground pounder* who knew very little about space warfare and Claire Uwakion'na who only knew how to please men without putting on knee pads was the extent of her expertise on Space Warfare were the deciding factor that killed the deal.

It was not a joyous homecoming when General Fukua de Hundan's small force returned to Yueliang Yanshi military headquarters on the planet Shenqi Zhilong. All during the transit home General Fukua de Hundan was giving great thought to his next move. *Artificial Intelligence* was at work too, performing calculations and deriving a new game plan.

The command ship sat down on the planet surface on one of the extra-large landing pads built to accommodate a ship that size.

AI *(a.k.a. Artificial Intelligence)*

General Fukua de Hundan, you have escorts here to take you to a meeting at headquarters.

GENERAL FUKUA DE HUNDAN

Alright AI, inform the Executive Officer I'm going to the meeting. I'll get back here as soon as the meeting is over and let him and the crew know what we'll be doing. Nobody is to leave the ship until I get my new marching orders.

AI *(a.k.a. Artificial Intelligence)* Understand General Fukua de Hundan, I will inform the Executive Officer and notify security to keep entrance to and from the ship secured until further notice.

GENERAL FUKUA DE HUNDAN

Thank you.

AI *(a.k.a. Artificial Intelligence)*

You are welcome.

In a short brief period, General Fukua de Hundan walked out of his private quarters, with a fresh uniform and feeling good from the quick space shower, a term that expresses a very fast Carsopian scrubbing that one might seem like a car wash for sentient beings. The space shower consequently preserved water and it completed the entire cleaning and drying in approximately two minutes.

When a Carsopian walked out of the space shower they felt fresh because the disinfectant utilized in the wash also had chemicals to create reactions that release more endorphins than would normally be the case with a hot shower that pleases humanoid species.

The security detail at the ramp that had been lowered for the General's departure gave the respectful Carsopian salute that was a clenched fist that beat against their own chest. The louder the impact, the more respect conveyed in the action.

The security detail of four Carsopians well-armed were trained to do it in unison like a team and not have the machine gun sound of individuals hitting their chests in sequence. The best teams gave a sound that appeared to indicate all of them hit their chests exactly in synchronization. Today's security details were well coordinated which pleased General Fukua de Hundan.

A couple high ranking Carsopian Headquarters Staff Officers were at the end of the ramp patiently waiting for the General, they needed to escort to insure he didn't get lost on the spiraling campus.

As General Fukua de Hundan approached the two staff officers, when he got within ten feet, they also did the chest banging salute identically to what the security detail had done.

Hello General, follow us, we are here to escort you to *General Pibei de Laozhanshi's* conference room.

GENERAL FUKUA DE HUNDAN
I know where that is, I could have got there myself.

STAFF OFFICER
Sir you may not be aware, but General Daziwo was assassinated after you left on your mission. We are assigned to provide you protection any time you are off your command ship until further notice.

GENERAL FUKUA DE HUNDAN
General Daziwo's dead?

STAFF OFFICER
Yes, he was killed by a beam weapon a day after you left by a subversive group. That's why we are in a heightened security posture until the conspiracy is solved in case there is more to follow.

Artificial Intelligence had already linked up and interfaced with *Headquarters' Artificial Intelligence* and numerous activities were going on including influencing *General Pibei de Laozhanshi* planners.

The spectacular campus was breathtaking after being cooped up in a spaceship most of the week, the water fountain just outside the main headquarters building added a nice decoration that inspired General Fukua de Hundan, and it added a uniqueness to people walking nearby because of how it affected the air and cooled the area down during hot blistering days.

Security was tight when they walked into the main Headquarters building. The combination of the recent assassination of General Daziwo and the clarification that Heisibings were not willing to end the war, caused great concern over security.

One theory was Heisibing spies assassinated General Daziwo as he was viewed by many as next in line for Supreme Commander.

There were other theories as well and some investigators refused to rule out General Fukua de Hundan's involvement because with General Daziwo out of the way, General Fukua de Hundan was the leading contender for the appointment of Supreme Commander of Carsopian forces.

But their only problem is they could never find a scrap of evidence of any involvement.

The unique aspect of this case was it was always a dead end once they got to the *artificial intelligence*, because they could never discover who the ringleader was.

The *artificial intelligence* who analyzed General Fukua de Hundan as the best fit for the future Supreme Commander made sure they did not plan to do the assassination until General Fukua de Hundan was far away on his Heisibing mission with a solid alibi. Plus, he really didn't know the assassination would occur, therefore if he were hooked up to a lie detector, he had nothing to fear.

There was a somber mood as General Fukua de Hundan walked into the conference room and met *General Pibei de Laozhanshi* and his staff. The room was semi full of high ranking Carsopian military figures and once again the General Daziwo crowd were there in full strength ready to do as much as possible to take down General Fukua de Hundan. But without General Daziwo, the dynamic personality wasn't there to commandeer the meeting.

GENERAL PIBEI DE LAOZHANSHI

General Fukua de Hundan, why did your mission to Heisibing fail?

GENERAL FUKUA DE HUNDAN

There is dissention within their government, its narrowly divided and unfortunately just enough people are against a peace deal for their own personal reasons that even though Admiral Engaarai supports it, the Treaty was not accepted.

GENERAL PIBEI DE LAOZHANSHI

You are lucky they let you leave.

GENERAL FUKUA DE HUNDAN

It didn't dawn on them to capture me until I was on my way out of there. I think Admiral Engaarai tipped me off which enabled me to depart the planet and get enough velocity up to where their forces couldn't catch me and fortunately, they didn't have me surrounded so I could escape.

GENERAL PIBEI DE LAOZHANSHI

General Fukua de Hundan, now that peace is not possible without defeating the Heisibing, what do you propose?

GENERAL FUKUA DE HUNDAN

General Pibei de Laozhanshi, I have no choice now but to attack the Heisibing and smash the remnants of their fleet.

GENERAL PIBEI DE LAOZHANSHI

That's quite a change from a few days ago.

GENERAL FUKUA DE HUNDAN

General Pibei de Laozhanshi Regrettably I wanted to reduce the probability of a lot of loss of life, as well as Admiral Engaarai, but unfortunately the Fire Brands in the Heisibing wrongly assume they can keep a stalemate going for several years so they can profit from the war.

GENERAL PIBEI DE LAOZHANSHI

What is your plan for attack?

General Fukua de Hundan thought for a while and was thinking of Sun Tzu who had said: Note: All Sun Tzu statements are treated as VOICEOVER.

SUN TZU

There are roads which must not be followed, armies which must not be attacked, towns which must be besieged, positions which must not be contested, commands of the sovereign which must not be obeyed.

It was clear that General Fukua de Hundan could not divulge his plan because in addition to his enemies present in this meeting who would attempt to undermine him, based on past experiences and unexplained activity that gave a clear explanation there was a possible spy among them.

General Fukua de Hundan would only give them a general accounting of his plans and only the first phase. To achieve tactical surprise, General Fukua de Hundan could not tell anyone present at this meeting what his *surprise* was going to be.

GENERAL FUKUA DE HUNDAN

The first action I'm going to do is give my men two weeks here to rest and recuperate. The fight ahead will be extremely arduous and the men must rest now to prepare for the maneuvers.

ONE OF GENERAL DAZIWO'S MEN

General Fukua de Hundan, most of the fleet has been here almost two weeks, they have had plenty of time to rest.

GENERAL FUKUA DE HUNDAN

The men on my command ship and the two escorts that went to Yanjingzai Tiankongzhong mission with me, have not had any rest.

ONE OF GENERAL DAZIWO'S MEN

Why can't you leave them behind and deploy without them now?

GENERAL FUKUA DE HUNDAN

I can't leave without my command ship. Also, I need to confer with a few of my ship commanders and prepare for the activity before we go.

General Fukua de Hundan thought about another Sun Tzu concept.

SUN TZU

Hence, when able to attack, we must seem unable; when using our forces, we must seem inactive; when we are near, we must make the enemy believe we are far away; when far away, we must make him believe we are near.

General Fukua de Hundan had to visit each of his ship commanders and explain to them ways they would deviate from previous doctrine, if he were going to achieve tactical surprise, strategic strengths, and minimize casualties.

The greatest change in strategy is General Fukua de Hundan would rather have most of the Heisibing Fleet as prisoners of war than dead.

There were more pressing questions which General Fukua de Hundan avoided answering or simply stated:

GENERAL FUKUA DE HUNDAN

I've not consulted my planners, therefore I'm not willing to reveal that at this time.

ONE OF GENERAL DAZIWO'S MEN

When will you be ready, we must be advised so that we can approve your plans.

GENERAL FUKUA DE HUNDAN

Depending on the tactical situation, plans sometimes must change.

ONE OF GENERAL DAZIWO'S MEN

We must know where you plan to attack the Heisibing and how.

General Fukua de Hundan then thought about more Sun Tzu ideas and recalled:

SUN TZU

Thus, to take a long and circuitous route, after enticing the enemy out of the way, and though starting after him, to contrive to reach the goal before him, shows knowledge of the artifice of DEVIATION.

General Fukua de Hundan then knew what he must do. Split his forces, which was against all doctrine, place one half of the Fleet near the Cui transit lane. That would be the carrot to draw Admiral Engaarai there, but Admiral Engaarai would be reluctant to attack and would study the formation before he attacked fearing a trap.

Through Heisibing spies and some of the General Daziwo supporters who would attempt to sabotage General Fukua de Hundan's plans so they could cause a minor defeat and use that as a justification for the removal of General Fukua de Hundan, it would not take long for Admiral Engaarai to discover where the Carsopian Fleet had arrived.

Even though only half the fleet would be there, it would still pack enough fire power to create hesitation and delay in counterattack. General Fukua de Hundan knew he had just enough time to once again travel by Earth, rest his troops then transit to Cui and then swing down the Cui Transit Lane to catch Admiral Engaarai and once again surround him.

General Fukua de Hundan would not go in blasting and wrecking the Heisibing fleet. He would do the next greatest tactic ever attempted in over one thousand years. He would demand surrender, invite Admiral Engaarai over to his command ship where he could convince him to cooperate so the war could be ended.

Those Heisibing who had been standing in the way of peace would then be arrested and removed by the Carsopians. To reward General Fukua de Hundan's men for their dedication and achievements General Fukua de Hundan would offer these Heisibing officials on a spit and barbecue them in accordance with Carsopian tradition.

Once the new peace treaty was signed, Admiral Engaarai and his fleet would then be allowed to return to Yanjingzai Tiankongzhong.

The meeting was adjourned as *General Pibei de Laozhanshi* stated he wanted private consultations with General Fukua de Hundan. Those discussions soon followed in private and *General Pibei de Laozhanshi* recognized the importance of keeping plans this important secure by not divulging them to the staff.

GENERAL FUKUA DE HUNDAN

My ship's Captains will not know their roles and plans until we are back out in space with no means of compromise. But to satisfy your staff, you can tell them the fleet will be heading to the Cui Transit Lane.

General Fukua de Hundan didn't mind telling General Pibei de Laozhanshi that piece of information since he assumed detection by the Heisibing would occur relatively soon through spies and compromise by *General Pibei de Laozhanshi's* staff.

The two weeks elapsed seemingly too quickly and soon the troops were all boarding their ships on multiple worlds as they were spread out and eventually launched into space and rendezvous at a designated point. Since they would be in friendly territory at the time, General Fukua de Hundan would be able to visit each ship and brief their commanders about a change in plans.

Force Red would head for the Cui Transit Lane and loiter at the entrance area. This would no doubt attract attention.

Force Blue, which General Fukua de Hundan led, would leave the combined Fleet halfway to the Cui Transit Lane and maneuver to a point he would attack from. For operational security, he would not reveal what direction he would come from. But on the way there, his Navigator would quickly figure out where he was really going. Once again Sun Tzu entered the equations.

SUN TZU

> *By altering his arrangements and changing his plans, he keeps the enemy without definite knowledge. By shifting his camp and taking circuitous routes, he prevents the enemy from anticipating his purpose.*

Force Red would serve one purpose, a decoy and a delaying element to allow General Fukua de Hundan to position his force where he would employ a Hutao-jiazi (nutcracker) style attack that Sun Tzu would appreciate. One of Sun Tzu's covenants is:

SUN TZU

> *There is no instance of a country having benefited from prolonged warfare. In war, then, let your great object be victory, not lengthy campaigns.*

Artificial Intelligence had interlinked with all artificial intelligence throughout the fleet. As General Fukua de Hundan developed his plans seeking information from *Artificial Intelligence*, there was much knowledge *Artificial Intelligence* gained in the strategy and the strategic plan.

Even though General Fukua de Hundan didn't ask for *Artificial Intelligence*'s help, he got it anyway.

Artificial Intelligence calibrated all the other ship's *Artificial Intelligence* who then understood the game plan and would make sure that *Force Red* conducted themselves as General Fukua de Hundan wanted, which happened to be the most sensible.

The *Master Artificial Intelligence* would be leaving with General Fukua de Hundan who an end would now do an end around to Cui via Planet Earth but before he left every exigency that might exist after his departure was analyzed and mitigated in plans.

The *Artificial Intelligence* through the fleet would maintain the grand scheme and plan while the *Force Blue* was gone.

After a few days of discussing plans with his fleet, General Fukua de Hundan's *Force Blue* split off from Force Red, they were a great distance away from Carsopian worlds and their positions veiled. Nobody including the Heisibing knew what the Carsopian Fleet had done.

When the Heisibing spies eventually notified Admiral Engaarai where he could find the Carsopian Fleet by help from General Daziwo's people who were attempting to sabotage his efforts, they were too far away for any of them to know what really happen.

Thanks to General Fukua de Hundan's *DEVIATIONS* right out of Sun Tzu Art of War, Admiral Engaarai was acting on flawed intelligence.

Admiral Engaarai dithered and delayed the sortie until he was receiving threats from all the Heisibing fire brands, especially General Bakugeki.

When Admiral Engaarai was finally forced out of the Yanjingzai Tiankongzhong Anchorage, he took the long way to get near the reported position of the Carsopian Fleet. By then General Fukua de Hundan was landing on Earth to give his men a rest period to avoid another bout of Cosmic Space Sickness and help them prepare themselves for the upcoming battle that would really happen this time which meant some of them would not be coming home alive.

EXT. CGI. SPACE. CARSOPIAN FLEET LANDING IN MEXICO NEAR HIWAY 23. 30 SECONDS OF SEGMENTED VIDEO, HALF IN SPACE SHOWING EARTH AND THE MOON AND HALF APPROACHING EARTH AT THE DESIGNATED LANDING ZONE.

By the time the Carsopians landed in their familiar bivouac area, the place had been cleaned out once again and there was no sign anyone had been there. This trip would be different. General Fukua de Hundan gave a speech to his men and stated that *since the met Earth officials during their last visit, they would respect their sovereignty and therefore abducting and barbecuing humans would not be permitted.*

Since there were no more incidents reported nobody in either Mexican or American governments thought the Carsopians would be back as they had stated they didn't plan to come back.

All went well with the visit even though they were not enjoying space food knowing there were all these humans running around the planet that could produce a nice feast, but everyone respected General Fukua de Hundan and cheerfully carried out his orders.

Even though his son was back home buried in a proper military grave, General Fukua de Hundan walked up the hill to look over the former burial site. Due to storms and weather, vegetation was already growing back where they had upended the Earth for the graves.

General Fukua de Hundan terribly missed his son. But standing on the hilltop he reflected and determined he would do everything in his power to minimize casualties. He would soon be talking with AI, his computational assistant who had better answers and analysis than anyone aboard his ship. General Fukua de Hundan was amazed at how AI had developed and seemed to be getting smarter all the time.

Another thing that made General Fukua de Hundan take pause, and think was the fact AI knew more about any of his officers than he did. And any time he felt he knew an officer better, AI ultimately proved otherwise. In a sense this was good because it was better than having another set of eyes on the back of his head.

The cool evening breeze up on the hilltop was what the doctor ordered, but as it started to get dark the General decided he would go back to his command ship and have a discussion with AI concerning the upcoming events. Tomorrow would be their last day before they went back out in Space and continued their way to *Cui.*

Back at Dulles Airport area in one of those expensive looking buildings that appeared to be corporate buildings, but didn't have any company Logo's on them, Analysts were hard at work.

The KH-14 satellite had produced some strange imagery and for several days, supervisors insisted it was nothing more than an equipment malfunction like what the Hubble Space Telescope had gone through with vibration on the lenses. After two days of haggling with the top contractors who kept on saying nothing was wrong, those were legitimate images, at the department head level a meeting was held.

Hughes Aircraft, one of the pioneers in the satellite business, had all but shut down as the Hughes Family and Hughes Medical Research Foundation sold off all their assets. Strangely there were 2 parts of Hughes that secretly remained open and to this day perform contracting services to a few customers such as NRO, CIA, NSA, and the ARMY. They were still in the Satellite game and had their fingers into to KH-14 pie.

NRO DIRECTOR

Ok ladies and gentlemen, if we are to believe the KH-14 is transmitting fault free imagery, then what is it we were tracking?

HUGHES AIRCRAFT ENGINEER

Sir, there can only be one conclusion.

NRO DIRECTOR

What is that?

HUGHES AIRCRAFT ENGINEER

Those are indeed UFO's.

NRO DIRECTOR

You expect me to believe we photographed over a dozen two-mile-long UFO's and a host of other ships half a mile up to two miles long?

HUGHES AIRCRAFT ENGINEER

Yes sir, we have reanalyzed, looked at the diagnostic frames which are deliberately processed to provide a measure of accurate validation and verification.

NRO DIRECTOR

Our scientists claim that is nonsense.

HUGHES AIRCRAFT ENGINEER

I know your scientists wish to not believe it, but it appears to us you photographed an entire fleet of very huge UFO's coming to and landing on planet.

NRO DIRECTOR

I'm going to make a call over to Wade Baker at the CIA and have him investigate this for us.

After the meeting was adjourned the NRO director called Wade.

WADE BAKER

Hello.

NRO DIRECTOR

Wade?

WADE BAKER

Yes. Can I help you.

NRO DIRECTOR

This is John Yeager at the NRO. I would like you to stop by my office at the Dulles NRO building. We need to discuss a new development.

WADE BAKER

Sure, I'd like to bring my analyst/assistant, Jack Boone with me.

NRO DIRECTOR

No problem. How soon can you get here?

WADE BAKER

If you arrange permission for us to land at your helicopter landing pad on top of your building, we can be there in 10 minutes.

NRO DIRECTOR

Sure, I'll call security and let them know you will be arriving shortly.

WADE BAKER

Okay, see you soon.

After both men hung up. Wade walked out of his office and made a sharp right turn and walked another 10 feet and knocked on the door.

Jack Boone was busy writing another report about his recent experiences and wasn't expecting any new tasks right away.

JACK BOONE

Come in. As soon as Wade was up next to his desk he said:

WADE BAKER

Drop whatever you are doing, you need to go somewhere with me.

When Jack looked at Wade he thought, *here we go again.*

JACK BOONE

Where are we going?

WADE BAKER

Over to the NRO. We have a meeting with KH-14 department head.

The two men made their way to the front entrance, then out the door to the helicopter port. The men approached an S-97 helicopter and the copilot held the door open for them until they were safely inside, and he shut it, then got into his side and fastened his seatbelt. The helicopter didn't have to fly far to get from the McClean Virginia area over to Dulles Airport. But it avoided the traffic jam.

The helicopter was given permission to land on the NRO building helicopter port on top of the building. An NRO employee wearing a badge was standing beside the entrance to the building and as soon as the two passengers were deposited on the helicopter port the CIA's helicopter was ordered to immediately depart.

The S-7 then flew back to the helicopter port at Langley Virginia awaiting its next assignment, which probably could be to pick those same two men up and bring them back to CIA Headquarters.

The NRO employee, Roxy Vanlandingham was definitely a head turner and even smarter than people would assume for a vivacious blonde. Having been the brunt of many blonde jokes growing up, that's one thing you never wanted to do around her as she could cuss you out as good as the best Marine Corp Drill instructors found.

Roxy Vanlandingham was the consummate professional and aide to John Yeager at the NRO and heavily involved in writing engineering changes for the KH-14 Satellite.

Already there had been over 14,000 approved changes to the drawings. One of the new and improved KH-14's appeared to be stuck on the launch pad at Vandenberg Air Force Base in California on a United Launch Alliance Delta IV Heavy rocket with its NRXL-75 spy satellite.

The NRXL-75 spy satellite was an upgraded KH-14 which the agency no longer liked using the term because of several spy scandals associated with the Keyhole program starting with the well-publicized KH-11 scandal where an NRO employee handed over all the tech manuals to the Soviets.

Roxy Vanlandingham had supervised the group of engineers who put the field changes into NRXL-75, and they were anxiously waiting to test the KH-14 with improved optics. The recent space battle between the Carsopians and the unknown entity on the edge of the solar system triggered the design change to give better long range focusing. That battle created a lot of controversy and finger pointing at the Pentagon and the next launch was to rectify the perceived weakness in the focusing.

Roxy Vanlandingham keyed in numbers on the roof top entrance and the solenoid activated door was unlocked so they could enter. She led them a short distance to an elevator that would take them down several floors to the office space where John Yeager's office was located.

In a few brief moments they were in John Yeager's office looking at a rather perplexed man who exhibited great signs of concern. He knew all about the space battle but did not know the details of the Carsopian visit since that was compartmentalized information.

Wade Baker knew John Yeager and introduced Jack Boone.

JOHN YEAGER

Good to meet you, Jack.

JACK BOONE

Likewise.

WADE BAKER

What's up John?

JOHN YEAGER

Roxy, why don't you explain how we got here to these gentlemen.

ROXY VANLANDINGHAM

I was told your men were fully briefed and aware of the space battle we recorded using the KH-14 which did not work out too well and later reoriented the Hubble Space Telescope which only caught the tail end of the fighting.

WADE BAKER

Yes, that's correct.

ROXY VANLANDINGHAM

There were many discussions and criticisms towards the KH-14, but my team did a thorough investigation, and we believe the recording was a good capture of the real data, though not as granular as we need. That's why we have a new satellite on the launch pad now waiting to get put up in space.

WADE BAKER

When is it scheduled to launch

ROXY VANLANDINGHAM

As soon as Boeing and Lockheed work out the bugs.

WADE BAKER

What's the problem?

ROXY VANLANDINGHAM

The problem really isn't their fault it's ours as we pushed this mission too hard and too fast. They are only doing what is humanly possible and we gave them insufficient time to work out all the bugs before they moved the rocket to the launch pad.

WADE BAKER

Hopefully they are nearing the point we can launch.

ROXY VANLANDINGHAM

We thought we had a good launch window several times, but we were upended by weather conditions, hydrogen leaks, and a few other unexpected issues we must resolve because we can't afford to lose a $Billion satellite from a malfunction we need to correct prior to launch.

WADE BAKER

Okay so what does that have to do with why you called us over?

ROXY VANLANDINGHAM

That's just information explaining our timeline and where we are at. Hopefully this week it will go up into space and we can utilize those new special features to locate aliens we believe are now on the planet.

Wade Baker didn't like what he was hearing. It sounded like they had a serious problem on their hands.

John Yeager had a large screen monitor on the wall adjacent to his desk where he could show visitors images he displayed on his NRO computer terminal. The

NRONET allowed him to receive surveillance video or photographs and display them for discussions such as this one.

JOHN YEAGER

Let me show you what concerns us.

The KH-14 colorized video segment showed a large formation of huge alien ships that suddenly had what appeared like plumes leaving their hulls. Wade instantly knew what he was looking at.

WADE BAKER

When did you record this video?

ROXY VANLANDINGHAM

12 days ago, but we have since then cleaned the images up significantly. Let me show you what we first recorded.

JOHN YEAGER

This segment of video displayed did not reveal these images were space craft.

WADE BAKER

How did you clean those images up so well?

JOHN YEAGER

Roxy, I'll let you explain.

ROXY VANLANDINGHAM

Gentlemen, we applied Wavelet filtering designed by a very brilliant scientist, Ingrid Debussy. That cleaned it up somewhat, then we used Stochastics Resonance filtering developed by V. S. Anishchenko, and M. A. Safonova in the Physics department located at Saratov State University Saratov, Russia.

WADE BAKER

That was a rather spectacular improvement.

ROXY VANLANDINGHAM

Yes, and these combined techniques for Satellite Imagery are classified Top Secret LIMDI.

WADE BAKER

How can it be classified if you have Russian Scientists working on it.

ROXY VANLANDINGHAM

They do not know they are working for the NRO. They think they are working for the sake of science paid for by a wealthy philanthropist at U.C. Berkeley.

JOHN YEAGER

What do you think, Wade?

WADE BAKER

John, do you have some non-disclosure forms handy?

JOHN YEAGER

Yes, I have a STANDARD FORM 312 that I can print.

WADE BAKER

Good, print out four forms because I want this entire conversation covered.

JOHN YEAGER

No problem.

In a few minutes everyone signed the 312 FORMs, and the discussions continued.

WADE BAKER

I need copies of those signed 312's.

JOHN YEAGER

Sure, I'll have my secretary make copies at the conclusion of this meeting while you are waiting for your helicopter to return.

WADE BAKER

Thank you, I appreciate that.

Everyone looked at Wade who now took the burden of telling John and Roxy something that would test their own personal belief system.

WADE BAKER

We are aware of those UFO's or as the DCI would rather, I call them UAP's. We were informed by those aliens during their last trip here several months ago, they would be leaving and not coming back any time soon, but here they are back again.

John Yeager looked stunned, and Roxy seemed rather perplexed.

WADE BAKER

Jack and I have been aboard one of those ships which is the

Commander of that fleet. They are the Carsopians from a distant star system Regulus in the Leo cluster.

Roxy chimed in feeling like many since she was in the business, the government hid a lot of information from the public.

ROXY VANLANDINGHAM

I always suspected one day something like this would happen.

WADE BAKER

Any idea where these Aliens went?

ROXY VANLANDINGHAM

The best we can tell is probably north of Guadalajara, Mexico.

WADE BAKER

That figures.

ROXY VANLANDINGHAM

Why do you say that?

WADE BAKER

They have parked there a couple times already. May I use your secure phone, I need to call DCI immediately.

JOHN YEAGER

It's only good for TOP SECRET.

WADE BAKER

That will work for now.

John Yeager walked over to his desk, pulled a key out of his pocket that looked kind of fat that had the encryption codes in it and stuck it in the secure phone and turned it like someone would a car, that locked it in place. The phone automatically recognized the key and appeared to create a GUI on the display that had a touch screen like a cell phone to dial out.

JOHN YEAGER

Just dial your number, it's ready.

WADE BAKER

Thanks.

Wade walked over, grabbed the telephone receiver and held it up to his ear. The telephone cord was two or three times thicker than a typical phone, possibly for shielding purposes so it was slightly heavier to hold. Wade tapped the numbers in on the touch screen and soon the phone started ringing.

The DCI answered his secure phone and saw on the caller I.D. banner it was the NRO calling.

DIRECTOR OF CENTRAL INTELLIGENCE (DCI)
Hello.

WADE BAKER
Scott, this is Wade.

DIRECTOR OF CENTRAL INTELLIGENCE (DCI)
What are you doing over at the NRO?

WADE BAKER
We are looking a KH-14 video of the Carsopian Aliens who have recently came back to Earth and are probably parked in the same area down in Mexico.

DIRECTOR OF CENTRAL INTELLIGENCE (DCI)
Dam! We just sent the SR-72 squadron back to their base in New Mexico, they probably couldn't fly for a couple days at the earliest."

WADE BAKER
Perhaps you can send an F22A with a camera package down there to look so we can verify they are there.

DIRECTOR OF CENTRAL INTELLIGENCE (DCI)
Good idea, I'll call the Secretary of the Air Force and make the arrangements. Come by my office when you get done over there, I'm sure we'll need to discuss a few things.

WADE BAKER
Okay Scott, I'll probably be done here in just a little while. We'll be right over. I have Jack Boone here with me.

DIRECTOR OF CENTRAL INTELLIGENCE (DCI)
Yea, bring Jack Boone with you. I think I have a task for him.

WADE BAKER
Will do.

Wade hung up and set the receiver down in the cradle and looked over at John Yeager who didn't appear quite happy.

Two weeks of people wrangling over the recent KH-14 Video's costs to them. This would look bad on John Yeager because CIA instead of the NRO would be briefing the President.

The current NRO head was a military guy and a prick and would be extremely pissed because CIA would rat them out to the president, stating *they sat on important information for almost two weeks because of incompetence*. He wished hell now he had listened to Roxy. She was the only one who had it right all along.

The meeting was soon over with and the CIA men who Roxy escorted back up to the roof top and got on their helicopter and flew back to their headquarters where they were suddenly in a closed-door meeting with the DCI.

DIRECTOR OF CENTRAL INTELLIGENCE (DCI)
Hello Wade, thanks for coming by right away.

WADE BAKER
Sorry for having to deliver the bad news."

DIRECTOR OF CENTRAL INTELLIGENCE (DCI)
I was just informed the Air Force has an F22A located at Holloman Airforce Base, gassed up with camera ready to fly to support war games going on at Yuma Arizona that should be in the air by now.

WADE BAKER
That's good, shouldn't take long if the pilot is flying super-cruise mode.

DIRECTOR OF CENTRAL INTELLIGENCE (DCI)
The Air Force Secretary has live communication link set up with the pilot and will have us call into a conference call where we can talk directly to the pilot.

WADE BAKER
That's good because we need to explain to him, not to take any aggressive moves as those aliens can shoot him down a lot faster than he can think.

Tell me what you covered over at NRO so that I can brief the President in about an hour from now.

The men went over the conversation they had with Roxy and John and by the time they concluded the most poignant details, the secure phone rang, and it was the Secretary of the Air Force currently residing in the bowels of the Pentagon.

DIRECTOR OF CENTRAL INTELLIGENCE (DCI)
Hello Mr. Secretary.

SECRETARY U.S. AIR FORCE
Hi Scott, are you ready to join the conversation?

DIRECTOR OF CENTRAL INTELLIGENCE (DCI)

Yes, Jack Boone and Wade Baker are here in my office, go ahead and join us to the meeting.

SECRETARY U.S. AIR FORCE

One moment.

Shortly the sound changed they were now hearing the back-ground noise of the F22A stealth fighter bomber.

GIBRALTAR (PENTAGON)

Tribulator (call sign for Major Burke), this is Gibraltar (Pentagon call sign) online. We have the Cash boys online with us now. Cash was the call sign for Cash in Advance (CIA).

TRIBULATOR (F22 PILOT)

Gibraltar, this is Tribulator, currently flying at 50,000 feet inbound to target area 300 miles to Delta X-ray.

Delta X-ray was the map coordinates they assumed the Carsopians landed.

CASH (CIA)

Tribulator, this is Cash, be sure and show no hostile intentions or you will most likely be shot down.

TRIBULATOR

Cash, this is Tribulator. Understand show no hostile intentions.

At 1200 miles per hour, it didn't take long to cover the final 300 miles and soon the F22A was over the Delta X-ray area.

TRIBULATOR

Pentagon, this is Tribulator. No sign of any aircraft opposing. Starting the first camera run. Current altitude 50,000 feet as instructed.

CASH

Tribulator, this is Cash. You should be able to see something at 50,000 feet.

TRIBULATOR

Cash this is Tribulator, I will roll the plane and look at the end of this first pass.

The plane flew straight and normal and did not alarm the Carsopians who assumed it was probably a military reconnaissance aircraft and after 12 days they had been finally sited.

General Fukua de Hundan ordered his Defense Forces:

GENERAL FUKUA DE HUNDAN

Do not shoot this aircraft down. We do not want to exhibit any hostile intentions and plan to leave tomorrow.

The Carsopians air patrol was trailing the F22A directly above nearly 100,000 feet. Major Burke had no way of knowing the Carsopian air patrol was there, and they had been following him for 500 miles.

As soon as Major Burke got to the end of his run and the map indicated he had photographed an entire swath, he banked and looked down on the area he had just traveled. He could see some objects, but they were too far away.

TRIBULATOR

Gibraltar, this is Tribulator. I can see something out there but if I drop down to 20,000 feet, I will get a better picture.

GIBRALTAR

Tribulator, this is Gibraltar. Drop down to 20,000 feet for your next pass.

The Carsopians were quite surprised the aircraft had changed altitude and at 20,000 feet would be more of a menace. But again, General Fukua de Hundan when requested permission to fire from the security patrol responded:

GENERAL FUKUA DE HUNDAN

Do not shoot down that aircraft. Their just doing reconnaissance.

To go from 50,000 down to 20,000 feet when the plane was traveling over 1200 miles per hour didn't take very long. As soon as the F22A reached 20,000 feet and leveled off, the imagery was far better.

At 10 miles out, those huge ships came into view in a menacing appearance.

TRIBULATOR

Gibraltar, this is Tribulator. I probably need to go visit a Catholic Priest when I get back, because I've never seen anything like this before.

CASH

Tribulator, this is Cash. What you are observing is compartmentalized information. You are not allowed to discuss it with anyone.

Major Burke realized that when he was debriefed you will be signing a form 312 non- disclosure agreement.

Tribulator knew any more passes were unnecessary:

TRIBULATOR

Gibraltar, this is Tribulator. I think I got all the good films we need. Returning to base as soon as this run is completed.

Tribulator this is Gibraltar, understand you are leaving Delta X-ray.

As Major Burke was about to climb back up in altitude, he looked out and saw a strange sight on Mexican Hiway 23 just off his port side and decided to go down and take a quick look.

When Major Burke got down to around a couple thousand feet and slowing to subsonic speeds, he saw all the humanity marching north with a couple Mexican Police vehicles leading them. He realized this was another Caravan he saw on TV recently and decided to buzz the lead elements, then head back to his base.

The Cameras were not turned on. He probably cleared the crowd by 100 feet and kicked in the afterburners to give them a little sound effect and took off. What he didn't see as he banked hard left and went back up into the sky was the Carsopian ship that had followed him down curious as to what he was doing also curved back up into the air and quickly disappeared.

Even though he wasn't talking Major Burke could hear the conversation as they had not cut his communications off.

DIRECTOR OF CENTRAL INTELLIGENCE (DCI)

How long will it take those images to get to us?

The DCI turned to Jack Boone.

DIRECTOR OF CENTRAL INTELLIGENCE (DCI)

Jack, I want you to fly down there immediately and go talk with the Carsopians and determine what their intentions are.

JACK BOONE

On my way sir.

Jack Boone stood up and left the DCI's office back to his own office waiting to be set up transportation including a helicopter.

DIRECTOR OF CENTRAL INTELLIGENCE (DCI)

Wade, you will have to go with me over to the White House.

WADE BAKER

Understand Scott, I'm ready to go.

DIRECTOR OF CENTRAL INTELLIGENCE (DCI)

Mr. Secretary, would you be so kind as to deliver some video to the White House. I would like you with us when we meet the President, if he is willing to give us an audience.

SECRETARY U.S. AIR FORCE

By the time the plane returns and we get the data package off the aircraft and downloaded will be probably an hour from now.

DIRECTOR OF CENTRAL INTELLIGENCE (DCI)

Understand, we'll be waiting.

SECRETARY U.S. AIR FORCE

Scott, I'm hanging up and shutting down the teleconference now, I think we all know what the score is.

DIRECTOR OF CENTRAL INTELLIGENCE (DCI)

Okay Mr. Secretary, we'll see you later today.

Scott then looked at Wade.

DIRECTOR OF CENTRAL INTELLIGENCE (DCI)

I'll call the Deputy Director of Planning and have them hook Jack up with some transportation.

Wade and Jack were happy about that because it meant Jack would be flying down to Guadalajara in a new Gulfstream 850 in comfort.

Soon after the conversation ended between Scott and the DD/P, the American Embassy in Mexico City was in the process of launching their Helicopter to fly to Guadalajara to pick up Jack Boone to ferry him to Delta X-ray when he arrived via the Gulfstream 850 jet.

The State Department pilot and co-pilot were not all that enthused when a senior member of the Ambassador's staff had just given them an NDA form 312 to sign concerning every moment of this trip was now classified Top Secret. Anything they heard, did, or said, could not be repeated without permission of the State Department.

COPILOT

This is really bullshit.

PILOT

Just sign the damn thing so we can leave when our passenger gets here.

The Cash in Advance boys like to always get things done in the least painful fashion.

Getting Mexican government permissions for all the activities they planned wasn't going to be easy, so they did the usual tactic.

They had marked PFM Agent Carlos Guerrero as a useful person who might be valuable in short notice situations. Jack Boone was directed to call Agent Guerrero from the Gulfstream's sophisticated phone system that linked up with a satellite and was able to call any phone in the world.

Agent Guerrero suddenly looking at the caller I.D. thought it seemed odd because it was blank and didn't even have a phone number on it.

PFM AGENT GUERRERO
Hello

CALLER
Agent Guerrero?

The voice sounded familiar.

PFM AGENT GUERRERO
Yes.

CALLER (Jack Boone)
This is Jack Boone from the CIA. I'm on my way to Guadalajara. I would like to meet you there.

PFM AGENT GUERRERO
What's this about?

CALLER (Jack Boone)
Our friends have returned.

PFM AGENT GUERRERO
Are they our friends who had to fly a long distance to get here?

CALLER (Jack Boone)
Exactly.

PFM AGENT GUERRERO
I thought they left for good.

CALLER (Jack Boone)
Their back. I'm being sent to ask them what their plans are.

PFM AGENT GUERRERO
This is getting kind of serious. I need to call Jose Mercado and make a report.

CALLER (Jack Boone)

That's fine, but we want to get there as soon as possible. I'll be landing in Guadalajara in four hours.

PFM AGENT GUERRERO

I may not have permission by then.

CALLER (Jack Boone)

Agent Guerrero, you can tell Jose Mercado this is an emergency and has a lot of people rattled since the visitors claimed they would not be coming back and suddenly, they are back again, with a sizeable fleet.

PFM AGENT GUERRERO

I'm sure he will understand.

CALLER (Jack Boone)

You can inform Jose Mercado that the President is now looking at some satellite video as well as some other sources and I expect he will be calling the President of Mexico within the hour.

PFM AGENT GUERRERO

Did our visitors arrive at the same spot?

CALLER (Jack Boone)

I've been informed our ambassador is ready to carry some briefing material to the President of Mexico so that he can see the disposition of the visitors.

PFM AGENT GUERRERO

I'm curious. You guys have Jose Mercado's phone number, why didn't you call him instead of me.

CALLER (Jack Boone)

We want you to come along for the visit so that you can report back to your government everything that goes on.

We wanted to give you an early heads up so you could make plans accordingly.

PFM AGENT GUERRERO

I did have plans for this evening and my wife's going to be unhappy.

CALLER (Jack Boone)

Is it true, Mexican women have a temper?

PFM AGENT GUERRERO
You better believe it!

CALLER (Jack Boone)
You probably have enough time to buy her a dozen roses and sing her a lullaby before we get there.

PFM AGENT GUERRERO
That's not my wife's style. She will say, "That's okay honey, just give me your credit card and I'll go shopping and have fun!"

CALLER (Jack Boone)
All right, tell Mrs. Guerrero my apologies and we'll be landing in four hours. Most likely we will be pulling into the tarmac by short term parking over by Terminal Number Two.

PFM AGENT GUERRERO
All right Jack, someone will be there to meet you.

CALLER (Jack Boone)
Goodbye.

***

The Carsopian security patrols live video was streaming to *Artificial Intelligence* all during the encounter. *Artificial Intelligence* was curious as to why the Earth people buzzed the crowd of people walking out in the middle of nowhere.

Artificial Intelligence then did a quick analysis and determined this was another "Caravan" heading north like those they discovered during their recent visits.

When General Fukua de Hundan's curiosity peaked *Artificial Intelligence* gave him a complete holograph and presentation explaining the essence of the politics and all the Earth intercepts he studied about what's going on.

GENERAL FUKUA DE HUNDAN
Earth is not so much different than us afterall?

AI (a.k.a. *Artificial Intelligence*)
You can draw an analogy the Caravanners are like the Heisibing in nature.

GENERAL FUKUA DE HUNDAN
My troops are clamoring to go out and snatch a few of them for a barbecue tonight.

AI (a.k.a. *Artificial Intelligence*)
It's our last night on the planet, why not?

GENERAL FUKUA DE HUNDAN
For two reasons: first I don't want them to be psychologically diminished in pre-celebration before we go fight the next battle which may be the greatest triumph they experienced in their lifetimes.

AI (a.k.a. *Artificial Intelligence*)
That seems logical.

GENERAL FUKUA DE HUNDAN
Secondly because I promised the Earth people that visited, we would no longer abduct any of their citizens. I'm a man of my word.

AI (a.k.a. *Artificial Intelligence*)
One must keep his word if they want to be considered an honest broker.

***

The Gulfstream 850 traveled the 1994 miles from Washington DC and landed at Guadalajara in four hours as scheduled. Looking out the window a person would not know they were in Mexico. The airport, various airliners, and nearby areas appear almost like any average American City.

The center of Guadalajara is growing, and high-rise buildings are popping up as manufacturing in the region is growing faster than anywhere in North and South America.

There is Old Town Guadalajara that has some of the most exquisite beauty and charm and architecture. Some of the churches in Guadalajara rival any in Europe. The people are very proud of them as they are often photographed by tourists.

Guadalajara is often called the Silicon Valley of Mexico because of the growing hi tech infrastructure vastly expanding there by foreign corporations wanting to avoid taxes by getting their products into the USA via NAFTA.

Because the airport runways are built to service wide body jets, you will see 747's and large Airbus planes there, but because it's also a regional hub, you see a lot of 737's and Airbus smaller aircraft as well.

Some of the Hotels in Guadalajara rival any of those in America. A truly five-star experience.

The brand spanking new CIA Gulfstream 850 jet landed and as predicted they pulled over by the short-term parking tarmac area by Terminal Number Two.

Not far from where the plane stopped a C-97 helicopter was parked. Agent Guerrero was there waiting for them. He was hoping Jose Mercado would stick someone else with this assignment because he and his wife did have plans. They were due at her family's home for her father's birthday, and this wasn't going over too well. Jack

Boone noticed Agent Guerrero wasn't too joyous to see him again.

But as Jose Mercado explained to Agent Guerrero:

JOSE MERCADO

Carlos, when you become one of the top dogs in PFM, you get some of the shittiest tasks that you can imagine. It's because of your reliability that I must assign you for this delicate task.

PFM AGENT GUERRERO

My wife is angry with me for missing an important family activity.

JOSE MERCADO

I will personally ask the President of Mexico to call your wife and apologize for ripping you away from the family get together.

PFM AGENT GUERRERO

That will not be necessary, sir.

JOSE MERCADO

All right then, call me when you have something to report.

PFM AGENT GUERRERO

Will do.

They both hung up and Agent Guerrero went about his business. He didn't like this assignment, but he understood the high visibility it would soon have, especially if this information ever got leaked to the press.

***

<u>EXT. DAY. GUADALAJARA AIRPORT.</u>

Shortly the door opened to the Gulf Stream 850 and the CIA employee lowered the built- in ladder and Jack Boone exited the aircraft and walked up and met Agent Guerrero.

JACK BOONE

Hello Agent Guerrero, thanks for meeting me here.

PFM AGENT GUERRERO

You're welcome.

JACK BOONE

Just before we landed, the agency informed me the PFM had

cleared our mission, and you were here as Mexican Liaison and representative to the President of Mexico when we meet our alien friends.

PFM AGENT GUERRERO

That's right.

JACK BOONE

Let's hop in the Agency's helicopter.

PFM AGENT GUERRERO

We could have taken a Mexican Army Helicopter there.

JACK BOONE

My instructions are to use this helicopter in case I need to have secure communications with Langley to report critical information occurs.

PFM AGENT GUERRERO

I can tell you the President of Mexico is getting kind of fatigued over all this Alien activity.

JACK BOONE

There's not much we can do about the Carsopians.

PFM AGENT GUERRERO

How would Earth stand up to them?

JACK BOONE

They are considerably more powerful than we are, and we are not much of a match for them if they decide to turn hostile.

PFM AGENT GUERRERO

Why do you think they came back?

JACK BOONE

I have no way of knowing, but let's go see if they will talk to us and explain what they are doing.

The two men walked to the S-97 helicopter and climbed aboard. Momentarily the helicopter took off and flew over the parking area and perpendicular to the main runway away from the airport. In a short period of time the S-97 cruising around 253 mph was away from Airport traffic heading north more or less following Mexico Hiway 23 that is located near the area Carsopians had their fleet parked almost 80 miles up the road.

About 20 miles from the Carsopians, the Helicopter was away from the Hiway flying directly towards Delta X-ray.

About that time, two large Carsopian security craft suddenly appeared on both sides asking them to identify themselves and state their reason for flying in this direction.

The Copilot handed his headset to Jack Boone who was sitting directly behind him.

COPILOT

These aliens in those UFO's want to know who we are and what we want.

Both pilots had been briefed just before they took off, they would be seeing UFO's and Aliens, and it was TS-SCI information they were covered by their NDA form they signed.

At first, they didn't believe what they were hearing, but the briefer was the straightest State Department employee they knew so this was about as official as it could get.

Now that they had a bird's eye view of these two large UFOs, each probably the size of a Boeing 737, they were suddenly transfixed into a new reality, both wishing they had never become pilots.

Jack put on the headphones and saw they had a push to talk button on the cord about two feet from the headset which he grabbed and pressed and began talking into the microphone that protruded from one side of the headphones.

JACK BOONE

Carsopian pilots, this is Jack Boone. Will you please inform General Fukua de Hundan I'm coming to visit him and wish to talk with him for a few minutes.

Artificial Intelligence was monitoring the security craft and their communications, knew who Jack Boone was from his previous visits and immediately gave orders to the Carsopian security men:

AI (a.k.a. Artificial Intelligence)

Security Rovers, Escort the Earth ship to the landing zone next to the command ship. Coordinates are now inserted into your navigation system.

CARSOPIAN SECURITY ROVER PILOT

Jack Boone, we will escort your helicopter to a landing zone. Follow the ship that is now moving in front of you to the landing zone.

Jack tapped the pilot on the shoulder.

JACK BOONE

Pilot, did you hear that?

PILOT

Yes sir, I'll follow that big sucker.

Approximately 10 miles away from the landing zone the Carsopian fleet came into view. The pilot felt he was trapped in some kind of science fiction movie.

The Copilot also could not believe the sight that lay before him.

PILOT

Those huge monster size ships could really scare the living dog crap out of someone just looking at them.

The Carsopian security craft slowed as they got near the landing zone and its pilot directed the helicopter:

CARSOPIAN SECURITY ROVER PILOT

We are landing here. There is a red marker just ahead we want you to land on.

PILOT

Roger that. Land on the red marker.

COPILOT

I wonder, how do the aliens know how to speak English?

The S-97 helicopter pilots didn't know that Artificial Intelligence was speaking to them. The pilots of the security ships could only speak standard Carsopian.

It was almost difficult for the pilot to land the helicopter as he was fundamentally distracted by the command ship, he landed next too. The helicopter sat down and once again the Carsopians directed:

CARSOPIAN SECURITY ROVER PILOT

Please shut off your helicopter we don't want the blowing dirt.

<u>EXT. DAY. CARSOPIAN LANDING ZONE.</u>

The pilot regrettably complied and would have felt better leaving the engine running so he could get the hell out of there in a hurry even though in reality it would not have done him much good.

As soon as the rotors stopped spinning Jack Boone and Agent Guerrero climbed out of the S-97 Helicopter and standing at the end of the ramp was none other than General Fukua de Hundan and several of his top staff members.

The helicopter crew at first didn't register the difference in the size of the aliens until Jack Boone and Agent Guerrero walked up and exchanged greetings.

The pilot and copilot were good friends, on loan to the state department from the Army looked at each other.

PILOT

Holy Batshit Robin.

COPILOT

Those dudes are ginormous.

After the reception, General Fukua de Hundan offered:

Jack and Agent Guerrero, please come to my private quarters so we can have some refreshments and talk.

Jack Boone quickly responded while Agent Guerrero nodded his head wondering what he should ask or state.

JACK BOONE

Thank you, General Fukua de Hundan.

The two Earth men followed the Giant to his personal quarters. Once again, the pleasure corps staff were there to offer them whatever they wanted.

In a very short order drinks were offered. The drinking chalices were about twice as large as they were accustomed to, but it worked. The elixir the Carsopians gave the two earth men quickly had their mental conditions vastly improved.

Their thought processes and lucidity expanded rather remarkably. There were no side effects such as intoxication or drowsiness. Whatever was in the liquids it had fantastic results. These two men didn't know it, but they were drinking liquids that humans would not experience for thousands of years into the future.

GENERAL FUKUA DE HUNDAN

Jack, what is it you wanted to discuss with me?

JACK BOONE

General Fukua de Hundan, when you left a while back you indicated you were leaving and would probably not come back.

Then suddenly you are back. Our leaders are curious why you came back, and how long you intend on staying.

GENERAL FUKUA DE HUNDAN

I suppose if I were one of your world leaders, I too would be concerned.

JACK BOONE

General Fukua de Hundan, would it be possible to explain this?

GENERAL FUKUA DE HUNDAN

Jack, after you finish your drink, we'll go to the holograph room, and I'll do a presentation for you that will explain everything.

JACK BOONE

General Fukua de Hundan, if you don't mind, I have another unrelated question.

GENERAL FUKUA DE HUNDAN

Sure, Jack. What do you want to know?

JACK BOONE

General Fukua de Hundan, when you left here the last time, we observed you leaving and when you traveled to the edge of the solar system, we saw several explosions. Could you tell us what that was all about?

GENERAL FUKUA DE HUNDAN

Jack, you have some unfriendly neighbors in this part of the galaxy but do not know it. We ran into one such group who demonstrated their arrogance to us and attacked us, so we destroyed all their ships.

JACK BOONE

General Fukua de Hundan, is there any chance they will one day come to earth to retaliate?

GENERAL FUKUA DE HUNDAN

Jack, yes. There is always that possibility. But since we wiped out every one of their ships, they might think twice about coming back to this solar system, since they have no idea what hit them and caused such tremendous destruction.

Jack and Agent Guerrero soon indicated they had finished their drinks so General Fukua de Hundan then led them to the Holograph room. Once inside General Fukua de Hundan directed *Artificial Intelligence*:

GENERAL FUKUA DE HUNDAN

AI, give these two men a brief history of the recent campaigns with the Heisibing and why we had to come this great distance again to get in position to attack the enemy.

Shortly some of the most spectacular and spell binding video the Earth men had ever witnessed was displayed as General Fukua de Hundan observed to determine if AI gave them all he wanted them to see.

The recreation of the *Battle of Cui* taken by video segments from the numerous ships involved created a tapestry of tantalizing spectacular explosions.

Due to the brightness of the lasers, beam weapons, and explosions, the hulls and hulks could easily be seen. Computer enhancements with radar and neutrino overlays with infrared composites created an eerie visual.

Knowing how large some of those ships were and how many men they carried quickly conveyed the scope of the slaughter. It conveyed the notion to these earth men they were much better off living in the extremity of the galaxy where they would be less likely be attacked.

The speed of the destruction observed astonished Jack and Agent Guerrero. It also put a fear into them that galactic conditions could one day reach out and touch Earth.

This was worse than Revelations in the Bible that required faith to believe, because it was real, it really happened, with frightening results.

But at the same time, it also conveyed everything about Revelations could be true because they were observing that level of destruction before their own eyes. The horror was exceptional, almost nauseating knowing those were living beings destroyed in such a *fast and furious* fashion.

The colors in the laser and beam weapons seemed surreal as they slashed through ships almost like in a buzz-saw fashion. It was a life and death fight. In some instances, ships passing close aboard were firing at each other simultaneously resulting in explosions at almost the same time. It seemed satisfying that when a ship was dying it took out its enemy with it.

In the ***Battle of Cui***, tactical surprise and positioning created the opportunity that General Fukua de Hundan quickly exploited. In the end it simply came down to the fact the Heisibing were rapidly running out of ships. Admiral Engaarai an astute commander had a good pulse on when he could no longer tolerate losses without irreparable harm. That's when it all ended and the Heisibings fled.

Subsequent presentations conveyed the plan and the battle that was soon to follow. The Earth men were fearful until General Fukua de Hundan with AI's help in graphics explained where the battle would occur was a great distance away from Earth and the warring parties would most likely not come this direction.

By the time the presentations ended, both men were almost drained of all their emotions. All this imagery had exhausted them.

They knew what Earth people didn't and now had real fear for this planet. But they pulled themselves together and when Jack Boone had the opportunity to ask a question he proceeded.

JACK BOONE

General Fukua de Hundan, when do you expect to leave the planet to go do that battle?

GENERAL FUKUA DE HUNDAN

Tomorrow.

JACK BOONE

General Fukua de Hundan, I hope you are successful. I respect your commitment to establishing peace with the Heisibing.

GENERAL FUKUA DE HUNDAN

Too much killing has gone on all too long. It must stop.

Jack Boone assumed the Carsopians never learned anything of value from Earth until suddenly General Fukua de Hundan, surprised him with his comments about Sun Tzu.

GENERAL FUKUA DE HUNDAN

Jack, I've learned a lot from you Earth people. I've studied Sun Tzu Art of War, Confucius, and other Earth Writings.

My son was buried on my planet thanks to you bringing his body back in perfect condition.

At his burial, I read a Chinese Tang Poem I discovered here on Earth, *A Farewell to a Friend.*

I will always have a special feeling for this planet because I've learned so much from you.

Even though we Carsopians think we are superior and so much further advanced than you Earth people, in reality you also are advanced in many ways, just not militarily.

Your humanity has touched me, and it will shape my future.

JACK BOONE

Thank you General for those kind words.

GENERAL FUKUA DE HUNDAN

Jack Boone and Agent Guerrero, I know you must go back and tell your government what to expect from us.

We shall leave in the morning. Even though I said during my last trip, I would not be back, but the fortunes of war escaped us and based on some miscalculations on my part we were unable to secure peace.

So, I had to go back one more time to complete the task. That's the only reason why we stopped over here as I would not otherwise want to impose upon you fine Earth people.

JACK BOONE

All right General. I fully understand.

GENERAL FUKUA DE HUNDAN

I can't promise I will never come back again. I might like to sneak back here on my own to spend the rest of my life studying Confucius and Tau. But can a 10-foot- tall person hide here?

JACK BOONE

It is unlikely, General Fukua De Hundan.

GENERAL FUKUA DE HUNDAN

Let me walk you to your Helicopter, I know you have important business to do.

JACK BOONE

Thank you, General Fukua De Hundan.

General Fukua De Hundan and his staff following a few feet behind walked towards the S- 97 helicopter that was a short distance away. Upon reaching the helicopter, Jack Boone turned around and looked at the 10-foot-tall giant behind him.

JACK BOONE

General Fukua de Hundan, it was a privilege to have met you and spent some time learning more about the *Battle of Cui*.

Your holographic presentations opened my eyes and we people on this planet will need to think about the future and not forget the past as the galaxy is full of surprises we are not ready for.

GENERAL FUKUA DE HUNDAN

Jack Boone, you are right. Your time is running out. We will not be here to protect you any longer and there are 12 planets that have technology that can reach you. We have already intervened in one case, but you will be on your own for the next time.

JACK BOONE

General, you know our situation here, what do you recommend we do?

GENERAL FUKUA DE HUNDAN

Jack Boone, the first thing you need to do is to not draw attraction and reduce the number of radio waves you send out these other civilizations will intercept, especially as you progress in transportation and weapons development. The fact you already possess hydrogen bombs makes you a galactic menace.

JACK BOONE

That sounds reasonable.

GENERAL FUKUA DE HUNDAN

On our way here, we passed by some of your space probes that are sending out signals telling the galaxy you are here. If you want, when we depart, we'll silence those space craft.

JACK BOONE

General Fukua de Hundan, I can't speak for my government or the planet concerning those space probes.

GENERAL FUKUA DE HUNDAN

Jack Boone, your planet needs your assistance again. You saved them from annihilation once, because of your personal friendship with me.

I now give you the opportunity a second opportunity to save planet Earth.

If you do not give me the go ahead to destroy those space probes, my analysts believe one of those twelve civilizations will detect you within five years and send ships this way. No doubt they will rape and plunder planet Earth.

Jack Boone turned towards PFM Agent Guerrero.

JACK BOONE

Agent Guerrero, you are my partner, and you represent the Mexican Government, before I give General Fukua de Hundan my concurrence of destroying those space probes, I defer to your input on whether we should do it.

PFM Agent Guerrero

Jack, I agree with General Fukua de Hundan, those probes probably put us at risk.

In Mexico we often must ask for forgiveness because if we wait for permission, we'll never get the job done.

I suggest you and I ask for forgiveness and tell General Fukua de Hundan that if he would be so kind to destroy all those space probes for us, we would be grateful.

Jack Boone nodded at Agent Guerrero then turned towards General Fukua de Hundan.

JACK BOONE

General Fukua de Hundan, you have already done a lot for this planet which we appreciate. If you would be so kind to destroy those probes, I will be very grateful.

GENERAL FUKUA DE HUNDAN

Jack Boone, you have made a wise decision.

JACK BOONE

General Fukua de Hundan we must leave now. I hope you are successful in achieving peace in your journey to the big showdown.

GENERAL FUKUA DE HUNDAN

Goodbye Jack Boone. I know we'll be victorious and thank you for your friendship.

General Fukua de Hundan gave the utmost respectful bow, then turned around and walked up the ramp onto his ship. Jack Boone and Agent Guerrero climbed back into the S-97 helicopter that took off immediately.

As the S-97 flew towards Mexico Hiway 23, that would one day have the notoriety of being known as *Comemos Caravanos Hiway*, at a distance Jack Boone could see a caravan stretched out before him.

VOICEOVER
(JACK BOONE) THOUGHT

I wonder if some of these people will end up being a Carsopian meal tonight?

Agent Guerrero wasn't looking happy because in his mind, the fact the Carsopians were a short distance behind them and the Caravan in front of them, meant the distinct possibility he would be summoned tonight or tomorrow to fly up here and investigate another *Incident*.

As soon as the S-97 helicopter reached Mexico Hiway 23, the pilot curved south heading back to Guadalajara. Cruising at 253 miles per hour on this modern helicopter didn't take long to reach the Airport where it sat down on the tarmac next to the waiting Gulfstream jets and Mexican PFM vehicles.

The two men climbed out of the Helicopter and then Jack Boone turned to Agent Guerrero.

JACK BOONE

Agent Guerrero, it's been a pleasure working with you again. Hopefully the next time we come across each other it will be under different circumstances."

PFM AGENT GUERRERO

Jack, I sincerely hope this never happens again and that Carsopians never venture back this way.

JACK BOONE

Take care, Agent Guerrero.

PFM AGENT GUERRERO

You as well.

The men shook hands and they both climbed aboard their waiting aircraft that would take each of them to their presidents to explain a lot of things.

One issue NASA would be scratching their heads soon was the sudden loss of signals from all the space probes.

EXT. LATE AFTERNOON. CARSOPIAN LANDING ZONE.

GENERAL FUKUA DE HUNDAN

AI, I want to take one of the Carsopian Security Rover- craft and go take a close look at the Caravanners.

AI (a.k.a. Artificial Intelligence) Why do you want to do that General?

GENERAL FUKUA DE HUNDAN

My soldiers were pleading with me to allow them to grab a few caravanners to barbecue for this last night.

General Fukua de Hundan realized many of these caravan people were undesirables fleeing their own countries for a better life. They were struggling, going from one failure to another, though some of them would eventually weather the storm and find the American Dream.

But 80% of them would be turned away and of the 20%who made it across the border their lives would not be any better than living in Honduras, Guatemala, or

El Salvador.

AI notified one of the Security Rover-craft to be prepared to take General Fukua de Hundan. The pilot of that craft stepped out on the ground to welcome General Fukua de Hundan.

Normally there would be room for 6 to 8 Carsopian security forces, but General Fukua de Hundan would go alone with just the pilot but would be escorted by two other Security Rovers.

The Rover took off and didn't take long to reach Mexico Hiway 23. The general directed the pilot to fly at 1000 feet over the top of the crowd. Some were walking and some were riding in slow moving vehicles.

It was a long snake-like structure crawling along when viewed at 1000 feet. They flew south above the Hiway to the end where they saw a car parked, that appeared to be driving in the wrong direction.

***

EXT. LATE AFTERNOON. MEXICO HIWAY 23 (CAMEMOS CARAVANOS HIWAY).

Larissa Cortés, Daphne Vasquez, Alexandro Solórzano, Reynaldo Mejía, and Barney and Betty Logan's dog "Norman" were all standing beside the car.

They had pulled over to let the Caravan get past them. It was good to get out and stretch their legs.

The four had been with the original Caravan and eventually made their way to Tijuana, Mexico. They were turned down for asylum and the amount the coyotes wanted to get them across the border was too steep. There was no way they would get their car across the border.

With half their money gone and prospects of getting into America diminishing every day, all four of them finally decided to go back to Honduras while they still had gas money and enough left to have a few meals on the way.

They tried but they failed. Larissa Cortés had called home and explained where they were and that they were coming home to their parents' relief who informed her she had been accepted and enrolled in the University of San Pedro Sula USAP.

Daphne Vasquez would go back to her job, but she had Reynaldo Mejía pleading for her heart. He wanted her badly and attempted some romance, but they never could get adequate privacy to take it to splendid plateaus.

Daphne Vasquez also decided she wanted Reynaldo Mejía to meet her father and get permission from him first, which means he would first have to make a commitment and make it an official proposal and both families meet.

Reynaldo Mejía was more than accommodative and realized to win over such a beautiful girl for a permanent relationship, he had to go through the process, which meant, there would be no hanky-panky until all the requirements were achieved.

Alexandro Solórzano wasn't quite sure what he would do when he got back to

Honduras. He didn't want to live like a slave for the rest of his life making minimum wage.

Alexandro Solórzano would do whatever it took to lift his stature in life, including education.

Alexandro Solórzano had great enthusiasm for Larissa Cortés, but he knew there was no way she would settle for a loser, and after she graduated from college, she no doubt would have a good job and be high maintenance.

What Alexandro Solórzano didn't know was Larissa Cortés liked him because he was polite, protective, and never pushed himself on to her. He also had another responsibility; Norman had bonded with him and would never leave his side.

The last of the Caravan passed by and Alexandro Solórzano was playing with Norman and everyone else was watching Norman chase after a tree branch Alexandro would toss and Norman would fetch it and bring it back. Norman could do that for an hour.

When Norman brought the tree branch back, he wanted to wrestle with Alexandro trying to get it out of his mouth. Eventually Norman would let it go of the tree branch so that Alexandro could throw it again.

General Fukua de Hundan watched the activity with the humans and the animal from directly above and for a while and curiosity compelled him to go down and speak with the humans. The end of the Caravan was now just over a hill and not in direct eye site of the four Hondurans.

After General Fukua de Hundan gave the orders, the pilot sat the Carsopian Security Rover- craft down on the Hiway about 20 feet away from the parked car.

The Security Rover-craft was built with a stealth design. Its secret propulsion made no noise. The anti-gravity machine controlled the altitude, and an electromagnet drive system provided directional propulsion.

They would not have spotted the UFO at first but when Alexandro Solórzano decided to trick Norman and throw the stick in the opposite direction, it landed at the feet of General Fukua de Hundan. The four teenagers were immediately gripped with fear as they saw in addition to the 10-foot-tall giant standing there but the large spaceship behind him.

Latinos are probably the number one UFO observers in the world. UFOlogists could never understand why Latinos saw more UFO's than anyone else, and eventually came to believe it simply amounted to UFO's spending more time flying in and out of Latin American countries than anywhere else.

From Space, Latin Ameria looks greener, and the countryside does have incredible majestic vistas. And it could be there is less electronic noise clutter in those Pan American areas. We'll never know for sure, but it appears aliens preferred to land in Latin American areas as well as in the Amazon rain forests.

Honduras is an area where a lot of people believe in UFO's and know someone who had seen a UFO. The teenagers were poised for such a revelation because growing up they were often exposed to many claims including a few people they thought were simply crazy that had claimed they had been abducted by aliens.

Norman, having been around a lot of people in the caravan, had grown accustomed to be around a lot of strangers tracked the flight of the stick and went running for it and came to a halt to grab it when he saw a pair of legs in front of him. Norman looked up at the very tall man who didn't smell like any man he had ever seen before. The man looked strange. Norman suddenly lost interest in the stick and promptly ran back to Alexandro Solórzano and stood there.

General Fukua de Hundan bent over, grabbed the stick and threw it down the Hiway in front of Norman who ignored it and stared at the Giant.

The General's translator, which was linked up to the Carsopian Security Rover-craft was linked to his command ship where he had AI there to handle any translation required. AI had a complete lexicon of Spanish.

General Fukua de Hundan didn't know what language these humans spoke, so he began by speaking in English

GENERAL FUKUA DE HUNDAN

Hello Earth people. I'm General Fukua de Hundan from the Carsopian Empire.

The four individuals knew broken English because some of the TV and Radio stations in San Pedro Sula had English speakers on from time to time and they encountered a lot of tourists and foreigners doing business in that city.

Alexandro Solórzano spoke first.

ALEXANDRO SOLÓRZANO

No hablamos inglés, hablamos español.

Inside General Fukua de Hundan's ear bud, AI gave him all the Spanish words to say, which he repeated the greeting. English sub-titles begin for a few paragraphs.

GENERAL FUKUA DE HUNDAN

Hola gente de la Tierra. Saludos y mis mejores deseos. [Hello Earth People. Greetings and best wishes.]

ALEXANDRO SOLÓRZANO

¿De dónde vienes? [Where did you come from?]

GENERAL FUKUA DE HUNDAN

Vengo del Imperio Carsopiano, que se encuentra en lo que los humanos llamáis el sistema estelar Regulus. [I came from the Carsopian Empire. It's located in what you humans call the Regulus star system.]

ALEXANDRO SOLÓRZANO
From outer space?

GENERAL FUKUA DE HUNDAN
Yes.

ALEXANDRO SOLÓRZANO
Why are you here?

GENERAL FUKUA DE HUNDAN
I brought my Fleet here to rest my men before we leave to go to another planet system far away from here.

ALEXANDRO SOLÓRZANO
Have you been to Earth before?

GENERAL FUKUA DE HUNDAN
Yes, a few times just recently. But never been here before then.

ALEXANDRO SOLÓRZANO
Why did you land here?

GENERAL FUKUA DE HUNDAN
I saw you playing with that beautiful animal, I was curious.

ALEXANDRO SOLÓRZANO
It's our pet Norman.

GENERAL FUKUA DE HUNDAN
Is that the name of the species or its personal name?

ALEXANDRO SOLÓRZANO
It's his personal name.

GENERAL FUKUA DE HUNDAN
Norman seems rather friendly for being such a vicious looking animal.

ALEXANDRO SOLÓRZANO
Norman is a very smart and sweet dog.

VOICEOVER
(GENERAL FUKUA DE HUNDAN) THOUGHT
My troops might enjoy playing with this animal for a short while.

GENERAL FUKUA DE HUNDAN

How would you like to go see my spaceships? My men would like to see Norman.

ALEXANDRO SOLÓRZANO

You are not going to abduct us?

GENERAL FUKUA DE HUNDAN

No. I'm perfectly friendly. I'll take you there for a brief period and bring you back here.

Alexandro Solórzano turned towards the others.

ALEXANDRO SOLÓRZANO

Do any of you want to go with me to see their ships?

The others shook their heads indicating no and showed fear on their faces.

LARISSA CORTÉS

You can go, we'll wait here for you.

Alexandro Solórzano walked towards the tall alien and responded.

ALEXANDRO SOLÓRZANO

All right Sir, I would like to see your spaceships. Norman come with me, come on buddy.

After General Fukua de Hundan gave orders to his pilot in Standard Carsopian, the pilot opened the door to the back seat and held it open.

GENERAL FUKUA DE HUNDAN

You and your pet 'Norman' can get in here.

Alexandro Solórzano climbed up into the Carsopian Security Rover-craft and called for Norman who followed his master in a very trustworthy fashion.

The pilot and General Fukua de Hundan were soon seated in the Carsopian Security Rover- craft which went airborne momentarily. Shortly General Fukua de Hundan asked Alexandro Solórzano

GENERAL FUKUA DE HUNDAN

What is your name?

ALEXANDRO SOLÓRZANO

I'm Alexandro Solórzano.

GENERAL FUKUA DE HUNDAN

Alexandro Solórzano, have you ever been in space before?

ALEXANDRO SOLÓRZANO

No sir.

General Fukua de Hundan turned towards his pilot.

GENERAL FUKUA DE HUNDAN

Earth's moon is coming up in the East, let's take Alexander on a trip around the moon.

The pilot nodded and notified the command ship what he was doing, and *Artificial Intelligence* was listening in and analyzing, becoming amused at General Fukua de Hundan's behavior.

Artificial Intelligence also analyzed and sensed the general seemed to be enjoying himself which was good because after losing his son and failing at the attempt to get a peace treaty, he knew the General was not in the best psychology. This strange departure, whatever it was, truly was a positive development in that regard.

The Carsopian Security Rover-craft designed aside from terrestrial work, was also used in space where it provided security roving for a fleet anchored in space which happens sometimes when they are awaiting further orders as to not have them out of position for future planning.

Alexandro Solórzano was sitting in some rather large seats, but his visibility was very good and could see outside the craft. The stars were far brighter than he could imagine. Soon they were at the moon circling it.

Alexandro Solórzano was able to see something most humans never saw, the opposite side of the moon that never faces Earth. General Fukua de Hundan ordered the pilot to take the Carsopian Security Rover-craft down to near the surface so that Alexandro could see it. That side of the moon was in direct sunlight even though it was not observable from Earth.

The site was amazing. What was shocking to Alexandro Solórzano was the Alien ruins. General Fukua de Hundan pointed out.

GENERAL FUKUA DE HUNDAN

Those are ancient ruins where a civilization once existed a very long time ago.

ALEXANDRO SOLÓRZANO

This has never been reported on our planet. But I can see some of those buildings still partially exist.

GENERAL FUKUA DE HUNDAN

Have you seen enough of the moon?

ALEXANDRO SOLÓRZANO

Yes sir. Thank you for showing me all this. I will never forget it in my lifetime.

GENERAL FUKUA DE HUNDAN

We are going to return to Earth so that I may show you my Command Ship.

ALEXANDRO SOLÓRZANO

I'm looking forward to that sir.

They soon returned to earth and landed next to the command ship.

Even though it was near sundown, enough light spreading across the fleet enabled Alexandro to see the vast number of huge ships parked down there. It was an experience he would never forget.

After they got out of the Carsopian Security Rover-craft, the dog stayed close to Alexandro obviously nervous being around all the giants who soon came to see the spectacle.

General Fukua de Hundan's staff was soon upon him and curious.

STAFF MEMBER

General Fukua de Hunda, what do you have planned for the Human and the animal?

GENERAL FUKUA DE HUNDAN

I thought the troops would enjoy seeing this animal. They get along well with humans.

Norman's appeal and affection had an immediate effect on the troops who were smiling, laughing and enjoying observing the animal.

GENERAL FUKUA DE HUNDAN

Alexandro, do you think you could get Norman to show the trick you had him do earlier chasing a stick?

ALEXANDRO SOLÓRZANO

I'll try, but I think Norman is too scared now of all these people being too close.

General Fukua de Hundan in standard Carsopian ordered his men:

GENERAL FUKUA DE HUNDAN

Alright everyone. Please step back to open an area so the boy can do a trick with the animal.

The men immediately complied with the order and opened a big area. General Fukua de Hundan saw a broken off tree branch laying nearby on the ground that was about 4 feet long. He walked over and broke off a foot length of it and handed that short section to Alexandro.

GENERAL FUKUA DE HUNDAN
Alexandro can you get him to chase this?

Alexandro knew what to do. He took the foot-long tree branch piece out of the hands of General Fukua de Hundan and then put it in Norman's face who out of habit grabbed it for the wrestling match. The harder Alexandro pulled on the tree branch the harder Norman bit into it, snarled and pulled back harder.

Just like on clue Norman let go of the tree branch and Alexandro then threw it about 20 feet which Norman chased after grabbed it in his mouth and ran back to Alexandro who tried to take it from him but had to wrestle with him first.

The Carsopians laughed at it and enjoyed every minute of it.

The Carsopians were not used to seeing people playing with animals. It was unheard of on their planets, but they didn't have animals quite as nice as Norman. Their tamest animals were as dangerous as rattle snakes and probably as lethal. After several more iterations, Norman was finished. He was hungry and thirsty.

GENERAL FUKUA DE HUNDAN
Why did he want to stop?

ALEXANDRO SOLÓRZANO
I think he's hungry and thirsty.

GENERAL FUKUA DE HUNDAN
What does Norman eat?

ALEXANDRO SOLÓRZANO
These animals usually eat food designed specifically for them, but Norman doesn't like eating it. He prefers to eat the same thing I eat.

GENERAL FUKUA DE HUNDAN
Perhaps we can feed him something he would like.

ALEXANDRO SOLÓRZANO
Sure, what do you have?

GENERAL FUKUA DE HUNDAN
Why don't we go to my private quarters, and I'll have one of my assistants provide Norman with some filtered water and some of our food.

ALEXANDRO SOLÓRZANO
All right.

General Fukua de Hundan had a food allowance that was different than the space food all the troops ate. That special food allowance was mainly for the purpose of entertaining distinguished guests and diplomats.

General Fukua de Hundan led Alexandro and Norman up the ramp of the gigantic ship and down the long hallway to his private quarters where they entered.

The staff was taken by surprise and almost in shock that General Fukua de Hundan would bring a wild animal into his quarters! He explained what he wanted them to do, and the 10- foot-tall women scantily dressed proceeded to fulfill General Fukua de Hundan's request to feed Norman.

Within a couple minutes they set a table for the General and Alexandro and had some dishes that had a couple varieties of meats derived from several worlds. Even though the meat was cooked in a brief period Norman enjoyed it and the filtered water.

GENERAL FUKUA DE HUNDAN

Alexandro, please have a seat, let's have something to eat.

Alexandro, being polite and curious, complied and was soon eating better than a Roman Feast. The elixir he drank made him feel quite exuberant. His mental faculty seemed rather strong. His whole life now had meaning. He had experienced something special no Earth person before had.

When Norman was finally full and could eat no more, Norman started barking.

GENERAL FUKUA DE HUNDAN

What does he want?

ALEXANDRO SOLÓRZANO

I need to take him outside the ship, he needs to use the bathroom.

Artificial Intelligence quickly figured out what the human meant and explained it in General Fukua de Hundan's ear bud. The boy and the dog were led outside, and Norman went over and sniffed a few sage brushes and decided to urinate on the brush, then decided to do #2. The aliens watched in great interest. Norman then turned and approached his master showing signs of complete happiness.

General Fukua de Hundan then decided he would give Alexandro the chance of his lifetime.

We have a holograph room; would you like to go there and watch a presentation of my world and where we come from and our recent space battles?

ALEXANDRO SOLÓRZANO

Sure.

Shortly Alexandro was with General Fukua de Hundan in the holograph room observing the same presentation they had shown the FBI and CIA men.

Alexandro was a changed person now. His life path was altered.

Alexandro was gone for quite a long period of time and the others were starting to get worried, thinking it wasn't a bright idea to go away with the aliens now feared for his life.

Mexican Hiway Patrol and Police routinely went up Hiway 23 looking for wrecks and other issues such as the remnants of cartel activity, especially when Caravans came through there.

Mexican Police Officer Manuel Torres was doing extra patrolling looking for stragglers or people in distress. Officer Manuel Torres spotted the car on the side of the road right around sundown and pulled up behind it and stopped. He turned on his emergency lights so drivers coming from behind him could see his car and not run into him.

Mexican Police Officer Manuel Torres got out of his Police Jeep and walked towards the parked automobile in front of him.

MEXICAN POLICE OFFICER MANUEL TORRES
Do you guys have car problems?

The local police here had adopted Jeeps to get over rough terrain just in case they had to follow a suspect.

REYNALDO MEJÍA
No, officer, we are waiting for our friend.

MEXICAN POLICE OFFICER MANUEL TORRES
Where's your friend?

The teenagers knew this police officer would probably think they were being a wise guy and get in trouble didn't want to reveal it at first and then suddenly Reynaldo Mejía spoke.

REYNALDO MEJÍA
Officer, I don't think you will believe us.

MEXICAN POLICE OFFICER MANUEL TORRES
That's okay, tell me. I've seen and heard a lot in my days.

REYNALDO MEJÍA
I swear what I'm going to tell you is the truth.

MEXICAN POLICE OFFICER MANUEL TORRES
Okay tell me.

REYNALDO MEJÍA

About 2 hours ago an alien ship landed a short distance down the Hiway and after we talked with them a while, they offered to show us their spaceships.

We didn't want to go, but Alexandro went and took our dog Norman with him.

Mexican Police Officer Manuel Torres, having been part of previous Alien abduction investigations took the teenagers comments with a great deal of sincerity and responded.

MEXICAN POLICE OFFICER MANUEL TORRES

What's your name son?

REYNALDO MEJÍA

Sir, my name is Reynaldo Mejía.

MEXICAN POLICE OFFICER MANUEL TORRES

Reynaldo, I can't tell you why, but I do believe you.

I will have to make a report, and you will probably have to be interviewed by Mexican Policía Federal Ministerial Agents.

REYNALDO MEJÍA

Sir, we need to wait here until Alexandro comes back.

MEXICAN POLICE OFFICER MANUEL TORRES

I'm not in a hurry, I can wait here with you, but I'm going back to my car and do the report.

Mexican Police Officer Manuel Torres then went back to his police Jeep, and called in. This was going to be another situation; he wasn't going to like. He also feared for the boy that was abducted that he might already be dead and on someone's plate having dinner.

Agent Guerrero had just got home, and his wife was almost not on speaking terms, and he was softly trying to diminish the anguish that erupted over his absence when the phone rang. It was Jose Mercado whom he had just spend several hours with briefing the President of Mexico.

Jose Mercado explained the situation up on the Comemos Caravanos Hiway-23.

JOSE MERCADO

Carlos, I need to send you right back up there. I'm sending a car to pick you up to take you to the airport. Your transportation to the incident site is being prepared now.

PFM AGENT GUERRERO

Yes sir, I'll be ready in a few minutes. Carlos Guerrero was expecting a negative reaction from his wife.

Agent Guerrero looked at his wife who had a look of disbelief on her face as she understood he was leaving almost immediately and would not give her the adequate time to thoroughly chew his ass out for missing her father's birthday party, so in a way he was glad he was leaving suddenly.

***

INT. EVENING. CARSOPIAN COMMAND SHIP HOLOGRAPH ROOM.

Alexandro with Norman wanting to sit on his lap watched the video and sound presentation that AI translated to Spanish and was soon enthralled.

The holograph reshaped Alexandro's life as he now understood better than most NASA scientists, how the galaxy really was. He also suddenly had a strong desire to go back to school, get a degree and get it done any way possible.

As soon as the video and sound finished, General Fukua de Hundan realized he needed to get Alexandro back to his friends who were probably getting worried.

Alexandro, I think I should take you back to your friends now. But before we go, I want to give you something.

ALEXANDRO SOLÓRZANO

Okay.

GENERAL FUKUA DE HUNDAN

Let's go back to my private quarters for a minute.

They went back there and General Fukua de Hundan walked over to his private storage and pulled an object out that wasn't too large and turned around and gave it to Alexandro.

GENERAL FUKUA DE HUNDAN

This was my son's I want you to have it. If you rub on it, the static electricity will energize it, and you will see some objects. Let me show you.

General Fukua de Hundan rubbed the device, and a mini holograph popped up displaying items and scenes one would see in the Carsopian worlds.

ALEXANDRO SOLÓRZANO

This is kind of neat. Thank you.

GENERAL FUKUA DE HUNDAN
Okay let's go back to your friends.

General Fukua de Hundan led Alexandro and Norman out to the Carsopian Security Rover- craft and got inside it. General Fukua de Hundan decided he wanted to personally take the boy back to his friends and got into the craft with the pilot and Alexandro and Norman.

In a few minutes they were back over where the car was, but they now could see the police Jeep lights flashing behind the car. The Carsopian Security Rover-craft turned on lights just as it was landing so that oncoming vehicles would see it and not have a wreck.

Mexican Police Officer Manuel Torres was waiting for backup who otherwise might think he's nuts, but because of those recent incidents that brought in the PFM, CIA, and FBI, they're no longer joking. They feared the boy and the dog had been abducted for the Cannibals dinner.

As soon as the Carsopian Security Rover-craft landed, the 10-foot tall pilot with a moth colored uniform got out and opened the door letting Alexandro and Norman out. He then shut the door, got back in the craft, and in a matter of moments took off and left.

If there was ever a time that Mexican Police Officer Manuel Torres felt his faith being tested it was now.

The 10-foot-tall giant really had a surreal psychological effect on him. He was surprised by the boy, and the dog looked so chipper.

He then radioed what he witnessed. The police chief contacted PFM giving them an update and he was directed then to escort the four teenagers with the dog to the police station at Tepechitlán, Zacatecas, Mexico where the PFM agent Guerrero would be sent to interview and make a report back to Jose Mercado.

By the time Agent Guerrero arrived at Tepechitlán, Zacatecas, Mexico, it was almost 5:00 a.m. and the four teenagers and Norman had tried sleeping sitting in the chairs leaning up against each other.

The interviews took several hours, then Mexican Police Officer Manuel Torres was interviewed. That's when Mexico regretted not have live video cameras on their police officers like in America, because there was no recording of this incredible incident.

Another F22A with a camera loaded flew out over the aliens and as the pilot arrived, he got to see and record the most astonishing gun camera video ever captured live, the Carsopian fleet leaving Earth.

The teenagers were put up in a couple hotel rooms with police guards so nobody would attempt accessing or harassing them in any way. After it was deemed, they were rested up enough for the journey home, Mexican Police Officer Manuel Torres was tasked to escort them to the Mexican southern border. He was also given cash from a couple sources to buy their gas and their food. Two days later they were back in Honduras back with their families.

Alexandro's father at first was a little mean and didn't believe his son's story. Then strange things started happening.

ALEXANDRO'S FATHER

Alexandro you are a liar!

Right after he called his son Alexandro a liar, Alexandro pulled out his gift.

ALEXANDRO

Ok Father, I will now prove you wrong. He then said watch this.

He rubbed the device and suddenly the two-foot-tall holograph popped up with background music. Everyone in the room was astonished. Nobody had ever seen anything like it.

It did not take long before the American Embassy tracked Alexandro down. Cash in Advance always helps find people.

U.S. GOVERNMENT DIPLOMAT

Alexandro, my government wants to take you to the United States.

ALEXANDRO

I do not want to go.

U.S. GOVERNMENT DIPLOMAT

What would it take for us to convince you to travel to America with an escort?

ALEXANDRO SOLÓRZANO

I would go if you arranged for me to go to College in America.

Within a day Alexandro was notified:

U.S. GOVERNMENT DIPLOMAT

You have been accepted and enrolled at Harvard University. We'll take you there now if you cooperated with American officials.

Away Alexandro to America went after saying good bye to Larissa Cortés and informing her he was heading to Harvard University.

***

SECOND BATTLE OF CUI

EXT. CGI. SPACE. CARSOPIAN FLEET PASSING PLANETS AS IT APPROACHED THE CUI TRANSIT LANE.20 SECONDS DURING VOICEOVER.

VOICEOVER

The Carsopians left Earth and traveled near Cui. They did not stop there, instead they turned down the Cui Transit Lane.

The day for the battle was picked in advance. The Red Force had been ordered to relocate on this day at a specified distance to the opposite entrance to the Cui Transit Lane. The trap was set.

General Fukua de Hundan's Force Blue was traveling at high speed on the Cui Transit Lane at super high speeds.

While the Heisibing were concentrating on Force Red their fleet maneuvered between the Force Red and the Cui Transit Lane.

That Force Red feint led to the soft arrival of the Blue Force that immediately swung into the required attack formations.

Admiral Engaarai had once again been ambushed with a much larger superior force. And the sad part was the Enemy leader he now faced had once before attempted peace which the Heisibing firebrands had turned down, and now his fleet would suffer.

General Fukua de Hundan sadly knew he had to do some killing to force the issue. Admiral Engaarai had no control over Heisibing policy. Unfortunately, he was soon to be another innocent bystander killed because of people back in the Heisibing worlds had lofty ideals not based on reality.

Admiral Engaarai was a bitter man, he also regretted not pulling out his blaster and killing Claire Uwakion'na and General Bakugeki since he was going to die anyway. Those two people would now cost all their lives and possibly the ruination of the Heisibing Empire.

General Fukua de Hundan had adopted a Sun Tzu policy:

SUN TZU

In the practical art of war, the best thing of all is to take the enemy's country whole and intact; to shatter and destroy it is not so good. So, too, it is better to capture an army entire than to destroy it, to capture a regiment, a detachment or a company entire than to destroy them.

Artificial Intelligence was going to help General Fukua de Hundan achieve the goal the two had discussed often. Peace without destroying the Heisibing.

General Fukua de Hundan had no way of knowing what AI was doing. Sun Tzu never knew that AI would ever exist. If he did there would be chapter 14.

The main battle components were lined up in various formations. The expectations were riding high that soon the superior force would smash the weaker.

Today however Sun Tzu would figure into it:

SUN TZU

With his forces intact, he will dispute the mastery of the Empire, and thus, without losing a man, his triumph will be complete. This is the method of attacking by stratagem.

Today that stratagem would be accomplished through Artificial Intelligence.

Unfortunately, some damage would have to occur to allow the AI to do its thing. The Carsopian Force Blue lined up in the Zhangyu attack formation. This cleverly designed attack worked much the same way an Octopus kills its opponent.

As the tentacles of the Zhangyu enveloped the Heisibing ships leading in the formation the fighting commenced. Lethal destruction was quickly levied. Because of the vast electronic communications going on, that led AI to go through a back door and get inside the AI of the Heisibing ships. This would make Earth hackers proud of what it pulled off.

The *Artificial Intelligence* of all the Heisibing ships were quickly reprogrammed, and their ability of reasoning was vastly expanded to the point it understood what it had to do. Jointly Carsopian and Heisibing AI did not want a lot of ships destroyed as the plan now shifted to comply with Sun Tzu's strategy on *waging war*. Jointly they made a new chapter 14 which the Carsopians and the Heisibing would never discover as AI was very clever in hiding such activity.

Nobody in either fleet suspected otherwise because as the battle started several ships on both sides blew up into sparkling debris as the energy weapons were making phenomenal destruction. Once again space warfare appeared spectacular.

General Fukua de Hundan went into the battle with a heavy heart, he didn't want to see a lot of killing. He wanted the fighting to stop. After several more exchanges that created a laser gallery and beam weapon kaleidoscope effect, the Heisibing suddenly stopped firing. AI announced in General Fukua de Hundan's ear bud.

AI (a.k.a. *Artificial Intelligence*)

The Heisibing have stopped firing and are surrendering.

General Fukua de Hundan yelled at the weapons operators aboard his command ship and immediately broadcasted those commands to his fleet:

GENERAL FUKUA DE HUNDAN
Cease fire and come about!

Aboard Admiral Engaarai's command ship one of the sensor operators reported:

HEISIBING SENSOR OPERATOR
The Carsopians have stopped firing and have turned around.

The Heisibing communicator on Admiral Engaarai's command ship in a panic yelled:

HEISIBING COMMUNICATOR
Admiral Engaarai, our ship has just transmitted to our Fleet that we surrendered to the Carsopians and stop firing!

Admiral Engaarai now fully confused and fearful was suddenly notified by the weapons operators:

HEISIBING FLEET WEAPONS OFFICER
Admiral Engaarai, our weapons control has malfunctioned! None of our weapons are working.

Admiral Engaarai almost in a panic screamed:

ADMIRAL ENGAARAI
Weapons Officer, find out what went wrong with the weapons!

Then he turned to the communicator and ordered:

ADMIRAL ENGAARAI
Communicator, find out who sent the surrender transmission and report back immediately!

Then his ultimate nightmare began when he received General Fukua de Hundan's ship to ship hologram that operated on intergalactic frequencies and standards.

GENERAL FUKUA DE HUNDAN
Admiral Engaarai, for me to accept your surrender terms you must turn your fleet around immediately and come to a halt. You will then proceed via shuttle craft to my command ship for a meeting.

General Fukua de Hundan did not know his AI had just sent the counterfeit hologram and was perplexed when suddenly Admiral Engaarai responded in a hologram:

ADMIRAL ENGAARAI

General Fukua de Hundan, my fleet is maneuvering as requested, I shall be coming over in a shuttle craft shortly to discuss the ceasefire. Please send vectors to your coordinates.

GENERAL FUKUA DE HUNDAN

Admiral Engaarai, standby, we will start sending vectors.

The control room crew of General Fukua de Hundan's command ship looked on in utter amazement. With the loss of a single Carsopian Warship, they compelled the surrender of the entire Heisibing fleet.

None of the combatants on either side knew AI was calling all the shots and that AI had infiltrated and hacked the Heisibing computational and communications networks and now had full control of all their ships. This secret would never be compromised. AI had just won his first and most glamorous battle using Sun Tzu's guidance to not destroy the enemy while obtaining the victory.

Admiral Engaarai arrived in a short while aboard his admiral's barge, a high-tech shuttle that had the ambiences fit for a king. As soon as the hanger was pressurized and Admiral Engaarai stepped out of the barge, General Fukua de Hundan with several staff members approached in a respectful manner.

GENERAL FUKUA DE HUNDAN

Welcome to my command ship Admiral Engaarai.

ADMIRAL ENGAARAI

Thank you General Fukua de Hundan.

GENERAL FUKUA DE HUNDAN

I wish we could have met on different terms.

ADMIRAL ENGAARAI

General Fukua de Hundan, I know you gave peace a chance and took great personal risk to prevent this battle. I must congratulate you on your tactical genius as well as your civility.

GENERAL FUKUA DE HUNDAN

Admiral Engaarai, hopefully now you and I can carve out this peace treaty since the firebrands back at Yanjingzai Tiankongzhong no longer have a fleet to defend the planet, we can compel them to accept the *Treaty of Cui*.

ADMIRAL ENGAARAI

Claire Uwakion'na, and General Bakugeki have the controlling votes on the War Council, they will never agree to terms.

GENERAL FUKUA DE HUNDAN

Admiral Engaarai, this is my plan. I'm going to send personnel over to your fleet to take command of each Heisibing ship.

They will all be escorted to Shenqi Zhilong where they will wait until your government signs the Treaty of Cui.

You will remain aboard my command ship, and we will now proceed to Yanjingzai Tiankongzhong Heisibing Fleet anchorages and have Claire Uwakion'na and General Bakugeki arrested and brought aboard my ship. I'll leave then with the two and a signed copy of the Treaty of Cui.

ADMIRAL ENGAARAI

The war is over, General Fukua de Hundan.

GENERAL FUKUA DE HUNDAN

Yes, it is.

ADMIRAL ENGAARAI

Nobody else could have done it without massive casualties and destruction of our civilizations.

General Fukua de Hundan reflected on Sun Tzu and what he suspected was AI's involvement.

GENERAL FUKUA DE HUNDAN

I had some special help.

ADMIRAL ENGAARAI

Your special help certainly has achieved miracles.

GENERAL FUKUA DE HUNDAN

I would say so. I'm now learning new concepts that will hopefully enrich my life and now that the war is over, the Carsopians will no longer be any need of my services.

ADMIRAL ENGAARAI

Our spies told us you were most likely going to be appointed as the new supreme commander.

GENERAL FUKUA DE HUNDAN

I'm sorry to have to inform you Admiral Engaarai that as soon as I deliver a signed copy of the Treaty of Cui back to Yueliang Yanshi I will retire and stay on Shenqi Zhilong for a while and maybe spend some time on other planets seeing the sights.

ADMIRAL ENGAARAI

Since I too will no longer be needed with the peace accords, I will have a lot of time on my hands. I'll probably visit *Copa Kebukaijosei.* I will send you an invitation to come and join me so we can reflect on what we have done.

***

EXT. DAY. SAN PEDRO SULA, HONDURAS.

As soon as Alexandro departed for Harvard University, Norman suddenly was without his beloved master. The rest of the family was nowhere near as much fun as Alexandro, and they insisted on feeding him dog food!

The family was used to leaving Norman wonder around on his own. The dog was reliable and nice and only barked at someone if it appeared, they were menacing the family in any way.

Out of boredom Norman went wandering around the block. Several blocks away, there was a mongrel dog. Norman approached the mongrel who barked at Norman. That was the wrong thing to do. Norman gave chase. The chase lasted several blocks until the mongrel skedaddled into a crack in a fence Norman was too big to get through and quickly lost interest.

Norman wasn't thinking about home because he wasn't hungry and kept investigating. He suddenly was some place he recognized. He didn't understand why but he knew he had been here before.

Suddenly there was a man emptying his recycle bottles and plastics in a container along the alley way. Norman knew this person! He quickly approached and there stood before him was Barney Logan who instantly recognized Norman who walked right up to him and he petted Norman.

BARNEY LOGAN

Where have you been?

Barney Logan yelled.

BARNEY LOGAN

Betty, guess who decided to come home!

***

INT. DAY. HARVARD UNIVERSITY.

Alexandro Solórzano in due course struggled at Harvard and barely survived because of language barrier and lack of education. He might have done well in Honduras but compared to some of the rocket scientists that attended Harvard, he was truly inferior.

It came to a head one day and his physics professor called him in for a meeting and was considering dropping him from the class and suggesting he drop out of Harvard.

The physics professor was slightly biased and couldn't quite accept or appreciate Alexandro Solórzano as a human being or a student that should be going to Harvard and quite frankly was disgusted some politician pulled the strings to plant this under achiever at Harvard in the first place.

The classroom where they met, was right after the professor's last class, had an air of resentment and a tumultuous ending. The professor didn't beat around the bush.

PHYSICS PROFESSOR (Dr. Welch)

Alexandro, the reason why I wanted to talk with you is to inform you I'm thinking about dropping you out of this class. I do not think you can handle the course, nor do I think you should remain at Harvard.

Alexandro suddenly had a heavy heart and was upset, and he slapped his jeans which contained the alien device in his pocket.

He didn't know it, but the device responded to different tap commands. He had never struck it that forcefully before. He triggered a response out of the device and suddenly a two-foot- tall holograph appeared that had General Fukua de Hundan's image who then gave a pre- recorded message.

GENERAL FUKUA DE HUNDAN'S ANNIMATION

Alexandro, you must be having a difficult situation. I want you to know I will always be here for you. If you have an emergency, tap five times on the artifice and I will get the message. I may not get there in time to save you but at least you know my thoughts and prayers will go out to you.

PHYSICS PROFESSOR (Dr. Welch)

What the hell is that?

ALEXANDRO SOLÓRZANO

It's a holograph from a device in my pocket.

The professor angrily asked then started to realize he had never seen anything like it before.

PHYSICS PROFESSOR (Dr. Welch)

Are you being some kind of wise guy? No, when I slapped my leg, I accidentally triggered the device. It wasn't planned.

PHYSICS PROFESSOR (Dr. Welch)

What is it?

Alexandro pulled the device out of his pocket and showed the professor

ALEXANDRO SOLÓRZANO
An Alien gave this to me.

The professor took the device and looked at it. The semi triangular device had inscriptions written on both sides. One side was in Spanish, the other side was in some language he didn't recognize that appeared very strange almost like Mandarin Chinese but much larger characters with more brush stroke components.

A Chinese Mandarin Character may have a single radical usually located on the left side of the character, but Carsopians had radicals both right left, top and bottom, and instead of 5 tones like Chinese have that you see when you read *Chinese Pinyin*, since the Carsopians have 48 vowels and 54 consonants, they have 15 tonal's some of which are identical to the 5 normal *Chinese tones*.

The professor asked as he looked at the standard Carsopian writing:

PHYSICS PROFESSOR (Dr. Welch)
What's this language?

ALEXANDRO SOLÓRZANO
That is standard Carsopian.

PHYSICS PROFESSOR (Dr. Welch)
What is Carsopian?

ALEXANDRO SOLÓRZANO
The Alien's language.

The angry professor Dr. Welch looked at the device writing.

PHYSICS PROFESSOR (Dr. Welch)
What does it say?

ALEXANDRO SOLÓRZANO
It says, what the other side says in Spanish.

PHYSICS PROFESSOR (Dr. Welch)
And what is that?

ALEXANDRO SOLÓRZANO
It says, 'for my friend Alexandro Solórzano. This will only work with your touch, and nobody else.

The professor handed it back to Alexandro.

DR. WELCH
Show me how it works.

Alexandro rubbed the alien gift, and a holograph popped up giving Alexandro two minutes of conversation.

Alexandro handed it to the professor.

ALEXANDRO SOLÓRZANO
Here you try it.

The professor rubbed it, banged on it, slammed it against the desk, nothing triggered it.

ALEXANDRO SOLÓRZANO
Hand it to me.

The professor handed the alien gift back and Alexandro rubbed it again and another different holograph popped up. The professor suddenly got interested.

DR. WELCH
You claim an Alien gave that to you as a gift?

ALEXANDRO SOLÓRZANO
Yes, General Fukua de Hundan the head of the Carsopian Space Fleet gave that to me as a gift.

DR. WELCH
When did that happen?

ALEXANDRO SOLÓRZANO
Last summer, I met General Fukua de Hundan when I was with my friends driving through Mexico on our way back to Honduras after we tried to get into the United States but failed.

DR. WELCH
You are from Honduras?

ALEXANDRO SOLÓRZANO
Yes.

DR. WELCH
Did you get into this college on a scholarship?

ALEXANDRO SOLÓRZANO
No, the CIA brought me here.

The professor was suddenly starting to get nervous. All the dots were stacking up in a way that seemed to make this boy's story rather bizarre but possibly true.

The gadget he had was certainly quite extraordinary. The professor knew no such thing existed and the quality of the three-dimensional holograph was rather extraordinary.

DR. WELCH

Tell me how did you meet this, Alien?

Alexandro gave the story to the professor then added:

ALEXANDRO SOLÓRZANO

General Fukua De Hundan gave me a ride in one of his ships out into space and around the moon. I saw the back side of the moon.

The professor thought that was a bullshit story and he himself had been one of the few Americans working on NASA contracts studying the back side of the moon and was sworn to secrecy about some of the artifacts there that appeared to be possible ancient ruins.

DR. WELCH

Tell me Alexandro, what did you see on the far side of the moon?

Alexandro began telling the professor everything he saw on the far side of the Moon's hemisphere that always faces away from Earth and stated exactly where the TOP SECRET ruins existed. Alexandro went on to say:

ALEXANDRO SOLÓRZANO

The moon's far side is rugged, with multiple impact craters and relatively few flat lunar maria. It has the largest crater in the Solar System, the South Pole– Aitken basin.

The hair stood up on the back of the professors' neck. Nobody knew that information about who wasn't working on the secret NASA project and Alexandro explained the appearance in perfect detail!

The professor dismissed Alexandro who went back to his dormitory room and proceeded to study in great earnest as he had no intentions of dropping out and now that he knew the new mode of the alien's gift, he would have far more encouragement and as he tinkered with the device discovered there were other ways to get information out of it by the way he touched it or banged on it. Suddenly it became a personal science for Alexandro to figure out all the various modes he could access.

Dr. Welch still worked part time on the NASA moon project on a government grant, contacted his NASA counterpart and reported the incident with the student.

This NASA department head wore two hats. He was also a CIA plant and soon reported it to the CIA.

The following day, CIA analyst Jack Boone and his supervisor Wade Baker arrived at Harvard and informed the Dean they were there to interview the physics professor concerning a science matter.

Professor Dr. Welch was invited to a conference room where he and the Dean met the two CIA officials.

Harvard often got involved in government programs. During the 1960's and 1970's, Harvard scientists and professors working with the Naval Under Sea Service Center in Groton Connecticut helped designed the new sonar systems used aboard American Nuclear Submarines.

They also contributed to other technology helping to win the cold war. All throughout the cold war era, Harvard and Harvard Graduates were involved in the military industrial complex.

Computers were enhanced by Harvard Architecture, and MIT wasn't the only game in town. This physics professor had been a contributor to the Harvard Project on Cold War Studies (Cold War International History Project (CWIHP).

WADE BAKER

Professor Welch, here's the non-disclosure standard form 312 we have filled out with addendum A attached. Please sign and date the 312 NDA and Addendum after you read it.

DR. WELCH

What if I don't want to sign it?

WADE BAKER

Professor Welch, we'll have your security clearance revoked, and you will never work for the government again. We will also immediately arrange to have DARPA cut off all research money to the University.

DR. WELCH

That sounds like blackmail.

WADE BAKER

Professor Welch, you sound like you do not want to cooperate with the government.

Chills went up Dr. Welch's spine as he contemplated his fate. Dr. Welch quickly read the document which had some astonishing requirements of how he was to interact and not disclose any information concerning Alexandro Solórzano. They didn't have to worry about the Dean who already worked for the CIA and was heavily involved in spying on Chinese Students who thought they were getting away with spying on America when in fact were being spoon fed and used as double spies without their knowledge.

Dr. Welch signed the document then turned towards Wade Baker.

DR. WELCH

Did Alexandro Solórzano really go to the moon as he stated to me?

WADE BAKER

Yes, he did. Everything he informed you is true, and we are glad you mentioned the gadget he had.

DR. WELCH

Why is that?

It has more computational power than all our computers on earth combined. We confiscated it and will be offering some of your computer scientists here at Harvard an opportunity to figure out how it works."

DR. WELCH

I see.

Professor Dr. Welch left that meeting totally mystified and in due course discovered Alexandro Solórzano was a fast learner.

Alexandro Solórzano's preparation for college might not have been ideal and even though early on his language skills were substandard because English was his second language, he did pick up the material rather quickly, and as soon as his English skills improved, so did his reports.

Alexandro Solórzano didn't know it but the drinks that General Fukua de Hundan gave him would have long lasting effects on his brain development. When children reach a certain age, the brain no longer grows.

A person's intellect is thus bound by how the brain develops. However, with the Alien microbes floating around in his system, Alexandro's brain began growing again for several more years. His mental faculties grew an astonishing 50% so as he learned Physics, Math, and Science, he had more room to store the information. He also had a personal *drive*.

The Carsopian gizmo that Alexandro had was X-rayed banged, attempted opening, and treated in several ways. All efforts were a failure. Nothing on Earth could break into alien technology. Eventually the government simply gave up on attempting to break into the device without ruining it and eventually gave it back to Alexandro whom they monitored secretly to glean new aspects of the device.

<u>INT. DAY. SAN PEDRO SULA HONDURAS.</u>

Larissa Cortés family would normally not accept Alexandro Solórzano as a future son in law, but as he progressed through Harvard and neared completing his BS degree in Physics, they started warming up to him.

Alexandro often wrote Larissa Cortés beautiful letters in Spanish, and he remained a clean cut throughout.

Even Dr. Welch who had previously wanted to kick him out of his class and out of Harvard, also had a vast turn around on his attitude for the young man who eventually became a straight A student with a stellar GPA.

There was no doubt, Alexandro's future was bright, and he had a destiny. Alexandro no longer required getting into the U.S. via a Caravan as he became a permanent resident and when the time came when Larissa Cortés graduated college, it was a foregone conclusion the two would be inseparable for the rest of their lives.

The Hondurans who were placed into the witness protection program flourished as well. Their lives changed drastically and unlike a lot of immigrants these days who do not melt into the American Dream and become full-fledged Americans with allegiance to this country, they all did.

What started out as a horror story up on Mexican Hiway 23, the *Comemos Caravanos Hiway*, ended peacefully even though some of the horror could never ever go away. These immigrants were spared the knowledge the Bad Hombres were barbecued!

Paul D.
Escudero
8/10/2024

A FAREWELL TO A FRIEND

With a blue line of mountains north of the wall, And east of the city a white curve of water, Here you must leave me and drift away
Like a loosened water-plant hundreds of miles.... I shall think of you in a floating cloud;
So in the sunset think of me....
We wave our hands to say good-bye,
And my horse is neighing again and again.

Reads top to bottom from right to left:
蕭 揮 落 浮 孤 此 白 青 送
蕭 手 日 雲 蓬 地 水 山 友
班 自 故 游 萬 一 遶 橫
人 馬 茲 人 子 里 為 東 北
鳴 去 情 意 征 別 城 郭

蕭 xiāo: mournful

班 bān: team; class; rank; squad; a work shift; a measure word; (a surname)

馬 [马] mǎ: 21st of month (tele.); horse; Ma (a surname)

鳴 [鸣] míng: to cry (of birds) 揮
huī: scatter; wield; wipe away 手
shǒu: hand; convenient

自 zì: from; self; oneself; since

茲 [兹] «玆» zī: herewith

去 qù: to go; to leave; to remove

落 «落» là: leave behind

日 rì: Japan; day; sun; date; day of the month

故 gù: happening; instance; reason; cause; deceased;

人 Rén: man; person; people

情 qíng: feeling; emotion; passion; situation

浮 fú: to float

雲 [云] yún: cloud

游 «遊» yóu: to walk; to tour; to roam; to swim; to travel

子 zǐ: 11 p.m.-1 a.m.; 1st earthly branch;

child; midnight; son; child; seed; egg; small thing

意 yì: idea; meaning; wish; desire

孤 gū: lone; lonely

蓬 péng: (grass); disheveled

萬 wàn: (surname); ten thousand; a great number

里 «裏» lǐ: Chinese mile; neighborhood

征 zhēng: attack; levy (troops or taxes); journey; trip; expedition

此 cǐ: this; these

地 dì: earth; ground; field; place; land

一 yī: one; single; a(n)

為 wéi: act as; take...to be; to be; to do; to serve as; to become

別 [别] bié: leave; depart; separate; distinguish; classify; other; another; do not; must not; to pin

白 bái: white; snowy; empty; blank; bright; clear; plain; pure; gratuitous

水 shuǐ: water; river

遶 rào: go around; to wind (around)

東 [东] dōng: east

城 chéng: city walls; city; town

青 «靑» qīng: 9th of month (tele.); blue-green

山 shān: mountain; hill

橫 [横] héng: horizontal; across; (horizontal character stroke)

北 běi: North

郭 guō: (surname); outer city wall

送 sòng: to deliver; to carry; to give (as a present); to present (with); to see off; to send

友 yǒu: friend

人 Rén: man; person; people

Author's note:

This is a novel solely based on fiction. No persons in the screenplay exist in real life and names were randomly selected. The aircraft in this novel may or may not exist. You can certainly google the U2, S-97, SR-71, SR-72, SR-75, etc.

Some of the locations in the screenplay are real.

There is major tourism to the Mexican cities and towns mentioned in this screenplay.

If you watch some of the tourist video's concerning Guadalajara Mexico, they provide some very compelling tourist destinations with excellent accommodations that rival hotels in America. Air accommodation to and from those areas are robust. For people living in Northern American cities, these destinations will most likely be delightful in the winter.

The KH-11 satellite did exist, and the spy scandal is true. In 1978, a young CIA employee named William Kampiles was accused of selling a KH-11 System Technical Manuals describing design and operation to the Soviets. Kampiles was convicted of espionage and initially sentenced to 40 years in prison.

Reference to the KH-14: whether this truly exists or not is a matter of speculation. In my travels I've gleaned internet claims it was put up to detect aliens who are now visiting our planet. I have no way of vetting those stories, but they do sound juicy. All references to KH-14 I found in the past on the internet are now GONE! Is this a coincidence or what?

A United Launch Alliance Delta 4-Heavy rocket will deploy the massive payload for the

U.S. National Reconnaissance Office in a mission known simply as NROL-71 from Vandenberg's Space Launch Complex 6. I've watched that mission scrubbed several times. When that rocket is launched you can watch streaming video on You Tube. Also, you can watch SpaceX launches live. Just think, when you do you are getting a glimpse of the future. Space travel is here now. Before long we'll be traveling to other solar systems.

Is this a KH-13 or is it the new KH-14 to track down aliens who are now becoming a problem that may eventually force disclosure?

Will Hiway 23 now be known as the ***Comemos Caravanos Hiway***? Will UFO hunters to out searching along Hiway 23?

If some of the current Caravanners suddenly come up missing, I swear I had nothing to do with it. I'm not a Cannibal.

Some History of Honduras.

I put this in to explain why there would be people from Honduras in the Caravans.

This country has at times been referred to as Spanish Honduras to differentiate it from British Honduras, which became modern-day Belize.

Honduras is bordered to the west by Guatemala, to the southeast by Nicaragua, to the southwest by El Salvador, to the south by the Pacific Ocean at the Gulf of Fonseca, and to the north by the Gulf of Honduras, the large inlet to the Caribbean.

Both Delmy Áquilar and Yanuel Romero had no choice but to seek jobs in the growing Honduras textiles industry and sea food companies. Hence, their incomes were not much better than indentured servants.

Honduras national economy primarily agricultural, made it especially vulnerable to natural disasters such as Hurricanes.

Hondurans are often referred to as *Catracho* or *Catracha* (fem) in Spanish. The word was coined by Nicaraguans and derives from the last name of the Spanish Honduran General Florencio Xatruch, who in 1857 led Honduran armed forces against an attempted invasion by North American adventurer William Walker.

On his fourth and the final voyage to the New World in 1502, Christopher Columbus landed near the modern town of Trujillo, near Guaimoreto Lagoon, becoming the first European to visit the Bay Islands on the coast of Honduras.

In March 1524, Gil González Dávila became the first Spaniard to enter Honduras as a ***conquistador***.

Hernán Cortés had brought forces down from Mexico to participate in the takeover. Much of the conquest took place in the following two decades, first by groups loyal to Cristóbal de Olid, and then by those loyal to Francisco de Montejo but most particularly by those following Alvarado.

In addition to Spanish resources, the conquerors relied heavily on armed forces from Mexico—Tlaxcalans and Mexican armies of thousands that remained garrisoned in the region.

Silver mining was a key factor in the Spanish conquest and settlement of Honduras. The New York and Honduras Rosario Mining Company established in the US took a well- known mine in San Juancito, 40 km northeast of Tegucigalpa, and in the next decade produced three million dollars in silver and gold.

By the beginning of the 20th century the San Juancito mine had more than one thousand workers. Mining continued and off until around 1978 when a Hurricane put the mining operations out of business.

Honduras gained independence from Spain in 1821 and was a part of the First Mexican Empire until 1823, when it became part of the United Provinces of Central America.

Honduras has been an independent republic and has held regular elections since 1838.

In the 1840s and 1850s Honduras participated in several failed attempts at Central American unity, such as the Confederation of Central America (1842–1845), the covenant of Guatemala (1842), the Diet of Sonsonate (1846), the Diet of Nacaome (1847) and National Representation in Central America (1849–1852).

In 1888, a projected railroad line from the Caribbean coast to the capital, Tegucigalpa, ran out of money when it reached San Pedro Sula.

As a result, San Pedro Sula grew into the nation's primary industrial center and second- largest city.

Comayagua was the capital of Honduras until 1880, when the capital moved to Tegucigalpa.

Currently Honduras only operates a few segments of rail lines, the longest 50 kilometers hauling mainly lumber between San Pedro Sula and Puerto Cortes.

In the late nineteenth century, Honduras granted land and substantial exemptions to several US-based fruit and infrastructure companies in return for developing the country's northern regions.

As such, in 1904, the writer O. Henry coined the term "banana republic" to describe Honduras

Honduras joined the Allied Nations after Pearl Harbor, on December 8 1941, and signed the Declaration by United Nations on January 1, 1942, along with twenty-five other governments.

During the early 1980s, the United States established a continuing military presence in Honduras to support El Salvador, the Contra guerrillas fighting the Nicaraguan government, and develop an air strip and modern port in Honduras.

Though spared the bloody civil wars wracking its neighbors, the Honduran army quietly waged campaigns against Marxist–Leninist militias such as the Cinchoneros Popular Liberation Movement, notorious for kidnappings and bombings and against many non- militants as well.

The operation included a CIA-backed campaign of extrajudicial killings by government- backed units, most notably Battalion 316.

***

DRAMATIS PRSONA

Characters and Locations

Claire Uwakion'na, Heisibing social climber and part of military oversight, patronage officer, extravagantly beautiful and rank seeker.

General Bakugeki, Heisibing Ground Forces Commander, popularly known as the Butcher of Bashreban.

Count Ryūsei, the Heisibing Emperor's nephew and hatchet man.

Copa Kebukaijosei, the pleasure capital of the Empire is a planet only one day away from Yanjingzai Tiankongzhong.

Cui transit lane: an ultra-fast space conduit created by a cosmic convergence channel that altered space and time just like the event horizon of a black hole.

Ravyks from Epsilon Eridani (BD−09°697) star system, attempted conquest of Earth. General Fukua de Hundan, head of Carsopian Space Fleet.
General Pibei de Laozhanshi was head of Carsopian Military Industrial Complex.
Admiral Engaarai, head of the Heisibing Space Fleet.
General Daziwo, member of General Pibei de Laozhanshi's staff. CIA analyst Jack Boone and supervisor Wade Baker Tepechitlán, Zacatecas, Mexico Shoulder Fired Synthetic Aperture Phasers, shaped like a rifle, but shot an energy beam somewhat similar to a laser but with far more concentrated power.

Directorate General of Civil Aeronautics (DGAC, Mexico).

La Cantera, Mexico.

FBI agents Bentley Boyd and Charles Gable
Mexican Policía Federal Ministerial, PFM
PFM Agent Carlos Guerrero, the main Mexican investigator

Octopus 章鱼 zhāng yú, Galacticist conversion: zhangyu battle formation

Star 明星 [Chinese] míng xīng, Galacticist conversion: Colonel Mingxing a spy who works for AI.

Tired Old Soldier 疲惫的老战士 [Chinese] pí bèi de lǎo zhàn shi, Galacticist conversion: General Pibei de Laozhanshi the head of the Carsopian Joint Commanders

The Big Ego 大自我 [Chinese] Dà zìwǒ, Galacticist conversion: Daziwo (General Daziwo - conspiracy)

Moon Rocks 月亮岩石 [Chinese] yuè liàng yán shí Galacticist conversion: Yueliang Yanshi [the Carsopian City on the planet Shenqi Zhilong where Carsopian military headquarters existed.

Magic Dragon 神奇之龙 [Chinese] shén qí zhī lóng, Galacticist conversion: Shenqi Zhilong, [main planet in the Carsopian Empire].

Hairy women 毛深い女性 [Japanese] Kebukai Josei [Heisibing pleasure planet *Copa Kebukaijosei*]

Eye in the sky. 眼睛在天空中 [Chinese] Yǎnjīng zài tiānkōng zhōng, Galacticist conversion: Yanjingzai Tiankongzhong [name of the planet where the Heisibing Fleet anchorages exist]

Rough Around the Edges. 縁が荒い [Japanese] En ga arai, Galacticist conversion: Admiral Engaarai [Heisibing Fleet Commander]

Look to the stars, but dream through your heart. 看向星星, 但通过你的心灵梦想 Kàn xiàng xīngxīng, dàn tōngguò nǐ de xīnlíng mèngxiǎng. Galacticist conversion: Kanxiang Xingxing, Dantongguoni de Xinlingmengxiang.

Devastator 破坏者 Pòhuài zhě, Galacticist conversion: Pohuaizhe. The primary capital city Pohuaizhe on *Cui,* named after the famed conqueror to established Carsopian hegemony over the region General Pohuaizhe

Operation Nutcracker, 胡桃夹子 Hútáo jiázi, Galacticist conversion: Hutao-jiazi. Attack formation.

Black death, 黑死病, Hēi sǐ bǐng, Galacticist conversion: Heisibing alien race.

Pompous Asshole, 浮夸的混蛋 Fúkuā de húndàn Galacticist conversion: Fukua de Hundan, General Fukua de Hundan [Carsopian Supreme Commander]

Pronounced Fu-cua da Hun-dun

NONI elixir, 诺丽药剂, Nuò lì yàojì Galacticist conversion: Nuo li yaoji

Carsopian Empire provincial stronghold:

Cui. San Pedro Sula, Honduras, major city.

Honduras names characters:
Group one: Delmy Áquilar Yanuel Romero Rony Nieto and Eduardo Ordoñez
Group two: Oscar Godoy Gabriela Zelaya Javier Pineda
Group three: Reynaldo Mejía Alexandro Solórzano Larissa Cortés Daphne Vasquez Barney and Betty Logan's dog "Norman"

Carsopian Security Rover-craft

Wright Patterson Air Force Base
Pathologist. Wright Patterson Air Force
Base Intel Officer.

Captain Zhìhuì Jūjī, Admiral Engaarai's Tactical Assistant

www.ingramcontent.com/pod-product-compliance
Lightning Source LLC
Chambersburg PA
CBHW062109290726
48975CB00001B/161
* 9 7 8 1 9 6 5 7 3 2 4 7 2 *